I0646799

ANGLEZARKE

Nicholas Whittle

Copyright © 2024 by Nicholas J. Whittle

All rights reserved.

No part of this publication may be reproduced, distributed, or transmitted in any form or by any means, including photocopying, recording, or other electronic or mechanical methods, without the prior written permission of the publisher, except as permitted by U.S. and international copyright laws. For permission requests, contact the copyright holder at anglezarke@protonmail.com.

This is a work of fiction. Names, characters, places, and incidents are products of the author's imagination or are used fictitiously and are not to be construed as real. Any resemblance to actual events, locales, organisations, or persons, living or dead, is entirely coincidental.

ISBN 978 1 7636 1403 1 (paperback)

ISBN 978 1 7636 1400 0 (ebook)

ISBN 978 1 7636 1406 2 (kindle)

Cover design by the author © Nicholas Justin Whittle 2024

First edition 2024

For EJ
… both of them

Prologue

Lake Maracaibo, Venezuela – 1973

Jasper Moffett III wiped the driving rain from his eyes, slung his kitbag onto his shoulder and started down the companionway to the supply boat. Mid-afternoon thunderheads were all too common on Lake Maracaibo, and the hawsers creaked loudly as the vessel swayed in the choppy water at dockside. He'd been making trips like this to his father's oil rigs in Texas and the Gulf of Mexico since he was nine years old. Now as the Head of Exploration & Production for Wolverine Petroleum, his family's company, he needed to see that their newest and most expensive investment was finally going to make them money. The expansion into oil-rich Venezuela was a very big bet for an ambitious company, and Jasper had put everything on the line to make this rig happen – things needed to turn around down on Lake Maracaibo, and fast.

The dockhands released the moorings. The supply boat shuddered as the helmsman opened the throttles. They eased away from the berth, picking up speed as the vessel turned in a long arc toward the navigation buoys that marked the lake's deep-water channel. The trip to Wolverine's concession blocks in the south-west corner of Lake Maracaibo would take a good six hours. At these equatorial latitudes, dark would fall quickly, but tonight there would be a full moon to steer by. Jasper stowed his gear in the small passenger saloon amidships and headed back out to the open cargo deck aft. The boat was heavily laden with equipment for the drilling rig, a variety of pumps, piping and colour-coded toolboxes lashed to eyebolts on the checker-plate deck. He tested a couple of the heavy slings to make sure they were tight. Then he looked back and could see the lights and neon of Maracaibo's Avenida de los Milagros shimmering between the curtains of rain, while the flares from the Venezuelan government's huge oil refinery on the far shore reached long, orange reflections across the dark waters.

Once in the channel, the helmsman turned the boat south, changing course every so often to steer around the thick floating beds of water hyacinth that were a feature of the lake, especially in its brackish northern reaches near the ocean. The lights of the city receded to a dim glow on the aft quarter, and the tang of salt on the breeze disappeared, to be replaced by the sharper scent of gasoline from the oil which constantly seeped into the lake from below. Jasper leant on the rail and grinned. He had convinced his father and brothers – not to mention the bankers in Houston, New York and London – to bet the company on this Venezuelan venture. It was a huge risk for a small independent producer like Wolverine: Lake Maracaibo sat on an ocean of oil, some of the lightest, sweetest crude in the world, but thus far the drillers had hit nothing but dry holes or deposits which looked good for a few days and then petered out to a trickle. Jasper knew that the big score, the motherlode, sat waiting for him somewhere under these shallow, oily waters, but his time was running out as the operating losses mounted into the stratosphere. He couldn't keep the bankers off Wolverine's back for much longer, and if he didn't hit paydirt soon, his Daddy would stake him to the ground and let the fire ants eat him for lunch. Those had been Daddy's exact words to him as he left Houston, but Jasper could taste the big strike, as easily and vividly as he could taste the oil on the air around him as it evaporated off the lake's surface. When he hit it, he'd take Wolverine straight to the top, and neither the bankers, nor his father, nor anyone else would be able to stand in his way.

The supply ship maintained a steady speed through the late afternoon and entered the oil-rich blocks of the southern lake. The captain slowed the engines as the navigation lights and outlines of the derricks and other oil installations that dotted the waters on either side of the channel came into view in the evening haze. The rumble of thunder now began to rival the constant thrum of the ship's twin diesels, and the sky flashed with lightning, welcoming them to the unique phenomenon that was Catatumbo.

Jasper moved round to the bow. He never tired of watching the lightning storms of Catatumbo, a combination of the geography and air currents where the Catatumbo river entered Lake Maracaibo, a microclimate which produced an almost constant barrage of thunder and lightning. In fact, he mused, he had become something of a connoisseur of the spectacle, and felt a shudder of disquiet as he surveyed the bruised and sullen storm clouds that loomed low and ominous ahead. Suddenly, the ship lurched beneath him, and he had to grab for a hawser to stay upright as a vicious blast of wind and rain tore at him and the remaining light of day was obscured. Deafening thunderclaps rolled like an artillery barrage as the lightning intensified. Jasper looked back to the bridge. He could make out the helmsman frantically signalling him to take cover, but could not hear a single word above the tumult. He tightened his grip on the cables and faced forward into the Catatumbo storm, while the ship pitched and yawed beneath him and he was pelted with rain and spray.

For a few seconds, the rain abated and half a dozen rapid bolts of lightning allowed Jasper to see ahead clearly. Some two or three hundred yards away on the starboard quarter was a small island, the trees on its nearer shoreline standing out in chiaroscuro detail as the lightning pulsed, whipping from side to side in the tempest. The next bolt of lightning hit the island with an ear-splitting crack of thunder, and an explosion of splintered trees and shattered rock blasted into the air. From its centre rocketed the huge shape of a dragon, straining to climb as flames tore at its ragged wings and a blue caul of electricity coruscated around its body. At the zenith, the dragon seemed to hang in front of the moon as it was speared by another thunderbolt, before it collapsed back toward the ground. The dragon's anguished scream as the second bolt of electricity smashed through it sent Jasper crashing to his knees. He clapped his hands to his ears but he could still feel the creature's pain rolling though his mind in sickening waves as it plummeted to earth. For a moment there was silence, and Jasper tried to struggle to his feet, but was thrown to the deck once more as an ancient voice filled his mind, and screamed, "HELP ... ME!"

Jasper gasped for breath. "Who … what … are you?" he groaned, still pinned to the deck by the dragon's torment.

"HELP ME…"

"I … AM…"

"I … AM…"

"I … AM … OIL!"

1 Ormerod

You could hear the motorbike climb the hill into the village from the main road, the crescendos between the hedgerows as good as markers on a map, the occasional chuffing sound of a misfire as good as a fingerprint for those in the know: Elizabeth Jade Carver had finished her last exam that morning and was on her way home. At last, Norton Magna could breathe easily again.

Though no one in the village ever called her Elizabeth Jade: She was just known as EJ (pronounced Edge) by the whole of Norton Magna, or at least the ninety-nine per cent of it that passed through the doors of *The Grouse and Hare*, the village pub on the south side of the Green. They'd all known her since the pub's landlords, George and Maureen Carver, had adopted her when she was barely two years old, and had shared in all the significant moments of her upbringing. That morning, EJ had sat her final A-Level in English History. George, Maureen and the whole of Norton Magna were on tenterhooks.

EJ swung around the Green and turned her motorbike down the side of *The Grouse and Hare* to the broad cobbled courtyard behind the pub. The air smelt of freshly mown grass, and the barest of breezes ruffled the leaves of the tall beeches and chestnuts beyond the pub's outbuildings. The engine made its usual wheezing complaint as she switched it off, and EJ wondered whether she'd ever manage to get her old 'bike fixed. She gave the tank an affectionate pat then dismounted and hurried in through the back door to the pub's ample kitchen. George and Maureen were happily preparing sandwiches and other fare for the lunchtime trade, working in tandem in that comfortable way of married couples that EJ found so endearing. She stopped at the door to unclip her chinstrap and take off her helmet. George Carver looked up and smiled broadly. "Hello, EJ. How'd it go, then?"

"Alright, I suppose, Dad. The first essay was a bit tricky, but the rest were fine."

"Oh, I'm so pleased," said Maureen, wiping her hands on a chequered tea towel and bustling over to hug her daughter. "Hardest three weeks of my life, these exams!"

EJ grinned at her mother's relief. "Haven't been much of a picnic for me either, Mum," she said, disentangling herself from Maureen Carver's embrace.

"Oh EJ, I know, dear. You've worked ever so hard, and we're so proud of you! Now, you go on upstairs. Everyone knows your father wouldn't open up today until you'd got home. They'll all be dying of thirst on the doorstep."

EJ shrugged out of her battered leather jacket and rummaged amongst the assorted coats, scarves and waxed jackets at the back door until she found an empty hook on which to hang it. She kissed both her parents, picked up her rucksack and headed for the stairs to the family's rooms on the pub's second floor.

"Come down when you're ready and get some lunch. The usual suspects'll all be wanting to see you," her mother called after her.

The pub was a large one, and had been in George Carver's family for six generations since its beginnings as a coaching inn. The three of them lived comfortably in the spacious suite of upstairs rooms. At the top of the stairs was an occasional table that by custom received the morning post and any other items of general family interest. As EJ passed it, she noticed a parcel there and was surprised to see that it was addressed to her.

"Mum," she called down the stairs, "This parcel's for me?"

"Came this morning, love. One of those motorbike fellas delivered it and had your dad sign for it."

Intrigued, EJ picked up the packet. It wasn't especially heavy, and a tentative shake didn't reveal much about it either. Just a normal parcel wrapped in brown paper. She tucked it under her arm and went into her room.

EJ dropped her rucksack by her desk, fished out her laptop and phone and checked her emails, DM's and other feeds. Nothing required her immediate attention, so she sat down on the bed and inspected her parcel. It was an oblong roughly ten inches long and four wide, wrapped in waxed brown paper. There was no return address, and EJ knew she'd been way too busy to order anything online in the past few days. She fished the small Swiss Army knife that she always carried from her jeans pocket and carefully slit open one end of the package. EJ eased the wrapping paper aside and sat back, her eyes widening. Inside was a plain wooden box of varnished oak with a simple clasp. She lifted the lid to find an envelope addressed to "Miss Elizabeth Jade Carver" in a bold copperplate hand. She took it from the box and laid it on the bed beside her. Beneath the envelope lay a small pouch of cordovan leather fastened at the neck with a crimson silk ribbon. EJ untied the ribbon and shook out the contents. Onto the bedspread dropped a white gold pendant of a dragon on a fine gold chain, its body studded with tiny sapphires and garnets, its eyes two brilliant small diamonds. EJ gasped. The dragon was exquisite, with even the smallest details of scales and claws clearly visible. EJ held it up in the sunlight and studied it carefully, its body seeming to come to life as the tiny jewels caught the light. She was overcome with an intense feeling that she had seen the pendant before, but couldn't quite grasp the hazy memory.

The envelope was of a heavy, cream stock. Turning it over, EJ saw that it was sealed with crimson wax that bore the impression of a dragon – the very same dragon as the pendant that she held glittering on its golden chain. EJ felt another strong frisson of recognition.

With great care and no little difficulty, she eased the seal up with the tip of her knife and lifted the stiff flap of the envelope. Inside was a single folded page written in the same bold copperplate hand:

Dear Miss Carver,

May I congratulate you on your completion of the A-Level examinations. I have every confidence that you will be rewarded with a superlative set of results.

Acting in loco parentis for your paternal grandfather, Joseph Simeon Livesey, as I am so empowered by your grandfather's deed to this effect lodged with the Lord Chancellor at Westminster on the 29th of May, 2011, I have been instructed by my client and your grandfather's business partner, Michelangelo de St. Exupéry-Antoine, to extend to you an annual stipend of £500,000 as well as certain other assets and benefits to be determined in due course.

The above stipend and benefits are subject to your meeting with my client at his residence in the village of Anglezarke in Lancashire within seven days of the receipt of this letter. Please be kind enough to visit with me at my bureau, No.16A Albemarle Street, London W1, tomorrow at midday, at which time I shall endeavour to answer the many questions you no doubt have, with as much clarity and empathy as I am able. I remain,

Your obedient servant,

Selwyn Ormerod Esq.

EJ folded the letter and replaced it in its envelope. Anglezarke? Her grandfather? She had a grandfather? EJ had known for several years that her biological parents had died in a car crash when she was barely a toddler and the Carvers had adopted her soon after. When at eight or nine she had inevitably become curious about why her unruly blond curls, green eyes and olive complexion were such a far cry from George Carver, whose ruddy face and prop forward's build were so perfect for a publican, or from her mother, who could have starred in any number of television serials as a typical English farmer's wife, George and Maureen had been conscientious in their explanations. They had told her that they had already been on the local authority's waiting list for adoption for two years. When they had received a phone call that she had been orphaned, they had jumped at the chance to adopt her. EJ loved them both very much as the only real mother and father she had ever known, but even then, she had been more than intelligent enough to realise that there must be more to her story.

EJ leant back and closed her eyes. As she thought about the letter and the dragon pendant, it was as if a key had been slowly turned in a lock, and once fleeting memories began to form, breaking the surface of a dark, still pool. She remembered a tall man with large hands and a ready smile. There had been a sprawling, unruly garden behind a large stone house, and a rambling orchard beyond, and she recalled clumsily running in the dappled sunlight between its gnarled apple and plum trees. Then she remembered the steep hill that rose beyond the orchard, and a stone arch with a heavy, iron-studded door, and it was as if a curtain of midnight blue velvet had been pulled aside in her mind. With absolute clarity, EJ remembered being taken through that door and into the hill by her grandfather on her second birthday, to a large, well-lit chamber that smelt pleasantly of leather and tobacco, to be introduced for the first time to

Michelangelo, and EJ wondered how on earth it was possible that she could ever have forgotten that Michelangelo de St. Exupéry-Antoine was a dragon.

*

EJ opened her eyes and stood up. She turned the pendant over in her hands and contemplated it again, then put it around her neck, fastened the clasp and looked at herself in the mirror. She would be eighteen in two months' time, and was a tall young woman with a mop of medium length blond curls that seemed to refuse, Medusa-like, to behave in any reasonable manner, no matter what preparations or techniques she tried – and EJ reckoned that by now she had tried them all. Basing her opinion more on instinct than experience, she felt that she might not be considered pretty in a conventional sense, but there was something about her face that could certainly be called attractive. Her nose was maybe a little small and her lips could have been a little fuller, but her emerald green eyes were intelligent and expressive. She was blessed with flawless skin, and her light olive complexion offset her other features well. Tomboyness as a child had morphed into an easy athleticism, and her long legs were strong and shapely. She knew she looked good in a dress, and enjoyed the opportunity to wear one, but normally preferred the comfort, as today, of worn jeans and a flannel shirt. EJ looked once more in the mirror at the dragon pendant, then tucked it inside her shirt. She picked up the envelope from where it lay beside the open box and shoved it into the back pocket of her jeans before she ran back downstairs, where she could already hear the pleasant hum of voices from the bar.

*

The Lounge Bar was already half full of regulars. Her father stood in his customary position behind his beer pumps, slowly polishing a pint glass and chipping in with an occasional bon môt to the usual barroom banter of weather, football and politics. He looked over inquiringly at his daughter as she slipped in behind the bar.

"Not too tired, are you? Did you open your parcel?" he asked.

"I'm fine, Dad. Let me get an apron and I'll help out with the food. The parcel was … interesting. I'll show you later."

George nodded and set to pulling a pint of bitter. "Well, if you're sure. Check with your Mum – Gibby's usual should be about ready."

EJ pushed through the serving entrance to the kitchen, where Maureen Carver was ladling mushy peas onto a large plate of fish and chips. She looked up as EJ came in and smiled broadly.

"I knew you'd be down to help. You don't have to. Not today, love."

"I want to, Mum. Anyone else besides Gibby?" asked EJ.

"There's a platter of beef and mustard sandwiches for the table in the corner. Be a love and take them too."

"Okay."

EJ added the sandwiches to the tray and took the orders back to the Lounge. She served the two local businessmen their sandwiches and then brought the fish and chips over to the spritely older man seated on his usual stool at the corner of the bar. He put down his copy of *The Times*, turned as ever to the crossword, and examined her at length over the top of his half-moon spectacles as she placed his meal in front of him.

"Am I to understand you did battle with old Oliver Cromwell and his cohorts this morning, EJ?" asked Archibald Gibson.

EJ grinned broadly and said, "Took him and his roundheads to the cleaners in two of the essays, Gibby."

"Good girl! God bless the Lord Protector and his little cotton socks! I expect great things, EJ, great things."

EJ grinned at the usual repartee. "Enjoy your lunch, Gibby."

Gibby tucked into his fish and chips. EJ spent the next hour and a half in a relaxed mix of filling lunch orders, pouring drinks and satisfying the regulars' curiosity about her A-levels and what she planned to do with the stellar results that all were convinced she would receive. By two-thirty, the lunchtime's drinkers had departed, all except for Gibby. He drained the last of his pint, handed the empty glass to EJ and said to her quietly, "Did I ever show you my signet ring, EJ? Here, you really should take a look."

EJ leaned over the bar a little to inspect the gold signet on the little finger of Gibby's left hand. She'd seen it a thousand times of course, but had never paid it any real attention. She now saw that the insignia was a dragon – the same dragon as her pendant. She was silent for a few seconds, then stepped back and looked Gibby in the eye.

"I suppose I should be surprised, Gibby, but to tell you the truth, I've remembered quite a bit already. Before anything else, I think I really need to have a chat with Mum and Dad."

"That, EJ, would be an excellent idea. Great things, my dear! Great things!" Gibby folded his spectacles into their case, and picked up his newspaper. "Give my regards to Selwyn when you see him, won't you?"

EJ followed Gibby to the pub's front door and watched him leave, then turned the key in the latch. She could hear her parents moving about the bar as they cleared the last of the glasses and tidied the room ready for the evening, so she wandered back to the kitchen in search of her own lunch and to wait for them there. A large plate of assorted sandwiches and quarters of pork pie sat on the kitchen table, together with a fresh pot of tea. EJ poured herself a mug and realised just how hungry she was. It had been quite a day so far. She picked up a random sandwich – cheddar and chutney as it turned out – and took a ruminative bite. She briefly wondered whether George and Maureen would be upset or worried by the parcel and its consequences, but quickly realised that they probably already had a pretty good idea of what was going on.

EJ had just picked up a piece of pork pie and was giving it a generous swipe of mustard when her parents came into the kitchen. She looked up at them and smiled, and could see the wave of relief on their faces as the tension was released. She put her hand to her throat and lifted her dragon pendant from beneath her shirt. George and Maureen Carver looked at it as if mesmerised, and EJ imagined she could see the sparkling diamonds and gold of the dragon reflected in their wide eyes.

"You've always known, haven't you," she stated gently. EJ took the envelope from the back pocket and handed it to her father. He read the contents intently then passed it without a word to his wife. George Carver looked at Maureen, who nodded for him to answer.

"We've always known. When I signed for that parcel this morning, I had the feeling it might be from Selwyn. He arranged the adoption ..."

Maureen interrupted him impatiently and continued, "We'd tried everything to have a child, but it just seemed like it would never happen, and then one night came this 'phone call, and it was Selwyn Ormerod."

George put his arm around his wife and continued, "He said he'd heard about our situation and that there was something he could do to help. Well, we were sceptical at first, of course we were. But the next day he came into the pub and introduced himself."

"Oh, EJ, he was ever such a nice man," added her mother, tucking the letter back into the envelope and placing it on the table in front of their daughter. "Anyway, Selwyn explained everything and we thought it all sounded so ...

hopeful, so right. He picked us up the next morning and we all went up to see your grandfather. That was the day we met you for the first time." There were tears in Maureen's eyes, but EJ could see that they were tears of happiness as her mother relived the day in her mind.

George Carver took up the story. "Your grandfather was worried. For your safety, EJ. He and Selwyn had decided it'd be best if you were hidden in plain sight. Those were his very words."

George got up and walked over to the kitchen window. He stood there and EJ could see that he was gazing back across the years to the day in Anglezarke that had changed his life forever. He then turned back to EJ and said, "Your parents died in that car crash, but your grandfather said it was no accident. He said they were murdered. You always were a perceptive girl, EJ. You're not upset we kept this from you?"

She touched the pendant at her throat and said, "This opened up memories … Ones I didn't know were there. But now that I've begun to remember, everything seems to fall into place. My grandfather. Michelangelo. Even Gibby. No, Dad, I'm not upset at all." EJ looked at the two people who meant the most to her in the whole world. "You'll always be Mum and Dad, and I love you very much."

"Gibby moved here not long after we brought you home. Selwyn said he and Gibby had done something together in government, and Gibby'd be on hand to keep an eye on things," explained Maureen. "Those first few months we were so worried something awful was going to happen. We couldn't bear to have you out of our sight. Many's the night Gibby'd look after you on his own. He was a Godsend."

"But nothing ever happened," continued George. "And pretty soon we all just seemed to forget about how you'd come to be here. To be honest, until this morning it had been quite a time since I'd even thought about Selwyn Ormerod."

"But what do they want from me?" asked EJ hesitantly.

"We met Michelangelo," said Maureen. "That same first night we went to Anglezarke. Came as quite a shock, I can tell you! He explained he'd never interfere with your upbringing, but if you ever needed anything we only had to ask. He hoped to see you again when you were old enough. I suppose this is what he meant."

"It's strange though, isn't it? The letter says they're acting on my grandfather's behalf. I don't understand that bit." EJ looked at them both in turn, then quietly asked, "What do you think I should do?"

George Carver took EJ's hands in his own and said, "You're our pride and joy. There's not a parent anywhere could ever have wished for a more wonderful daughter. But there comes a time when you have to find out for yourself who you really are."

"Dad! I already know who I am! I want to know who these two think I am!" laughed EJ.

"What I mean is, all this money and meetings in London and what have you. Must be something pretty important," said George, nodding at his own wisdom.

"I'd better run you to the station in the morning. You go down to London and find out what's going on."

2 Pol Roger

The following day, EJ woke early to a morning warm and bright, the June air already busy with the hum of insects and the soft round coos of wood-pigeons. She showered and dressed in her best suit, a navy jacket and skirt with a faint chalk-stripe, a simple white blouse, and low-heeled black pumps. Her blond curls were tied back, but still managed to squirm free in their usual manner, and she realised that this morning, as every other, was to be a losing battle in the hairstyle stakes. She studied herself in the mirror, and with a flush of pride made sure that the dragon pendant was visible at the open neck of her blouse. EJ put her iPhone and wallet into a Chanel handbag that had been a Christmas present. She'd thought it quite extravagant at the time but now understood how she could have received such an expensive gift. By nine o'clock, after a pleasant breakfast of toast and tea, she was in the car with her father and on the way to the railway station.

Norton Magna was a small village a little over an hour's commute from London. Once the railway had arrived in the nineteenth century, a place that had barely registered on any maps now acquired a new life as a desirable location to bring up a family amongst the middle-class comforts and away from the grime of the capital.

"You've got money and your 'phone?" asked George.

"Yes, Dad. Don't worry, I'll be fine." She kissed him fondly on the cheek, got out of the car and, waving as he pulled away, went into the station. She bought a return ticket from the automatic vending machine then strolled onto the southbound platform to wait for the London train. Gibby was sat on the bench half way down the platform reading *The Times*. He raised a hand in greeting.

"Why, Gibby, what a surprise," said EJ with mock sarcasm and a broad grin. "Quite the country gent this morning, aren't we? Going up to town for anything special?"

Gibby was resplendent in a Donegal Tweed suit over a Tattersall check shirt and a yellow silk tie with a motif of racehorses, the ensemble topped off by a battered brown felt Trilby, which he now doffed in mock recognition.

"Why don't you join me? Humour an old man."

"I suppose you're my chaperon for the day?" asked EJ.

"Not at all, my dear, not at all," laughed Gibby. "Just on my way into town for a spot of lunch at my club. Now you mention it, Selwyn did say in passing that he expected you on this train. Suggested it might be an idea if I saw you as far as Piccadilly."

"How very gallant of you."

Gibby looked over his spectacles at her and smiled. "Thank you, my dear. We do try, you know."

The train was pulling into the station. They climbed aboard and found a pair of facing seats.

"Got an explanation for any of this, Gibby?" asked EJ, once they had settled and the train was under way again.

"Oh, no one tells the poor bloody infantry what's going on, EJ. You should know that, especially after yesterday's exam! It's like this, I suppose: Selwyn and I have known each other for many years, and when he asked me to help it was very much as a watching brief," Gibby said kindly. "Best if you held on to your questions for him. I'm sure your grandfather and Michelangelo have their reasons. Selwyn will do his utmost to help you understand."

EJ patted Gibby on the arm and said, "Thank you. For everything."

"Oh, stop it. You'll make me blush."

They spent the rest of the journey in companionable silence, Gibby ticking off clues in the crossword while EJ scrolled through mail and updates on her iPhone.

Marylebone Station was its usual maelstrom of confused and harried travellers, none of whom spared more than a passing glance at the incongruous pair. They took the Tube to Piccadilly, and tried as politely as they were able to make their way out of the station through the waves of Chinese tourists, whose large bags from the boutiques of Regent and Bond Streets formed a colourful obstacle course. Once above ground, the day was already humid and overcast, a typical London morning in mid-June with the lime trees in flower and the chance of a shower ever-present. Gibby bade her goodbye and headed south toward Pall Mall, while EJ set off west through the crowds on Piccadilly. A crocodile of small children in bright red school blazers were thronged noisily in front of the Royal Academy as she passed, and she resisted the urge to nip into Burlington Arcade to window shop. She turned into Albemarle Street and headed north, past the boutiques, the international jewellers and a number of galleries, the landscapes in their windows bland and uninspiring.

Farther along the street toward the Royal Institution, EJ soon found No.16A. A typical Mayfair townhouse, the ground floor with its colonnaded portico painted an immaculate white, the floors above plain London brick. Yet unlike so many of Mayfair's former grand residences which had been remade into offices, the portico of No.16A did not boast a varied collection of brass and brushed steel nameplates at its entrance to guide its visitors to the assorted enterprises housed within. EJ had no need to read down a list of company names to find her destination: in splendid isolation, a single, somewhat Edwardian-looking brass plate simply read:

SELWYN ORMEROD ESQ.

EJ pressed the old-fashioned bell-push. After a couple of seconds, the large front door clicked open. She entered a short lobby tiled in black and white. From a speaker on the wall came a cultured, rather booming voice.

"Miss Carver! A pleasure indeed! I have so looked forward to making your re-acquaintance. Would you be so kind as to hold perfectly still for a moment?"

A small grille slid back from the ceiling and EJ felt a mild tingle of static and smelt the tang of ozone as a blue actinic beam scanned her from head to toe and back. The door at the far end of the lobby then slid aside to reveal the burnished mahogany interior of a small lift.

"What was that?! Mr. Ormerod? What did you just do to me?" shouted EJ, looking around to see if there was at least a security camera upon which she could focus her irritation.

"Come now, Miss Carver, it's just a security scan. Quite a sophisticated one, I'll grant you, but nothing to worry about! We've learnt to take precautions over the years, and you will too. One cannot be too careful, you know. Now please, won't you join me?"

Feeling like she'd just been told off by a rather pompous headmaster, EJ stifled a stream of curses under her breath and strode forward with as much bruised dignity as she could muster. The lift took her up to open onto a wood-panelled vestibule, simply decorated with a Persian carpet and a pair of tall blue and white Chinese vases on either side of a set of double doors. These opened to reveal a tall, elegant man in an impeccable grey worsted suit, worn over a blue-striped shirt and a dark silk tie. He had an aquiline nose, on which perched a pair of modern frameless spectacles, and, her anger evaporating, EJ had to suppress a giggle as she realised that he bore a striking resemblance to pictures she had seen of the Duke of Wellington. He extended his hand in greeting and said, "Miss Carver! You've brought your appetite, I hope? I thought we might have a spot of lunch, so I asked the bar at Claridge's to send something round. An aperitif first? I've a quite acceptable bottle of Pol Roger. Churchill's favourite, you know."

"Thank you, Mr. Ormerod. To be honest, I'm famished. Champagne would be lovely, but maybe a little later?" EJ replied. "And just call me EJ, like everyone else … since you have known me for so long," she added pointedly.

Selwyn Ormerod paused as he ushered EJ into an expansive living room and examined her. His eyes twinkled, and the hail-fellow-well-met tone was replaced by something considerably more business-like.

"Of course, EJ. Ha! Sixteen years down here but you're still a blunt Northerner. Like your grandfather. And me, for that matter. I do hope George and Maureen weren't too upset with me? Splendid people, the pair of them."

"Actually, they seem to think Selwyn Ormerod is the dog's danglies."

"And you don't! You have questions, and I'll answer them all as best I can. You deserve to hear the truth. Remarkable as it is," said Selwyn Ormerod with a sad smile. "The main point is, Joe, your grandfather, has decided to go AWOL. Wandered off the reservation, so to speak. We think you may be the only one able to find him."

He straightened the crisp white handkerchief in his breast pocket and seemed to brighten. "Anyway, it's my experience no one ever made a wise decision on an empty stomach, and Claridge's still runs a damned fine kitchen. Come, sit down and eat first, and then we'll talk."

Selwyn Ormerod led EJ through a pair of French windows to an enclosed terrace. There were large tubs of white and pink rose bushes, and a purple wisteria covered the south-facing wall. A table for two had been laid with simple white linen, silver and crystal, while a sideboard held warmers and chafing dishes on small spirit lamps. Selwyn took off his jacket and hung it on the back of his chair, and proceeded to serve EJ and himself. To start, there were Beluga caviar and blinis, and a platter of fresh rock oysters, and as entrées the hotel had sent a splendid Côte de Boeuf with steamed spinach and minted new potatoes, and a Lobster Wellington simply served with a green salad and French fries. Selwyn had placed a bottle of Burgundy and a bottle of mineral water on the table, together with a well-chilled bottle of Chablis in an ice bucket. EJ sipped a little of the latter out of politeness, while Selwyn probed her about her exams and regaled her with stories of his own school and University days. EJ began to warm to Selwyn Ormerod as he talked. She realised that she had overreacted earlier. She had never really doubted what she would find when she met him – she had too much faith in her parents' own sound judgment for that – but it was nonetheless reassuring that he seemed both genuine and good-natured.

Selwyn dabbed at his lips with his napkin and topped up his glass of Burgundy. He pushed his chair back from the table and selected a Montecristo cigar from a humidor on the sideboard. Clipping the end neatly, he smiled and asked, "So, where would you like me to begin?"

"I remembered some things when I read your letter last night. Images from when I was very small. I saw my grandfather, I think, and I remember that he took me to meet Michelangelo, but I couldn't remember very much else … and I've known about my parents – my biological ones, I mean – for ages. But now Mum and Dad tell me the car crash wasn't an accident but was murder. Why? And why did I have to be hidden away? I mean, why all the cloak and daggers?"

EJ paused to gather her thoughts and took a sip of wine before continuing. "Michelangelo's a dragon, for God's sake … I mean, I realise I've met him, and for some reason that doesn't seem at all strange, even though it should. But who are you? What the hell is going on? And what does any of it have to do with me?"

Selwyn lifted his glass of wine from the table and looked at her for several long seconds, then smiled and said, "Hmm, that would seem to cover just about everything. I was born in Anglezarke too, you know. Joe and I grew up and went to school together, then on to Cambridge. I've known Michelangelo de St. Exupéry-Antoine since I was a lad. Proud to count the pair of them as my closest friends.

"Your grandfather and I are, sadly, all too human, but there have always been other races that call Anglezarke Moor home too. Not just in Anglezarke either, but across the world. Human mythology's built on them, the fairies and dwarves and goblins … and the dragons. Every culture has told its stories about them since time immemorial. Oh, each one gave them different names, different skills and attributes, but the point is they've always been around us. Part of us even. The more perceptive humans recognised it long ago, and its only recently that people have forgotten that – probably thought they were too busy for such nonsense! Now most of the other races, those that are left, just try to make their way in this world as best they can. Like the rest of us, I suppose."

"So, where do all the stories about ogres and goblins and evil, fire-breathing dragons come from then?" asked EJ. "I mean, you don't see many reports of dragons burning down villages or carrying away virgins on Sky News or videos of them on YouTube, do you?"

"Oh, don't get Michelangelo started on the subject of the rotten press dragons have had for all these centuries. He'll bore you to tears," chortled Selwyn.

Selwyn sighed and lit his cigar with some deliberation. He brushed a tiny crumb from the tablecloth and continued. "There used to be quite a few places like Anglezarke, especially up North … but Anglezarke's special because it has a dragon, and such places have always been rare. It really all comes down to the dragons."

EJ reached for her wine glass and realised she hadn't noticed that she had drained it as she listened with rapt attention. She poured herself some more Chablis.

"Other races are naturally drawn to a dragon, even humans. Because a dragon is elemental," explained Selwyn, watching her reaction closely. "Each of them reflects the Earth itself in some way. Michelangelo is a Golden Dragon, or rather **the** Golden Dragon."

"What do you mean, **the** Golden Dragon?"

"Michelangelo embodies gold. He senses gold. He knows where gold is. He feels it as it flows and moves. For most of history that didn't mean much at all. But the world moves on and everything changes. Mostly for the better I might add.

"For instance, the dwarves reckon the Industrial Revolution was the best thing to have happened to them in donkey's years, and some of the younger ones are dab hands at computers – they do all our programming. Most of the elves fared okay, too. They're an artistic lot, so they usually fit in pretty well among the painters and musicians. They had a ball during the Arts and Crafts movement — most of Art Nouveau wouldn't have existed without them. Then the Sixties and flower power – well, you can imagine, that was right up their street."

"You mean all the elves were hippies?" laughed EJ incredulously.

"Well, maybe not all of them, but I can think of a few that sold an awful lot of records! Threw some damn good parties, too." Selwyn blew a thin stream of smoke skywards and pointed at her with his cigar. "The dragons changed as well, though I doubt Michelangelo would put it that way. The things for which gold was used – trade, banking and the like – well, they all multiplied and 'morphed into what we now call finance. Turned out that it makes no difference to Michelangelo at all. He can still sense the movement – the value – whether it's an ingot of the purest metal or a list of shares on the back pages of the FT. It's been a very long time indeed since Michelangelo just went to sleep on a hoard of gold and jewels! That dragon has an uncanny flair for making money. Plus, he finds sleeping on a pile of coins plays merry hell with his back."

EJ stared at Selwyn Ormerod wreathed in cigar smoke, utterly enthralled by the fantastic tale he was placing before her.

"But something else changed, didn't it?" pointed out EJ. "That's where you and my grandfather fit in," she surmised.

"You're right, something did change. As far as Joe was concerned, Michelangelo had always just been the dragon at the bottom of the garden. Your grandfather had joined the Foreign Office when he left Cambridge, so his work often took him overseas. Then in the late Eighties, he jacked in the service, got his gold watch, and went back home to Anglezarke.

"You see, Joe had been posted to some dodgy places during his time at the FCO. He'd seen his fair share of war, famine and the like, but he realised he could do something about it, because he had this amazing advantage."

"A dragon at the bottom of the garden."

"Exactly. Michelangelo. So that's what we do: we make a difference. Or try to, at least. Michelangelo makes the money, a lot of money, and we basically give it away. Call it supporting worthy causes."

"So how did you get involved, Mr. Ormerod?" asked EJ.

"After my Articles, I'd gone into government as a junior lawyer. Different departments from Joe, but he and I kept in touch, of course. I hadn't heard from him in a couple of years, then, out of the blue, there's this letter from him. Come up to Anglezarke for the weekend, he said. Well, I was happily settled in London getting on with a career, hadn't been back to the village in years," explained Selwyn Ormerod, watching his cigar smoke billow gently into the air. "But he insisted, so I went up to see him and Joe and Michelangelo explained what they wanted to do. Back then, I think Michelangelo thought it was bonkers, but he'd already agreed and he wasn't going to break his word to Joe. Said they needed someone they could trust who knew his way around contracts, companies and the like. So, I resigned from Whitehall. We bought this house when I joined the firm. Looking back, I suppose we started out quite small but we've learnt an awful lot. Become quite sophisticated over the years. You'll see."

Selwyn Ormerod rested his cigar on the ashtray at his side and regarded EJ. "So … Still interested?"

"I think I'll have that glass of champagne now. If I may."

*

They had moved back inside from the terrace to Selwyn's study, a narrow book-lined room with a view across Albemarle Street. The study contained a simple Swedish modern desk on which sat a pair of monitors and a keyboard. A silver service of coffee and a platter of biscotti had been laid on the low table in front of a leather sofa which faced Selwyn's desk, and he busied himself serving two cups before he spoke again.

EJ spun her champagne flute slowly by its stem and said, "That still doesn't explain all the security and cloak and dagger stuff, does it? Or why I ended up an orphan."

"No, EJ, it doesn't … Interesting creatures, dragons. Each one's linked to a different material. Not just metals or minerals, either. There are dragons that feel the changes in ice and water. Others which seem symbiotic with the seasons or the winds."

"So, they're like Chinese dragons, then? Different aspects of the world."

"Yes, they are. But the thing to remember is that dragons don't create or control the minerals, or what have you. Quite the opposite: Gold exists, so Michelangelo feels its essence and exists too. There's a dragon in China that's all things jade, one in Siberia that's diamonds, though we don't have that much to do with him, and another in Java that's the essence of coal. You get the picture?"

Selwyn had taken his coffee and sat down behind his desk. He popped a biscotti into his mouth, before he continued.

"That, of course, is the problem. I'm not saying that we're always on the side of the angels, but over the centuries there have been men who have used dragons for more selfish ends. Recently, one man in particular.

"About fifty years ago, it appears something terrible happened to a dragon in Venezuela. Michelangelo felt it at the time, but it was only years later that we started to put the story together. We now know that dragon was the Oil Dragon, and for whatever reason he's helped one man become very rich and powerful … and willing to do anything to protect the secret of his success. Even kill for it."

Selwyn Ormerod would never forget how proud he felt of the young woman in front of him as he watched her set her jaw while she fingered the pendant at her throat. Her eyes sparked as she asked, "How did my parents die, Selwyn?"

"They'd been to a concert in Manchester and were driving home to Anglezarke. It looked like an accident. The police and everyone else were convinced. A wet road, a sharp bend, driver error. The car exploded on impact. But we now know they were followed all the way that night. It was no accident."

3 Nightstick

At about the same time EJ was learning of a past of which she had forgotten, Jasper Moffett III stood at the full-length window of the small office in his private suite on the ninety-seventh floor of Wolverine Tower and smiled grimly down as dawn broke across the city of Houston, Texas. Wolverine Petroleum's worldwide headquarters covered an entire block of downtown Houston at Texas Avenue and Preston Street, a hundred-storey cylinder of mirrored black glass and anodised steel that dwarfed every other building around it. One of the city's more perceptive radio jocks had nicknamed it 'The Nightstick', and the name had stuck. The whole of Houston knew that the top floors of the tower were the private domain of Jasper Moffett and his two brothers, by far the richest men in Texas and reputedly the richest men in the world. The Nightstick looked like the Devil had sliced a doorway to Hell through south-east Texas' clear blue skies, and while many Houstonians might privately harbour the uncomfortable feeling that the three Moffett boys were in league with Satan himself, this was Texas, and Texans admired money and oil above all things – and the Moffett's had more of both than just about anyone else.

Jasper Moffett III cared little about the view from his window, but savoured the dark satisfaction he took each morning as he surveyed the skyscrapers below him and thought how every boardroom in these shining monuments to the power of oil and wealth literally had to look up to him each day. It hadn't always been so, but the family's spectacular rise over the past fifty years had been a case study in the brutal realities of business and Jasper Moffett's unbending desire to win at all costs. Of course, mused Jasper, they'd had a significant advantage over their competitors, but that was quite another story ...

Dressed that morning in a crisp white Charvet shirt open at the neck, tailored blue jeans and a pair of handmade, anaconda-skin cowboy boots, Jasper Moffett III was a big man with a trim, square beard, his silver hair still full and slicked back from his forehead. Six foot four and a gifted athlete in his youth, he had earned a fearsome reputation as a rattlesnake-quick and malevolent linebacker at the University of Texas, where he had graduated summa cum laude in petroleum engineering before starting his career at the bottom as a roustabout on one of the family's small land rigs in the Texas Panhandle, as his grandfather and father had done before him. Now nearing seventy-five years of age, he might have lost a step or two on the football field but the waistline remained trim and he was still an imposing sight. Jasper Moffett had a prodigious knowledge of the oil business, and as those who had dealt with him would attest, he'd lost none of his malevolence over the years.

Jasper turned from the window and sat down at his battered and scarred oak desk. It had been his Granddaddy's, back in Jasper Moffett I's wildcatting days when he had founded the company Jasper now controlled, but was now heavily though invisibly modified with the latest technology. Nevertheless, Jasper could still pull open the bottom drawer to rest his boots upon. He sipped from a large mug of strong coffee, as he watched one of Wolverine's black and gold jet helicopters swing in from the west and approach the tower, its posse of security drones keeping station around it. The helicopter was bringing his brothers, Warren and King, to the office from the family's sprawling ranch in the hill country toward Austin, some 200 miles away. Jasper gently tapped the desktop and said quietly, "Marvin, have the boys meet me for breakfast."

"Y'all want I should tag along, Jasper?" replied the voice of the man dressed in black who kept station beyond the security door of his inner office, where a secretary might normally be expected to sit.

"Let me hear what these boys have to say for themselves first. Don't expect they'll tell me anything I don't know already. Happen we'll want to go talk to our friend. Y'all stand by."

"Sounds like fun," said Marvin, in his lilting, Louisiana drawl.

Marvin Thibodeaux was a man whose Narcissism was only rivalled by his capacity for backstabbing ruthlessness. He favoured Cuban heels on his hand-tooled boots, not because of any aesthetic charm they might bring, but for the extra two inches of height they afforded him, and he disguised (or so he thought) his baldness with a selection of toupees crafted for him by one of Paris' finest, and most discrete, manufacturers of bespoke wigs and hairpieces. In fact, Marvin's baldness was the worst kept secret in the whole of Wolverine Petroleum, but not even Jasper Moffett III himself would dare mention one of the numerous 'Marvin's wig' jokes within a thousand yards of the man's hearing. As Head of Security and Special Situations, just the mention of Marvin Thibodeaux's name could put the fear of God into every one of Wolverine's eighty-five thousand staff, no matter how high they might sit up the corporate totem pole, and his arrival at one of the company's rigs or refineries inevitably heralded pain and suffering for someone.

Jasper kicked his boots off the open drawer and rose from his desk. As was his wont, he looked up at the two full-length portraits of his father and grandfather that dominated his quarters and nodded his good morning. Raising an eyebrow as he passed Marvin, who was now relaying orders quietly into a headset, Jasper headed across his suite to the more spacious and comfortable surroundings of the dining room.

*

The helicopter settled on the landing pad on the roof of Wolverine Tower. Magnetic shackles clamped the 'chopper firmly after it landed, and as the rotors cycled down, the three hydraulic rams that held the landing pad in place disengaged and the whole section descended smoothly down two levels into the top of the building before coming to a stop. The aircraft's doors opened. Warren and King Moffett hurried down and headed for the secure airlock set into the inner wall, while technicians dressed in black and gold Wolverine Petroleum jumpsuits appeared to begin their routine checks of the aircraft.

As seemed to happen in certain families, it was hard to believe that Warren and King Moffett were even related to their elder brother, Jasper. Maybe the genes that had made Jasper such a dominating individual had skipped a couple of beats when Warren and King came along. Whatever the reason, the three of them made an unlikely trio. Warren Moffett was of medium height and somewhat portly, with a bad comb-over and a doughy complexion that neither exercise nor a healthy diet had ever been able to improve. Where Jasper Moffett had the easy elegance that came from a simple wardrobe of beautifully made clothes worn well, Warren had the uncanny ability to make even the finest Savile Row suit look sad and rumpled within minutes. This morning, despite the fact that he was wearing a brand-new grey bespoke herringbone from Anderson & Sheppard with a red and gold Hermès foulard silk tie over his white button-down shirt, he gave the impression of being a harassed and underpaid accountant slipping into middle age while others passed him by on the career ladder. Yet appearances could be deceiving, for behind Warren's shabby exterior lay a superior mind that collated the facts and figures about Wolverine Petroleum's business with frightening ease. While Jasper could stand under the spotlights when required to be the company's public face, Warren's gifts preferred the background, guiding the business from the shadows with a practiced hand.

Following Warren through the airlock wheezed the youngest of the three, King Moffett. King had fallen in love with computers at an early age and gone on to earn a doctorate in computer science at M.I.T., and a life of late-night programming and junk food had left him overweight and habitually out of breath. His mop of dirty blond curls, thinning at the crown, sat above a pair of protuberant eyes and a fleshy mouth, which all combined to give King the look of a rather louche monk. Nevertheless, the two elder Moffett boys had quickly recognised King's unique abilities, and Wolverine Petroleum had a well-earned reputation for the use of cutting-edge technology, often with spectacular results.

Warren and King passed through the retinal scans and biometric monitors that guarded the building even at this most private of entrances. It never paid to keep Jasper waiting, and they knew that the news they brought with them would do nothing to improve their brother's state of mind this morning.

*

A half dozen large flat screens dominated the main wall of the open plan dining room of Jasper's quarters, each silently playing one of a selection of 24-hour news and business channels from around the world. Jasper scanned them quickly as he fixed himself a plate of salad and smoked salmon at the sideboard, then took his customary seat at the head of the huge slab of mahogany that served as a dining table. The double doors at the end of the room swung open silently and Warren and King Moffett entered to join him.

"So, it's confirmed then?" stated Jasper, dabbing his lips with a white linen napkin.

"Yep, it's true," answered Warren. "Don't see why nor how, but production's falling at every well we own."

"I've run all the simulations I know," added King. "And we've got the mother of all problems."

"Y'all can forget about the earnings hit. The way things are stacking up, we'll be writing down our reserve levels. I don't have to tell you what that means, Jasper," said Warren, loading his plate with pancakes and syrup before he sat down heavily beside his elder brother.

Jasper regarded his two siblings silently and sipped his coffee. No, he thought, Warren did not have to spell things out for him. If he had to announce to the world that the reserves in Wolverine's oilfields were now substantially lower than their previous estimates then the markets would go berserk. The company's share price would crumble, and all those executives and bankers that Jasper so enjoyed looking down upon would quickly smell the blood in the water and come seeking their own pound of flesh. It did not bear thinking about, so Jasper did not. He was not going to allow such an eventuality to take place. Warren and King waited nervously for him to speak, picking at the food before them.

"So, what does he say?" asked Jasper slowly.

"The dragon?"

"No, dummy, the prize bull in the North Forty! Yes, the dragon! What does the dragon say?"

"He says the same he's been saying for the past don't-know-how-long if King or I talk to him, Jasper. Says he'll talk to you and you alone," answered Warren quietly, trying not to catch his brother's eye and the look of disdain that he knew it would contain.

"You know that one-eyed old devil won't tell us nothing no more," blurted King. "I can't stand having him inside my head."

Jasper returned his attention to his breakfast, and for the next several minutes the only sound inside the dining room was the soft chime of cutlery on fine porcelain.

"I know you boys don't like it one bit, but that ol'dragon made this company. He's the reason y'all get to fly here for breakfast. If our oil's drying up, then he's the one that knows why … and he's the one that's going to have an answer." Jasper pushed back his chair and stood. "You boys go on downstairs now. I believe we still have a company to run here."

He flicked the intercom on the table. "Marvin, get my aeroplane ready. We're heading out West."

4 Mostro

EJ's arrival at the entrance to No.16A Albemarle Street had not gone unnoticed. High up on the wall of the rather exclusive hotel on the opposite side of the street, sat a small, nondescript box of electronics. From below it didn't merit a second glance, disguised as it was to blend in with all the other junction boxes, cable points and assorted electronic paraphernalia that seemed to have proliferated on every building in the city, and which had therefore become invisible to all but the most attentive. A very discreet gentleman who specialised in such clandestine work and had been recommended to Marvin Thibodeaux by an acquaintance in the British security services, had placed it on this particular wall a number of years previously. The equipment it contained piggybacked the hotel's power and wireless networks, and King Moffett's ingenious programming made sure that it left no electronic footprint and removed all trace of its activity after it was activated.

It had been some time since this box of electronic tricks had been called upon to do its job, but it had functioned perfectly. Disturbed by EJ's entry, the beam from a low-powered laser rangefinder trained on the portico activated a pair of tiny cameras, which auto-focused and took a rapid burst of shots. To avoid unnecessary alerts, image recognition programming compared these pictures against a library of regular arrivals, such as postmen or couriers – the types of everyday activity that one would expect at any central London address. Not finding a match, the new pictures of EJ immediately uploaded to a server in Wolverine's headquarters to which access was severely restricted. It was now just a question of when Marvin Thibodeaux would get round to reviewing them.

Of course, Selwyn Ormerod had his own list of contacts in the upper reaches of Britain's intelligence services, and thus was well aware of the little box and its purpose. Indeed, he and Michelangelo were counting on it.

*

"It's time we took a look at a few details for you. Then we'll nip and say hello to the lads downstairs," said Selwyn Ormerod, reverting to what EJ had now silently decided was his 'business' voice. He opened a drawer and withdrew a slim blue folder which he laid on the desk before him, steepled his fingers and said, "EJ, you have for the past fourteen years owned thirty-seven percent of Anglezarke Holdings Limited through a trust which was established in your name. Certain monies were made available to your parents from time to time, but these were relatively small sums – school fees and the like. Michelangelo and I now propose that on your eighteenth birthday you take direct control of your shareholding, and that you should also become a Director of the company at a basic salary of £500,000 per year.

"As I said in my letter, this is subject to a meeting with Michelangelo in Anglezarke, when you and he can best decide your role. I know he has some ideas about what is going on and how best to proceed. Do you agree?"

EJ touched the dragon pendant at her throat. "Last night, my dad said that at some point everyone needs to go out and find who they really are. He said you and Michelangelo must have something important for me to do. I think it's time I found out what that is, don't you?"

Selwyn Ormerod smiled. He brought his hands down and placed them on either side of the folder, and studied the dragon engraved on the signet ring on the little finger of his left hand. "You know, Michelangelo and your grandfather gave me this ring twenty-five years ago. Since then, I think I've done the most important work I could ever have imagined ... and the most interesting. If you'd asked me at the start, I'd have said you were bonkers, but I've discovered more about myself along the way than I thought possible, and each step has been an adventure."

Selwyn opened a desk drawer and removed a slim envelope. He slid it across the desk to EJ.

"Here's £1,000 in cash to cover immediate expenses, together with the details of an account opened in your name. Your first month's salary has been advanced to the account. And there are Amex and credit cards drawn on the company. The PINs are inside the envelope.

"Right! Next thing is to get you on your way up to Anglezarke, and for that we need to go downstairs and see young Mr. Mortensen. He's got everything else ready for you."

Selwyn Ormerod tapped one of his computer screens. "Stan, put the kettle on. EJ and I are coming downstairs for a brew."

They took the same lift EJ had ridden in earlier down to the basement, where they entered a lobby of plain concrete, bare except for a pair of CCTV cameras and a touchscreen panel set next to a steel fire door. Selwyn placed his hand against the panel, which chirped once, and then bade EJ do the same.

"We've all your biometrics already from the scan upstairs. Brussels'd get its knickers in a twist if it ever found out. European directives? Ha! Won't keep me awake at night," said Selwyn with a derisive snort.

Another electronic chirp and the steel door clicked open and swung smoothly inward. Selwyn led EJ past a room full of server racks behind a glass wall, their LEDs flickering in green and red pulses. She briefly placed her hand on the glass and could feel the steady background hum of air conditioners in the room on the other side.

"One part of our systems," explained Selwyn. "Mostly hooked into trading platforms here and in New York, Tokyo, Zurich, a few other places. There's a much bigger server farm up in Anglezarke that handles most of the business and the communications. Two of Stan's brothers look after that one," Selwyn pointed out as they walked through another fire door and into a room divided into four spacious cubicles, each with an impressive array of computer monitors.

A flat Lancastrian accent greeted them from behind the large bank of monitors in the furthest cubicle. "Give us a sec, Selwyn! That bloody high-def feed's on the blink again."

There were a couple of loud thumps and a muffled curse, then a dwarf's cheery face, his hair and beard both plaited with silver rings, popped out from the stack of equipment. He grinned and shouted, "Ay up!"

"EJ, may I introduce you to Ragnar Mortensen, a.k.a Stan to his friends," said Selwyn.

"Call me Stan. It's an old joke, but they're the best, or so I'm told," said Stan Mortensen jovially, extending a be-ringed hand. He was wearing a rather faded Iron Maiden tour t-shirt, jeans and heavy motorcycle boots. EJ noticed that both of Stan's arms were heavily and expertly tattooed.

"Pleased to meet you, Stan," said EJ. "Love your ink! Mr. Ormerod says you're the man to see before I go up to Anglezarke."

Stan Mortensen nodded in recognition of EJ's compliment. "Well, Selwyn's not wrong there. The lads should have the tea brewed by now, and we can run through a couple of things. Have you got your 'phone with you?"

EJ fished into her handbag and handed Stan her iPhone, as a rather solemn dwarf with long grizzled hair and large mutton-chop whiskers came into the room carrying a tray with three large mugs of tea.

"This here is Albrecht, known as Lemmy for obvious reasons, who besides making a reasonable cup of tea is a dab hand at all things cryptographic. He'll make your 'phone a damned sight safer from eavesdroppers and the like," said Stan, tossing EJ's iPhone over to Lemmy.

Lemmy moved off to the farthest cubicle and set to work at his keyboards and computer terminals, while Selwyn dragged a pair of office chairs over to Stan's workspace and the three of them sat down.

"Stan," began Selwyn, "why don't you fill EJ in on your side of the operation. Then we need to get her kitted out and on her way."

"Ay, Selwyn. Well, EJ, Selwyn's probably told you about Michelangelo and money, right? Loves it even more than us dwarves, and that's saying something! The thing is, Michelangelo's a damned quick learner. He took to trading like a natural. So, me and the lads here run the front-end tech for him to be in the markets in real time, but most of the business comes from the desks up in Anglezarke. Basically, between us we process whatever positions he wants to take. The big servers are the ones back at the mill in Anglezarke, and they're the primaries, so with ours here we've got redundancy built into the system," explained Stan, playing with one of the silver skull rings on his fingers.

"Besides all that, I take care of most of the other tech when it's needed – personal communications gear and the like. Which brings me to you." Stan pulled open the deep double drawer to one side of his desk, removed a slim leather rucksack and handed it to EJ.

"This is keyed to your right index finger alone. You'd best test them now. Just press your finger onto the locks."

There were three thin, matt-black locks to the three compartments of the rucksack, each looking like a small blank luggage tag. EJ did as Stan had instructed and pressed her right forefinger to each in turn. Tiny diodes on the side of the locks changed from red to green as they released.

"Go on, open it up. We've stuck one of our laptops in the back for you. It's already set up to our encrypted VPN. The charger and everything are in the front pockets," said Stan.

EJ removed a sleek MacBook Pro from the rear pocket of the rucksack and flicked it on. She was unsurprised to see that the screen background was the stylised dragon of her pendant, and wondered whether this had now become her logo too.

Lemmy had obviously weaved his programming magic on EJ's iPhone, as he now brought it back in a new leather cover and set it down next to the rucksack with a small bow.

"EJ, do you know what a Faraday bag is?" asked Stan, lifting the rucksack from the desk. EJ looked up from the laptop and shook her head.

"Well, a Faraday bag shields its contents from electromagnetic waves. We've put a copper mesh between the leather and the lining. It should stop most electronic snooping. Not completely foolproof, but it's a lot better than nothing. There's a shielded wallet for your passport etcetera inside, and Lemmy's put your 'phone in one too."

Stan Mortensen then got up from his chair and reached for a large, flat cardboard box on a shelf behind him. He brought it down and laid it on the desk in front of EJ and said, "I hear you're a 'bike rider. Reckon you're any good?"

EJ sensed the challenge in the dwarf's voice. "Pretty good," she replied. "I ride every day, and I've done a fair bit of motocross at weekends. No track riding yet, though."

Stan grinned and said, "You're gonna like this then." He opened the box with a flourish. Inside was a set of crimson bike leathers. The workmanship was exquisite. EJ gasped and instantly fell in love.

"Oh Stan! These are beautiful!" she exclaimed. "Can I try them on?"

Stan looked at Selwyn Ormerod, who sighed and said, "Bloody dwarves. Always did have a flair for the melodramatic. Go on then, take EJ into the garage and show her."

"Show me what? No, you're kidding!"

"Well, these aren't much use if you've nothing to ride, are they?" laughed Stan. "Come on, we've got her in the lift to the mews house."

The three of them went through the back of the workroom past a small kitchen, EJ clutching her new leathers and rucksack and feeling rather giddy, like a little girl on Christmas morning who has asked Santa for a pony and suddenly realises that she's actually got one.

The mews lift was a spacious and brightly lit cargo lift, in the middle of which stood a bright red Ducati Mostro 797, with a red full-face helmet and a pair of racing boots sat on the lift floor next to it. EJ looked from Selwyn to Stan and back, her mouth open in delighted astonishment.

"OMG! That's a Ducati!" whispered EJ.

"Yeah. Pretty cool, huh?" replied Stan, obviously equally enamoured of the motorbike.

"I hate to break up this tender moment between the three of you, but there's a reason for all this," said Selwyn Ormerod. "EJ, you need to get up to Anglezarke quickly, and we'd prefer no one notices you too much when you do." He looked pointedly at Stan Mortensen and added, "Though how a bright red motorbike and leathers are supposed to be inconspicuous is beyond me."

"Give over, Selwyn," laughed Stan. "EJ needs something fast for the highway and agile for the smaller roads up on the moors. This is perfect. And red? Well, of course it's red – it's a Ducati."

"Oh, I suppose you're right," admitted Selwyn, looking at his wristwatch. "Come on, take the lift up to the mews house. EJ can change upstairs there."

*

Stan slid the lift doors closed and pressed the control to take them up. He picked up the boots and put them on top of the leathers in EJ's arms. "Leave your clothes and bag upstairs. We'll send them home for you tonight. Come back down when you're ready. The doors'll all open to your palm print. Just come straight through and we'll get you on your way."

The lift rose and EJ's excitement mounted. Yesterday now seemed a lifetime away. Ahead of her lay the meeting with Michelangelo and all that might follow from that, but first – first! – was the ride to Anglezarke on an amazing new 'bike! A Ducati! She still didn't want to say it out loud in case by uttering the magical name the spell might break. She realised that Stan was talking to her.

"… so, we just replaced the whole floor with the lift. Makes it easier to bring equipment and stuff in and out of the workshop."

"I'm sorry, Stan. I was miles away," EJ apologised.

The lift came to a stop and EJ realised that Stan had been explaining to her that the lift fit perfectly into a whole section of the ground floor of the mews garage. The back wall now showed a doorway with stairs leading to the second floor, while at the front was a steel concertina door through which the muffled hum of Mayfair traffic could be heard.

EJ ran to the doorway and up the stairs. There were two doors leading off the landing, and EJ guessed that they had once been the coachman's quarters. She recognised the touchpads next to them and placed her palm on the nearer of the two. The door clicked open and lights came on in the small room beyond, which held nothing more than a desk and office chair. She went in, pulled the chair across to her and started to change out of her clothes.

EJ unzipped the leathers from the collar across the chest and then down the right-hand side and sat down to pull them on and re-zip them. The leather was soft and warm. She stretched to either side and then did some leg lifts. The suit moved perfectly with her, its strengthening and protective pads staying exactly in place. She clipped the collar studs and sat again to pull on the boots. Once again, they were a perfect fit.

"Oh, I could so get used to this!" she said out loud, and then had to sit down again as a paroxysm of giggles left her helpless. EJ finally pulled herself together and hurried back down to the garage, where Selwyn and Stan waited patiently for her next to the Ducati. She put the rucksack on her back and walked admiringly round the motorbike. Stan handed her the helmet, a pair of red gloves that matched the leathers, and the 'bike's keys.

"We've programmed the routes to Norton Magna and Anglezarke into the maps app on your 'phone, and you can Bluetooth it into the bike's audio system. Take it easy to start with – this is much more powerful that you're used to. We changed the tyres to a heavier tread, so they should handle country roads better, but you might feel them a bit here in town. She handles like a dream though, so you should get used to her pretty quickly."

Selwyn approached and said, "As Stan said, your laptop and 'phone are now both on our private network. You can get hold of either of us any time day or night. Go home now, then head out first thing tomorrow. You'll be in Anglezarke by mid-afternoon, and you'll be expected."

EJ looked at them both, and then hugged each of them fiercely, tears pricking the corners of her eyes. "I won't let you down."

As Stan rolled the garage door aside, EJ settled the helmet on her head, adjusted the chinstrap, and got on the Ducati. She hit the starter button and the bike came to life with a low growl. EJ selected first gear and eased out into the mews.

She immediately found that Stan had been correct – while the bike was not a great deal larger than machines she had ridden before, it was a lot more powerful, and its balance and agility, even in low gear, made the ride a pleasure. Confidence growing, EJ started to slice smoothly through the mid-afternoon traffic of Mayfair, running up through Berkeley Square into Grosvenor Square, then bearing north toward the heavier traffic of the Marylebone Road. She relished the fact that the gorgeous Ducati and her crimson leathers were so easily visible to the rest of the vehicles around her, and was soon merging onto the A40 and heading out of London. Traffic was heavy but the rush hour had yet to build, and EJ was finally able to open up the Mostro as the wide road headed out through Uxbridge and on into suburbia.

Fifty exhilarating minutes later EJ eased back on the throttle and took the exit for Norton Magna. It was about three miles more through the rolling chalk hills to the village, the narrow roads between the tall hedges of hawthorn and hazel dappled in the late afternoon sunlight, the heady scent of cowslip strong from the verges. She eased back on the throttle and flicked the visor of her helmet up as she cruised, the wind on her face, and thought about all that had happened. The idea of answering her mother's stock question of "So how was your day, love?" made her laugh out loud with the absurd joy of it all. Well, let's see, Mum. I had a splendid lunch in Mayfair with a rich dragon's personal lawyer, who told me that I was now rich myself, and then a dwarf who looked like a roadie for a heavy metal band gave me all this cool stuff, and all because my grandfather … Ah yes, she thought, the smile fading from her lips. My grandfather. She dropped the visor and gunned the throttle again, the Ducati's engine screaming as the revs jumped and EJ scorched the last few hundred yards into the village.

EJ pulled to a breathless, skidding stop behind *The Grouse and Hare* and killed the engine. She sat and thought about how, of all the gifts with which she had been showered in the past thirty-six hours, the most precious was the knowledge of her grandfather, his big hands reaching out for her, the two of them fused in that moment, raw from the pain of their loss to greed and self-interest. She could feel him out there somewhere, and knew that this whole surreal adventure was now in deadly earnest and meant more to her than anything she had ever known. EJ took off her gloves and released her helmet. She pulled off the rucksack and dug into it for her iPhone. Scrolling down the contacts, she called Selwyn Ormerod's number.

"Selwyn? I'm home in Norton Magna … Selwyn, I don't know what my grandfather's got himself mixed up with, but I'm going to find him."

*

Seated once more behind his desk, Selwyn Ormerod ended the call and carefully placed his phone in the centre of the blotter in front of him. He

53

straightened it with the tips of his fingers and stared through the windows into the middle distance. So it begins, he mused. With any luck, the curiosity of a certain bewigged gentleman in Houston should be about to be piqued. Selwyn sighed. He had fought long and hard with Michelangelo and EJ's grandfather to continue to leave her out of things, but in the end, they had won the argument as he had known they would. He picked up the 'phone again and rang downstairs. A couple of minutes later, Stan Mortensen appeared in the doorway.

Selwyn regarded the young dwarf. "You know Michelangelo instructed me not to monitor her journey."

"I know he did."

"So where did you plant the tracers?"

Stan looked at him steadily and said, "I've got three different GPS tags – one on the 'bike and two more low frequency transmitters sewn into the leathers. She'll never find 'em."

"Good lad," said Selwyn, getting up from his desk. "Right, let's go see if there's any more tea in that pot."

5 Jacky Boy

Jasper Moffett settled back into the soft cream leather of his seat as his VTOL aircraft climbed away from Wolverine Tower and set a westerly course across the city's sprawling suburbs. He contemplated the conversation he was planning to have with the Oil Dragon. Closing his eyes, he thought back to that extraordinary evening on Lake Maracaibo and the weeks that had followed. Weeks which had set the course of his life, and, through him, the lives of so many others. Weeks which had now led to this.

No sooner had the dragon collapsed back to earth to scream out its agony and need in Jasper's head, than the maelstrom on the lake had subsided, replaced by an eerie stillness. Jasper had cautiously picked himself up from the deck and staggered to the davits that held the supply vessel's Zodiac outboard. With the help of a pair of crewmen he had lowered the boat with himself in it over the side. He raced across the short distance to the island, hardly slowing as he beached the launch on the narrow strand. The low prickly scrub and mangrove of the shoreline quickly gave way to more mature trees and rocks set in sandy soil. Finding the dragon had been easy – the splintered trunks and smouldering wreckage of the lightning explosions' devastation increased as he headed further inland, but even if the forest had remained pristine, he would have only had to follow his nose. Jasper remembered he had tied a bandanna over his face but it did nothing to stop the acrid reek of burnt flesh and gasoline. The stench seemed to pulse around him in waves, as if some gigantic barbecue had been overturned ahead. All the while the mental anguish of the dragon battered at his mind and pulled him forward.

He had burst through the last stand of broken palmetto to a sight that would forever remain seared in his memory. The dragon writhed in agony before him. The right side of its head was flayed raw, and blood as black and thick as crude oil seeped from its wrecked eye socket. It flapped a tattered right wing, but the left one lay unmoving at an unnatural angle, while the powerful body smoked and smouldered from the terrible wounds that it had endured. Nevertheless, even severely damaged, Jasper's breath had caught in his throat at the animal's magnificence. It was probably about forty feet long and, Jasper supposed, looked pretty much like the dragons he had seen in picture books as a child, but its jet-black scales glinted and shimmered with the rainbow iridescence of oil on water as the massive muscles of its haunches flexed and the long, barbed tail scythed to and fro.

In that instant, Jasper Moffett III had understood that his destiny now lay here before him. The noise of the dragon's agonies and the buffeting of its onslaught on his mind seemed to melt away, and he had spoken the words which had sealed his life's path.

"You called me so I'm here. I'll help you. Now tell me how you will repay me."

With effort, the dragon had slowly turned and brought its fearful and ravaged head close enough to Jasper that he could hardly breathe for the acrid fumes. The remaining reptilian eye focused on him, and in the new silence of his mind Jasper heard the dragon speak slowly and clearly for the first time.

"I shall bring you that which you desire. I shall bring you oil. By dragon's blood I, Jacinto Saavedra Cervantes i Domenech, bind myself. Hold out your hand."

Jasper had done as he had been told, and the beast had flicked its tongue, like some obsidian dagger, to lick the black blood that flowed from its ravaged eye. It had stretched further forward and dragged it across the man's outstretched palm. Jasper's own blood welled from the shallow cut that the dragon's tongue opened across his hand with the finesse of a surgeon wielding a scalpel, to mix with the reptile's jet black ichor.

*

Sunlight flooded the cabin as the plane banked smoothly. Jasper studied the thin white scar that ran diagonally across his right palm. He smiled ruefully, then looked across to where Marvin Thibodeaux sat dozing. Marvin had been the Drilling Superintendent on the Maracaibo rig that day, and with his help Jasper had gathered together a barge, winches and lifting equipment, and a crew to handle them. By daybreak, Jasper and his team had been back on the island, and through a combination of physics, manpower and the Oil Dragon's own sheer bloody-mindedness, they had somehow managed to move the injured beast onto the barge deck. After years of rig work, both Jasper and Marvin were both reasonably accomplished field medics, and between them they had set to tending the worst of the Oil Dragon's wounds with all the medical supplies that the rig's dispensary could provide them, but it had been clear that more specialist help would be required. They had lashed together a crude tent from all the tarpaulins they could find to shroud their cargo and begun the tow North. Jasper chuckled to himself as he remembered his merciless bribing of the port and customs officials in Maracaibo with the ten thousand dollars in cash he always carried – his 'walking around money' as he called it – and by the end of the second day they had been clear of Venezuelan waters and headed for Houston.

Jasper had sailed the Caribbean often both before and since, but he could not remember a smoother voyage. Indeed, he had become convinced that just as the weather had been the Oil Dragon's downfall on the lake, somehow it had now been working in its favour. He and Marvin had ferried back and forth between the ocean tug and the barge several times each day during the three weeks it had taken them to reach the Gulf Coast, and by the time they had reached port the worst of the Oil Dragon's wounds had been well on the mend.

Throughout the voyage, the great dragon had studiously ignored Marvin, though it had allowed him to examine and change its dressings, but it had soon began to communicate more openly with Jasper. Its answers to his questions, which had been begrudging at first, had become fuller and more nuanced as the two of them had begun to learn how to talk to each other. The sensation of Jacinto

Saavedra Cervantes i Domenech – Jacky Boy as Jasper had quietly dubbed him – speaking directly into Jasper's mind had quickly become second nature to him, and as time passed Jasper had come to realise that the telepathy only worked at close quarters and was most fluent when the Oil Dragon had direct eye contact. All Jasper had needed to do to gain some respite had been to put some distance between himself and the creature. He had asked the dragon if it could read his thoughts, and the creature had seemed mystified by the idea that it would even bother. The only thing they had talked about, then and ever since, had been oil. Jasper understood that the Oil Dragon not only had no interest in any other subject, but that it was the creature's very essence. In that respect, they were kindred spirits.

Jasper had never needed reams of paper covered in facts and figures. He carried it all around in his head, and when there had been a particular detail that he had not had to hand, Marvin Thibodeaux had been sure to be able to supply it from his own seemingly inexhaustible store of drilling data. Jasper had told the dragon about rock formations and sediments, inclines and declines, drilling depths and pressures, and all the other technical minutiae of the Maracaibo rig's operations. To begin with, Jacky Boy had seemed non-plussed, but when Jasper had translated everything into a language of colours and shapes, it had been as if a light switch had been thrown and the dragon had begun to reveal its own precise knowledge of the oil held locked beneath Lake Maracaibo. With mounting excitement, Jasper and Marvin had barricaded themselves in the tug's radio room each night to relay instructions to the drilling crews, and within a couple of days the rig was striking the oil that Jasper had always known would be his to find. By the time they had docked in Houston the news of Wolverine's Venezuelan success was everywhere, and Jasper Moffett was the toast of Texas.

Jasper had ordered the largest of Wolverine's warehouses near the port to be cleared for his arrival, which hadn't been difficult since every piece of equipment it contained needed to be shipped to Maracaibo to keep up with the supercharged drilling program that he had set in motion. Under cover of darkness, and with another shower of bribes to keep people looking the other way, they had moved the dragon into his temporary home. Over the next three months, Jasper Moffett III used some of the tidal wave of money that he and Jacinto Saavedra Cervantes i Domenech had created to turn Texas' finest veterinarians into millionaires as they brought the dragon back to health under the strictest confidentiality that money – and threats – could buy.

A stroke of luck and an overheard conversation had solved the problem of where to house the dragon on a permanent basis. One of Jasper's high-up lobbyists in the military had learnt of a huge empty tract of land owned by the US Army in New Mexico near the border with Arizona. A mad jumble of canyons and arroyos, it was pretty much the middle of nowhere, and Jasper had paid the largest bribe yet to secure it for Wolverine and have it removed from the maps. If anyone checked the records, all they'd be met with were vague signs that indicated an Army testing ground, with no mention of Wolverine or what the quarter of a million acres of nowhere really contained. A month later, they had moved the Oil Dragon overland disguised as a wide load bound for a refinery, and installed him in the high mesa far from prying eyes.

And so, the years had passed, and Wolverine had grown spectacularly to dwarf its rivals. Jasper would bring Jacinto Saavedra Cervantes i Domenech samples of rock and drilling cores from anywhere on the globe, as his company ploughed wave upon wave of money into more and more concessions, often after they had been dismissed as unpromising by the competition, and the uncanny magic would be repeated time and again as the dragon's sense for oil had guided them to some of the biggest strikes in the history of the petroleum business. The circle of people who knew the real reason behind Wolverine's success remained small, and Marvin Thibodeaux had made sure that it stayed that way, sanctioned by Jasper Moffett to use whatever means necessary to do so.

Now, thought Jasper, he needed answers. This conversation with Jacinto Saavedra Cervantes i Domenech would be the most important he had ever had since that day long ago on the forgotten island in Lake Maracaibo. He hadn't come this far just to watch his whole empire collapse around him. No sirree, Jacky Boy! That one-eyed old devil best know why all of a sudden Jasper's oil was disappearing quicker than water down a plughole.

6 Xiaolongbao

To her surprise, EJ had slept like a log, in spite of the excitement of the previous day and the sheer, delightful improbability of it all. The cooing of the wood-pigeons in the tall chestnuts and beeches around the pub had woken her just after first light, and she had risen to pull on her jeans and a sweatshirt before padding downstairs. She went into the kitchen to put on the kettle, and then slipped out of the back door and into the yard. There was still a chill to the air and wisps of mist in the hollows and under the trees. EJ hugged herself as she crossed to her Ducati, on which a fine film of condensation had formed. Hesitantly, she wiped it away with the tips of her fingers, admiring the bright red machine — attentive, almost alive.

EJ shook the image from her head and wrapped her arms around herself. She turned and hurried back to the warmth of the kitchen. The kettle had already boiled, and George and Maureen were sat at the kitchen table in their dressing gowns, a pot of tea and three mugs before them. EJ had seen little of her parents the night before, as they had had the pub's evening trade to look after: her own bright red arrival back in Norton Magna meant that *The Grouse and Hare* was even more abuzz with gossip, and hence thirsty customers, than usual. There had been some appreciative "ooh's" and "aah's" as she had shown off her new motorcycle to George and Maureen, but little time for a real conversation. By the time George had seen the last of the regulars on their way, the rush of adrenaline had long subsided and EJ had been fast asleep. She pulled out a chair and sat down as Maureen poured the tea.

"I had a wonderful day," she said, somewhat superfluously.

George Carver guffawed.

"Wonderful day! I'd say you had a day for the ages, my love!"

George's laughter was infectious, and in no time the three of them were gasping for air with tears rolling down their cheeks. Finally, EJ managed to pull herself together enough to speak.

"Well, it was wonderful, and Selwyn is just as nice as you remember him, Mum. And I suppose I know that it all makes sense in the strangest way … I mean, it all fits with the bits and pieces I've been remembering …"

EJ fingered the dragon pendant at her throat. "Oh, I don't know what I mean! But it seems that everything he wrote in his letter is true and I'm now quite wealthy and have something important to do. That's if I want to do it."

George sipped at his mug of tea as he watched his daughter struggle with the reality that now faced her.

"It would seem to me, that all that's changed is you have more choices open to you this morning than you had yesterday. You can still do all the things you wanted. Maybe not in the same order, or at the same time, but those decisions are still yours, and yours alone," he said deliberately.

"I suppose you're right, Dad. Anyway, I still have to go up and meet Michelangelo today, and I expect he has the final say."

"We know, love. Gibby had a quiet word with us last night," said Maureen, taking EJ's hands in her own. "I can't rightly say I understand what's going on, but it seems to me that you owe it to yourself to keep going and find out. I've laid out some clothes and whatnot, though there's precious little space to put them on that fancy motorbike of yours."

EJ squeezed her mother's hands and grinned. "It's not very practical, is it? But it's so cool!"

*

Breakfast over, washed and changed, and with as much as she could fit in her backpack and the two small panniers, EJ fired up the Ducati and rolled slowly out of the yard with a final wave to George and Maureen. She tapped the visor of her helmet into place. She and her parents had agreed that she should spend the night in Anglezarke and then travel back down to Norton Magna the following day, no matter what transpired when she met with Michelangelo. The engine barely ticking over, she let the 'bike roll smoothly round the Green in the middle of Norton Magna toward the road out of the village, and wondered if she would be able to keep to that promise, or whether other plans were already afoot. It had already occurred to her that the last time she had truly been in control of her own destiny had been her final 'A' Level exam three days previously. Since then, she seemed to have allowed herself to be directed, manipulated even, by this fantastic cast of characters that had gate-crashed her life. Oh, it had all been lovely thus far, and she certainly enjoyed the attention and the toys, not to mention the sense of a new life opening before her, but she was determined that none of it should change the plans she had for Cambridge and her future. EJ gunned the throttle, and as the Ducati leapt forward like a thoroughbred given its head, resolved that whatever the result of her conversations with Michelangelo, she was not going to let it distract her.

She wound down the long lane that led from Norton Magna to the main London to Oxford road, revelling in the feeling of becoming as one with the agile motorcycle. The cool haze of early morning had already burnt off, and the sky was clear and blue with the promise of another glorious summer's day. EJ maintained an easy pace through Buckinghamshire and across into northern Oxfordshire, allowing herself to soak in the beauty of the verdant countryside around her before she would have to concentrate more fully on the road and her journey North when she joined the heavier traffic of the motorways. At Bicester she stopped briefly and bought a couple of bottles of mineral water that she stowed in her backpack, before she dropped down the ramp onto the M40, ran the 'bike smoothly up though the gears and sped on toward the Midlands.

About an hour later, EJ pulled into one of the motorway services to refuel and take a break. Her trip thus far had been a blast, and the looks of other drivers as she passed them, ranging from the appreciative to the downright envious, had left her grinning from ear to ear. EJ parked and dismounted, giving the Ducati an affectionate pat. She removed her helmet and shook out her curls, now heavy and sweat-darkened, and headed for the amenities of the station. Inside the busy rotunda of restaurants and convenience stores was another story: her euphoria quickly began to wane as she felt heads turn and eyes watching her, and EJ began to feel a creeping disquiet. The conspicuousness of the red 'bike and leathers, which Selwyn had commented upon the previous day, now began to weigh upon her. She hurriedly bought a sandwich and a cup of coffee, but rather than sit in the food court, she took them back outside to one of the picnic tables set back nearest the line of trees on the edge of the parking area. Was this how it was going to be from now on, she wondered. It struck her that of all she had seen so far of Anglezarke and Michelangelo's activities, she was currently the most obvious, and this realisation was jarring. A very small voice in the back of her mind started to ask whether this was by accident, or could something more be at play? One more thing for her to ponder, but for now there was little she could do about it except continue on her way to Anglezarke and the greater anonymity that she presumed awaited her there.

EJ drained the last of the coffee, stood and tossed the cup into a nearby waste bin. Pulling on her gloves and helmet, she remounted and swung slowly out of the services, winding up through the gears once more to rejoin the motorway. The volume of traffic built steadily as she hit the busy industrial heartlands around Birmingham and she had to reduce her speed, so that by the time she joined the

M6 and was heading into Staffordshire, she had put her concerns out of her mind and was wholly concentrated on the road and vehicles around her. She stopped once more, relieved at the chance to take a break from the thunder of heavy goods vehicles around her and dismount to stretch her legs. The day's warmth and humidity had continued to build and clouds were now massing in the heavy, moist air. EJ sat for a while on her 'bike and drank from one of her bottles of water. By the looks of it she'd be lucky to make it to Anglezarke in the dry, so there was no point in hanging about. She flipped her visor back down and hit the starter button.

The skies had continued to darken, and EJ felt the first fat drops of rain hit as she slowed to leave the motorway. She knew it was probably her imagination, but she thought she could hear the hiss as the heavy drops hit the hot tarmac of the slip road beneath her, the shower intensifying while distant thunder rumbled its own welcome to Lancashire. Off the motorway the traffic was light, and she followed the glowing tail lights of a small van as it turned at a road sign for Anglezarke Moor, and headed off the main road.

Even in the rain it was easy to follow the line of this new road as it gently snaked up the escarpment that formed the edge of the moor ahead, the hillside a wash of purple heather and yellow gorse, even in the gloom the luminescent black and white road markers twinkling into view as they caught the lights of passing vehicles. The rain began to ease, and it took her less than ten minutes to crest the hill. EJ pulled over to the side of the road and took in the view: Anglezarke Moor stretched before her, a wide plateau that formed a shallow bowl before it rose again toward the foothills of the distant Pennines to the East. The village of Anglezarke itself sat toward this further side, spreading up and away from the centre of the bowl, the tall brick chimney of its former cotton mill vying with the spire of the church for dominance of what passed as the village's skyline, curved rows of tidy terraced houses running up the gently rising slope from the village's centre, where a utilitarian stone bridge crossed the broad stream which had once fed power to the mill's great steam engine. Of course, the passing of that age was clearly evident in the sodium street lights which were now winking out as sunlight returned to the afternoon in the downpour's wake, and the numerous solar panels affixed to many of the houses' roofs. EJ reached round and removed her phone from her backpack, unsurprised to find a strong cellular and data signal. Well, that's a relief at least, she thought wryly.

As the far side of the village rose away beyond the terraces the land was more noticeably wooded. A trail of smoke among the dense greenery of oak and ash betrayed the presence of a house: Her destination. Set into the hillside among the trees beyond stood the door to Michelangelo. Her back wheel spun on the loose, wet gravel and EJ fishtailed the Ducati back out onto the lane to swoop down through the series of gentle curves that led into the village of Anglezarke.

*

EJ had spent most of her life in Norton Magna, a place so picturesque that it regularly featured on television in one of Britain's longest running murder-mystery series as one of those quintessentially English scenes for genteel gruesomeness which charmed viewers the world over. In contrast, the tidy brick and slate-roofed terraces of Anglezarke offered a very different aspect of England. As the road crossed the stone bridge, the centre of the village broadened into a handsome street of late Victorian frontages and shops – a Post Office, a grocer's, a bakery and a fish and chip shop cum Chinese takeaway, who's reassuringly steamed-up windows showed the blurred outlines of a queue of customers inside, and made EJ's stomach rumble as she rode past. There were two pubs, each with vibrant displays of hanging baskets which resonated with her, and which she assumed (rightly, as it turned out) to be evidence of the sort of publicans' floral arms race with which she was intimately familiar. The sort of traffic and the number of people on the street was as one might expect in any village: All in all, Anglezarke appeared a pleasant, hard-working and altogether ordinary place.

The larger of the two pubs stood next to the imposing iron gates of the old mill, which had clearly been subdivided to become the home to several other companies, including, EJ noticed, a sign for Mortensen's Metals Ltd., which must be the family business that Stan had described during their conversation in London the previous day. The mill's iron railings, painted an elegant British racing green, curved alongside the road as it gently rose, the still damp tarmac gleaming in the late afternoon sunlight, more neat terraces lining the slope of the hillside opposite. Two old ladies stood chatting near the open mill gates, and they turned to wave cheerily to EJ as she rolled past. Well, she thought, there's something you wouldn't see in Norton Magna!

At the top of the slope stood the parish church, its stones darkened by the soot of former times. Modest and of plain design, the church could have passed for a non-conformist chapel if not for the impressive steeple that dominated its Western end, providing architectural interest to an otherwise forgettable building. The bay windows of the more substantial terraced houses which faced it from across the road caught the sun as she passed, their net curtains maintaining a discreet silence to the outside world.

And here the village of Anglezarke abruptly ended. A low stone wall began on the side of the road opposite the church, beyond which stood a dense mixture of oak, ash, beech and chestnut. EJ realised that this must be the boundary of Michelangelo's estate, and sure enough, two stone gateposts, lichen-stained with age, came into view as the road continued its gentle curve ahead of her. She slowed and turned into the tree-lined gravelled drive.

EJ slowed further to little more than walking pace, the Ducati's engine now barely noticeable as the raucous blackbirds and thrushes sang their warnings of her arrival. At the end of the avenue, the trees opened out, the drive branching, the left fork straight ahead while the right curved around a broad lawn to end in front of a substantial Georgian villa faced in dressed stone blocks. EJ pulled to a sudden stop and gasped. She fumbled for the catch of her chinstrap, dragged her helmet off her head and didn't notice as it slipped from her fingers and fell to the ground at her side. Transported back to another summer, she saw the large house in front of her, its stone portico and evenly-spaced sash windows exactly as her mind's eye saw them on a long-distant day not unlike this one. She could see the same warm afternoon light and feel the gentle southerly breeze. The door had been black, now repainted a glossy red, and the Virginia creeper that had covered most of the two-storey frontage had been cut back and tamed, but EJ felt the sudden dislocation as the two timelines spun and merged. A new memory of her grandfather opening the big front door in welcome flooded her mind, the most vivid so far as she caught the sounds and scents of that long lost afternoon, and EJ realised with a shudder of delight that she must have been in her mother's arms. She fumbled for the handlebars in front of her as reality reasserted itself and she was jolted back into the present.

EJ blinked. She was breathing hard and it took several seconds to recompose herself. "Pull yourself together," she muttered, grabbing her helmet from the ground and thumbing the starter, then chided herself for her trite reaction to such a life-affirming experience.

She'd never been one for front doors, probably as a result of living in a pub, so she flicked the Ducati back into first gear and swung the 'bike left down the fork in the driveway which continued toward the back of the house. As she'd expected, and then realised she already knew, the rear of the house, its walls still faced in the broad stone blocks of the facade, backed onto a flagged courtyard. This was bordered on one side by a line of outbuildings, with to the right the long, high wall of the kitchen garden as the third side of the quadrangle. Ahead of her and set off to the side closer to the trees, stood a more modern structure; clearly a garage ample enough for several vehicles. The overall layout was somewhat larger than the pub's backyard at home, but not dissimilar. She pulled to a stop to park the 'bike next to the garage and dismounted. A pair of huge hounds, one jet black its sibling pearl white, emerged from the corner of the house and loped silently toward her, tongues lolling, their eyes seeming to glow a dull red in the waning light, and another frisson of recognition washed over her.

"Balthazar and Akitafelt, my beautiful hellhounds," she whispered hoarsely. The two great dogs stopped a couple of yards from her and stood patiently, watching as she removed gloves and helmet and unclipped her leathers at the neck. EJ knelt down, and the black Balthazar and white Akitafelt came to her, nuzzling her as she wrapped her arms around them and buried her face in their necks in an embrace.

"You made it then?" called a woman's voice, laced with good humour. EJ disentangled herself and turned to find she was being watched from the back door by a short figure with a broad smile. She got to her feet, and shaking her hair loose, picked up her helmet and rucksack and wandered over, Balthazar and Akitafelt flanking her. There were two stone steps up to the back door where the woman stood waiting for her, but even with this advantage she barely reached EJ's shoulder. She was dressed quite unremarkably in a red-and-black plaid shirt over a pair of jeans, her ruddy face framed by two thick plaits of auburn hair which sparkled in the sunlight. EJ realised with a start that each of the plaits was wound through with gold and silver thread. Her fingers flashed with gold rings, though the overall effect was rendered more mundane by the damp tea-towel she was holding.

"OMG, I love your hair! You have to teach me how to do that!" gushed EJ, as she shook a be-ringed hand, immediately feeling foolish and turning as bright red as her 'bike leathers for having nothing better to say.

"And a how-do-you-do to you too, love," laughed the woman kindly. "Welcome to Anglezarke. I'm Molly Mortensen. I look after this place." She lifted her chin toward the two guard dogs and added, "I see these two certainly remembered you. Wouldn't have let you anywhere near if they didn't know you already."

"Oh Molly, that was so rude of me. I am sorry," apologised EJ. "First the house, and then the dogs … I know this place, I know their names. How much more will I remember?"

"Oh, don't worry yourself, love. Past few days must have left your head in such a spin! Anyway, Michelangelo already knows you're here, but there's no rush. He'll keep. Tell you what, why don't you freshen yourself up and have something to eat first? You look like you need a good cup of tea."

EJ ran her fingers through the thick fur at the napes of the two dogs' necks, and they turned and padded silently back across the yard to the garden gate. Molly led EJ into a kitchen of polished granite, brushed German stainless steel and recessed lighting that could have walked straight off the pages of a design magazine. The earlier rain now no more than a waning scent on the late afternoon air, the kitchen's large sash windows suffused the room with dappled light. Two blue and white-striped mugs of tea already sat on the countertop with a plate of chocolate digestive biscuits beside them.

"Milk and one sugar. Stan already told us," said Molly, grinning.

EJ sat down on one of the leather and chrome stools at the island counter and picked up her mug. "So, you're a Mortensen as well? Let me guess. Stan's sister?"

"Cousin actually. Not that it makes much difference in a family the size of ours," answered Molly, taking the stool next to EJ.

"Does the whole family work for … I don't know what to call this whole thing yet. The Firm? Oh no, can't be that!" laughed EJ.

"Aye, most of us. We usually just call it Anglezarke," Molly replied, patting EJ's hand kindly before picking up a biscuit and merrily dunking it into her tea. "Bit of a shock for you, all this then?"

EJ looked through the large kitchen window toward the hillside that rose beyond the orchard and the kitchen garden. "It feels like I stepped out of one skin and slipped into another," she said. "Does that make any sense?"

"Not really my place to be giving advice, but you just take care to keep a good tight hold on who you really are deep down, EJ," counselled Molly. She paused, a soggy digestive biscuit halfway to her mouth. "Do you know what a glamour is?"

"You mean like an enchantment?"

"That's right. It ain't magic per se. No such thing if you ask me, but gold creates its own kind of magic. I should know, I'm a dwarf after all!"

Molly twiddled her fingers and laughed happily as her rings twinkled in the kitchen lights. EJ smiled and thought back to her own musings about her life and future. Molly's words, though couched in kindness, were not lost on her.

"I've ordered some Chinese food from the village," said Molly, finishing her tea and getting up from her stool. "Why don't I show you up to your room first? Everything's laid out for you – Michelangelo insisted – but I'll bring your things in from the 'bike in a minute. Food'll be here by the time you're washed and changed."

EJ took a last hurried gulp of tea and followed Molly out of the kitchen to the front hall. A vibrant Persian runner, its pattern a swirl of midnight blue, silver and gold, lay on a black-and-white tiled floor, walls half-panelled in pale oak. There was a stillness to the house, broken only by the tick of a long-case clock. At the foot of the broad staircase sat a large brass statue of a coiled dragon. The top of the stairs opened onto a generous landing with several doors leading away down the upper hallway. Molly opened the second of them and said to EJ, "Make yourself at home."

*

The bedroom looked out onto the front lawn, and the meadow and park beyond. The walls were painted in subdued coffee tones, and it was comfortably appointed in modern, blond oak furniture and cream cottons and linens. A separate door clearly led to an ensuite bathroom. The most striking thing about the room at that particular moment were the bags and boxes bearing the names and logos of Bond St. boutiques which sat stacked at the foot of the bed. EJ stuffed her fist into her mouth to stifle a scream and had to summon all her willpower to hold herself back from falling on them like a wolf on the fold. She set down her rucksack, thumbed the locks and retrieved her 'phone, her eyes never once leaving the shopping bags in case they suddenly developed a mind of their own and decided to leave. EJ called her mum to let her know she had arrived, and then scrolled through a mountain of texts and messages from school friends, all wondering where she had managed to hide herself, and why she wasn't answering. EJ half-heartedly resolved to try better, though how she was going to explain any of this eluded her. At the bottom of the list was a message from Selwyn Ormerod:

'Glad you've arrived safely. Hope you approve of the room and that its contents are to your liking.'

She quickly tapped out a reply: *'You certainly know how to spoil a girl!'*

After a few seconds, EJ's 'phone vibrated and a line of laughing face emojis appeared in answer.

EJ stripped out of her leathers and hung them over the back of the sofa, still eyeing the shopping bags warily, then went into the bathroom. The countertops were covered with yet more bags and boxes of cosmetics and scents, and this time she really did shriek with delight!

*

Showered and refreshed, moisturised and perfumed, she emerged some three-quarters of an hour later, ready to reward her patience and get down to the serious business of opening the shopping bags. Dusk had fallen while she had bathed, and the curtains to her room had been drawn, presumably by Molly. The bedroom's subtle lighting and the scent-heavy steam from the bathroom combined to turn the scene into a Santa's grotto of discarded boxes, strewn ribbons and torn tissue paper. Leather and silk, cotton and suede, all bearing the labels of the leading designers of Paris, Milan, Tokyo and London were each reverentially laid out on the bed. EJ sat back and surveyed the glories around her. The angels and demons of her nature were gathered on her shoulders and cavorting as they whispered into her ears, one side telling her that life could be one long cavalcade of catwalk shows and afterparties, the other warning her not to get distracted like some magpie eyeing a diamond ring. She touched the dragon pendant at her throat and thought back to the questions with which she had wrestled during the day's ride North. If the roles were reversed, and it were she who was bringing someone new into an organisation, would she be showering them with gifts to test their resolve? This test – if test it was – had certainly managed to wake her up before her meeting with Michelangelo, and the questions remained to be answered.

EJ went back to the bathroom to see what she could do about her hair. She added a little makeup, as she had taught herself, from the gorgeous selection that had been provided – just enough to feel good – and dabbed some Shalimar behind her ears and at her throat. She selected a simple white linen shirt and a pair of midnight blue trousers, cut beautifully from Shantung silk, then a pair of light brown suede Chelsea boots with a low heel. EJ admired the result in the full-length mirror and adjusted the collar of the shirt so that her dragon pendant was more visible. She picked up an Italian leather jacket and went out onto the landing.

She didn't need a map to find her way back to the kitchen. The whole house was suffused with the most delicious mix of scents and flavours. Ravenous after a day of service station sandwiches and production line coffee, EJ flew down the stairs two at a time. The round dining table at the far end of the kitchen had been laid with a bright yellow tablecloth. A Lazy Susan at its centre was covered with platters and serving bowls of Chinese blue and white porcelain. There was a solitary place setting, clearly intended for EJ, with an elegant handwritten menu set before the bowl and teacup. Feeling somewhat self-conscious, EJ sat down at the table to read the menu.

'The Fair View', Anglezarke – Fish & Chips · Chinese Cuisine

Shanghai-style Xiaolongbao Shrimp Dumplings

Cantonese Char Siu Bao Dumplings

Hong Kong Barbecue Pork and Fragrant Roast Goose Platter

*

Hangzhou Beggar's Chicken

Suzhou Taihu Lake Steamed Fish with Braised Sichuan-style Spicy Bean Curd

Guangzhou Abalone with Oyster Sauce

*

Fujian Double-boiled "Buddha Jump over the Wall' Soup

*

Zhou Dynasty Eight Treasure Rice

Kowloon Lobster E-fu Noodles

*

Long Jing Dragon Tea

"There you are! My, don't you look lovely," exclaimed Molly, as she bustled back into the kitchen, both delighting and embarrassing EJ at the same time. EJ looked up from the menu, and asked, "Aren't you going to eat as well, Molly? Oh, please come and join me. I hate eating by myself, and this looks amazing!" She lifted lids from the bowls on the table and almost swooned at the heavenly sights and smells within.

"Oh no, I couldn't do that, love," protested Molly, waving away EJ's entreaties.

"But you have to!" continued EJ, slyly wafting fragrant steam from the table in Molly's direction. She thought she saw Molly's nostrils twitch and flare and knew she had the housekeeper hooked.

"Go on then. It does smell lovely," conceded Molly, with a show of overcoming her hesitancy that deserved an Oscar. She rummaged in a couple of the kitchen cabinets and hurried back to the table with a place setting for herself.

Molly poured EJ a cup of tea, and EJ returned the courtesy, obviously impressing the dwarf, who said, "It's not just a Chinese custom, it's good dwarven manners too. Though of course in our case, we're usually not drinking tea!"

With that, the two women set to and tucked in, laughing and swapping stories in the way that good food will always allow.

"I've never eaten Chinese food like this! No way this is from the village takeaway!" said EJ, serving herself another helping of Beggar's Chicken.

"All your grandfather's fault,' replied Molly. "A few years back he returned from a visit to Jade Dragon and brought home a whole pile of recipes. Of course, Jade Dragon's not exactly proletarian, and his understanding of food is only fit for an Emperor's table. So, your grandfather presents them to Mr. and Mrs. Kao – they own the chippy – and says have a go at these then. The Kao's weren't too keen, but their eldest was into his haute cuisine and decided to stick them on the takeaway menu! There were a few diehards moaning about missing their chicken chow mein, but the rest of the punters loved it! Jade Dragon and his people think it's a hoot, so they send over new recipes about once a year to keep things fresh," explained Molly, polishing off one final bowl of Eight Treasures Rice. "And they still make cracking fish and chips," she added.

"I noticed the chip shop was full when I rode past," said EJ. "Now I know why. That was SO GOOD!"

Molly laughed. "Had enough? Why don't you wander over to see Michelangelo and say hello? He'll be watching the New York markets, but it's a quiet day so far. Leave me to tidy up here."

Molly pushed her seat away from the table and began to gather up the ruins of their glorious meal. "The path will light up for you, but you know the way already, if you think about it. I'll see you in the morning."

EJ gave the older woman a quick hug, and headed outside to the back yard, well-lit by security lights on either corner of the house. She crossed to the garden gate set into the high wall, where the red diodes of another bio-lock glowed beside the gate. EJ placed her palm against the sensor, feeling again that pleasant shiver of being part of a very exclusive club as the diodes flicked to green. The locks clicked and the gate swung smoothly aside. Balthazar and Akitafelt materialised from the darkness on the garden side and fell into step with her, as EJ had known they would. EJ sensed their alertness, and knew that these two otherworldly, un-ageing creatures were bound to her, and she in turn to them, as surely as any blood oath of fealty. With her guards now in place on either side, she set off across the garden and its neat beds of vegetables and herbs toward the orchard and the hillside beyond.

As Molly had said, small halogen lamps set into either side of the path lit up ahead of her as she walked, each three or four yards around her glowing into life as she moved forward, creating a rolling nimbus of soft light that then gently faded as she passed. The lights continued under the trees as the ground steepened. Michelangelo's hillside loomed ahead, the shadows of its gullies and contours lengthened by the moonlight, while a soft breeze played in the treetops, which creaked and rustled gently. EJ's thoughts inevitably turned to the memory of the only other time she had taken this path. Now as then, she had felt no apprehension as she stopped a few feet in front of the stone arch with its heavily studded oak door. In her toddler memory the door had seemed enormous, towering above her, the work of giants rather than men. Now seeing it once more, EJ realised that it was really quite an ordinary doorway, a plain arch of dressed stone blocks standing some nine or ten feet high, with simple stone flags set before it. The door itself had an impressive dragon's head knocker at its centre, a detail which had seemingly eluded her memory, but another set of winking diodes below showed that the knocker was for decoration alone. Balthazar and Akitafelt moved behind her to lay down, barring the path, their eyes glowing once more in the moonlight. EJ checked her appearance and tidied an unruly curl of hair back behind her left ear, then pressed her palm to the security panel.

7 Mesquite

Though Jasper had spent many, many millions on his dragon hideaway, it had been easy enough to run the cost through a maze of Wolverine's exploration budgets and other expenses. He'd even been able to take a tax write-off on most of it. This was a harsh landscape of high sierra, gullies and rockfalls, it's monotony broken by the occasional stand of sagebrush or piñon pine, mesquite and prickly pear. To an old drilling hand like Jasper Moffett, there was a certain austere beauty and interest to the meandering story its ancient geology told across its crags and escarpments, a tale of titanic forces and immeasurable time. Well, thought Jasper, immeasurable to most men at least. Over the years, they had covered the canyons with a spider's web of cables and steel hawsers anchored into the rockfaces, onto which military-grade camouflage netting had been slung, obliterating the chance of aerial or satellite surveillance. As technology improved, a network of sensors and other monitors had been installed, but beneath the camouflage nets was very much the dragon's demesne.

The VTOL's propellers swung up and out of their forward thrust position and the aircraft slowed into her descent to a broad landing pad whose concrete had been carefully and expertly painted to blend seamlessly with the desert surroundings. The engine pitch rose again as the pilots engaged just enough power for the aircraft to taxi, and she ran smoothly forward toward the hillside ahead. Motion sensors reacted to the stream of encrypted instructions from the plane's transponders and camouflaged doors rolled open to allow entry to the hangar complex that Jasper had built inside the hill. In the passenger cabin, Jasper slipped on a pair of mirrored Aviator sunglasses and picked up his Stetson from the seat beside him. Followed by Marvin, he descended and marched across the hangar space to its far side, where a line of ATV's stood ready. The main hangar doors had already rolled shut, and under the bright overhead lighting, Jasper felt the big room's turntable floor engage to swing the aircraft round so that it would be ready for their departure.

The two men were well used to the arrival procedure and its tasks, and worked quickly in a routine that they had practiced more times than they cared to remember. While Jasper checked that the ATV was fuelled and ready to go, Marvin grabbed two 12-packs of mineral water bottles from a stack by the wall and stowed them in the vehicle's cargo bay, together with a pair of rucksacks that carried emergency rations and medical supplies. His last task was to place both of their Stetsons in a carrying case that had been designed for just such a purpose, and clip it into place behind the seats. Checking that his toupee was still properly fixed to his head, he grabbed helmets and face masks from a locker, tossed one pair over to Jasper and climbed aboard the ATV. Jasper drew his mask up over his nose and mouth, pulled on his helmet and adjusted his sunglasses. He fired up the ATV, and they peeled down a short ramp to emerge from the shadow of an overhang of rock into the full white glare of the relentless New Mexico sun.

Marvin checked the screens in front of him. "He's about twenty miles north of us. In the big canyon."

"Uh huh. Reckoned he'd be somewhere in there, this time of day," nodded Jasper in reply. He opened the throttle and the ATV picked up speed along the well-worn track into the wilderness, leaving the fine dust from its six tyres hanging like a contrail in the still air. It took them an hour or so to reach their destination. At the top of the canyon, where the ATV could go no further, Jasper pulled to a halt in the shade of a stand of mesquite and desert juniper, the canyon's grey and orange sandstone cliffs rising to either side. He got out and stretched, pulling a bottle of water from the cargo bay, and drank deeply. Marvin handed him his Stetson from the carrying case, before carefully seating his own on his head.

"Let's get to it then," said Jasper, fitting another two bottles into one of the backpacks and hoisting it to his shoulder. Reluctantly, Marvin grabbed the other pack and levered himself out of the ATV. Marvin Thibodeaux prided himself that he had never disobeyed an order or a request from Jasper Moffett, and the list of unpleasant and downright illegal tasks he had performed over the years had, to his dispassionate outlook on life, been well worth it. They had made him wealthy beyond the dreams of most men, and more importantly (at least to his way of thinking) had brought him near equal measures of respect and fear in those whose paths he had crossed. Nevertheless, he had grown to loathe the dragon, and the canyon opening before them looked to him like the jaws of Hell itself.

The noon sun was now high in the sky, but obscured by the camouflage nets some thirty metres above them, so the heat in the canyon's manmade twilight became less oppressive as the two men began the steep trek downhill to the canyon floor. Jasper was well aware of Marvin's feelings about being in this place, but kept his own counsel as they descended the narrow path, stones and scree skittering over the edge as they scrambled along. He had understood long ago that the dragon had chosen him alone, and that the creature suffered the presence of his two brothers and Marvin as part of the complex web of respect that underpinned their relationship.

The snakes and lizards had learnt over many generations to stay in the sunlight away from the canyons, and it was rare that any bird or mammal was foolhardy enough to venture in, though there were always enough fresh bones and bleached carcasses lying around to show that the dragon remained adept at punishing any that did. At the bottom of the path, the cliffs opened out into the broad, sandy floor of one of the widest points in the whole canyon complex. They had no need of a tracking device down here. Jasper could already feel the dragon's presence on the edge of his mind, so while Marvin hung back and leant against a boulder, he walked forward and said out loud, "I'm here. We need to talk."

Jasper felt the pressure change in the air above and behind him, and turned to watch the dragon drop from the cliff face above, it's great shadow flashing past him as it swooped. Marvin had felt it too, but as usual had ducked too late, and the dragon, with exquisite care, had flicked the Stetson from his head with the tip of its tail. The cowboy hat bowled across the sand, Marvin cursing a blue streak of Creole invectives as he chased after it. The dragon wheeled awkwardly. Its left wing had never recovered its full range of motion and gave the creature a lopsided gait in the air as it overcompensated on every wingbeat for the weakness. There was a blast of sand and heat as it landed some twenty yards in front of Jasper, folded its wings slowly and walked forward. A dozen feet from him, it stopped, flicking its great tail to coil around it as it sat.

Jasper smiled dutifully as the dragon played out its theatrical entrance. He understood the creature needed to demonstrate some level of control in their relationship, even if the unspoken truth between then was that Jasper was the master here. A smile was a small price for their continued collaboration, and for a man who smiled so seldomly, he found it a pleasant change. Even Marvin realised that being made to play the fool on these visits was the fee the dragon exacted in order to ignore his presence and allow him to watch its conversation with Jasper from afar.

"You know why I've come," stated Jasper, foregoing any preamble.

"I know. The oil. It is always the oil," said the dragon, its voice in Jasper's mind measured, restrained. This was no accusation, just a simple statement of fact.

"You know it is disappearing. Why? What is happening to my oil?"

The dragon closed its single right eye and seemed to sigh. "Look at me. I am dying. As I diminish, so too does the oil."

Jasper stepped closer. The dragon's good eye flicked open and it watched him intently, waiting. The rainbow lustre of oil on water that had always played across the great beast's muscles and marked its power had dimmed, and only remnants danced and flickered in and out of Jasper's vision as he examined the great haunches, the sheen and ripple of light at play now missing from the dragon's scales. The great scars and gouges that had healed so well over the years as to be nearly invisible were now clear once more, and the empty socket of the missing left eye was a livid bruise of pain and damage again.

"I believed you immortal. Was I wrong?" he asked.

"Not immortal. Never so. As the world craved oil, so my strength grew. Now the world changes. No creature is immune to that. Not even the dragons."

"What do you mean, 'as the world changes'," scoffed Jasper indignantly. He moved back and sat on the edge of a low sandstone shelf.

"The world moves forward. It wants our oil no longer. I sense this. I feel this. Thus, you and I no longer wield the power we once did. The world has decided, and I diminish."

Jasper and the Oil Dragon watched each other intently, silent and unmoving. The crude oil that Wolverine Petroleum pumped to fill its coffers was the dragon's very lifeblood. They had both known for all these years that the pact he and Jacinto Saavedra Cervantes i Domenech had sealed in blood on that nameless Venezuelan island was a bond forged in single-mindedness, greed and naked ambition. The more oil that Jasper and Wolverine controlled, the greater the strength the dragon had enjoyed. The contract it had sealed with Jasper Moffett had been one of necessity to save its life, but it had brought it a vitality it had never known previously and to which it had become addicted. And now that vitality was ebbing. Yet, while the dragon now appeared resigned to its fate, the same could not be said of Jasper Moffett. He had built Wolverine Petroleum into the most powerful oil company the world had ever known, and that was the way it was going to stay.

"So, the oil in my wells is drying up, and my company's going to go to the wall? No sirree. Not going to happen. You've been whisperin' in my head for half my life? Well, I've learnt a thing or two about you as well, Jacky Boy. I can sense you too, you cunning old bird, and I know you don't give up easy. I was there the last time this big old world tried to get rid of you, remember?"

The dragon's pupil narrowed. Jasper held his gaze steady and knew that he was right.

"You would wish another outcome?" asked the dragon, thrusting its grizzled snout toward Jasper and flicking its long black tongue. Jasper Moffett did not move a muscle, despite the provocation.

"You would not surrender, Jasper Moffett?" it continued. "Then nor shall I. Follow me."

The dragon lifted itself and turned, moving off along the sandy canyon floor. Jasper realised that it meant to put some distance between them and Marvin, and he quickly motioned for him to stay where he was. Whatever needed to be said, the dragon intended it to be heard by him alone, or at least wanted no reply that Jasper might make to be overheard. Jasper pulled his Stetson lower on his head and followed. After forty or fifty yards, the dragon stopped and turned to face him once more.

"You must find the egg. You must bring me the egg."

"What egg? A dragon's egg?"

The voice in Jasper's head took on the familiar, ancient tone the dragon used when it looked at the rocks and samples that Jasper would bring him and taught him how to find the oil they contained. Whatever would be said now was a secret that few if any men had ever heard, but inside he felt the stirrings of hope, for this meant that, maybe, a solution was at hand.

"A dragon is of the earth. As I am of oil, other dragons feed from other … streams. This much you already know. We are not born, we are made. Ask me not how, for I do not have the words. But I diminish, so an egg will appear. Somewhere. You must find the egg. You must bring it to me."

"And when I find this egg and bring it to you, what then?"

"I shall destroy it, and in its destruction, I shall grow strong once more."

"And if you don't get this egg, what happens then?"

The dragon brought its head forward until it was just inches from Jasper's face.

"Then, Jasper Moffett, you and I shall both perish."

8 Old Gold

There was a rapid series of heavy clicks as security bolts in the door released. EJ had half expected a whoosh of steam or dry ice, like some special effect in the movies, but the door simply swung open smoothly. Bit of an anti-climax, she thought, as she stepped inside. The passage was disappointingly normal too, well-lit with walls of dressed stone blocks and a smoothly paved surface. It was about fifty feet long and sloped gently toward a balustrade and the bright lights of the larger chamber beyond. EJ stood for a moment. So, this was it, she thought, maybe not crossing the Rubicon, but she realised that she had been steeling herself for this moment from when she had left Norton Magna that morning, which now seemed a lifetime ago. Now, some of her questions could finally be answered. As EJ hesitated, a voice like honey dripping from an axe blade entered her mind and said,

"I am most pleased you have come, Elizabeth. Won't you join me? We have so much to discuss."

EJ steadied herself against one wall with her hand. Well, she thought, that was unexpected. She decided to try something and composed a reply in her mind, but it was met with silence, so she spoke instead.

"I have to speak to you, don't I? If I want to talk to you, that is."

"Yes," came the reply. "I may speak into your mind, but I cannot read it. My hearing is exceptional, but a dragon's mouth is not designed for conversation."

EJ hurried forward and stopped at the low balcony. Before her was a huge chamber that looked like the whole hill had been scooped out and a lid then put back on. It was roughly oval, and probably a hundred feet high at its centre. A complex array of lights and sound deflectors hung from the ceiling, while several large passageways opened from the walls either directly or via slopes and stairs onto its floor. It felt rather as if one was stepping into the Royal Albert Hall, or better yet the Royal Albert Hall if it were turned into an enormous cinema, for the front wall was covered by a huge screen split into different areas of coloured charts and graphs, spreadsheets and lists of codes and numbers which flickered green and red as their values changed. Along the top and bottom of the grand screen ran live news tickers, relaying the day's events and the gyrations of markets around the world. EJ was looking out onto the heart of Anglezarke's activity – its trading room.

Arrayed in shallow terraces around the great chamber sat numerous workstations. Some were active, with dwarves studying their racks of monitors, or talking into headsets as they typed at their multiple keyboards. Others stood idle, their screens blank. At the room's centre sat the dragon, Michelangelo de St. Exupéry-Antoine. He was watching her closely.

"Welcome home, Elizabeth. I am no judge of these things, but you have grown into a beautiful young woman," resonated Michelangelo's voice of honeyed gold in EJ's head.

EJ descended the short stone stair that led down from the balcony and approached. Michelangelo did not impress by his size, but by his presence. There was the gleam of gold to everything about him: his scales glowed with the old gold of burnished breastplates, his talons glittered like inlaid ivory, and the irises of his great eyes flared like sunbursts. It was somewhat disconcerting then to see him sprawled across a pile of cushions each the size of a wool bale, and apparently wearing a pair of large reading glasses. EJ giggled.

"Hello, Michelangelo. Why are you wearing glasses and sat on a big pile of cushions?"

Michelangelo shifted slightly and looked at her. There was a moment of silence, then EJ felt a low rumble that seemed to begin in the back of her brain and then roll and build into a ringing laugh, lambent and bright as bells, as Michelangelo guffawed.

"Ah, Elizabeth! I am found out, and so quickly! We dragons are vain creatures, but we are also old. My eyes are not what they once were, and, to be honest, my back hurts."

One of the several dwarves, his sleeves rolled up and long hair held back in an impressive plait, had hurried forward with an office chair from one of the empty workstations, which he placed next to EJ with a low bow. EJ, who was starting to see the family resemblance and reckoned this was yet another of the ubiquitous Mortensen clan, thanked him for his thoughtful gesture.

"So, this is what you do?" she asked, settling herself in the chair and turning to face the wall of screens. "I don't really understand it, but this looks a lot like one of those business news channels on television," she added.

"Yes, Elizabeth. This is what I do. I believe Selwyn and Ragnar – Stan – explained some of it to you." Michelangelo turned, his eye caught by a change in one of the charts on the screen. For a moment, EJ was left in silence. She had felt the dragon snap out of her mind, as if a telephone conversation had been cut off in mid-sentence, and then just as suddenly she knew that he was back.

"Forgive me, Elizabeth. I had to give the instruction to sell one thing and buy another."

"Because of what changed on the screen? Over there, in that big chart on the right with the white and blue lines," she asked, beginning to feel a tingle of excitement.

"You noticed that?" replied Michelangelo, a hint of pride in his voice. "I can see that you should not be underestimated. Yes, because those numbers changed. Though to me they are not numbers, even though the dwarves have spent many hours teaching me the concept. To me, they are shapes, they are patterns, they are colours."

"And you understand these shapes and patterns?"

"Of course, Elizabeth. They are the patterns of the great ebb and flow of gold. The great current of treasure by which the world turns, the very engine of the world. It is what made me."

EJ got up from her chair and walked over to the nearest of the unoccupied desks. She picked up one of the slim folders that lay in front of the keyboards and dark monitors and began to leaf through it.

"How do you keep track of it all? I mean, each of these guys handles something different, right? So, how do you know if you are making money?" she asked, putting the file back in its place and turning to the dragon.

"I keep track of it?" Michelangelo's voice barely concealed his amusement. "I do not, as you put it, keep track of it. I see the movement, I sense the flow. I know. It is for others to keep the score. You must ask that question of Selwyn Ormerod. It is he and the dwarves who keep track of it."

"But surely you care what happens to the money? How it is spent?" she asked him, genuinely curious for his answer. "Don't Selwyn and the dwarves – and I suppose my grandfather too – report it to you?"

"They do. They insist that I should be told. It matters not. The gold is there, the gold flows somewhere else. That is its nature. Why should I care where it finds its final home?"

From this angle, Michelangelo's eyes were opaque behind his spectacles. EJ watched the reflected lines of numbers and charts dance in the lenses. In that instant, she understood what Selwyn Ormerod had meant when he had called Michelangelo and the other dragons elemental. Men like her grandfather and

Selwyn Ormerod, and dwarves like the many Mortensens, had created this grand, complex edifice that was Anglezarke. It was they who took pleasure and pride in the people and places that it helped, the projects it supported, but most of all they took pleasure in Anglezarke itself. Because that is what men and dwarves did – they built things, the more complicated the better, and then they made them work, bent them to the purpose for which they were designed. Michelangelo de St. Exupéry-Antoine and, she supposed, the rest of the dragons were different. It was not simply that Michelangelo took no interest in the results of his work. What he did and what he was were one and the same, and EJ now understood that in that sense the dragon before her stood apart from the world.

EJ sat back down and rolled the chair forward until she was at Michelangelo's side. She reached out and ran her hand along the dragon's neck, watching the hues of gold, bronze and silver shift and shimmer. The great dragon's skin was cool to the touch, and EJ could hear the metallic clink as the scales rippled under the movement of her hand across Michelangelo's neck.

"It doesn't matter to you, does it?" she said gently. "It's not that you don't care, it just has no meaning for you. You are elemental. You are the Golden Dragon."

EJ felt Michelangelo heave a kind of sigh.

"I do not measure time in the same way as you, Elizabeth. The last time you were in this hall, your grandfather held you up to me and you ran your hand along my neck. Few are they who touch a dragon once in their lives. Fewer still those that have done so twice."

The dragon pressed himself closer to her hand, and EJ leant in to rest her head against him.

"I am of the earth. I am of gold. You see this clearly, Elizabeth."

"I do, but what about my grandfather? All this, and you can't find him."

"On the contrary, Elizabeth, I know exactly where to find your grandfather. I have always known. It is for you to return him here before he gets himself into too much trouble. The world turns. It is your time."

EJ stepped back, delighted and dumbstruck in equal measure.

"You are surprised, Elizabeth. You believe I have lured you here with lies and trinkets?"

"Yes, but why?"

"A good response. The correct one. This is not the first time that your grandfather has taken it upon himself to follow his own instincts, nor the first time that he has done so despite my entreaties, or the warnings of Selwyn Ormerod. Why should this time require you to learn of your true history and return to Anglezarke Moor? Why this time should I convince you to rejoin me? Because I fear that your grandfather is correct, and that he has knowingly placed himself in mortal danger. He believes that those who killed your parents are ready to wager everything to save their position in this world. He has never forgiven himself for that night. His penance was to watch you from afar grow into the young woman that stands before me, even as he accepted the need for your safety."

EJ sat back down. The hall was now deserted except for her and Michelangelo at its centre, the dwarves all appearing to have realised that Anglezarke Holdings and its many interests and affairs would transact no further business this night, and that the conversation now taking place, so long in the making, was not for their ears. Michelangelo had fallen silent, and he watched her coming to terms with his words.

"You're telling me he's off on his own some place, planning to take his revenge?" she asked the dragon, that now familiar set of her jaw signalling her defiance.

"He is, as you say, off on his own. For now. Revenge? I doubt it. He has had plenty of opportunities over the years to seek his vengeance, should he have so wished. No, he and I believe that a much greater wrong may be about to occur. Your grandfather decided he would find out if our fears are real or misplaced."

EJ bubbled over with questions, but Michelangelo gently rebuffed her and suggested that she retire to the house and get a good night's sleep. She quickly admitted to herself that the day's ride and the evening's revelations, not to mention a stomach full to bursting with the most delicious food, now all weighed heavily on her. Michelangelo was right, it was late and a good night's sleep was in order.

"Can I come back tomorrow?"

"This is your home, is it not, Elizabeth? You may come and go as you please. Mortensen and I will begin to show you more tomorrow. There is much for you still to learn," replied Michelangelo, settling himself more deeply into his nest of cushions.

EJ kissed the dragon on the cheek, and grinned as she felt his small thrum of pleasure. She walked back to the short stair that led to the hillside entrance. On the balcony she turned to wave, but the dragon was looking straight ahead, clearly focused on the screen in front of him. She headed down the passage to the door, and felt his words in her head one last time.

"Think hard, Elizabeth. The coming days may not be easy. You alone can choose which path to follow."

Balthazar and Akitafelt were on their feet, snouts raised to the currents of scent on the breeze, as EJ emerged into the darkness at the hillside door. She steadied her hands on the two great dogs' backs as her eyes adjusted to the moonlight. The great door closed behind her and she sensed rather than heard its locks click into place. The trio moved off down the path back to the house, where Balthazar and Akitafelt again melted away into the darkness. Lost in thought, EJ didn't even notice lifting her palm to the security panel by the back door. The small gestures and routines of this new life were becoming automatic, and she passed through the kitchen and headed for the stairs to her bedroom. Opposite the foot of the staircase with its coiled brass dragon, the double doors stood ajar, their varnished panels reflecting the soft glow of firelight. EJ knew they had been resolutely shut when she had come down to dinner earlier that evening. Her curiosity now piqued, as she was sure had been the intention, EJ pushed the doors open further and slipped inside.

The long room was a combination of library and study. Heavy velvet curtains were drawn across the three oblong sash windows that gave onto the front lawn, but each of the other three walls was lined from floor to ceiling with books housed in oak cabinets, some open and others with glass doors to protect their contents. A broad stone fireplace dominated the middle of the long wall, the hearth decorated with Majolica tiles in swirls of greens, reds and blues, the remains of several logs still burning. Two well-worn Chesterfields faced each other before the fireplace with a rather faded and somewhat threadbare Turkish carpet between them, and the room was lit by the colourful glow thrown by the stained glass shades of two Tiffany lamps sat on the sofas' mahogany end-tables.

She ran her fingers reverently down the leather spines of the volumes nearest the doors, examining more titles as she moved further into the room. She had always been a voracious reader and an avid student, and was immediately caught under the spell, the secret power of the books. This was an eclectic collection, a working library for reference and pleasure that had grown organically over time, not just impressive leather bindings bought by the yard by some interior designer. There were oversize collections of art books, as well as architecture and business, thrillers and literature of all kinds. Nearer to the fireplace, the shelves housed volumes in French, Spanish and Italian, as well as treatises in German and Russian that appeared to be concerned with matters religious and philosophical.

The far end of the library was dominated by a huge Victorian desk, and EJ envisioned the original mill owner sat there, mutton-chop whiskers and dark frock coat, surrounded by heavy Moroccan-bound ledgers as he tallied the credits and debits of his great enterprise and wrote his correspondence. Not much had changed then, she thought, in the intervening decades. At the centre of the desk's scarred, green leather blotter sat a single cream envelope. EJ didn't even need to look to know that it was addressed to her.

She realised that she was holding her breath, and forced herself to take in a long, shuddering draft of air, feeling the catch of the fragrant woodsmoke in her throat before she slowly approached the desk. An old-fashioned roller chair sat behind it, its leather worn and cracked, the indentation left by her grandfather in its cushion as he had sat there over all these years clearly visible. EJ did not sit down, but picked up the letter and carried it over to the nearer of the two sofas, where she pulled a couple of cushions towards her to make herself more comfortable. Molly had obviously anticipated her, for there were a mug and a small Thermos on the end-table beside her. EJ gratefully poured herself some tea and took another deep breath as she fingered the pendant at her neck. She was ready.

The same heavy cream stationery, and the same blood red wax seal with the Anglezarke dragon imprimatur, but this time the letter was simply addressed to 'EJ', written in confident italics in emerald green ink and underlined with a flourish. She forced the flap with her thumbnail and lifted out three sheets of rich cream writing paper. As she released the letter from its envelope, a pair of polaroid photos fell out into her lap. She turned them over, and even though she knew what she would see, couldn't stifle the cry of delight that quickly, and without any conscious decision, turned to sobs. She held the first of the two small prints up to the light of the Tiffany lamp beside her, and through a blur of tears looked at a picture of a young couple stood in front of the house, its ivy and creeper a riot of autumn reds and golds. The woman, her mother, held the swaddled infant EJ in her arms, and was half-turned to the man at her side, who stood smiling down at her, his arm around them both. Her father was a good head taller, with a mop of unruly blond curls that fell to the collar of a weather-beaten wax jacket. EJ's mother was also dressed for the country in jeans and a quilted stable coat over a ribbed turtleneck jumper, her chestnut hair tied back in a ponytail. EJ unconsciously patted her own hair as she examined the picture, proof at last, if proof had ever been needed, of the provenance of her own abundant curls. She set the photo down, and picked up the second one. Her breath caught at her throat once more. It must have been taken well over twenty years previously, for it showed her grandfather and Selwyn Ormerod stood together in front of the entrance to No.16A Albemarle Street, the pair of them suited and booted in crisp white shirts, sober silk ties and pinstripes. Her grandfather wore a red carnation at the buttonhole of his three-piece suit, while Selwyn Ormerod sported a gold watch chain across his waistcoat. The two friends were smiling at the camera, with the somewhat self-satisfied look of colleagues that had just concluded an important business transaction. Selwyn Ormerod's appearance had changed very little, the silver at his temples had of course spread to the rest of his hair, and EJ wondered whether the same might be true of her grandfather. In the photo his jaw was strong, and his dark blond curls, though cropped shorter than his son's, still betrayed the family resemblance. EJ looked more closely at her grandfather's eyes. She could discern the beginnings of crow's feet, but his gaze seemed to twinkle with amusement, as if only he had got the joke, and he was smiling with a lopsided grin. She laid the second photograph alongside the first and turned to the letter.

My dearest EJ,

For you are and have always been, Elizabeth Jade. Other details may have been changed, but I would not countenance any change to your names, as much for my own sake as for yours. It seems so very long ago now, but I am certain that the confident young woman whose progress I have observed with so much pride and joy, should instinctively understand that there is power in a name, and for these many years I have stubbornly held to the conviction that one day I would be able to write to you, EJ, my granddaughter.

Since you are now reading this letter, that means that over these past several days you have already learnt a great deal about who and what you are, and where you come from. Some of this may have surprised you, some maybe not, but I warrant that you have taken these revelations in your stride. For this, as for so very much else, I owe a debt of gratitude to your parents, George and Maureen. Make no mistake about it, EJ, for your parents they most assuredly are.

It is not yet time for me to welcome you personally back to Anglezarke, but such a time will come. In a life that has too often been tinged by regret, this latest failing on my part pains me more than words can say. Michelangelo and I discussed my decision over the course of many days and nights, and though the logic remains sound and rules my head, it does nothing to assuage the bleakness in my heart that, for the time being, I have willingly foregone a long-dreamt reunion.

Thus, we come to the matter at hand. I am sure you have been told that I have "gone off the reservation" or some other such euphemism for my current travels. I had become convinced that change was in the air. Great change, the like of which had not been seen in the world for many generations. Michelangelo sensed it too. Selwyn argued strenuously for me to hold back, to wait until we knew more, and in particular for you to remain uninvolved. Selwyn is a splendid man, a lawyer with a first-rate mind and, above all, my friend. However, like many of his profession, he has over the course of his career learnt to place caution ahead of endeavour. His yin to my more piratical yang is a counterpoint that has served us well over the years, and I fervently hope that it will continue to do so in our current circumstances. However, Michelangelo and I came to the conclusion that the time for caution was long past. I believe that you already understand. You are my granddaughter, and you are Anglezarke's future. I shall therefore assume that Michelangelo has already admitted to you that, in that uncanny way of his, he is well aware of my current whereabouts. If I am correct, and I firmly believe that I am, then matters are about to come to a head. Our first reunion will thus be away from Anglezarke, quite where in the world I cannot yet tell, though I have the feeling that it will be sooner than either of us imagine.

Trust your instincts, EJ, and trust in Michelangelo. There's never been much that you can get past him, you know, and I stopped trying long ago. Your own *opinions of Selwyn Ormerod and of our other colleagues, especially the estimable Mortensen and the clan, will take some time to form fully, yet you will not find them wanting on your behalf or in the defence of Anglezarke and all for which it stands.*

There are some tricks that might be considered obsolete in this age of technology and wonders, but which still serve remarkably well. One such is the handwritten letter, a splendid method to avoid prying eyes and unwanted records. I have found over the years that it usually pays to have a back channel open, and now is just the sort of time to use it to maintain contact with you directly. I have a very clear idea of where your own travels are about to take you, and shall leave further correspondence for you to collect from the poste restante in a number of the cities which I expect you to visit, beginning with London. Please enquire first at the Post Office on Grosvenor Street in Mayfair. I am confident that you will be passing by there in the very near future.

I deeply look forward to seeing you once again, and remain,

Your loving Grandfather,

Joseph Livesey

The remnants of a log shifted in the hearth with a shower of sparks. EJ looked up from the letter then emptied the last of the tea from the Thermos into her mug, stared into the dying embers and tried to make sense of what she had read. It was a mass of contradictions. More cloak and daggers. What, she thought, should she think of a man who after nearly a lifetime of separation from her would put his misgivings about the future of the world and the opinion of his beloved dragon ahead of welcoming his own granddaughter back into his life? Yet, wasn't it this whole idea that Anglezarke embodied some higher purpose that had drawn her back? At least he was right that Michelangelo had appeared to tell her the truth, and something, an understanding maybe, flickered at the edge of her vision but remained just out of reach. Well, as he had said himself, Joe Livesey was off the reservation, so she would rely on Michelangelo to guide her further. EJ picked up the two Polaroids from the table and studied them: At least now she could feel a more tangible link to him. She folded the letter and tucked it and the photos back into their envelope, then pulled her 'phone from her pocket to check the time. She was surprised to find that she had been sat deep in thought for far longer than she realised and that it was already late. EJ suppressed a yawn, stood and stretched.

Back in her bedroom, EJ carefully slotted the envelope and its contents into an inner pocket of her rucksack. The debris of earlier in the evening had been cleared away, and the clothes, including those her mother had packed for her that morning, had all been neatly hung or folded in the wardrobe. EJ changed into a loose sweatshirt and shorts and, not wanting to make a bad impression with Molly, carefully hung her evening's attire up as well. She switched off her lights and got into bed, the room dim in the moonlight. How would she explain this swirling carnival of events and impressions to her parents? Before any kind of answer could form, EJ had fallen fast asleep.

9 Mademoiselle

The sun was falling into the West. The shadows on the cliffs crept higher and the canyon floor sank into a deepening twilight. Jasper watched the dragon retreat into the darkness, his tattered bulk becoming more indistinct.

"Where do I find this dragon's egg?" he asked. The last he saw was a rasping flick of the barbed tail, and then the dragon was lost to the shadows.

"Seek out the other dragons. They will know. One will know. One may tell you," echoed the reply in his mind.

"One? Ask each of 'em until one admits? Is that it? Why don't you know yourself?"

"I saved myself all these years past, Jasper Moffett. I made a pact sealed in blood. You remember this?" the dragon answered deliberately, an edge of angry regret in the voice in his head that Jasper had never heard before. "You received your heart's desire that day. Yet to live, I gave up something precious. I am oil. I am dragon. Since that day I no longer sense the others. I know not where the egg may be found."

"You saying you sold your soul to the devil that night?"

"I sealed my pact with you, Jasper Moffett, in dragon's blood. Are you the devil?" came the reply.

"Goddamn you!"

Jasper Moffett knew his voice had betrayed him. He knew that even here, in this most secret of places and conversations, he should have stayed silent, not risen to the bait. Instead, he had let his frustration and fear show, and was disappointed with himself that he had offered the dragon any hint of weakness. The dragon made no reply. Jasper's mind and the canyon had fallen silent.

He cursed quietly and headed back toward the cliffside path at the head of the canyon. At his approach, Marvin Thibodeaux levered himself from the boulder on which he had been waiting. He tossed a full water bottle to Jasper, who passed him without breaking stride and headed back up the track toward the ATV. Marvin fell in behind. He knew from long experience that Jasper was rarely in a talkative mood after visiting the dragon, so stayed quiet as they climbed back out of the arroyo. Jasper would tell him in his own good time whatever the two of them needed to discuss.

Jasper hung his Stetson on a dry mesquite branch and poured half the bottle of water over his head, scrubbing the fine grey dust from his face. Beard glistening wet, he finally looked Marvin in the eye.

"Old bird says he's dying."

Marvin wiped his own face and scratched an ear as he pondered Jasper's pronouncement. "He beat them odds once already. We were there. Why's he so certain this time?" he asked.

"Says the world don't need our oil, so the world don't need him. That's why our wells are drying up," explained Jasper, stowing his hat and climbing aboard the ATV.

"Merde, Jasper. Didn't that old salaud have any suggestions?"

Jasper settled himself into his seat and slowly drank from his water bottle. He turned to Marvin and grinned.

"Yep. He said find him a dragon's egg and he'd take care of the rest. I reckon we've got ourselves a dragon hunt."

With that, Jasper pulled on his goggles and mask and slammed his foot down. The ATV spun out from under the stand of scrub in a fountain of dust and gravel, and they set off at full tilt for the hangar base.

The first stars began to show themselves as the broad, clear sky shifted from the waning orange glow of sunset that still hung like a crown of fire to the tops of the distant mountains, to the violet of early evening, and the temperature was rapidly falling by the time they arrived back at the hangar. The VTOL was already fuelled, prepped and turned to face the hangar doors ready for departure. The pilots ran through their final pre-flight checks while Jasper and Marvin squared away the ATV and other gear. Marvin would send one of his small security teams of former Special Ops guys up to the base the following day to clean and restock with fresh supplies and aviation fuel, all routed and hidden behind half a dozen shell companies and never to appear in Wolverine's records. Within minutes they were airborne and heading east back to Houston.

Unlike Jasper and his brothers, Marvin Thibodeaux did not keep an apartment in Wolverine Tower, preferring the ostentation of the mansion he had constructed in the upmarket River Oaks neighbourhood of Houston. Nevertheless, a comfortable guest suite was always at his disposal in the tower for when he might need it, and he had stayed there after their return from the high desert. He was an early riser, and was at his desk before sunrise the following morning.

Jasper Moffett might be the face of Wolverine Petroleum, a man with the wealth and power to compel even presidents and potentates to wait upon him, but Marvin was the company's eyes and ears. He accessed the computer on his desk with a long alphanumeric password and a pair of biometric tests, and entered a set of servers that existed entirely separately from Wolverine's operations. Marvin had spread his net widely over the years of Wolverine's ascent to build a web of contacts both formal and informal. Some were direct employees responsible for security and safety at Wolverine offices and facilities across the world and Marvin quickly ran through their regular reports, annotating some and replying to others. Then he entered a new window which required further passwords to proceed. At this point, Marvin always intoned a short prayer of thanks to King Moffett and his paranoia about encryption and data security. Back in the day, before the computer had taken over the world, King's concerns and doom-laden warnings had been treated as a joke by his two brothers and the other senior Wolverine executives, but as information technology had become ever more critical, they had changed their tune and realised that King had been ahead of his time. He now oversaw an IT budget of eye-watering proportions, and a good chunk of this outlay was spent on the darker side of technology. Marvin and King used their skills to keep Wolverine ahead of their competitors through a parallel network of informants, both human and electronic. Some of this intelligence was secured legally, some not so, while a small proportion came from sources that remained so black that, should they ever come to light, neither Jasper Moffett nor the Good Lord himself would raise a finger to save him.

Marvin liked to picture his intelligence gathering as a city map, and he knew and tended every route and byway. There were the major avenues and landmarks, which might signify a government minister or a senior executive at a rival company that Jasper or Marvin had suborned or blackmailed and put on their payroll. Further from this city centre might sit a residential street, a place of comfortable villas or a pleasant local pub, and these might represent an academic or the head of a think-tank, ostensibly opposed to the oil industry but secretly feeding Marvin their thoughts on policy, which gave the company the chance to put its considerable lobbying powers to work. If you studied the map more closely still, you would discover the dark alleys and quiet backstreets where Marvin's most secret watchers and listeners lurked. The flow of information his city map delivered, whether the steady stream from the well-lit boulevards or the intermittent drips from its more clandestine addresses, was a constant source of joy for a man like Marvin Thibodeaux, who like spooks everywhere derived a visceral pleasure from simply knowing something that others did not.

Each day, he would compile a dossier of messages, rumours and illegally copied documents and present it to Jasper. Together they would decide what was of value and what of merely passing interest, and on the appropriate courses of action they should take. Occasionally, Marvin's most subtle watchers – the dark alleyways of his imaginary city – would provide him a nugget of pure gold, and this morning he noticed a flashing alert from a snooping device he had had installed high on a wall in a fashionable London district. A device which had delivered nothing of note for a very long time.

He opened the attachment and studied the dozen or so photographs of a young blond woman elegantly dressed in a smart navy suit, stood the day before at the entry to No.16A Albemarle St., the London offices of Anglezarke Holdings. A couple of the shots were rear view only, but one was a clear side-on profile of her face, while two more showed her entering the building.

"Well hello, Mademoiselle," said Marvin to himself, "and who might you be?"

Marvin scanned through the photos again and uttered a favourite Creole curse under his breath. There were no pictures of her leaving.

He sent a selection of the best shots to his printer and slipped them into the folder he had prepared for Jasper. The two men might be close, but Jasper was the boss and Marvin would never presume to just walk in on him. He keyed the intercom, knowing that Jasper would already be at his desk, and given the okay he picked up the dossier and went in to see him.

Wolverine was in a tight spot, but Jasper was not a worrier. That morning, as he had so often found, he felt refreshed by his visit with the dragon, even though their conversation had been tense. As Marvin entered the small private office, he was in his customary position, hand-tooled boots resting on an open desk drawer, a mug of strong coffee in his hand, leafing through the day's edition of *The Wall Street Journal*.

"Share price off another couple of points yesterday. There are whispers in the market that we've got problems," he said without rancour, looking up from his newspaper. "What you got for me today?"

Marvin opened his dossier and slid the glossy photographs of the young blond woman across the desk. Jasper folded his newspaper, setting the mug of coffee down to one side. He arranged the photos according to their time stamps, and viewed them silently for several minutes.

"Well butter my butt and call me a biscuit. It has been a long time, young lady. How old must you be now? Seventeen?"

"Almost eighteen," confirmed Marvin, "If it is who you think."

"Why? You don't?"

"Nah, I think it's her as well. She never left the building. Leastways, not by the front door."

Jasper leaned back in his chair, deep in thought.

"Is that right? It's her, but you get some confirmation first. Tell King to do his thing and poke around in some of their computer systems. London's got cameras thicker than fleas on a farm dog. One of 'em will have seen her. Let's see where she upped and disappeared to."

Jasper paused and picked up his coffee cup again. "I'll be. The one dragon on earth we can't get to. Old Michelangelo under his hill. Best we keep an eye on what he's up to, and she might be just the ticket...

"Don't it seem a mite suspicious that she reappears after all this time, just when our friend in the sierra has his first attack of conscience? Now, I don't believe in coincidences, Marvin, and neither do you. Maybe, finding this dragon egg is going to be easier than we thought. You find that pretty little girl for me, Marvin. Then we'll see what we shall see. Now, let's go fix us some breakfast!"

Jasper sprang up from his chair and came round from behind his desk. He slapped Marvin on the back, catching the smaller man by surprise, and led the way from his office to the dining room. Marvin followed, surreptitiously checking that Jasper hadn't knocked his toupee out of place.

*

Later that afternoon, King Moffett grabbed one of his laptops and took the short trip upstairs to Jasper's private suite. He found his brother in the dining room, in his customary position at the head of the table, with Warren Moffett sat to his left, shirt sleeves rolled to the elbow and a biro stuck behind one ear. An avalanche of reports, charts and spreadsheet printouts lay spread before the two men, but the atmosphere in the room remained relaxed. A white-liveried steward was placing two cut glass crystal tumblers filled with ice and an unopened bottle of whisky on the table. It was clear to King that whatever review of Wolverine's finances had been underway was now at a close.

Beyond the windows, the shadows thrown by Houston's skyscrapers had begun to lengthen and the crystal blue sky of another cloudless Texas day was softening to hints of aquamarine and teal as late afternoon approached. King opened the laptop he had brought with him and tapped in a series of short commands to cue up a pair of the screens in the centre of the array of monitors on the wall. A couple of still screengrabs appeared, the previous day's time and date stamps and other data prominent in the left-hand corner. Jasper recognised the one on the left as the photo from the hidden camera that Marvin had shown him that morning.

"What you got for me, King? You track down our mystery girl?"

"Oh yeah. I got her. Y'all have any idea how many cameras there are in London? They can follow you from one side of the city to the other! God, I love it!" enthused King, the light from the laptop screen turning his normally wan complexion a yet more sickly green as he hunched over it.

Jasper motioned to the steward to bring another glass for his youngest brother.

"Well, tell me what I'm looking at."

King shook himself free from his reverie on the boundless joys of a surveillance society. He set the laptop on the table and took a seat as the steward placed a fresh tumbler of ice before him and Jasper slid the whisky bottle over.

"OK," began King, filling his glass to the brim. "That picture on the left you've seen already. That's from our covert camera opposite 16A Albemarle Street in Mayfair, London, taken yesterday morning local time. The one on the right is a shot from a traffic camera in ...." King studied the notes on his screen. ".... Mary-le-bone Road taken at 3.12pm local yesterday afternoon."

This second photo showed a motorbike, its rider clad in crimson leathers, the mirrored visor of their helmet down. The 'bike was sat between a red double-decker bus and a pair of black London taxis, all clearly waiting at a traffic junction for the light to turn to green. King tapped a key and the picture came to life, the motorbike leaping forward to turn in front of the bus and disappear from the camera's view as the seconds ticked away on the readout to the left.

"How do we know that's her?" asked Warren as he gathered the stack of papers in front of him.

"The Feds wrote a clever little piece of recognition software that I got my hands on a while back. Compares a whole slew of measurements, plus the way someone moves, things like that. Anyways, the rider of that there Ducati is one and the same as our young lady on the left."

King cleared the screens and brought up a map of central London. He zoomed in on Mayfair and the grid of streets that ran north as far as Marylebone Station. A series of red dots appeared on the map, the first at the intersection of the Marylebone Road and Portman Street.

"Once I had a confirmed sighting, I just backtracked through the cameras," he explained.

Sure enough, Jasper and Warren could follow the line of red dots, each with its time stamp, back to their origin through the streets and squares of some of London's most desirable addresses. King zoomed in again on the dot that marked a camera in front of the Cartier boutique on New Bond Street.

"Makes sense," surmised Jasper with a small grunt, swirling the ice in his empty glass. "All them Mayfair townhouses have carriage houses round back. Most of 'em have been sold off and turned into residences over the years. Dollars to doughnuts she came out of a back entrance there."

"So, you're convinced that's her?" asked Warren, the Scotch thickening his Texan drawl. "Y'all sure spend enough on your fancy computers to answer that simple question."

By now King was enjoying himself far too much to be fazed by Warren's predictable jibes. He was well aware that while Warren Moffett had an accountant's view of his technology, what mattered was that Jasper had long ago been seduced by its possibilities. He focused the map view back on the red dot at 3.12pm at the junction of Portman Street and Marylebone Road and tapped a rapid series of keystrokes into his computer. The left-hand screen dissolved into a grid of smaller photographs, each clearly taken by a CCTV camera. At the same time the line of dots on the map to the right blinked into life and the three brothers watched it make its progress into the west of London and out along the A40, through the city's suburbs and on into rural Buckinghamshire.

King turned to Warren. "Y'all want to go snooping through half the cameras in London, as well as the Metropolitan Police's servers, their Home Office systems, without leaving a single goddamn trace, then be my guest. No? Then shut up and watch."

Jasper smiled at the slap down and poured himself two fingers of Scotch into a fresh glass of ice. "Carry on, King."

"I could track her out as far as this exit to a village called Norton Magna. She must have turned off there, because she's not on the cameras further up this main highway. So, I assumed she headed there, referenced that over to the UK passport and drivers' license databases, and bingo!"

King raised his glass and took a long pull of his drink, then tapped a single key with a flourish. The screens dissolved into the passport data page and driver's license of one Elizabeth Jade Carver, age seventeen and currently a resident of Norton Magna, Buckinghamshire, England. The two mugshots clearly matched the face in the surveillance photo of the entrance to No.16A Albemarle Street from the day before.

Jasper pushed himself back from the table and went over to stand in front of the monitors. Glass in hand, he addressed the photograph in front of him.

"Well now, Elizabeth … Is that what they call you? Lizzy? No, you don't look much like a Lizzy to me. I don't suppose you knew anything about old Michelangelo, now did you? That fancy red motorcycle looks just the kind of shiny trinket that wily old bird might dangle in front of a feisty young woman, assuming he'd followed her from afar and knew her tastes. And I'm damned sure he's been doing that. I reckon you've taken a trip on that there Ducati all the way to make your reacquaintance with Michelangelo de St. Exupéry-Antoine. In fact, I reckon you're there with him right now. Anyways, King here is going to find out everything about you, aren't you King? And I do mean everything."

Jasper clapped his hands and turned back to his two brothers sat at the table.

"Good work, King. Now you and Marvin work me up a file on Miss Carver here. I want it on my desk by the morning. Warren, you finish off those projections. We'll talk tomorrow."

King and Warren understood when they had been dismissed. They hurriedly drained their whisky glasses, gathered together their things and headed for the dining room's double doors. After they had left, Marvin Thibodeaux came in, quietly shutting the big doors behind him. Jasper had sat back down at the table and motioned for Marvin to join him.

"So now we have a name. Elizabeth Jade."

Jasper turned and looked out of the windows at the Houston skyline, the westering sun's reflection gleaming from the mirrored glass towers. Marvin knew that Jasper's mind was elsewhere, reliving a blustery, wet night on the moors above Manchester, England. Both men knew that that night had secured their future and their fortunes, but at a terrible price, as events had spiralled out of control and ended in the murder of Elizabeth Jade Carver's family, leaving her an orphan. Outside of this room, only Michelangelo de St. Exupéry-Antoine, the Golden Dragon of Anglezarke Moor, had always known exactly the deal that Jasper Moffett had made to satisfy his ambition, and from that fateful night on would never forget his crimes.

It had all begun innocently enough, thought Jasper, if 'innocent' was a word that you could use when a man such as he collided with billions of dollars and the power that brought. Wolverine Petroleum had already grown rapidly, and by the turn of the millennium was widely considered a 'major', even if the stuffed-shirt old money of the country club sets in Houston and Dallas continued to look down their noses at Jasper as some upstart, especially since he had become a darling of the business and fashion media in his hand-tooled boots and Savile Row suits. Jasper had always watched the Wolverine share price with an eagle eye, and knew that Wolverine had now become a key holding for most of the biggest pension and mutual funds in the world. He had begun to notice a regular pattern of trades that seemed uncannily prescient about the direction of oil prices and other factors. They weren't small bets either, often moving many millions of dollars and always coming out on top. Indeed, so extraordinary was their success rate that the financial authorities had become convinced that only Jasper himself could be so well informed, and they had investigated him on several occasions for insider trading. His own investigations had led him via layers of subsidiaries and special purpose companies to the investor that seemed to be behind it all, an operation called Anglezarke, but here he had hit a brick wall, for what few records and filings existed for this mysterious financial powerhouse soon dissolved into a tapestry of offshore trusts and other blind alleys. Jasper had been in the game long enough to understand that someone very rich, very knowledgeable and very, very careful was sat behind all this legal subterfuge, and his curiosity had been piqued.

Jasper had stumbled upon the key to the mystery by accident. He had travelled alone to the Oil Dragon's canyon to discuss some particularly interesting rock samples from Argentina, and as the conversation was drawing to a close and he was preparing to leave, he had mentioned the conundrum of Anglezarke.

"That is the Golden Dragon," the Oil Dragon had said, one of the very few times that it had ever said anything to Jasper that was not directly related to oil, and it stopped him in his tracks.

"What do you mean?" Jasper had asked. "There's a Golden Dragon?"

"I am of oil. The Golden Dragon is of gold," came the simple if enigmatic reply.

Jasper was by now long experienced in deciphering Jacinto Saavedra Cervantes i Domenech's more cryptic statements, but this was something new. He had thought for a moment, then asked, "This dragon senses gold like you sense oil? So, why's he trading my shares?"

"He is the Golden Dragon. He senses gold. Do you not turn my oil into gold?"

Jasper had stood deep in thought as he assimilated what he already knew about Anglezarke and added this new piece of information.

"If he knows about the oil then he knows about you."

"Yes. He knows. He knows that I am bound to you, Jasper Moffett."

Jasper had sat down on a nearby boulder and he and the Oil Dragon had begun a fresh conversation. He had never bothered to think that there might be more than one dragon. He realised how naïve he had been, swayed by the success and the money, and that he had arrogantly assumed that the Oil Dragon – his dragon

– was a secret that he alone enjoyed. As had happened in the early days, the Oil Dragon now found it difficult to explain something that it regarded as its own nature, but slowly Jasper built up enough of a picture of the relationship that these creatures had with the world, and that there were many more of them than he could ever have imagined. By the time he left the canyon that evening, the Milky Way was a shining carpet across the clear night sky, but Jasper felt little of the biting cold as he drove the ATV back to the base camp. Now he understood what he was up against in Anglezarke, he was more determined than ever not to let go.

10 Neon

EJ woke early. The warm southern breeze of the evening before had shifted and strengthened into a blustery south-westerly some time during the night, the greyish dawn light pallid and weak. EJ felt at her throat for the reassurance of her dragon pendant, then stretched, surprised that apart from the hint of stiffness in her thighs from the long 'bike ride, she felt fresh. The conversation with Michelangelo, which had loomed ominously over her for the past three days, had proven to be both a physical and mental release. Oh, she still had plenty of questions, yet one more key had been turned, another set of the jigsaw pieces had fallen into place, and she felt herself growing smoothly into this almost parallel universe that continued to open before her like some fabulous Fabergé egg.

She took a leisurely shower, sinking into the simple pleasures of steam and fragrance, before dressing in a pair of soft, cream moleskins and a denim safari jacket top from a well-known Paris couturier that belted at the waist and fit her like a second skin. She took five minutes to make up her bed and straighten the room, then dropped into the corner of her sofa nearest the window and, legs curled beneath her, simply gazed out over the damp lawn and watched the world awaken. EJ contemplated the quiet landscape of trees and meadow, and

Michelangelo's parting words of the night before came back to her. She allowed herself a small grin of self-satisfaction. It was all there, laid out before her. She only had to reach out and take it.

The outlines of the trees around the house had become more distinct and the dawn chorus was in full flow. A final glance outside and EJ returned to the bathroom to run a towel through her still damp hair and add a little makeup and some eau de parfum. She adjusted the pendant at her throat and appraised herself in the mirror.

"You might well be on first name terms with a dragon, Elizabeth Jade Carver, but you still can't do a thing with your hair," she said out loud to her reflection, and quickly pulled it back into its usual unruly ponytail. EJ made a mental note to ask Molly about fixing her hair in the dwarven style with gold and silver threads, snagged her 'phone from the bedside table and stuffed it into a pocket of her leather jacket, then grabbed her rucksack and went downstairs.

The kitchen was brightly lit but deserted, though the pot on the coffeemaker was freshly made and filling the room with its aroma. A note beside it read: *'Good morning, EJ! You know where the fridge is, so make yourself some breakfast and come down to the Mill. Everyone's dying to meet you. Love, M'.*

EJ poured herself a cup of coffee and followed Molly's advice. She opened the double doors of the immense fridge that dominated even this temple to the gods of stainless steel, and after a brief consideration of the merits of diving back into the leftovers of yesterday's Imperial blowout, she allowed the better angels of her conscience to win the day and took the far healthier choice of a bowl of berries and some yoghurt.

*

EJ had already decided that she would walk to the Mill. It wasn't far enough to warrant taking her 'bike, the fresh air and exercise would do her good, and she'd have a chance to explore the grounds and maybe a little of the village as well. She opened the back door and stood with her coffee cup, breathing in deeply. A hint of loam and wet summer leaves dusted with pollen scented the morning air. No surprise that Balthazar and Akitafelt stood patiently waiting for her in the middle of the back yard. She clicked her tongue softly and the two great hounds came to her, flowing like water across the flags, still damp from the early morning showers. EJ drank the last of her coffee, put the cup on the side with a twinge of embarrassment at not washing it up, and closed the door behind her.

EJ closed her eyes and pictured herself stood in this moment at the centre of something, like a pebble dropped into a still pool of water creates ripples and effects. The two mastiffs took up their now customary position to either side of her, Balthazar on the left and Akitafelt to the right, and they headed around the corner of the house toward the front lawn and the driveway. There was something almost Arthurian in the sight of this striking young woman, her blond curls already snaking loose from their bindings, as she strode ahead. She could feel it all – Anglezarke, Michelangelo, Balthazar and Akitafelt – wrapping around and through her. The trio headed down the tree-lined driveway towards the gates, the blackbirds and thrushes angrily scolding the dogs for their intrusion into the woodland. At the gateposts EJ turned toward the church and the Mill beyond. As if they had stepped from their enchanted realm into a harsher, more prosaic world, the birdsong abruptly ceased, replaced by the sounds of traffic and everyday life.

EJ passed the bay-windowed houses of the Church Terrace, and the great oblong mass of the Mill began to rise beyond its railings to the right as the road curved down the hill toward the building's gates. The two old ladies were stood chatting in exactly the same spot, as if they hadn't moved since EJ had waved at them as she passed the previous day, and they turned to watch her approach. They fell silent as EJ and her guard dogs neared, and then both broke into broad smiles. The shorter of the two, wrapped in a blue Macintosh, her hair crimped into a perm that looked like it could etch glass, said,

"Morning, love. I'm Mrs. Winters. Saw you yesterday on that fancy red motorbike of yours."

"Good morning, Mrs. Winters,' EJ replied, somewhat unsure of how she was expected to answer, but properly brought up to be polite to one's elders.

The taller of the pair, a string shopping bag hanging from her crossed arms, her head covered in a battered faux-fur hat that had seen any number of better days, took her turn, eyes twinkling mischievously behind a pair of rather ornate spectacles.

"And I'm Mrs. Summerbee. Nice 'bike, that. Fast. Lots of torque, them Ducati's. 'Specially a Mostro like yours."

"Um, yes. It's a great 'bike," managed EJ in reply, blindsided by the unexpected shift in the conversation.

Balthazar and Akitafelt clearly felt quite at home and wandered forward to get their ears scratched, while Mrs. Winters and Mrs. Summerbee stared silently at EJ, before looking at each other and bursting into laughter.

"Oh, the look on your face, love! Thought you'd have realised we're a bit different round here!"

EJ could feel the colour rising to her cheeks, but knew that, however good-natured the exchange, she had to take back the initiative or she'd never hear the end of it.

"Summerbee and Winters? Are you kidding?"

"Good, isn't it?" chortled Mrs. Winters. "A right double act!"

And now, the ice broken, EJ joined in the laughter. Mrs. Winters and Mrs. Summerbee both moved closer.

"Don't mind us, EJ. We're only teasing. Everyone's right glad to see you back here again," said Mrs. Winters kindly.

"Aye," added Mrs. Summerbee. "There's never been but a couple of people as knew where you were all this time. Them as are close to Michelangelo would never crack on. But we always knew you were out of harm's way and keeping safe and well."

EJ watched the faces of the two old ladies as they spoke. She felt that same embracing sense of place that she had experienced at the house and with Michelangelo inside his hillside, and understood that this was the real magic of Anglezarke.

"This whole village works for Michelangelo really, one way or t'other," continued Mrs. Summerbee. "It's always been like that, I suppose, and most of the families have been here long enough to know it. Once your Granddad came home with his ideas … well, that dragon's our guardian angel."

"Now that's quite enough of that, Esme. This young woman's very busy and doesn't need any of your maudlin carry on," chided Mrs. Winters amiably. She fished a rumpled paper bag out of her mac pocket, which she proffered to EJ. "Best we were getting along, and you're expected inside. Fancy a midget gem?"

Smiling broadly as they bickered, Mrs. Winters and Mrs. Summerbee turned and headed off in the direction of the Post Office. They left EJ grinning and speechless. She clicked her tongue to Balthazar and Akitafelt and entered the Mill yard.

EJ walked forward a few yards and then stood and took stock of the buildings in front of her. This was a long way from the idea of a Victorian cotton mill that she had learnt at school. Nothing dark or satanic here: The main building was a long box of four storeys, but the slender columns of brick between the large windows that ran the length of each floor were decorated with vertical stone finials, and these seemed to give the building a lightness and nimbleness that belied its size and brought it to life. At their tops the finials flourished into stone trefoils which flowed along the roof line, as if the whole structure was supported by a lattice of vines. At the front of the main building stood a smaller block, which must have been the offices for the factory in days gone by, and the architect had mirrored the larger building's lines and proportions with the same restraint and lightness of touch. Set in a stone portico at its centre, its columns carved with the same design of trefoils, stood a pair of modern glass entrance doors, their chrome fittings highly polished. The walls to either side of the portico were adorned with the names and logos of a number of companies, the largest being the sign for Mortensen's Metals that she had noticed from her 'bike the previous day. To the left across a broad yard laid with smooth granite setts, stood a lower building attached to the tall, squared mill chimney which soared above the Mill and all around it. This annex sat like the squat, powerful cousin to its larger, airier sibling, its brickwork columns thicker, its smaller windows running along an upper storey only. EJ understood this reinforcement of design marked it as the engine house, home to the boilers and great steam motors which had powered the looms and other machinery in the Mill's heyday, though its current purpose remained unclear.

"Are you just going to stand around all day admiring the view, or come in for a brew?"

EJ's architectural reveries were broken by the shout of a broad individual who now stood in front of the glass doors of the entrance, hands on hips and a broad smile on his face. EJ realised that he must be Mortensen – the tattooed forearms and a preponderance of gold and silver rings, earrings and other jewellery made it clear that he was a dwarf – but he was the height of an average man, and unlike most of his relatives that she had so far met, his head was completely shaven. However, he made up for this lack of hair with a splendid beard plaited into two forks that reached to his waist and was dyed an acidic shade of purple. A pair of silk braces that glittered with embroidery in gold and silver thread held up Mortensen's dark corduroys which tucked into a pair of knee-length riding boots burnished to a deep chestnut.

Mortensen strode forward and wrapped EJ in a hug, then stepped back and held her by the shoulders as he looked her up and down. EJ felt like she was being sized up for market.

"You are a sight for sore eyes, my girl! Come on, let's get you inside. Don't worry about these two, they'll find their own way home."

Sure enough, Balthazar and Akitafelt turned and slipped away toward the far end of the mill yard, while EJ followed Mortensen into Anglezarke Mill. The glass doors opened into a small reception area which apart from several large, luxuriant tropical plants, was completely bare, its walls hung with the sort of nondescript abstract prints that one might see in a thousand other corporate entries. Upon closer inspection, one would notice the solid door set flush into the wall ahead, the cameras at each corner which covered the whole lobby, the small blinking diodes of the biometric readers, and the soft hum of air vents set into the edges of the ceiling. This room had been constructed with care for the sole purpose of vetting any visitor that might pass through its doors. EJ placed her palm on the reader and watched the diodes flick from red to green. However, it was only when Mortensen did the same that she heard and felt the thuds of heavy electronic locks release and the security door swung open. Mortensen politely stepped aside to allow her to enter first.

"The whole mill belongs to Anglezarke, of course, but we mostly use this front part ourselves. Lots of folk have businesses in the rest of the place," explained Mortensen as they passed inside.

Accustomed as EJ was to the undertone of paranoia that surrounded Anglezarke, with all its security precautions and biometric scans, she was unprepared for the space into which she now walked. The ground floor was set with varnished brick pavia in a traditional herringbone. The building's original frame of fluted cast iron columns and braces had been cleverly used to create an open atrium at the centre which rose to the huge glass skylight that formed the roof. To her left, the halves of the first and third floors had been kept, while to her right it was the second and fourth stories which remained. These alternating galleries were linked to each other by wrought iron stairs which crossed the central space at either end of the building. Vines and other hanging plants festooned this space from each of the balconies, and all the foliage and light just reinforced EJ's earlier sense that Anglezarke Mill was as much organic as manmade.

She jumped as Mortensen stuck two fingers between his teeth and let out a piercing whistle. The gentle background hum of conversation common to any office ceased, and at every floor the balconies filled with faces between the lianas.

"A great day! A grand day! A day long in the making and for which we have waited patiently these many years. Please welcome our Elizabeth Jade back home to Anglezarke!"

The space rang with tumultuous applause, mixed with warm shouts of greeting. As the dwarves clapped, the air flashed and sparkled with the gold, silver and gems that adorned every hand, male and female. Mortensen stood and beamed broadly, then raised one eyebrow at EJ in invitation for her to speak. She looked up and around at the smiling faces, gulped and took a couple of paces forward.

"Hello, everyone. I'm afraid you have me at a disadvantage, since you all know me, but I've yet to meet you … Um, it's very kind of you all to be so welcoming, though I can't say I really understand what I've done to deserve it … Anyway, I promise that I'll get to know each of you just as soon as I can …"

As EJ spoke she could feel her iPhone vibrating. She was sure she had switched it off before she came out that morning, but she slipped her hand inside her pocket and thumbed the power switch again to shut it down. After a couple of seconds, the 'phone began to vibrate again. Distracted, and with her train of thought broken, EJ shook her head and tried to rally.

"… and I know that I've still got such a lot to learn … and I'm sure that I'll need you all to help me … Um, so you must all have lots to be getting on with and you don't need to listen to me all day … so, thank you."

Mortensen moved closer and asked out of the side his mouth," Everything alright there, EJ?"

"Yes, Mr. Mortensen. I'm fine. Really."

Her iPhone now began to vibrate with what appeared to be the first bars of Beethoven's Fifth Symphony. EJ fished it out of her jacket pocket and examined it. The screen filled with a message:

ask mr. mortensen to take you to the conference room on the third floor.
it's time we talked.

EJ studied the phone screen. This was something new, even by the extraordinary standards of the past few days. She glanced over at Mortensen, who was now watching her with undisguised disquiet.

"You're sure there's not a problem, lass?" he asked, the bonhomie of seconds earlier now faded from his voice, his manner business-like.

EJ realised that a decision faced her: she had no idea what the message on her phone could mean, but the fact that it had managed to appear on a newly-secured device gave it a significance which was not lost on her and she knew she couldn't ignore it. It was time to put her instincts to the test once more, and that meant trusting Mortensen. She handed him the iPhone.

Mortensen read the screen and looked at her. He remained silent for several seconds, and just as EJ was beginning to feel uncomfortable, asked her, "This the 'phone that Stan and the lads in London took a look at for you?"

"Yes, it is."

He handed it back to her and motioned for her to follow him. They walked to the nearer of the two staircases that cantilevered up the atrium. As they headed up, Mortensen said, "You noticed there's no name or number on that message then?"

EJ looked at the screen once more. It showed the familiar dialogue box of the popular messaging app that she always used for her chats and texts. She'd used it that morning to let her mother know she was fine and planned to head back to Norton Magna that afternoon. Mortensen was right, the normal details of sender and receiver were missing.

"So, what does that mean?" she asked.

"What that means, my dear, is that Stan and the lads down in London are bloody good with this kind of thing and they don't make mistakes," said Mortensen, as they passed a young dwarf on the stairs who politely pressed himself against the wall to let them by. "Whoever, or whatever, sent that is even better."

EJ stopped on the stairs and looked at Mortensen, who now stood a couple of treads higher than her. "Whatever?"

Mortensen threw his head back and laughed. "Have you forgotten where you are? This is Anglezarke, lass! Normal doesn't apply here, and you'd best not forget it."

They turned off the stair. Mortensen led the way to the door of a glass-walled room that took up half of the third floor and ushered her inside. The room was clearly designed to be self-contained and soundproof: A large plasma screen occupied one wall, a complex system of multiple speakers and cameras suspended from the lowered false ceiling. EJ felt Beethoven's four-beat dum-dum-dum-DUM again. A new message had arrived:

please ask mr. mortensen to leave. thank you

Mortensen stroked his beard as he watched her, then asked, "You need a bit of privacy, lass?"

"I'm sorry, Mr. Mortensen."

"No need, EJ," he replied, opening the door to leave. "And you can stop with the Mr. Mortensen business. Just Mortensen will do."

EJ smiled, relieved that he had sensed her awkwardness. "No, I think I'll stick to Mr. Mortensen, if you don't mind."

The door closed and EJ could hear Mortensen chuckling as he moved away. Then everything happened at once. The door locks clicked into place. The blinds at the windows and glass walls all closed. The lights dimmed, and EJ sensed rather than heard the hum of white noise from the speaker system above her. Unsure how to react, she pulled one of the chairs out from the table and sat down. She had little choice now but to play along.

The face of a dragon appeared on the plasma screen. Of course, thought EJ, why would it be anything else?

"Good morning, Elizabeth. Thanks for accepting my messages with such little fuss. Hey, apologies to you and Michelangelo for the intrusion into his cosy little world, but it can't be helped. Dude, in the end you'd have to talk to me.'

The avatar on the screen was amazingly lifelike and had a distinctly Southern Californian drawl. The scales of the dragon's face shimmered with aquamarines and teals, shot through with flamingo pinks and Ferrari yellows. The eyes glowed an emerald green.

"Allow me to introduce myself … I'm a man of style and taste," the dragon continued. "Sorry, dude, I always get carried away by that line. I'm Al-Khwarizmi Ibn Shams ad'Din, the Silicon Dragon. Call me Riz."

"Silicon?" asked EJ. "Silicon as in computers?"

"Right on the money, dude. Pretty good guess for someone who's only been riding this wave for a couple of days. Hey, kinda, sorta, kinda. I'm the dragon of all the ones and zeroes, all the code, all the comms, every network. If it's got a chip inside and any kind of electronic heartbeat then I can sense it. What? Not impressed?"

EJ watched the grinning dragon's head and ostentatiously placed her iPhone on the table in front of her. The avatar cocked its head to one side and grinned, bearing fangs that glittered with tiny blue sparks.

"I assume this isn't a social call, California. I mean, I might be new to this game, well, newer than you at least, but you dragons are not exactly the happy few, we band of brothers, are you?"

"No, dude, we ain't," replied Riz. "OK. In exactly 12.7 seconds from now one of your dwarf friends is going to knock on that door to find out if you are alright and whether you might know anything about why their system backtraces have just lit up like Times Square because of all the unauthorised transmission gateways I'm using to talk to you. I'll open the door, so you go on and reassure him."

Sure enough, the locks clicked free and EJ opened the door. A somewhat out of breath young dwarf, his blond hair tied up in a topknot, was just about to knock.

"Um … Miss Elizabeth … Are you alright in there?" he managed to pant after dashing up three flights of stairs. "Only we've got some rather unusual activity. I mean, really, really unusual."

EJ's face lit up into what she hoped was her most magnetic smile. She knew she'd feel bad about this later, and made a mental note to find the dwarf and apologise.

"Of course I am, but thank you for asking. I appear to have a visitor. No need to worry, but I'd keep an eye on your servers, if I were you. If you need anything else, just go and talk to Mr. Mortensen."

EJ closed the door slowly on the dumbfounded dwarf and heard the lock click back into place once more. She turned back to the screen, where Riz's avatar continued to grin at her.

"Wow, nicely done, Elizabeth! Your boys are a tad nervous 'cos I've taken over quite a chunk of their systems. Temporarily of course, but I really do need to speak to you. Appreciate it if you could invite me in. Good IT etiquette. That way your boys might feel a tad less uncomfortable."

EJ hesitated. If Riz was all he said, and everything before her pointed that way, then she could be putting Anglezarke's computer systems in real peril. Riz seemed to read her mind.

"It doesn't work that way, dude. I don't wreck systems, I am systems! All of them, everywhere. Once upon a time, not that very long ago, I was a real flesh and blood dragon. Then one day, I wasn't. Went from being the dragon of the sands living in some godforsaken cave in the middle of a North African desert to inhabiting a stack of memory in some bunker in San Cupertino! I guess critical mass and all that – the computers had taken over the world! You could say I've adapted to my new surroundings pretty well," said Riz, and he winked at her.

"Okay, you have my permission."

"Thank you kindly, ma'am. See, there's these three young Caltech PhD dudes down in Santa Monica, and when they're not surfing, they're coding up a storm. They've come up with something that will blow your mind! In fact, to make nice for my little intrusion and show my bona fides, I've just left a copy of all their work on your servers. I think your guys will love it. Now, watch the table."

As Riz finished speaking, the avatar dragon face disappeared from the screen. The two cameras on the ceiling at either end of the room shifted to point down at the middle of the conference table in front of EJ. The room lights dimmed further, and the cameras lit up to project a perfect hologram of Riz onto the table, three dimensional and apparently as solid as she was. EJ placed her hand against the dragon's flank and watched it disappear as she slowly pressed it forward, like Alice stepping through the looking glass.

"OMG! That is so cool! Okay, let's say you've convinced me now. So, what do you want?"

The hologram was about six feet long. EJ watched the electric kaleidoscope of colours swirl across his scales as Riz turned to face her. He moved his head closer to inspect her, and then shifted back, languidly flicking his tail around him.

"Pretty neat, huh? Sure, these cameras aren't quite up to spec for this, but I've left details of what you guys need, and hey, it ain't like you can't afford the upgrade! Just remember, you can't go selling this stuff. Got to let my boys on the PCH become gazillionaires. Now, let's get right down to it. Elizabeth, you are being watched."

EJ could feel the sound in the room coalesce into the hologram as Riz and his nifty projection software modulated the speakers. She knew that, rationally speaking, it was an illusion created by some very advanced algorithms, but her brain was telling her that the voice now came from the dragon's mouth in front of her. As Riz spoke, the volume decreased and the easy Southern Californian drawl of earlier slowly melted away, replaced by something more ancient that carried the hiss of sand being blown from the top of a dune by a hot scirocco wind, and the patience of centuries of waiting and watching as civilisations rose and crumbled around it.

"I am new. Yes, I am systems and networks and code, and I can span the globe in less time than the blink of an eye. Yet I am still dragon. As Michelangelo de St.

Exupéry-Antoine senses the others, so did I, even from the depths of my hidden desert caves. I sense them still. I sense those around them too, for now I have many more eyes and ears, many more ways to discover and know."

"You're talking about the Oil Dragon, aren't you? About Wolverine."

"Yes, Elizabeth. They know who you are. I have always paid attention to their systems, to computers which they believe cleverly hidden from prying eyes. Yet no system, no network can remain hidden to me. They do not bother to intrude here, but they have watched your London office for many years. They noted your arrival there. They are skilled at searching in the computers of others, and they went looking for you. It did not take them long to find you. That is why I am here today. You need to know this."

The dragon nodded toward the plasma screen. It lit up with a rapid series of images of EJ: Stood in front of No.16A Albemarle St.; on her Ducati; her driver's license; her passport; school photos; her 'phone bills; the application to Cambridge; and finally, on the front of an electronic dossier which bore the logo of Wolverine Petroleum.

EJ's mouth felt dry. She remembered the creeping disquiet of the turned heads in the motorway service station, the sense that everyone was watching her, and as the slideshow looped in front of her, the worst fears of the past few days mounted. She felt for the pendant at her throat.

"Did Michelangelo know all along?" she asked quietly.

"I have no answer to that question. Michelangelo de St. Exupéry-Antoine is a very ancient dragon. As old as I. He cares not for the technology which I now call my domain, even as those around him and in his employ use that same technology to execute his wishes every day."

EJ's ear for the nuances of a dragon's words were already well developed, even after so short a time.

"So, this was Selwyn Ormerod's doing? But why, and why now?"

"Again, I know not. However, I know that he placed tracking devices upon you and your motorcycle to monitor your position and your safety."

She had been right. They had dangled her out there like bait on a line. But to what end? She began to say to herself that Riz's appearance had changed everything, but stopped as the sentence began to form. Was that really true? she asked herself. Both Michelangelo and Selwyn Ormerod had already told her that something was happening that could change the world, and not just for the dragons. She felt another of those mental clicks that seemed to have become more frequent, as more pieces slid into place in her mind. Riz's warning didn't change a thing. Her fears about being watched were not fears at all. Rather, they were the realisation that she had willingly stepped into the role that had been offered her. It was time to talk to Michelangelo again.

"Can you appear like this in Michelangelo's chamber in the big cave, or only in this room?" she asked Riz.

Riz closed his eyes for a moment and was silent, as if surveying some mental schematic of Anglezarke. "The equipment there is older but it is adequate. However, if I am to manifest there, then Michelangelo must invite me to do so."

11 Alpha Male

Al-Khwarizmi Ibn Shams ad'Din's hologram slowly dissolved until only a disembodied head remained, grinning at her like the Cheshire Cat.

"Take young Man-bun along with you. I might need a guy who knows his way around a circuit board, just to make sure this thing works over there," said Riz, as he finally disappeared. The lights in the room came back on and the blinds at all the windows rose in unison. There was another vibrating burst of Beethoven from EJ's iPhone. She picked it up and Riz's face appeared on the small screen and winked at her again. EJ couldn't help but smile as she stuffed the 'phone back into her jacket pocket. She turned to the door and jumped at the sight of half a dozen dwarves stood in a silent semicircle in front of the conference room. They each carried a laptop or tablet, and when they weren't typing or furiously poking at their screens, they were stealing glances in her direction. 'Man-bun' as he had been christened by Riz, was a mask of concentration, nervously chewing the ends of his blond moustache. If this was going to work, EJ could see that it was up to her to regain the initiative.

"Right, Man-bun! What do I call you?"

Man-bun looked up and said, "Daniel, Miss Elizabeth. Daniel Mortensen, at your service."

"Brother? Cousin?"

"Cousin, Miss Elizabeth. We all are, really."

EJ paused and looked at her small audience until she had their attention.

"Two things: First, no one here calls me Miss Elizabeth anymore. I'm EJ. Secondly, you're coming with me, Daniel. I need to talk to Michelangelo."

"OK … um, EJ. We can take one of the golf carts."

Golf carts? That wasn't quite the answer she had been expecting, thought EJ, deciding to put it to one side for now. She was sure that all would be revealed shortly.

"Oh, and one last thing, before I forget. My visitor says that he has left us a present in one of our servers. Wanted to say sorry for his intrusion and all the commotion he's caused. Why don't you lot check it out while we head over?"

At EJ's words, the typing and swiping became even more frenzied, and it was the matter of only a few seconds before the first exclamations of delighted surprise.

Content with the results of her little speech, if a little self-conscious at her overacting, EJ took Daniel Mortensen by the arm and guided him to the head of the stairs. The other five dwarves formed up behind them, apparently unwilling to miss any further developments. The last in line was so engrossed in his screen that he shuffled straight into the back of the dwarf in front of him, but neither paid any heed as the code continued to scroll across their devices.

Mortensen awaited them at the foot of the stairs on the ground floor.

"Ay up, EJ. And where might you be off to with young Daniel here at this time of the morning?"

"EJ needs to see Michelangelo," explained Daniel, clearly anxious to be helpful. "And she says that I need to go too."

Mortensen stroked his beard and regarded the pair of them and their techie entourage.

"Does she now? I presume this has something to do with our recent visitor? Caused quite a stir in certain departments, I can tell you."

"Yes, Mr. Mortensen. 'Our recent visitor' as you call him has shown me a few things, so I think Michelangelo and I need to have a quiet word," replied EJ carefully.

"Right, best we went and saw him then," said Mortensen, and he turned to the rest of the dwarves.

"Make yourselves scarce, you lot! I'm sure our EJ's visitor has left plenty for you to be getting on with!"

As the other dwarves scurried off, Mortensen turned to EJ and winked.

"We did think he might make an appearance, you know. Never known him to leave gifts, though – I think he likes you."

EJ could feel the colour rising at her throat as Daniel's gaze ricocheted between Mortensen and her, as if a spectator at a tennis match. Mortensen clapped his hands and laughed.

"Lead the way, young Daniel! We'll take the tunnel."

The three of them went back outside and turned to the right to walk down the length of the Mill toward its far end. There they stopped in front of a large loading dock where a line of golf carts waited in front of a broad steel concertina gate, each one plugged into a charging point. The carts were painted British racing green with a discreet golden dragon stencilled on the front. Daniel busied himself checking the charge, then unplugged the nearest, took the wheel and reversed it out so that the other two could climb aboard. Daniel shifted gears and they trundled forward toward the tunnel entrance, stopping briefly at a biometric reader against the wall for them each to scan their palms. Instead of the usual diodes, traffic lights on either side changed to green and the door rolled smoothly aside. The tunnel was well lit and broad enough for two vehicles, its asphalt surface divided by a fluorescent white line, the curved walls lined with smooth, precast concrete panels.

"Probably the most dwarven thing any of us had done in decades when we dug this," said Mortensen conversationally as they headed inside. "Good fun! Felt like the old days. A lot of the younger dwarves had never even swung a pickaxe, let alone been down a mine. Ooh, did they complain! Not happy at all, being dragged away from their computer screens. Were they, young Daniel?"

Now it was Daniel's turn to blush, and he stared fixedly at the roadway ahead and remained silent. The tunnel curved gently to the right and then straightened. Another cart passed them coming from the other direction with a wave and a toot of the horn, and Daniel acknowledged them with a fanfare of his own.

The journey to Michelangelo's cavern took barely five minutes. The other end of the tunnel opened into a parking area very much the same as the one from which they had left at the Mill – with the obvious difference that it was underground. Daniel allowed the golf cart to roll to a halt, and EJ and the two dwarves disembarked. Daniel immediately grabbed his iPad, anxious to catch up with whatever he might have missed while he drove.

They passed through another security door, and EJ felt the atmosphere change: The familiar scents of leather and tobacco, and the feeling that the world was turning just that little more slowly the closer she came to Michelangelo. She had remained silent during the ride. Mortensen and Daniel stood politely waiting for her to lead the way. EJ fished in her jacket and pulled out her 'phone, but its screen was blank. For now, at least, she was on her own.

The main cavern was only a short distance ahead, and the hum of activity was more pronounced at this time of day than it had been the night before. As the three of them entered, EJ looked around and saw that all the workstations were busy, their banks of screens alive, their occupants marshalling the streams of money as Michelangelo gave his silent orders.

"Good morning, Elizabeth."

Michelangelo's voice in her head sounded like mead splashing into a golden goblet.

"Good morning, Michelangelo. May I speak with you?"

Michelangelo de St. Exupéry-Antoine reclined on his mountain of cushions, the reflections of the great screen in front of him flickering on his spectacles. He turned his head toward her, and EJ felt as if enveloped in a warm smile. She hurried forward and placed her face against Michelangelo's neck.

"I understand you have had a visitor."

EJ released her hold and moved round to face the dragon.

"You knew. You knew all along."

"Yes. Are you displeased, Elizabeth?"

EJ remembered a book she had read when she was seven years old. A famous story about hobbits and dwarves on a quest, and a great, sly, malevolent dragon that dealt in greed, disaster and death, all in the madness of gold and power. She looked at Michelangelo, and then around her at the desks of well-dressed dwarves as they traded and moved Anglezarke's billions. She wondered what the author of that famous story would have made of all this. This was something to be proud of. This was something worth fighting for.

"Riz has already shown me. They needed to know about me, didn't they? What does Wolverine want from me? How do I stop them, Michelangelo?"

Michelangelo leant forward and for the first time EJ noticed two wisps of smoke at his nostrils. They stood there in silent communion for several seconds.

"Mortensen has told me that Al-Khwarizmi Ibn Shams ad'Din has caused a great deal of excitement, but has made handsome amends for his presumptuousness. The dwarves seem most pleased with their new toy. You have made quite an impression, Elizabeth."

EJ smiled at Michelangelo's honeyed words, but could sense the glistening edge of the axe blade hidden within. She chose her reply with care.

"I think Riz is a little bit afraid of you, Michelangelo. He seems to think it's important, but he told me to ask your permission before he would try to appear here."

Michelangelo turned to Mortensen and said, "Please ask everyone to leave. Very well, Elizabeth, he may appear here, should he now so choose."

"Daniel has to stay. Riz said we might need his assistance."

"Daniel Mortensen. Stay. Now, Elizabeth, you may proceed."

As the dwarves closed down their screens, doffed their headsets and filed out of the cavern under Mortensen's watchful eye, EJ motioned for Daniel to join her. She pulled out her 'phone once more, but this time felt the Beethoven buzz as it vibrated. Riz must have been listening this whole time.

Daniel hurried over and whispered excitedly to her. "EJ, the lads are going bonkers! They've been taking a look, and this thing is amazing! Can he really turn himself into a hologram?"

EJ watched the young dwarf bounce up and down on the balls of his feet with excitement. She tossed her iPhone to him.

"Here you go. You're about to find out."

Daniel ran over to the nearest desk and flicked its screens into life, pulling the keyboard in front of him. Riz was clearly now in charge: The lights flickered as power systems rerouted. The atmosphere changed and the cavern seemed to get colder. EJ felt a shiver of static and sparks arced across the huge lights in the roof beams. The cameras around the perimeter and in the heights of the cavern focused down to fuse their beams of light on an empty area in front of Michelangelo's big screen, and in a blink the hologram of Riz appeared. He was putting on a show. He had manifested the same size as Michelangelo, and the psychedelic candy shades of his skin swirled and danced as he sucked more computing power through the systems. Michelangelo looked on impassively, but EJ could sense his smirk of quiet amusement as Riz turned to them. Daniel sat transfixed, his mouth agape at the sight of the two dragons eyeing each other warily.

Riz's voice boomed through the cavern's speaker system and dissolved into a squeal of feedback.

"Whoa! Sorry, dude! That's some gnarly top end you've got there. Sweet system, by the way."

The volume dropped to something more acceptable and Riz continued, "Hey, Michelangelo. Sorry for dropping in unannounced, dude, but thanks for agreeing to have me stop by. Could you be a sport and tell Man-bun over there to type whatever you want to say onto the screen? I've patched through another program

I found that'll turn it into speech. I know, that stuff's been around for years, but mine really is some world class coding."

Michelangelo clearly waited for a beat longer than necessary, in a manner calculated to remind Riz who was in charge. EJ looked on with mounting disbelief as the two dragons' inevitable alpha male contest of wills began. Eventually, Michelangelo yawned ostentatiously, then flicked out his tongue, and in her mind she heard him say, "Daniel Mortensen, please do as Al-Khwarizmi Ibn Shams ad'Din has bidden. If he has the means to give me voice, then so ..."

Daniel had already started to type, and his stream of text appeared on the big screen. Suddenly the speakers crackled and the cavern echoed to Michelangelo's words.

" ... be it ... Do I really sound like that?"

Riz quickly ran Michelangelo's last sentence through several different male British accents.

"That one!" shouted EJ. "Keep it on the last one."

That final accent was a cultured baritone, a voice that one might imagine of an Oxford don, wearing a comfortable tweed jacket and filling his pipe with dark tobacco. Michelangelo seemed pleased with the result. He shifted on his cushions as if satisfied that the conversation could now continue. EJ was about to speak, but Michelangelo beat her to it, and his artificial voice rang out across the cavern.

"Enough! You are skilled in these technological games, Al-Khwarizmi. As you should be, for such is your domain. You are welcome in Anglezarke. For now. Tell me what you wish me to hear."

The psychedelic kaleidoscope on Riz's flanks slowed, and EJ understood that the two dragons had reached tacit agreement. The Silicon Dragon turned to the big screen and it began to cycle through a yet more exhaustive display of the security stills and other photos and data about EJ that he had shown her earlier.

"They will follow her, Michelangelo. They know her now. I watch their systems, their networks. I see the methods embedded in their code. It is my language."

"Yes, they will follow her. They must," replied Michelangelo, looking at EJ as he spoke. "I know that they have always watched. It has mattered little for many years, but you understand that things are changing. You sense this as well as I."

The two dragons appeared to have forgotten about everything else in the room, and EJ's frustration now boiled over. She took a deep breath and pushed another lock of errant curls back behind her ear. She felt for the pendant at her throat, and then shouted at the top of her voice.

"Daniel Mortensen! You stop writing this minute! Not one more word, you hear, or I'll have your guts for garters! And as for you, Riz, shut up or leave. Your choice."

The cavern fell silent once more and Michelangelo and Riz both turned to face her again. She heard Michelangelo in her head once more, speaking quietly to her alone.

"Forgive me, Elizabeth. Forgive us both. You are correct, you deserve the explanation that has been promised you."

"Thank you, Michelangelo. Go on then, explain. Why must Wolverine follow me?"

"There will be an egg, Elizabeth. A dragon egg. All dragons can sense this. You already know that the world makes dragons, we are not born as you would understand that term. For an egg to appear is a signal of great change."

Michelangelo blew another smoke ring up toward the roof, and nodded at Riz to take up the story. Riz allowed a ripple of neon pink and yellow to flash down his sides and said in his SoCal surfer drawl, "Wolverine's in trouble, dude. The magic ain't happening for him no more. Jasper Moffett's wells are drying up 'cos his dragon's on his last legs. Dude, that dragon of his is the source of his wealth and power. He needs that dragon egg. He thinks it will save him 'cos his dragon has told him so. Like Michelangelo here says, all dragons can sense this … but only one dragon can read the guy's emails."

"But you still haven't explained why they have to follow me!"

"Because he must be made to believe that you are the key. That you will lead him to the egg. If not, he will seek out the dragons in every corner of the globe to satisfy his quest. We dragons have our power, but there are few indeed that can withstand the guns and bombs of men. Many will be hurt, and many will die."

"So your big plan is to save the dragons by letting Jasper Moffett and his goons hunt me down instead? How does that make sense? Say I find this egg and Wolverine is watching me, won't he just take it?"

EJ walked away from the two dragons and stood and stared at the big screen in front of her. Riz's dossier of security photos had been replaced between the two silent news tickers by one large graphic, a chart of the most valuable oil company in the world, Wolverine Petroleum. She studied it, not entirely certain that she understood what she was looking at, but certain enough that it represented the many billions that were at Jasper Moffett's disposal, and that he would go to any lengths to protect it. She turned away and returned to Michelangelo's side. The dragon laid his head on the floor and she sat down and leant against him. EJ looked over at Daniel Mortensen, who slowly nodded and got up from the desk to leave. He stopped briefly to look back at the three of them, and then hurried down the nearest tunnel. It was now just her and the two dragons.

"Can't you just destroy his company? Sell all his shares, or bankrupt him, or something?"

"No, Elizabeth. Wolverine Petroleum is too big for that. The repercussions would be very great, and many would suffer. Your father thought he could do that once, and he paid with his life and that of your mother. He must be stopped another way this time," answered Michelangelo slowly. "Our typist is no longer here. Please ask Al-Khwarizmi if he is willing to help you further."

EJ did so.

"You bet, dude! That's why I'm here. I can keep you and your guys one step ahead all the way. EJ dude, you gotta find the egg, and you gotta keep them looking for you while you do it."

With that, Riz's hologram abruptly disappeared. EJ's 'phone still sat where Daniel had placed it on the desk, but she heard it vibrate its Beethoven buzz, and while Michelangelo de St. Exupéry-Antoine blew another smoke ring into the heavens, she sat back against him and smiled.

The life of Anglezarke resumed around them. The charts and price indicators reappeared on the big screen, and dwarves returned to their desks in their ones and twos, chatting amiably as if coming back from their lunch breaks, which, EJ supposed, many of them were. The companionable silence that had enveloped the two of them was replaced by the buzz of activity. EJ roused herself.

"He wants me to lead him to the egg? So, let him follow me," she said. "But where do I lead him? Here?"

Michelangelo remained with his head resting on the floor beside her, his golden eyes closed. They flicked open at her question, and he regarded the defiant young woman in front of him, her fists bunched and arms akimbo. There was a sadness to his words in EJ's head when he finally spoke.

"It was many years before Jasper Moffett learnt of the existence of other dragons. Yet he is a man of great purpose. Once he knew of us, he made it his business to learn as much as he could.

"He knows where many of us are, but now he will watch you. Jasper Moffett wants the egg for himself alone. He will believe that I seek the egg for my own ends, and he cannot allow that to happen, for Jasper Moffett fears me almost as much as he fears the loss of all he holds most dear."

EJ had looked up at the chart of the Wolverine share price on the screen above them and smiled.

"Why would he fear you? He's the richest man in the world!"

"He fears that which he does not understand. I know Jasper Moffett's secret. I know his weakness. His is the weakness of so many rich men, for he believes that money bestows power. He has watched the gold of Anglezarke move and flow, yet Anglezarke remains hidden, a shadow. Anglezarke shuns such power. Use this weakness, Elizabeth. Do what he now expects of you. Visit the dragons."

EJ kissed Michelangelo fondly on the cheek and the two parted without another word needing to be said. She stood for a moment on the balcony at the mouth of the tunnel to her private entrance from the wooded hillside behind the house and looked back at Michelangelo and the great room. She could still feel him in her mind, but Michelangelo remained silent, his thoughts now turned to other matters, and EJ turned and hurried forward to the doorway, where Balthazar and Akitafelt awaited to escort her home.

The Mortensen bush telegraph had clearly been humming, for Molly Mortensen stood at the open kitchen door as EJ and her two hounds came through the orchard garden gate into the yard.

"Been a bit busy, haven't we?" stated Molly, delivering her verdict with a grin.

"Is it always like this, or is it just me?" asked EJ, hugging her friend tightly. Molly laughed, the tension broken.

"Come on. I've made a pot of tea and some sandwiches. There's enough to take with you for the ride too. Get your breath back and then we'll take a look at packing some of these fancy clothes. The rest can stay here or I can have them sent down to you, as you prefer."

EJ sat down at the kitchen counter and considered Riz's parting words in Michelangelo's cavern. If he lived up to his billing, she thought, then she pretty much had root access to any data or comms system that she cared to take a look at. Not to mention a backdoor into the heart of Wolverine. She rummaged in her jacket pocket for her 'phone and Facetime'd the Silicon Dragon, who answered without delay.

"Hey dude! What can I do you for?" drawled his grinning neon avatar.

"I'm going home tonight. To Norton Magna. Are you going to be watching?" she asked.

"Sure thing. I'm on it. I can track you via GPS, and I'll be in the cameras as well. Pretty certain your admirers in Houston will do the same."

"Really? How can they know?"

"Oh, that's so easy, man! Drop some triggers in the code to alert them when any camera picks up your tag. You Brits do like watching each other."

EJ thought about this briefly then dismissed it from her mind. She'd expected something of the sort, so there was nothing she could do to change it. Anyway, she had other matters to discuss.

"Okay, Riz, if you're going to help me then we can start right now. I want our London offices kitted out with all the gear for your little son et lumière show. Two sets. You say you've got the specs for the equipment. Is it all available in London?"

There was a pause and the avatar froze briefly, exactly as if Riz had suddenly left the call to do something else. Then he flicked back into motion on her screen.

"Just checked. Yeah, it's all there. Multiple suppliers, so it's harder to work out what it's being used for. I can have it all expedited for immediate delivery."

"Do it. Email the details and the specs to Ragnar Mortensen. I'm sure you can find his address. Then charge it all to me."

EJ pulled her wallet of pristine credit cards from her rucksack and recited the details of one of her new charge accounts to the dragon. Then, for a couple of hours she pushed aside all thoughts of dragons' eggs and went upstairs with Molly, to curl up on her sofa with a mug of tea and a plate of sandwiches while Molly Mortensen bustled around her room and they slowly whittled down the choices of which of her new wardrobe might fit on the Ducati and what would, for the time being, remain.

12 Beethoven

It had been past two in the morning when she had finally rolled to a halt in the yard behind *The Grouse and Hare.* She'd shut down the engine and sat quietly as she unhooked the chinstrap and pulled off her helmet. The light over the back door was on: her parents must have waited up for her arrival, but she could take a few minutes to catch her breath and gather her thoughts. The ride back from Anglezarke had been uneventful and the roads quiet, apart from the convoys of heavy goods vehicles slipstreaming each other on the motorways, but these professionals had had no interest in fast motorbikes and had left plenty of room for a rider whose head was still full of the tumult of emotions of this day of encounters and revelations. EJ had pulled her rucksack around and rummaged in the front pocket for her 'phone. There had been a slew of new message alerts clamouring for her attention, but only one of them had stood out for its background of swirling psychedelic colours. She had tapped open the message from Riz:

> *they hacked the traffic cameras. they noticed you.*
> *go to london tomorrow. see ya, dude.*

EJ swiped the message from her screen. Sure, see ya too, dude, she'd thought, but not tomorrow. She had really tried to build some anger and focus it on someone or something as she rode, but the effort had been futile. She had turned things over in her head and had kept coming back to the conclusion that if Wolverine was watching her, then what mattered was that from now on she gave them every opportunity to do so. The miles had sped by beneath her wheels, EJ had looked at her situation from every angle, and in the end had been reduced to a complacent smile behind her visor. Let's face it, she thought, avoiding the traffic cameras and the CCTV surveillance, was: a) futile, because there were millions of cameras in Britain, especially in London; and b) Wolverine would soon work out that she knew they were spying on her, and it seemed to EJ that that was the very last thing she should do. Let them watch, she decided, and let's give them a show!

So, EJ decided to go shopping. She had been brought up to value her independence and take her own decisions in life, and since there was still a nagging doubt at the back of her mind that the past few days might have somehow compromised this principle, it was time to take back control. She'd spent just a few pounds of the cash advance that Selwyn had given her after their lunch meeting, mostly on fuel for her Ducati, coffee and so forth during her travels up and down the motorways, and on reflection had been glad of the anonymity that the cash had allowed. However, she had money in the bank and a pile of credit cards in her own name. Time to follow Michelangelo's advice and take them out for a spin.

Despite her arrival in the small hours, EJ was up bright and early as the adrenalin started to pump. She pulled on her old jeans and flannel shirt, sat down at her desk with MacBook and 'phone, and half a bar of chocolate that she had picked up at a service station kiosk when she had paid for fuel the night before. Riz had implored her to come down to London, but she planned to spend the day at the pub helping her parents. If things began to happen as she now expected, then today might be the last chance for some time for her to enjoy the simple pleasure of the rhythms of home and family, and she did not intend to pass that up. Nevertheless, there was plenty she could do in the couple of hours before she went downstairs. Jasper Moffett wasn't the only one she planned to surprise when she got to London the next day! She pulled her credit cards from their secure folder in her rucksack for only the second time ever and set to work. The first order of the day was to Facetime Stan Mortensen.

"Morning, Stan. Hope I'm not disturbing you."

"EJ! Thought we might be hearing from you. I'm sat here looking at about a hundred messages and emails. By heck, you've got the place in an uproar." Inked and be-ringed as ever, Stan Mortensen was this morning resplendent in a vintage Slipknot tour t-shirt and, from the large mug of tea and the pile of greasy wrapping paper that he had hastily pushed out of sight, was obviously eating breakfast at his desk.

"Hmm … is there one from an address you've never seen before?"

"Hold on. Let me check."

Stan placed his mug back on the desk and EJ heard the staccato of a keyboard.

"Bloody hell! Excuse my French, but is this what I think it is?" asked Stan, his accent thickening.

"If you mean, is it a shipping list from a rather unusual dragon that can get anywhere he wants so long as there's a signal, then, yes, it's exactly what you think it is," EJ replied.

"Right, we heard all about Al-Khwarizmi and his magic show. In fact, the lads wouldn't shut up about it," commented Stan, with a chuckle. "What do you want me to do with this lot, then?"

"Riz said he'd put priority orders on everything, so you should receive it all today. Can you install it so it's up and running tomorrow?"

"Tomorrow?"

EJ watched Stan's brow furrow and swore she heard him suck air in between his teeth in the time-honoured reaction of every engineer and mechanic that had ever been asked to do a rush job.

"Two sets, eh? By the look of it, at least. Where were you thinking of putting 'em?"

"I thought one in Selwyn's study and one in the garage out back. How does that sound?"

"One in Selwyn's study? Oh, you're going to be popular. If even half of what young Daniel told me yesterday is true, then I think it sounds like a damned good idea. Let me and Lemmy take a look at some details first. In fact, sounds like the first of your couriers has just arrived, so I'd best be off. Later."

*

By the time she appeared in the kitchen for some breakfast, EJ wore the self-satisfied daze of someone who has discovered the surreal pleasure of spending real money for the first time in their lives. She had made a number of calls to establishments of one sort or another, mostly in Mayfair and the West End, to make certain enquiries and reservations. Her hesitancy and lack of experience in such matters had shone through to the professionals who had taken her calls, and had been reflected in their demeanours. However, once she had given them her credit card details, matters had rapidly improved – it was clear that her credit was of the very highest standing, and attitudes had changed accordingly. Emboldened by the sudden switches from superiority to obsequiousness, EJ had quickly cottoned on, and could already see that the coming few days were going to be a great deal of fun indeed. She grinned broadly as she imagined the reactions in Houston to some of the surveillance footage that she now had mapped out for them.

Maureen Carver was already at work readying the kitchen for *The Grouse and Hare*'s lunchtime trade, and was up to her elbows in flour from the enormous mixing bowl on the kitchen table. EJ came up behind her mother quietly and grabbed her around the middle in a suffocating hug.

"Morning, Mum!"

"Ooh, you gave me such a start!" yelped Maureen in delight. She wiped the flour from her hands with a tea-towel and kissed her daughter warmly on the cheek. "We heard you come in last night. Let me take a look at you! All those lovely clothes you told me about, and you're still wearing that same old shirt and jeans," she chided EJ gently.

"Well, if you want me pulling pints and whatnot wearing Yves Saint Laurent and Tom Ford I can go back upstairs and change. No? Thought not. Anyway, I left most of it up in my bedroom in Anglezarke. Not much room on my 'bike."

EJ saw the shadow pass across her mother's face at the words 'my bedroom' and realised that she had well and truly put her foot in it.

"I'm sorry, Mum. I didn't mean to hurt your feelings. It's just …"

"No, love, you've found your real home now."

"Don't you ever say that again!" shouted EJ, taken aback by the vehemence with which she'd spoken. She and her mother sat down at the kitchen table in shocked silence, each afraid in their own way of the sudden turn in the conversation and where it might be headed.

"You're never to say that again, Mum," EJ repeated more quietly, taking her mother's hands in her own. "This is my home, always has been and always will be. Anglezarke is like … it's a bit like one of those fantasy island programs on television, the difference is it pretty much belongs to me … or to Michelangelo … or to both of us. I think I need Selwyn Ormerod to explain some more about all that. Anyway, I can go there whenever I feel like it, and so can you for that matter. The thing is, there's stuff I need to do now to make sure that Anglezarke and places like it, and Michelangelo and the other dragons, can remain safe. I'll have to be away for a while. Is that okay?"

Her mother's face shifted from a look of relief to one of deep concern.

"Are you in danger, EJ?" she asked, with rather more perception than EJ might have previously given her credit for. EJ had convinced herself on the ride down to Norton Magna that she was safe from any harm, despite the evidence to the contrary in her own family history, and the knowledge that at least one participant in this great game believed that he was playing for the very highest stakes imaginable. Her mother's question jolted her back to the very heart of the matter. Was she in danger? The honest answer was that she really didn't know for sure, since the truth lay somewhere in that broad expanse between 'possibly' and 'probably'. However, she had never knowingly lied to her parents, and she jolly well knew that now was not the time to start.

"No, Mum, I don't think I am, but the same people who killed my parents, my birth parents ... well, let's just say that they haven't gone away. In fact, they've become much more powerful. And they've taken an interest in me, now that I'm involved again. I need to keep them interested. I've got a lot of help, and ..."

Maureen Carver knew her daughter. Like every loving mother she could decipher EJ's facial expressions with the precision of a surgeon. Maureen studied her profile in that moment, as EJ's voice tailed away and her daughter turned to look through the kitchen window into the middle distance. What Maureen saw was not fear, or even the hint of confusion, but determination. EJ was up to something. Heaven alone knew where this might end, but Maureen understood that there was no point attempting to dissuade her now.

EJ pushed herself back from the table and grabbed an apron and a tea-towel from the fresh piles on the dresser. "That can all wait for tomorrow. Today I'm here. Tell me what the specials are and I'll go and chalk them on the board."

*

The sun had appeared in some force mid-morning and the temperature had climbed rapidly. It seemed like half the village had decided to eat with them that day, and most had taken advantage of the continued shirt-sleeve weather to take their pints and sandwiches in the pub's ample beer garden. The atmosphere in and around the pub was leisurely and indolent and the conversation and laughter had flowed. EJ had been kept busy with a constant stream of orders, content to immerse herself in the life of pub and village for a few precious hours.

As the clock ticked toward closing time, Gibby was the sole occupant of the Lounge Bar, resplendent in a double-breasted suit in a herringbone weave of cornflower yellow wool and Shantung silk, a pale blue linen shirt and what appeared to be a Royal Artillery regimental tie. He was happily ensconced at his usual corner of the bar, but EJ knew him well enough to reckon that he was there in some semi-official capacity, and making a particularly poor job of trying to hide the fact.

"Love your suit, Gibby," said EJ, leaning over to clear away his empty plate and glass. "Off somewhere special, or is this in my honour?"

"I merely thought that it had been some time since I'd worn it, so I'd give the old girl a whirl, so to speak, and see how she felt. Only three of these ever made, you know. A rather dapper Italian clothier and the playboy heir to an industrial empire own the other two."

"It's very memorable," replied EJ, waiting for Gibby to speak.

"So, how was your trip to all points North?" he finally asked, somewhat sheepishly, peering at her over the tops of his half-moon spectacles.

"Lovely, Gibby, but I expect you knew that already. I met such a lot of interesting … people," answered EJ with a mischievous grin, her hand at the pendant at her throat.

"Yes, I expect you did. I don't suppose you've given any thought to what you'll do next?"

"Oh, Gibby, don't be such a bore. Of course I know what I'm going to do next! I'm just not going to tell you. Selwyn Ormerod will simply have to find out for himself, starting tomorrow. Can I get you another pint before I call time?"

Gibby grinned broadly. "I did tell him, you know. That you wouldn't crack on to me. Still, I suppose he needs to learn the hard way what the rest of us have known for years."

"And what might that be, Gibby?"

"My dear girl, that you're not to be trifled with! What else?"

EJ burst into laughter and set to pulling a fresh pint of *The Grouse and Hare*'s best bitter for her part-time confidante and bodyguard.

*

EJ sat at her desk the following morning, already changed into her crimson leathers and boots. She reckoned there'd be a fair few sore heads that day. The pub had been packed the night before, a carnival of jolly patrons from Norton Magna and the surrounding area, all revelling in a long summer evening of good food and drink. EJ had been rushed off her feet, more than busy enough to banish all thought of leaving. She slowly sipped a mug of tea that Maureen Carver had placed outside her door with a gentle knock while she watched her father in the yard below. He was moving a half dozen crates of assorted bottles from one of the storerooms to the pub's backdoor, and then back again. He'd made three such round trips while EJ had observed from behind the curtain, marking time as he waited for his daughter to come down., unwilling or unable to let her see how much it mattered to him. EJ blinked back the beginnings of tears. It was time.

Maureen Carver met her at the bottom of the stairs, wiping her hands on a tea towel. "Go and put him out of his misery. You know what he's like."

"I'm only riding into London," EJ replied, but the lack of conviction in her words was plain to both of them and EJ fell into her mother's open arms and buried her face in her neck. She tried with all her might to hold herself together, but to no avail. They stood in this embrace until Maureen gently pried herself from her daughter, brushed the tears from EJ's cheeks with a practiced hand and kissed her fondly.

"No, my love. It's like you said yesterday. There's things that you need to do. Go on now. He'll be alright. We both will."

EJ picked up her rucksack and helmet from where they had fallen to the floor and slipped through the back door into the yard. Her father had just stacked the last of his crates at the door to the storeroom, and turned to her with a brave smile, his face shining with sweat and his cheeks ruddy.

"Got everything you need?" George Carver asked.

EJ patted her rucksack in response. "I don't need to carry much. Dad. I've made sure there are clothes and things for me in London."

EJ waited by her Ducati as George Carver came over to her. He brought his hand up to his daughter's cheek.

"I know your mind's made up. Don't you worry, EJ, I'll look after your mum while you're away."

EJ held her father's hand against her cheek and kissed it. "That's just what she said. That she'd look after you," she replied with a grin.

"Ay, I suppose she would. Well, neither of us have ever been wrong on that score, have we?"

"I don't know how long …"

"Hush now, you'll be home soon enough. Never doubt it. I don't."

EJ held her father tightly, then dragged a hand across her face to wipe away fresh tears. George pushed the usual errant curl of hair back behind her ear, a gesture so familiar to them both since she had first arrived in Norton Magna, kissed her softly and stepped back. EJ pulled on her helmet and mounted her 'bike. Maureen came to stand at her husband's side and held his hand in hers as EJ started the engine to roll slowly from the yard and out onto the quiet road in front of *The Grouse and Hare*.

EJ took a little over an hour to make the journey into London. The worst of the morning rush had already subsided, and she made a conscious effort to ride at an even pace to give the traffic cameras every opportunity to pick up her progress as she passed by or beneath them. She'd never really bothered too much about them before, apart from the normal reluctance to being pinged for speeding, but was soon amazed by the sheer number that monitored the roads. She gave up counting with a small grunt of disgust.

EJ wound down into Mayfair from the north-west. Brook Street presented its usual obstacle course of roadworks, parked cars and delivery vehicles, which slowed even EJ's nimble progress, but eventually she was able to squeeze through and gun the Ducati into the right turn onto Bond Street. She slipped right again down the narrow mews that led to the rear of No.16A Albemarle Street and Anglezarke's London base. Without dismounting, she shook one glove free and pressed her palm to the reader at the garage door, then nudged the throttle again to roll inside.

Right on cue, she felt the buzz of her iPhone in her rucksack. Riz seemed to respect her privacy – well, most of the time at least – so if he stayed in the background while watching over her from the cameras and computer networks that he inhabited then that was fine by her. Right now, she needed to speak to him. She remembered reading somewhere in her studies that the BBC had used Beethoven's four opening notes to announce their nightly broadcasts into occupied Europe during the Second World War, because three dots and a dash in Morse code spelt the letter 'V' – for victory. EJ hoped it was a good omen. She switched off the 'bike and removed her helmet. The lights dimmed. The newly-installed cameras at the four corners of the ceiling immediately focused down onto the bare concrete floor in front of her and Riz's hologram appeared.

"Dude! You know this is the first time I've done this with the correct gear? Wow! What a difference! We really were winging it back in Anglezarke," exclaimed the Silicon Dragon. His fangs and talons glittered with sparks and yellow, pink and electric blue neon rippled along his flanks. As Riz's hologram spoke, the inner door to the garage flew open and Stan and Lemmy practically fell over each other into the room, but pulled up short at the sight of Riz in all his technicolour glory.

"Bloody hell! Will you look at that? It works!"

Riz turned his attention to the two dwarves. "Hey guys! Nice job on the installation. Chapeau."

EJ grinned as the two dwarves visibly swelled with pride at Riz's compliment.

"Morning, Stan. Morning, Lemmy," she added, before the tech love-fest could advance any further.

"Oh, yeah, hi EJ," replied Stan Mortensen distractedly, his eyes never once leaving Riz's simulacrum. He tentatively ran a be-ringed hand through the hologram and let out a long, low whistle, before finally turning to her.

"Spent all day and most of last night on this, so's it'd be ready for you. We knew it was all hooked up right, and that software is a real work of art, but we had nothing to test it with! I mean, His Nibs here wasn't around to help," he explained excitedly.

"Stan, I checked it out every step of the way, dude! Didn't EJ or your cousins up at Michelangelo's crib tell you? Man, I can go anywhere. Just give me 240 volts and some ones and zeros," replied Riz with obvious enjoyment, and he sent a full rainbow pulse of neon up and down the length of his holographic body, before he turned back to EJ.

"Was there something in particular, or are you just checking on the merchandise?"

"Did Houston clock me coming into town?"

"Oh, they saw you alright. I felt their little tripwires go off. Of course, it's still a tad early over there, even for those boys, but they'll have you up on their screens with their biscuits and gravy."

EJ nodded. Good, so at least part of their assumption appeared correct. "I've got some things to take care of here first, but stay in touch." She patted her iPhone. "I'll call you. You're going to love Selwyn."

"Your wish is my command, Milady. Ciao!"

With a final glittering grin, Riz winked out. For several seconds it felt as if all the air had been sucked from the garage, and then the background rumble of the city returned and EJ and the two dwarves began to breathe again.

*

The three of them moved back to Stan's basement lair. Stan waded through piles of boxes and plastic wrapping, then pushed aside empty cable reels and other remnants of the previous day's build from the chair in front of his desk so that EJ could sit down. Lemmy meanwhile had disappeared into the back. Probably off to brew another pot of tea, thought EJ.

Stan sat behind his monitors and fidgeted with the rings on his fingers. "I don't know what you're playing at, EJ. Believe me, one dragon's a handful. Now you've got another one in tow, and this one knows how to do things that most of us could never dream of. I hope you're being careful."

EJ leant forward in her seat and looked Stan Mortensen in the eye. "Hold out your hand, Stan."

The dwarf did as she had requested and EJ dropped three small electronic devices into his outstretched palm.

"Riz pointed out where I could find these. I must say, stitching a couple into the leathers was a particularly nice touch. So, since I'm certain that Selwyn Ormerod isn't a dab hand with needle and thread, let's not talk about playing games, shall we?"

EJ was pleased to see Stan Mortensen had the good grace to look suitably embarrassed, and her point made, decided to soften the blow.

"Anyway, no harm no foul, as Riz would say. I know you were only looking out for me, but as you've just seen, my security has undergone a significant upgrade over the past forty-eight hours."

Stan Mortensen rallied. "Listen, EJ, I'm dead sorry about not telling you. You know, about the trackers. But you understand we had to, don't you? … Is old techno dragon really watching everything for you?"

"Looks that way so far. I mean, he seems to be everywhere, but if I need him, I just drop him a message and up he pops."

"So, what do you want us to do now?"

"You've got to make sure that I always have a connection, no matter where I am. I have to be able to contact Riz, and you too."

"No problem. In fact, that's basically what we've been doing. We already have the transponder access if we need it. With Riz in the networks, we can pretty much guarantee coverage anywhere."

EJ stretched, got up from her chair and retrieved her rucksack from the floor. "I'll be staying in town for a couple of days, so I'm going to leave my 'bike here. Not going to pass up free parking in Mayfair, am I? I'll make sure that Riz knows to contact you, now that he can manifest here if we need him. Where's Selwyn?"

"He popped out earlier. Said he was off to his tailor for a fitting. He should still be there."

"And where does our Mr. Ormerod get his suits made?"

"Same place that's been dressing him and your grandfather for the past thirty years. Huntsman on the Row."

"Good. That's on my way. I'll nip in and say hello."

13 Chelsea Boots

EJ made a mental note to ask Riz to send her copies of the surveillance footage and stills from the next couple of days. She wanted to see them for herself – bright red motorbike leathers *sans* helmet in front of some of the world's most famous fashion houses and boutiques would make some great shots for her own portfolio, as well as turn heads in Houston. She stood for a moment in the vestibule of No.16A Albemarle Street, shook her hair loose from its ponytail and unzipped the leathers enough to expose the dragon pendant at her throat, then stepped out. She resisted the urge to look up and across the street to locate Wolverine's hidden camera on the opposite wall, and instead turned right and then around the corner into Bond Street, to most observers just an attractive young woman on a leisurely stroll through London's wonderland of luxury retail.

EJ headed south and crossed the street to walk the short distance east to Savile Row. In no time at all, she had completely forgotten about Texan oil magnates, dragons (golden, technicolour or otherwise) and any kind of higher purpose for which a twist of fate may have marked her out. Here she was back to being a young woman with a burgeoning love of high fashion, revelling in the chance to enjoy one of the great shopping playgrounds of the world. She might not have been dressed for the part – though she would rectify that shortly – but she could take her time to admire the designers' displays in the windows of their famous boutiques, relaxed in the knowledge that she was more than able to buy anything they had to offer. Who cared if the occasional shop assistant dismissed her with a condescending glance as just another motorcycle messenger idling away a few minutes between jobs?

Mayfair is not an especially large district of London, whose stratospheric real estate values mean that not an inch of that space is wasted. So, even at a walking pace reduced by frequent interruptions to examine the bounty on offer, it took EJ only a few minutes to turn into Savile Row and arrive at the front of the ornate wrought iron railings and burnished brass of H. Huntsman & Sons. EJ had meant to go straight into the tailors' and surprise Selwyn Ormerod, but instead spent several minutes admiring the display in Huntsman's front window. Behind a rank of terracotta pots of green, white and purple heather, and surrounding a large open picnic hamper filled with spotless white porcelain and gleaming silver cutlery, were arrayed four tailors' dummies, each dressed in a selection of Huntsman tweeds and other shooting attire. EJ's gaze was drawn to a woman's bespoke shooting gilet in a soft grey-green Donegal tweed with a burgundy windowpane check, finished at the shoulder and along the pockets in maroon suede. She was smitten, and decided then and there that first chance she got she would make her own fitting appointment, and discover what else the esteemed tailors might be able to do for her.

She skipped up the four shallow marble steps to Huntsman's broad oak door and rang the bell. The door was immediately opened by a slender gentleman in a dark double-breasted suit with high lapels, his silk tie perfectly knotted and silver hair swept back, a cloth tape measure around his neck. He clasped his hands behind his back and looked EJ straight in the eye.

"May I help you, Miss? If you are here for a pickup, then may I suggest you use our mews entrance," he asked without a hint of condescension, in a Cockney accent that a lifetime on Savile Row had done nothing to erase.

"No, no pickup," answered EJ jauntily. "Just a message for Mr. Selwyn Ormerod. I believe he is inside."

"Ah, yes!" beamed the tailor. "Mr. Ormerod. A most discerning gentleman. Delighted to convey your message to him."

"Thank you. Would you tell him that Miss Elizabeth Jade Carver requests the pleasure of his company for lunch at Le Gavroche at one p.m. sharp today. Oh, and be so kind as to remind him to be punctual. I find lateness so impolite, don't you?"

"I do indeed. Miss Carver, is it? I shall pass your message to Mr. Ormerod forthwith," replied the tailor, with the impeccable courtesy for which Savile Row was, among so many other things, renowned. EJ felt decidedly pleased with herself as she turned back to the street, the oak door closing softly behind her.

She turned right once more and continued up Savile Row and its temples to the sartorial arts. Now moving with more purpose, she allowed a couple of cars to pass before she jogged across the road and took another turn into Clifford Street.

At the corner, she re-joined Bond Street, this time heading north, before she cut along Avery Row toward the well-heeled chaos of Brook Street.

The entire walk from Savile Row had only taken her about ten minutes, and EJ was certain that the CCTV coverage of her progress would be comprehensive. Even mixed in among the hordes of tourists on Bond Street, EJ's blond curls and red 'bike leathers would be impossible to miss. Brook Street was now the domain of hedge funds and management consultants, who had gutted most of the buildings behind its stately frontages to create their state-of-the-art office spaces. EJ strode the last two hundred yards or so to the Art Deco entrance of Claridge's, barely noticed by the other pedestrians as they hurried to their destinations, eyes down and glued to their mobile 'phones.

There was very little in this world that the frock-coated and top-hatted doormen of one of London's grandest hotels had not seen before, so the arrival of a tall young woman dressed more for the motor racing track than a Mayfair soirée barely warranted a raised eyebrow. They stepped aside with a polite "Good morning" to allow EJ to push through the revolving doors into Claridge's lobby of black-and-white marble tiles and Art Deco luxury. She passed by the grand staircase as it swept up to the mezzanine, and headed for the Reception desk, pleased to note that, as she had fully expected, the fisheye dome of yet another surveillance camera was capturing her every move.

"Welcome to Claridge's. How may I help you?" asked the smart young receptionist, a hint of a French accent to his greeting.

"Good morning. Elizabeth Jade Carver. Anglezarke Holdings. I have a reservation." EJ passed the receptionist her driver's license and the credit card she had used to guarantee her booking. With slick professionalism, the young man had already begun to type the details into his terminal, and quickly looked back up with another smile.

"Indeed. Thank you, Miss Carver. I have you booked with us for three nights in one of our Corner Suites. Is that correct?"

"Quite correct," answered EJ, trying hard to suppress her excitement that she was really doing this. Of course, EJ had been brought up in a pub and had spent her whole life immersed in the hospitality business, so she was by no means a complete novice in an establishment like Claridge's. Nevertheless, she was about to take up residence in a suite at one of the world's most elegant hotels, so maybe a little giddiness was allowed.

"One moment while I confirm your card details. How many room keys shall you require?"

"Just the one for now."

The receptionist completed the check-in procedures and placed the necessary paperwork on the desk in front of EJ for her signature.

"Thank you, Miss Carver. I hope you enjoy your stay with us. Is there anything else that we can help you with?" asked the receptionist as he handed her the small wallet with its plastic keycard.

"Yes, I believe you are holding a number of packages for me. Would you be so kind as to send them up to my room?"

The receptionist checked his screen once more and them motioned to the Concierge desk. The concierge, a rather rotund, balding man resplendent in a black tailcoat with the crossed golden keys of his profession prominent at his lapel, hurried over.

"Madame has a number of deliveries."

The concierge checked the name on the screen and beamed at EJ. "Indeed, Miss Carver. And may I say that you have provided us with a most interesting morning! I shall supervise the delivery to your suite personally."

EJ inclined her head in acknowledgment and trotted across the lobby to the hotel's lifts. Her suite on the fifth floor was a compact jewel. Sunlight flooded the main room through the bay windows which looked out onto Brook Mews behind the hotel and Davies Street to its west. This sitting room was decorated in an eclectic mix of Regency, Chinoiserie and Art Deco pieces, its walls divided into classic panels of eau-de-nil framed in white stucco relief. The adjoining bedroom was simply appointed with a king-size bed, Art Deco side-tables and lamps, a pair of leather easy chairs and, in the window bay, an elegant writing desk and chair. EJ had researched her choice thoroughly before she had made the booking, but the thrill of actually being there was spine-tingling. The ring of the suite's doorbell shook her from her reverie, and she hurried to open the door. In the corridor stood the concierge at the head of a procession of bellboys, each laden with a stack of expensive boxes or bags – EJ's 'deliveries' had arrived.

"Shall we put everything in the drawing room, Ma'am?"

The concierge stepped aside and, like the minor despot that he was in his position, to whom the bellboys owed their absolute obedience, he only needed to clap his hands once. The crocodile moved forward smartly to deposit their loads on the seats and surfaces of the suite's drawing room. EJ had thought this moment through carefully, and knew that her stay at the hotel would be significantly enhanced, and hence that much more noticeable, if she showed her appreciation with a generous tip. She shook the concierge by the hand, leaving two folded fifty pound notes in his palm.

"One for the boys, and one for you. Thank you for your assistance."

Long years of experience had carried the concierge to the pinnacle of his profession, and he did not even glance down to know exactly how much this mysterious and wealthy young woman in the motorbike leathers had just deposited in his hand. How refreshing to have a proper guest for once who knew how to observe the proprieties, not like some of the ill-mannered upstarts with whom he often had to deal! He would make sure that everyone at Claridge's knew that Miss Carver was to be treated with the very highest regard during her stay, and he murmured his thanks to her as he ushered his troops from the room and away.

EJ surveyed her drawing room. In Anglezarke, the bags and boxes had been a delightful surprise, but as she looked over her purchases, her reaction was a good deal more measured. For one thing, she knew exactly the contents of every bag and box, as well as the amounts she had paid for them. She picked out the various cosmetics and perfumes – pretty much a repeat of the selection that had been bought for her in Anglezarke – together with some new underwear, and went into the bathroom. There was no time to dawdle today. She needed to keep one eye on the time, for it was already past eleven-thirty, if she was to be at the restaurant early as she intended.

After her shower, EJ put the finishing touches to her usual simple makeup and examined herself in the mirror. She'd do, she decided. EJ returned to the drawing room and retrieved two bags of ready-to-wear from a fashion designer who had once been a famous popstar and was married to an equally famous former footballer. She had chosen a pair of wide pleated trousers made from black seersucker cotton that belted high on her waist and draped perfectly to accentuate her long legs, and had paired it with a fitted cardigan top that was bright red with pink slashings at the sleeve. She decided to leave her hair down today, and admired the way the cardigan's severe V-neck drew the eye to her dragon pendant. A pair of low-heeled black Chelsea boots finished off the ensemble. She pulled a black leather clutch bag from another box and put her 'phone, cards, the letter from her grandfather and a sizeable sheaf of cash inside it before she took one final look around her suite. Everything else could wait until she got back later in the day. For now, it was time to continue the show.

EJ certainly made an impression. She had taken the lift only as far as the mezzanine floor so that she could then walk the rest of the way to the lobby down Claridge's famous staircase. Coffee cups and champagne glasses stopped in mid-air and newspapers were lowered. Every head turned to watch as she swept down the curving flight of steps. The ever-vigilant concierge bustled across to the foot of the staircase to meet her.

"Do you require a taxi, Miss Carver?" he asked obediently.

"Not today, thank you," EJ replied sweetly. "I'm only popping up the street for lunch."

The concierge understood her destination perfectly – for there was only one establishment that a Claridge's guest of Miss Carver's stature would consider, and nodded sagely. The folklore of Miss Elizabeth Carver thus added another chapter as she passed through the hotel's entrance with a pleasant wave and turned left to walk the short distance into Grosvenor Square and then along Upper Brook Street to Le Gavroche.

The moment EJ passed the fragrant window boxes on the restaurant's railings and mounted the three low steps below its glass canopy was a very special one. She had heard tales of this monument to haute cuisine for as long as she could remember. Her parents were skilful and enthusiastic cooks who, in addition to making their living from the strength of *The Grouse and Hare*'s kitchen, tried never to miss an episode of the many cookery programs on television. She had been regaled with tales of the men and women who had learnt their craft in Le Gavroche's kitchen under the benevolent dictatorship of its legendary chef patron, and how they had then taken these secrets across the world, as if Le Gavroche was more cathedral than restaurant and its alumni some form of monastic brotherhood.

EJ had requested a secluded table when she had spoken with the knowledgeable staff the previous day. Le Gavroche had exceeded her expectations by seating her in a semi-circular booth upholstered in dark green velvet that afforded a good deal of privacy from the rest of the dining room. A portrait in oils of the restaurant's founder smiled avuncularly down from the wall behind her while EJ sipped from a glass of Taittinger Blanc de Blancs and watched Selwyn Ormerod make his way over to join her, exchanging brief pleasantries with the staff as well as several of the guests seated at other tables.

EJ had been quite certain that the lure of lunch at Le Gavroche would prove irresistible to Selwyn, who had shown no aversion to displaying his love for the finer things in life. She stood to meet him as he arrived at her table. Selwyn took her hand and brushed his lips against it with the very barest of contacts.

"Am I on time?" he asked, with a twinkle in his eye.

"Don't be daft, Selwyn. Of course you are."

They sat down and regarded each other in silence as the sommelier poured another glass of champagne for Selwyn and then retired a polite distance. It was Selwyn who spoke first, just as EJ had intended.

"Firstly, you look wonderful. Secondly, I think that if you are planning to tell me off then we should get it over with immediately, shouldn't we? Then we might still be able to salvage a decent lunch at one of my favourite restaurants."

EJ watched him for a moment, then grinned. "I've no reason to tell you off. I thought I had, but I'm rather better informed now. We do however, have a lot to talk about."

She motioned for the waiter to approach the table to take their orders. "First we should eat. I thought I'd try the tasting menu. I've been told so many stories about this place, it seems a shame not to get the full experience now I've finally made it here."

Selwyn Ormerod guffawed. "A splendid choice! By the way, have you noticed the surveillance camera? It's very discretely placed, but it should still have a good view of us."

EJ smiled and raised her champagne flute to him. "Good, I'm glad you've worked out my little game for yourself. I don't need to waste time explaining it to you."

"No, you don't. Nevertheless, I apologise about the tracking devices. It now seems so unnecessary. I assume you're staying down the road?"

"I've taken a suite there for three days. I want to keep them interested, make them think I'm on a bit of a shopping bender. The sort of thing that a seventeen-year old girl with a big bag of money might do. If she cut loose, that is."

Selwyn nodded appreciatively. "Yes, I can see what you're thinking. Your new friend Al-Khwarizmi says they're taking the bait?"

EJ waited to reply as they were served their first course, a cheese soufflé that looked so light it needed to be tethered to the plate lest it float away. After they had both reverently tried the dish before them, she continued. "Riz says they have, but let's see what they do over the next couple of days. They've definitely opened a file on me. Plus, I think Riz is rather afraid of Michelangelo, so he's on our side. Do all the dragons treat Michelangelo that way?"

Selwyn polished off his last spoonful of the soufflé and closed his eyes in a silent prayer of thanks. "You know, I've lost count of the number of times I've eaten that, and it never ceases to amaze. I hope you enjoyed it too. Afraid of Michelangelo? I suppose in a way they are, though they're not the most convivial of creatures. I think in their own way they have a sort of grudging respect for him, or at least for the gold. They are dragons, when all's said and done."

As they waited for the next course, EJ slid the Polaroid photo of Selwyn and her grandfather across the table.

"Riz isn't the only one who's been in touch."

Selwyn lifted the photograph and examined it. "The day we bought the Albemarle Street house. I'd forgotten all about this picture. How did you get it? Mortensen, I suppose. I'll bet Joe didn't tell you where he is, did he? You must think we are a right pair of old fools."

"No, he didn't say where he is, but he seems to be on the trail of this dragon egg that's got everyone's knickers in a twist."

Selwyn continued to study the Polaroid while the sommelier refilled their glasses and their second course, a tartare of wild venison, was served. The food managed to drag him back from whatever memories had been holding his attention. He placed the picture face down on the tablecloth and pushed it with the tip of a finger back across to EJ.

"Shall we talk more about that later? Not here. I assume Al-Khwarizmi will be joining us? Stan and his sidekick practically threw me out of my study yesterday.

Said that you'd ordered it. I took refuge in the smoking room at my club rather than hang around."

The venison tartare was sublime, subtly flavoured with juniper and walnut. EJ was in heaven. "I did ask them to make sure that he could appear in your office. Selwyn, you're going to love it! His hologram is so neat."

Selwyn Ormerod regarded EJ balefully for a moment and then relented. "Hmm, I suppose it's better than trekking down to the garage every time he calls round. I must say, Stan did a lovely job. You'd hardly notice the work."

The most pressing points now covered, or at least postponed until they were back at Albemarle Street, their conversation moved into an easier familiarity as the remaining courses of lunch came and went. Selwyn wanted to know EJ's impressions of Anglezarke and Michelangelo, and EJ was more than happy to oblige. Although, inspired by their surroundings, she possibly overdid her description of the Chinese food that she and Molly Mortensen had demolished. A confirmed fan of Anglezarke's Fair View Takeaway himself, Selwyn didn't mind one bit, and by the time the coffee and petit fours were served, they were both sated in body and spirit.

"That was extraordinary," said EJ with finality, as if daring anyone to contradict her.

"It always is. There are some very fine restaurants in London nowadays, but Gavroche is …"

"Gavroche."

"Exactly."

Selwyn recognised that lunch was part of EJ's game plan, and remained silent as she paid the bill, though he noted her generous tip with approval. They left the restaurant and hailed a passing black cab to take them back to Albemarle Street.

*

"Who brings all these trays of tea and coffee? I never see anyone," asked EJ as she entered Selwyn's study, yet another silver service laid out on the low coffee table in front of the sofa.

"Oh, very stealthy when they want to be, these dwarves," replied Selwyn, looking up at her while he poured the tea into two cups. He pushed one across to her and picked up the other for himself. EJ set her bag down on the sofa beside her and pulled out her iPhone.

"I'll give Riz a buzz, shall I?"

"Hold on," said Selwyn, seating himself behind his desk. "Before we call your new guardian angel, may I see the letter that Joe left for you in Anglezarke?"

EJ pulled the envelope from her clutch bag and passed it across the desk to him. Selwyn read the letter twice and then folded it, returned it to her and checked his watch.

"I doubt our conversation with Al-Khwarizmi will take too long, so if you hurry once we're finished with him, you should be able to make the Post Office before it closes."

"You think there will be a letter?"

"I'm sure of it. Michelangelo and your grandfather have been planning this for a long time. I know it looks like some kind of idiotic treasure hunt, all cloak and daggers, but Wolverine must not know. Not yet. Not until Joe tells you the time is right."

"OK, I guess. So, I just play along?

"Yes, now that your security is guaranteed, you keep showing Wolverine exactly what they are expecting to see."

EJ tucked the letter back into her bag and then shot a message to Riz. The response with the new equipment was immediate: EJ hurriedly pushed the tea tray to one side as the hologram materialised in a circle of light on the coffee table. It was much smaller than she had previously seen it, barely three feet long, and fit snugly on the tabletop. However, the definition provided by the more powerful processors gave Riz a level of depth and detail that, if she hadn't known, EJ would have sworn that the Silicon Dragon sat before her, flashing and grinning in his normal manner, was as real as she or Selwyn Ormerod.

Riz's simulacrum looked around to get the measure of his new surroundings. "Hey, EJ! I guess this is the other rig, right? Cool beans. Very … cosy. Is the man himself around?"

"He's sat right behind you at his desk."

Riz turned and wrapped his tail around himself. "Mr. Ormerod, it is my pleasure to make your acquaintance, sir. Love what you've done to the place! How was lunch?"

EJ intoned a brief prayer and looked to the heavens in exasperation. She was already used to Riz's overfamiliarity, but sometimes his stream of consciousness approach to communication was like trying to bottle lightning. She watched Selwyn to gauge his reaction. She need not have worried.

"Al-Khwarizmi Ibn Shams ad'Din, Michelangelo gave you permission to enter our systems, and I do the same. You are serving EJ, therefore you are also serving Anglezarke, for which I give you my thanks. You are welcome here. Oh, and lunch was exceptional. Thank you for asking."

EJ looked on open-mouthed and understood that she had just witnessed a valuable lesson born of Selwyn's long years in Michelangelo's employ – dragon diplomacy 101. She could see by Riz's reaction, the way his usual light show slowed and his posture straightened, that the Silicon Dragon was now taking this conversation seriously. Riz inclined his head in a bow and spoke.

"You are well known to me, Selwyn Ormerod. You serve the Golden Dragon with honour. I, Al-Khwarizmi Ibn Shams ad'Din, am at your service." Riz looked over at EJ. "And at the service of Elizabeth Jade."

Diplomatic relations firmly established, thought EJ. Now maybe they could get down to business.

"Selwyn already knows about the surveillance, Riz. And he knows you're watching to make sure that Wolverine keeps on tracking my movements."

Riz nodded in assent and waited for Selwyn to open the conversation.

"The first person over there who'll see any of this stuff is their head of security. Who is also one of the few people to ever see the Oil Dragon," explained Selwyn Ormerod.

"Yes. Marvin Thibodeaux."

"Can you tell when Jasper Moffett receives this information from him?"

"Yes. I follow the files. If the files move, I know. If they are printed, I know. If they pass to a screen, I know." Despite the modern-day subject matter, Riz's voice had slipped back into the older accent of the desert that EJ had heard before. Selwyn Ormerod sipped his tea and regarded EJ and Riz then addressed them both.

"EJ now knows that I was against this little adventure from the very start." He saw that EJ was about to protest and held up a hand to stay her. "No, EJ, allow me to finish. I said that I was against it, but that was before Al-Khwarizmi here came into the picture. Al-Khwarizmi understands our adversary's reach and power. He will confirm my worries, but now that you're no longer running around blind, I feel a great deal more confident about your safety."

"They will watch, Selwyn Ormerod, but soon they will move. Jasper Moffett must find the egg. He means to own it for himself."

"You are correct, Al-Khwarizmi. However, neither we nor Jasper Moffett will find this dragon's egg. EJ's grandfather has already set himself that task. The dragons will feel its presence and will tell him where to find it, and then he will send for EJ to join him."

EJ felt a familiar frustration building within her. "But why, Selwyn?"

"We did not create this situation, but now we must make it work for us. The Oil Dragon cannot sense the others, and Michelangelo is certain that he cannot sense the egg, whenever it appears. That is why Jasper is taking such interest in your movements. He must have the egg and will follow you to get it. Instead, he will learn that he has lost, and you and your grandfather will finally have your revenge on the man who destroyed your family."

14 Serpentine

EJ threw back the light quilt and padded through to her suite's sitting room. The harsh sodium glare of the streetlights on Brook Street was slowly giving way to the grey light of dawn. She looked out of her window and watched a taxi quietly turn into the deserted street to pull up outside the hotel. The doorman in his top hat and black coachman's coat opened the taxi's door with practiced ease to welcome a couple in evening dress returning from some society event. EJ turned away with a small yawn and went back into the bedroom to change into the running clothes and shoes that had been among her purchases. In less than five minutes, she was downstairs and gently jogging along Upper Brook Street toward the trees of Hyde Park. She crossed Park Lane to enter the royal estate, still gloomy under its perimeter of planes and poplars, then headed north toward Speakers' Corner and the Marble Arch, which appeared to float as a floodlit, off-white glow through the trees, one of the day's first buses making its turn around it to head up Oxford Street. EJ angled southwest along one of the broad paths into Hyde Park's open meadows, the occasional pedestrian and dog walker now visible, the last vestiges of early morning mist receding.

Selwyn had been right, she'd made it to the Post Office on Grosvenor Street with barely five minutes to spare before closing time the previous afternoon, and the helpful staff had been happy to lock the doors behind her and allow her to wait while they checked the Poste Restante. Clearly, she was not the first customer to put them to this minor inconvenience. Sure enough, there was a letter addressed to her and awaiting her pickup, and once the formalities of identity check and signature had been completed, the door had been unlocked and she had been politely but firmly ushered out to head round the corner to her hotel. The letter had been postmarked a week earlier in Hong Kong. Back in her suite, she opened it to find a single page, little more than a hurried note, scribbled in green ink on Peninsula Hotel stationery:

My dearest EJ,

A flying visit to Hong Kong: I have always preferred to enter China via the tradesman's entrance, as it were. An old habit from my FO days, but I think more important now than ever. I will make my way up to Beijing to meet the Jade Dragon – he's always got his finger on the pulse, so to speak, and his powerful friends in Zhongnanhai might prove useful.

Book a ticket and meet me there. Don't worry about flight details – Jade's people will know when you're due to arrive and will make all the arrangements.

Must run! Love as ever, J

The path began to slope gently down in the direction of the Serpentine, the kidney-shaped ornamental lake that dominates the southern half of Hyde Park, and EJ lengthened her stride to quicken the pace. Watery sunlight finally broke through the banks of low cloud above London, and the Serpentine's dark waters shivered with the reflections of Knightsbridge to its south. EJ halted at the boathouse, leant on the railing and breathed deeply. She could feel the tension in the muscles of her neck ease and her shoulders relax. The run had cleared her head and let her think about her grandfather's letter and the instruction to travel to China. Her thoughts moved to how she might take advantage of this new development to sow some more confusion in Jasper Moffett's mind. As she heard and felt London come to life around her, the outlines of a plan began to form. For starters, another day leading Wolverine a merry dance around Bond Street wouldn't hurt. Now that she also needed to buy some luggage for her trip, she had every reason to take her time, make herself visible again and reinforce the impression she'd so carefully curated. Nevertheless, she had to assume that Wolverine would know her flight details almost as quickly as Riz when she bought airline tickets later, so the trick would be for them to create a trip that was believable. Then, if Riz could run some interference in the computers, it ought to give her the room she'd need to shake her watchers long enough for her to arrive in Beijing unobserved. Wolverine would work it out eventually, but even a head start of a few hours might prove very useful indeed. The real hurdle was that she knew next to nothing about international travel; apart from a couple of family holidays to the sunshine of the Mediterranean, her only real experience had been a school trip to France. EJ realised that she would need Selwyn Ormerod's help. Until now she'd been flying by the seat of her pants, but the installation of the holo projectors and the campaign of disinformation she'd played out so far in front of the cameras for Wolverine's benefit had clearly made a favourable impression. Their first meeting now felt so long ago, and EJ had often had the nagging feeling that, for all his undoubted loyalty, Selwyn tolerated her as a necessary distraction, a smokescreen for unwelcome attention while he and her grandfather got on with the real business of Michelangelo and Anglezarke. Thus, the change in Selwyn's demeanour toward her since her return from Anglezarke had been notable, especially the way he had opened up to her and Riz the previous afternoon. She needed his expertise if this was going to work.

That deep background resonance which never really disappears in any city had now built to a full-throated rumble. She didn't yet have all the details clear in her mind, but EJ felt the excitement building that another fascinating day lay ahead. A renewed spring to her step, she sprinted along the Serpentine's northern bank in the direction of Apsley House and Hyde Park Corner, now just another of the many runners starting their day on the royal park's paths and byways. Mulling over her options, EJ slowed to exit Hyde Park via the Queen Elizabeth Gate, then took the underpass below Park Lane to run back north to the heart of Mayfair and the joys of a Claridge's breakfast.

*

Early that evening, EJ and Selwyn Ormerod took an after-dinner table in the onyx and burgundy Art Deco splendour of her hotel's cigar lounge. His own familiarity in Claridge's notwithstanding, Selwyn had looked on with a mixture of admiration and bemusement as each member of staff that crossed their path addressed EJ by name as 'Miss Carver', and he had been pressing her throughout their light dinner to divulge her secret. He extracted his cigar case from an inner suit pocket and tried once more.

"I mean to say, you're not the first wealthy and attractive young woman to grace this hotel with her presence. Most of them don't get the attention you've received, no matter how well the place looks after its guests."

EJ regarded Selwyn over the edge of her glass of Riesling. "Oh, alright then. I bribed the concierge, of course."

"Really? How wonderful! I should have guessed," he exclaimed, as he sat back on the velvet banquette beneath the framed black and white portraits of film stars of a bygone era, and cut and lit his cigar with evident satisfaction. A waiter discreetly placed a balloon of Armagnac and a glass of mineral water on the table in front of him.

EJ had shown Selwyn her grandfather's letter from Hong Kong at dinner and they had chatted in the most general of ways about EJ's ideas for her travel plan, with Selwyn adding nuance and detail to the bare bones. Though there had been few other guests dining at that hour in the bar, neither of them had wanted to run the risk of even casual eavesdropping. The smoking lounge was a room accustomed to the hushed conversation of colleagues and conspirators, and the pianist in the corner playing selections from Gershwin and Cole Porter helped to keep matters private.

"I think that your Paris idea will work, if you and Al Khwarizmi can time things right," said Selwyn, his head now wreathed in a nimbus of fragrant cigar smoke. "The reservation at the Georges V is easy – Stan Mortensen could hack that and make it disappear without a trace, so Al Khwarizmi will have no trouble at all. What about the seat on the Air France to Beijing tomorrow night?"

"Plenty of room in either First or Business. I had Riz check for me. He says the flight's barely half full. I explained to him what I need, so he's keeping an eye on things."

"Take the first class seat. You'll disembark before the rest of the plane, which will be a help for Jade Dragon's people," suggested Selwyn, resting his cigar on an onyx ashtray the size of a dinner plate. "It sounds like you've got all the moving parts in place. Why don't you run the whole thing past me one more time and we'll make sure we've not left anything out."

EJ took her iPhone from the clutch bag that she had taken to carrying with her, and placed it on the table between them. She tapped the screen, brought up the icon that Riz had added and opened it. The pulsing, grinning dragon head appeared on the screen.

"Riz, just listen for now. If everything is clear then message me. OK?"

The Silicon Dragon winked at her and disappeared from the screen. EJ rolled her eyes and took a decent mouthful of wine in response.

"So, the idea is to make it look like I'm taking my shopping jones over to Paris. I have a flight booked for tomorrow afternoon. I'll leave here at lunchtime, and I've already asked the concierge to have a hotel car ready to run me to Heathrow. We've reserved a suite for three nights at the Georges V, but Riz'll make that disappear when we need to."

"Do Wolverine already know?"

"About Paris? Yes. That's why I had the new suitcases delivered here. Riz says that as soon as they saw them, they checked all the airlines. When they found the reservation, they immediately checked the Paris hotels too. They think I'm going shopping."

Selwyn lifted the brandy glass to his nose and savoured the aroma. "Once you pick up your luggage at Charles de Gaulle, you alert Al-Khwarizmi and he'll book the Beijing flight. You go upstairs one level to departures and check in. Can he do anything about the cameras in the airport?"

"Riz'll make sure I'm unobserved from the time I leave the baggage hall to when I board the Beijing flight. I could pretty much go straight from check-in to boarding if the flight from London lands on time. By the time they work out what's happened, I'll be half way to China, and Riz says Wolverine will think twice about hacking any of their systems."

"I dare say he's right," replied Selwyn looking rather smug. "You know, they really do revere the Jade Dragon, even the Chinese leadership – Zhongnanhai, as Joc called them. That's where the Central Committee all live, near the Forbidden City. Once you land in Beijing, don't be concerned if you're singled out and treated differently. Jade and his people will make sure you enter the country with the minimum of fuss … Jasper Moffett is going to throw a fit when he finds out."

EJ picked her 'phone up from the table. The emoji of a thumbs up flashed on the screen from Riz and she rose from her seat to lean forward and kiss Selwyn Ormerod on the cheek. She stood, straightened her jacket, and said to him,

"Isn't that the whole point, Selwyn?"

*

EJ had already been in bed for several hours when later that same day in Washington D.C., Jasper Moffett had a half hour before he needed to leave for the White House and a private dinner with the President. He sat back on the black leather sofa in the large office cum lounge reserved for his private use in Wolverine's spacious suite in the Watergate complex, the centre for his company's hugely powerful political lobbying operation. He'd bankrolled this President's election, as he had the three before him, but he liked to keep up the appearance that the occupant of the Oval Office was the most powerful man on the planet, and made a point of accepting the quarterly dinner invitations. The White House chefs were first class, and Jasper found the current incumbent tolerable, for a politician, so there was the small added benefit that conversation at the dinner table was occasionally interesting. Senators, on the other hand, came to him. The three senior Senators of Texas, Oklahoma and Louisiana had all paid court that afternoon, as was to be expected since he had put them in their positions and owned each of them outright, from the tops of their perfectly styled hair all the way down to the soles of their hand-tooled boots. They each knew which side their biscuits were buttered, thought Jasper.

"Bless their hearts," he said contemptuously, and loosened the tie at his collar. Marvin Thibodeaux had flown up to the capital with Jasper that morning, and chose that moment to enter the room with the black leather folder that contained the latest updates on the whereabouts of one Elizabeth Jade Carver. Jasper's mood immediately brightened.

"Well now, Elizabeth! And just what have you been spending your time and Michelangelo's money on today, young lady?"

"Same old, same old. Mademoiselle sure likes her fancy boutiques."

Jasper took the folder and began to leaf through the surveillance shots while Marvin watched from a respectful distance. He already knew the contents. For the past two days, he and King Moffett had collated screenshots from across Mayfair. The previous day, they had needed to scramble when it became clear that EJ had not just wandered by accident into one of London's most desirable hotels, but King immediately grabbed a keyboard and his fingers had become a blur as he coded. It hadn't been long before the crisis had been averted and they had slid like a stiletto into Claridge's mainframe. Marvin had laughed out loud as he and King had watched in real time the procession of bellboys carrying EJ's purchases, like slaves in some Ottoman palace. Today's selection was more conventional: EJ entering a dizzying variety of Mayfair shops, invariably exiting with a stack of expensive purchases being carried to her hotel by one employee or another, before she paid yet another courtesy call on the Anglezarke office at Albemarle Street in the mid-afternoon. She had then returned to her hotel for a light dinner in the Claridge's Bar and an after-dinner drink with Selwyn Ormerod, before retiring to her suite.

Marvin had performed enough covert surveillance during his career to be mostly unimpressed by the day's results. He considered the previous day much more interesting, having included the lunch at Le Gavroche, and he had lingered over the footage from the restaurant's security cameras and nodded sagely in admiration. Cajun born and bred, Marvin Thibodeaux was no stranger to good food, and had developed an avid appreciation for haute cuisine over the years. Indeed, he had himself eaten at this very restaurant several times, always alone, and considered it an establishment of the highest quality. Maybe it was the distraction of Le Gavroche's tasting menu, but Marvin failed to pay as much attention as he ought to the several photos that followed. He had noted the pair's return to Albemarle Street after lunch, as he had expected, and that EJ had later left there to walk back to her hotel. It was unfortunate for him that neither he nor King had recognised the discreet signage of the Post Office in Grosvenor Street, and that King had therefore not grabbed a feed from its cameras. If he had, then it is possible that a great deal of unpleasantness may subsequently have been avoided.

"She's holding a reservation until tomorrow afternoon," Marvin pointed out to Jasper. "And she bought luggage today. There's a photo near the back."

"Did she now?" Jasper flicked through to the picture in question, then clapped the folder shut and tapped it on his knee with one hand, the other stroking his beard. "Well, a young lady of means sure needs something to carry all them fancy clothes she's been collecting. Won't all fit on the back of a motorbike, now, will they?'

He continued to tap the leather binder on his knee. "This ain't your first rodeo. Where's she headed?" he asked Marvin.

"She's booked on an Air France to Paris tomorrow afternoon. A suite at the Georges V."

"My oh my, well ain't we one busy little fashionista!"

Marvin remained unmoved. "Maybe so. You sure she's gonna lead you to this dragon egg, Jasper?"

Jasper Moffett tossed the leather folder back to his head of security and stood, then strode across the room to the wet bar that took up most of one wall. He re-knotted his tie in the mirror, his eyes never once leaving Marvin Thibodeaux behind him.

"That's your job to find out. What's that suspicious old brain of yours telling you, Marvin?"

Marvin retrieved Jasper's suit coat from the back of the chair near the desk and took it over to him. Jasper shrugged it on and stood expectantly for an answer.

"Girl's just having a bit of fun, Jasper. You or I would have done the same at her age. Anyway, King says snooping around in the French computers is even easier than the British ones, so I guess we'll keep an eye on Little Miss Shopping Spree and see where she goes."

Jasper grinned. He shot his cuffs and adjusted the Irish linen handkerchief in his top pocket. Satisfied, he turned and led the way to the door. He stopped and looked at Marvin Thibodeaux.

"You boys do that. I want to know everything, and I mean everything. Where she goes, what she eats, what she buys. I happen to enjoy young Elizabeth's sense of style, but at some point, she's gonna have to start to pay the piper and earn that generous salary of hers. You can bet old Michelangelo'll insist on it. She's around for one reason only, and that's to find that egg."

With that, Jasper threw open the double doors and the cadre of burly security personnel in the outer office silently flowed around him into their practiced positions.

"Call the cars, Marvin. We've got a dinner date at 1600 Pennsylvania Avenue. Let's make sure we keep our host waiting and arrive fashionably late."

15 Le Monde

Though there's barely a moment when the roads of London can be called quiet, EJ's mid-afternoon departure from Claridge's the following day gave her as good a chance of a trouble-free run to Heathrow Airport as might be hoped for. EJ had appeared in the hotel lobby, unmissable in a crushed red velvet trouser suit that she had fallen in love with the day before at the Gucci boutique on Bond Street. The concierge had rushed across to the foot of the staircase to fuss over his favourite guest. He barked out instructions to his most trusted bellboys to treat her three shining aluminium suitcases with the utmost care, then he personally escorted EJ to the car idling for her at the hotel entrance. EJ was delighted: She couldn't have asked for a more visible fanfare at her departure, and slipped him another substantial tip while he held the door open for her to slide into the Mercedes' capacious back seat. According to Riz, her Mayfair escapades had been swallowed hook, line and sinker in Houston to glowing reviews, and EJ had every reason to believe that their little Paris ruse would be equally well believed by her secret watchers. Besides, she thought, with a huge grin as her limousine glided away from the hotel, how many other seventeen-year old girls got to spend three days splashing thousands of pounds on luxury hotels, Michelin-starred restaurants and shedloads of designer gear? Most of the ones she knew would sell their souls for half the chance!

The Mercedes swooped in near silence through Hyde Park towards Knightsbridge, and this gave EJ a new idea. She pulled her 'phone from her rucksack and tapped the Riz icon on the home screen.

"Riz, can you book a car from the Georges V to pick me up at Charles de Gaulle?"

The psychedelic dragon head on the screen raised an eyebrow in response, and then a message appeared below it:

booked. why?

"I'll give the driver a couple of hundred Euros to swing through the airport for five minutes and then drop me at the Air France departures. Enough time for you to make the Beijing flight booking, then scrub the car reservation? Leave the hotel booking for a few hours until I'm in the air."

EJ was now more than accustomed to Riz's avatar freezing as the Silicon Dragon zapped round the networks or performed more complex tasks, but in a couple of seconds he was back:

can do. there are a lot of cameras watching the airport roads

"Let Houston believe I'm on my way into Paris from the airport. They might think it a bit hinky if I don't keep up appearances, and a chauffeured limo from the Georges V fits the bill nicely. You manage the cameras to make sure I can get back to the terminal undetected. OK?"

Riz's avatar grinned one of his trademark toothy neon flashes:

sayonara. happy landings, dude!

EJ slipped her 'phone away and serenely watched West London slide by, feeling the surge of power press her back into the seat as the big car finally opened up to leave the mild congestion of the Cromwell Road and merge with the raised M4. Traffic on the motorway was light and they soon drew up in the reserved parking bay in front of Heathrow's Terminal 3. The driver politely asked EJ to wait in the car while he fetched a baggage trolley for her, and then courteously accompanied her to the first of the security checks at the terminal entrance – news of Miss Carver's tipping habits had clearly spread at Claridge's, and the smile on his face as he bade her bon voyage told her that she had not disappointed in that regard.

From check-in to boarding, EJ's passage through the airport was without incident. She rather liked the idea that her outfit meant that Wolverine once again had a bright red target to follow and, sure that they would try to hack Heathrow's surveillance systems, she wandered around the duty free and other shops for a while to make herself visible, stopping to admire watches and other trinkets, then made the long walk to the gate and was the first passenger to board. A light drizzle was falling as the Air France 737 pushed back on time, and it came as a delightful shock when the plane burst through the low cloud above South-east England to emerge into dazzling summer sunshine as it climbed and banked away toward the Channel and France. EJ happily tucked into the selection of hors d'oeuvres she was served by the attentive flight crew, and brushed up her French with a copy of *Le Monde,* immersing herself in the trenchant opinions of the Parisian press corps.

EJ was one of those fortunate few who happily confound the firmly-held British belief that whether at home or abroad no one in the country could, or should, speak any language other than English. She had always enjoyed studying French at school, and spoke passable Spanish and Italian as well. Indeed, her own expectations for the result of her recent French 'A' Level exam were probably higher than for the History or English Literature that she had also taken less than a month before. They were in the air barely forty-five minutes before she looked up from her newspaper to feel the gentle bump of the wheels as they landed in the golden glow of a Parisian summer evening, the top of the Eiffel tower visible in the distance as the aircraft turned off the runway. She folded *Le Monde* and slipped it into the seat pocket.

Baggage retrieved and through customs, EJ was expertly guided to the waiting car by the Georges V hotel's airport representative. Her driver was a dapper, middle-aged man of North African descent, with a pencil moustache and a widow's peak accentuated by his slicked-back hair. He listened without comment to her request, accepted her generous tip with a polite nod, then pulled the large black BMW sedan away from the Arrivals Hall to merge with the heavy traffic flowing around Charles de Gaulle airport and Paris's north-western suburbs. EJ had the distinct impression that this was not the first time that one of his well-heeled passengers had requested some kind of detour from him, and that hers was far from the most outlandish that he had ever entertained. Anyway, she thought, Riz would make the car booking disappear once he dropped her off at the departure level and no one would be any the wiser.

Thinking about Riz, EJ felt the tell-tale Beethoven buzz of her iPhone. She fished it out of its secure pocket on the front of her rucksack and settled back into the limo's cream leather seat to read the Silicon Dragon's latest update. He had added an Air France app to her home screen which she opened to find the confirmation and ticket details for her flight that evening to Beijing. EJ flipped the app closed and opened the latest message from Riz:

when the car turns back into the airport, i'll start to fritz the road cams

"You know, they'll probably think they've lost me in all this traffic. There's a ton of cars heading into Paris," said EJ.

roger that, dude. i've checked the lounge. take one of the privacy suites. i'll fuzz one camera and you're good. they'll fetch you when it's time to drive you to the plane

"Drive me to the plane?" asked EJ, immediately regretting her outburst.

first class, baby! knock 'em dead!

With that, the Riz avatar gave her one last conspiratorial wink and flicked out. EJ stared at the blank screen, her mouth still set in an 'O' of surprise, before she hurriedly shoved the 'phone away as the door was opened by the kerbside greeter at Air France's First Class reception area with a pleasant "Bonsoir, Mademoiselle Carver!"

*

Dusk had begun to fall as the Air France 777 taxied toward its arrival gate at the nearest of the low, burnished wings of Beijing Daxing International Airport. The building's flowing lines were picked out in bright strips of halogen, the rest of the huge structure sat behind it like the arms of some gigantic glass and aluminium octopus. Away to the west, the sun was a blood red ball on the horizon, while the north was lit by the growing evening glow of the huge city, its light diffused by the fine orange dust that so often blew in from the Gobi Desert to the north of the Chinese capital, and which made Beijing's hot, humid summers even more trying for its many millions of inhabitants.

Paris to Beijing is a long flight, some ten or eleven hours depending on the season and the prevailing winds. Sat in the expansive comfort of her first class berth, EJ's thoughts had inevitably turned to her grandfather. She knew she was just as guilty of getting caught up in the excitement and subterfuge, and tried to convince herself that it was all part of some grand plan to recover the dragon egg, wherever it might appear. Nevertheless, EJ knew the real reason for this extraordinary journey. What would her grandfather be expecting? More to the point, what was she expecting? Some older version of the little girl that had toddled at his side, her tiny hand in his, as they had visited Michelangelo in his lair under the hill? Or a young woman with a thousand questions and a pent up frustration at being sucked into this wild goose chase of a life by a man who apparently considered it some great game, no matter who he manipulated or deceived along the way? One part of her was thrilled by the adventure, by the romance of it all. Another seethed with anger that her whole existence, everything she held to be most true and dear, had been turned upside down by this man who, if Selwyn Ormerod was to be believed, was acting not out nobility or some higher calling, but from a coldblooded desire for vengeance. EJ sighed. The reality, she thought, was somewhere in the middle, as so often in life. She was both the little girl who longed to see her grandfather, and the wary young woman who could see through the shower of gold and gifts and cynically questioned his motives. She realised that aside from all these human machinations, she now felt most at ease when she was with Michelangelo or even Riz, so maybe the presence of the Jade Dragon would help. After all, he had been advising China's various rulers for centuries, so he must be used to some very complicated people indeed.

EJ had been the sole passenger in First Class that night, and had been looked after with all the élan and attention to detail for which the French carrier was famed. After a superb dinner, she had slept well, and so by the time the stewardess had asked her to fasten her seatbelt for their final approach, EJ was already breakfasted, washed and changed back into her Gucci velvet suit, which had drawn a slew of compliments from the chic stewardesses, who all knew a thing or two about haute couture themselves. She sat expectantly as the aircraft braked into its parking position and felt the gentle bump and sway as the air bridges connected with the doors. The order was given from the cockpit that the doors could be opened, and the purser approached her seat.

"Mademoiselle Carver, we have been requested by Beijing ground authorities to hold the rest of the passengers while you deplane. An escort is waiting for you on the air bridge." At that moment the young woman sat before him, elegant though she might be, looked very young indeed, and the purser couldn't hide the fact that this unusual instruction filled him with concern. "Mademoiselle, it has been our great pleasure to have you on board, and I thank you for flying Air France this evening. I very much hope that I will see you again soon on one of our flights."

With a graceful bow, the purser led EJ to the main door. She thanked the stewardesses for their attention and kindness, and looked back at the cabin one final time. The curtains to the rest of the plane remained tightly closed. She realised with a mounting sense of disquiet that whatever was about to happen would have no witnesses. Then EJ remembered Selwyn Ormerod's words of advice the previous evening that she should not worry if she was singled out from the rest of the passengers on arrival. Confidence a little restored, she stepped through the doorway.

Two Chinese soldiers stood silently at the door, blocking any passage to the air bridge. At least, EJ assumed by their bearing that they were soldiers, for they might equally be policemen or some other kind of security officer. Whatever they were, there was no way past them. Both stood at least six feet tall, their hair cut high and tight to their skulls, the thin wires of earpieces running down inside the collars of their immaculate dark grey suit jackets, which they wore over crisp, white dress shirts open at the neck. EJ stopped, unsure now of how to proceed. Then the imposing pair simply stepped to one side. Behind them stood possibly the most beautiful man that EJ had ever seen, who smiled and said, in an impeccably educated English accent that sent a strange tingle up and down EJ's spine,

"Elizabeth? Or may I call you EJ? Welcome to China. Would you kindly come this way?"

He was not quite as tall as the two guards, who fell into step behind EJ as their little party headed up the air bridge. Lean and lithe, he wore a Mao suit of a grey silk so pale as to be almost white, its high embroidered collar held at his nape with a clasp of limpid jade. His long hair was the palest platinum, pulled back from his forehead and held in a ponytail by two complex plaits that glittered with silver thread. The perfectly smooth features of his handsome face were clearly Chinese, yet his eyes were a striking sapphire blue. However, his most arresting feature, were his pointed ears.

"You're an elf!" blurted EJ in her astonishment, immediately wishing that a hole would open up and swallow her. Her escort laughed.

"Yes, I am. The ears are always a bit of a giveaway." He stopped and turned to her as they walked toward a lift, the door to which was being held open for them by yet another besuited guard. "You must think me incredibly rude. May I introduce myself? I am Xing Meng Hua, Chamberlain to my lord, Guanzhong Nai'En, the Jade Dragon. Please call me Meng Hua." He beckoned her forward into the elevator. "Now, if you'll accompany me, we have a car waiting to take us into the city. My people have already secured your baggage from the aircraft. The Jade Dragon is anxious to meet you, EJ. He has heard such a great deal about you from your grandfather."

"My grandfather is here, isn't he?" EJ asked excitedly.

"My dear EJ, he most assuredly is," replied Xing Meng Hua with another smile that made EJ's heart skip a beat.

The elevator had no visible controls. Once EJ, Meng Hua and the two guards were inside, the doors simply closed and EJ felt it descend. Meng Hua smiled reassuringly, as if all of this were the most natural thing in the world, and the doors opened onto a large, underground forecourt that could clearly accommodate a whole fleet of cars, if so required. Three Range Rovers sat at the kerb, their windows blacked out and engines running. EJ and Meng Hua climbed aboard the middle of the three vehicles, and the small convoy sped up a series of ramps and out into the early evening, policemen holding the traffic at the airports many intersections to allow them to pass at high speed onto the expressway that linked Beijing International to the city.

"Er, do you always travel like this?" asked EJ, the road outside the darkened windows passing in a blur.

"Nothing is too much for an honoured guest," replied Meng Hua, who tried to keep a straight face as he gauged EJ's reaction, but failed and burst out laughing. "No! Quite the opposite, actually. The Jade Dragon prefers a low profile nowadays, and our friends in the Party agree with him. Our presence is not exactly a state secret – the Jade Dragon has been part of China's consciousness far too long for that – but in these modern times, it is rare that we need to travel beyond the capital. As you have seen tonight, our colleagues in government are generous with their resources when we require them."

Though the subject was really quite mundane, Meng Hua's voice seemed to flow over and through EJ as he spoke, and gave a poetry to his words. In Beijing for less than an hour, the whirlwind of her arrival had left EJ disoriented, unable to catch her breath, especially with Meng Hua now sat next to her. EJ pushed such thoughts aside, and finally plucked up the courage to ask him the question that had been flashing in her brain like the neon signs in Piccadilly Circus.

"I didn't know there are elves in China," she said hesitantly.

Meng Hua half-turned in his seat and regarded the young woman beside him. A sardonic smile played across his features. "No, most people do not. Even here, it is not generally known, or remembered, and those who do know do not often speak of it. Tales of my people in our folklore are few. Yet China's history is a long one, and dragons have always been revered in our culture. If there are dragons, then why not the other races too?"

"You mean the elves and dwarves?"

"Yes, and much as in the West, as you have already learnt in Anglezarke, the dwarves and my kinfolk have always found our paths linked to the dragons."

The cars barely slowed to leave one expressway and join yet another, now heading west between modern blocks of apartments, pedestrian bridges and other roads criss-crossing it at regular intervals as it bisected China's huge capital city. Some distance to the east rose the brightly lit towers of the Central Business District. She turned back to Meng Hua, intrigued to learn more.

"So, my grandfather, and I suppose my whole family, had a dragon who lived in a hill at the bottom of the garden. Then they had the bright idea to work together, since this dragon knows how to make tons of money. For worthy causes, of course. I'm guessing your story is a bit different."

Meng Hua laughed once more and the sound of his joy transfixed her. "What a splendidly capitalist story that is! I've never heard your grandfather tell it quite like that. You know, a revered leader of this great nation once said that to make money is glorious … Yes, EJ, our story is very different. My clan has been at the Jade Dragon's side since the time of the Ming emperors. He embodies jade, of course, but his true place in things here is a complex one. In many ways, he embodies China itself."

Their three Range Rovers now slowed and turned off the expressway and onto a broad avenue that ran in a near straight line north. EJ looked ahead and saw the traffic lights at each cross street turn green in their favour as they approached, so that although they were no longer running at high speed, their progress continued to be rapid. Meng Hua realised what had caught her attention.

"Beijing's networks are some of the most sophisticated on earth now. You should ask your friend Al-Khwarizmi sometime. He's probably running around in them as we speak."

"You think Riz is making the lights change for us?" EJ asked incredulously.

"Not at all! Even Al-Khwarizmi knows better than to play games with our government's systems! No, we have been monitored since we left the airport. Call the green lights a welcoming courtesy," explained Meng Hua.

EJ dug into her rucksack for her iPhone and was happy to see that she had a strong signal. Stan in London had been as good as his word and made sure that she'd always be connected, no matter where in the world. She tapped the icon for Riz and had never felt more relieved to see the grinning icon wink at her. She tapped in a quick hello and then stuffed the phone back into its pocket. The cars executed a series of rapid turns onto ever older and narrower streets, and EJ began to lose her bearings. They were entering the heart of old Beijing. One final turn and they pulled to a halt in a broad courtyard. To their left was a high wall built of light grey granite blocks, set into which was a traditional Chinese gatehouse. Beneath its curved eaves stood a solid wooden gate lacquered a bright red of welcome, above which was placed an elaborate carving of a dragon on a solid panel of flawless white jade. To the right of the courtyard, a line of ancient willows bordered a low stone wall along the edge of a lake. On an island close to the opposite shore, EJ could see a building which she recognised from documentaries and travelogues about the city: the White Pagoda, lit by floodlights, its long stone jetties for pleasure boats picked out by red hanging lanterns. She was stood on the edge of the North Lake, part of the Forbidden City that had been the seat of Chinese power since the time of the Ming dynasty. The great lacquered gate behind EJ was opened by two more handsome elves. Meng Hua bowed deeply before her.

"Elizabeth Jade Carver, on behalf of the Jade Dragon, I welcome you. Please enter, my master awaits."

16 Adrenaline

Jasper Moffett had been in an excellent mood as he left his private office and took his customary seat for a solitary lunch at the head of the long mahogany dining table. The light, healthy meal of grilled fish and salad that the steward set before him would have come as a surprise to those who only knew Jasper by the meticulously curated public persona, but he rarely ate red meat any longer – an attitude that might be considered downright un-Texan in some circles. Let the good ole boys clog their arteries with prime rib and chateaubriand in the country club dining rooms then drop dead of coronaries, thought Jasper. He planned to outlive them all.

He had wrung yet another raft of concessions from the President over dinner the previous evening, and spent the morning instructing his PR people in Houston and Washington how he wanted the details leaked to their pet media outlets over the next few days, dressed up in spin and with no mention of either him or Wolverine. Pretty soon, the whole oil industry would be taking credit. They always did, but the big winner would be Wolverine Petroleum. Business as usual, boys.

This genial affability had been soured by the arrival of Marvin Thibodeaux and King Moffett. There was no sign of the black leather folder filled with pictures of Miss Elizabeth Jade Carver and her latest exploits. Instead, Jasper narrowed his eyes at the hangdog expressions of the two men stood before him, defendants in the dock. "What do you mean, 'We lost her'?" he now asked, his voice low and measured.

Like the hiss of a cottonmouth about to strike, thought Marvin, who knew that a bad situation would surely become immeasurably worse if he allowed King to open his mouth and whine. Marvin had been brought up to take his lumps, and knew that he understood Jasper Moffett's sense of frontier justice far better than either of the man's own brothers. Now was no time for a backward step, not if he planned to get out of this with his skin intact.

"She played us, Jasper. She played me. Don't know how, but as God is my witness, I will find out," he stated, staring straight at his superior. Never lose eye contact with a snake that's ready to bite, thought Marvin.

Sure enough, King Moffett decided this was his cue. "We followed her the whole time, Jasper! Watched her leave the Paris airport in a hotel car and all! Then we lost her on the freeway into Paris. She doubled back and sneaked into the terminal! How was I to know she had the whole thing planned out?" he blurted out.

Marvin had known King would not be able to stop himself. There had never been a snafu in his whole over-privileged existence that he hadn't tried to pin on someone, or something, else. He raised a silent prayer of thanks to heaven that he had spoken first, and spoken truthfully. It would still be a close run thing, but Marvin began to breathe a tad easier as he felt Jasper's wrath now focus on his younger brother.

Jasper rose from the table, the midday sun's glare creating a nimbus around him like the vision of some avenging angel. It took a great deal to faze Marvin Thibodeaux, but he swore he could feel the temperature in the room drop a degree or two. "I don't want to hear one more word from you, King. Not one! I'll deal with you later. Now get out of my sight. Leave this to the adults in the room."

"But, Jasper …"

"I SAID GIT!" roared Jasper. He and Marvin watched King Moffett scurry from the dining room, the great double doors crashing shut behind him. Jasper took a deep breath and briefly closed his eyes, then sat back down and resumed his lunch.

"Don't think you're off the hook, neither," he added calmly. "Now tell me what really happened, and mind you leave out nothing in the telling."

Marvin sensed that the immediate danger had passed. Now the two men could get down to what they did best, the assessment of how to take maximum advantage of any given situation. As for King, well, he'd make it back into Jasper's good books eventually. He always did. Though this time there would be a hefty price, thought Marvin ruefully.

"I don't know how she worked out we were watching her, but it's clear to me now that they knew about our camera on the hotel opposite. Someone in MI5 probably tipped them off to it years ago. I reckon that whole show of hers in Mayfair was pure theatre – she gave us exactly what we wanted to see, and like a damned fool I fell for it. I'm sorry, Jasper."

Jasper continued to eat, wrapped in his own thoughts. Eventually he looked up at Marvin, who hadn't moved an inch from where he had been standing this whole time.

"Alright. You can sit down now. Damned fool? You and me both! Oh, Elizabeth Jade. I hardly thought it possible you could impress me more, but hoodwinking the pair of us with that bravura performance has raised you even higher in my estimation. My oh my, haven't you had some fun at my expense, young lady."

"She ain't stopped, neither," continued Marvin.

"How so?"

"When it became clear that Paris was a ruse, King threw a fit and dived in on the airlines. Their systems have more holes than a Swiss cheese, so it didn't matter none that he was less than subtle about it. Anyway, upshot is this whole manoeuvre of hers was so she could fly to China."

Jasper carefully put down his cutlery and asked, "Where in China?"

"She made us look the other way so's she could jump on yesterday's Air France to Beijing. I got to hand it to her. She was real slick, Jasper."

"I told you that she'd be on the move, did I not?"

"Yessir, you did."

"And I told you that old Michelangelo has only one intent, his eye on the prize, and that's to get that dragon egg before yours truly, did I not?"

"Yessir, I believe you did."

"So, answer me this, Marvin: What do we have here? Our clever Miss Carver embarrasses you and makes me lose my temper with one of my nearest and dearest, even if he can be a self-absorbed clown most of the time. Yet she has now given you both an opportunity to redeem yourselves in my eyes, has she not? A golden opportunity, one might say. Michelangelo is being surprisingly generous to you, my friend."

"Well, not quite so generous, Jasper. Or so easy."

"And why not?"

"She knew what she was doing. We're blind in China. We can't track her. King says even he can't break into their systems. Or won't."

Jasper Moffett knew that his younger brother would not have strayed too far from the dining room. He motioned for the steward, who approached the table.

"Jorge, would you be so kind as to bring me my coffee, and then find King and ask him to come back in here? Thank you."

The steward quietly did as Jasper had asked, and King returned to the dining room.

"Sit. Now tell me why China is such a problem."

Realising that he was now on much firmer ground, and with a sense that his redemption might come sooner than he had feared, King Moffett slumped gratefully into a chair at the table.

"It just ain't like anywhere else, Jasper. I mean, there's systems and networks here and in Europe where even I have to tread carefully, you know, like the military or the security services, some of the Feds' better stuff. Hell, I could poke around in most of the Russians' gear if I had a mind to. But China? Over there, everything is either government-owned or government-monitored. And they're sophisticated too, Jasper. They build in all kinds of redundancies and false flags that are only there to trip you up. Those boys pick up a hack, or someone doing something they shouldn't, and they come looking for you. And they ain't too subtle about it, if you get on their wrong side."

Jasper regarded King over the top of his coffee mug. He knew how good his younger brother was with computers, even if some of his other behaviour might irritate him. It wasn't just King's MIT doctorate, or the state-of-the-art systems that he had created for Wolverine. He and Marvin had made discrete inquiries over the years with the sort of people who knew about these matters, and King Moffett was a legend in the free-for-all world of professional hackers. If King was spooked by the People's Republic, then he surely had good reason to be.

"But you're certain that Elizabeth faked you out to fly to Beijing?" asked Jasper, returning to his original line of questioning. Marvin and King could see that his mind was now focused on this new set of variables that had presented themselves.

"One hundred percent. She'd already been in the air almost four hours, but the flight manifest confirmed it. Only passenger in First Class," answered Marvin.

"The she's gone to see the Jade Dragon. And that is the only piece of good news that's come out of this whole mess. Beijing is his territory. How much surveillance could you give me, King? At a push. If we really needed it?"

"Really? They've got cameras everywhere, facial recognition, biosensors, the works. Their AI is the best anywhere. And that's just their civilian gear. God alone knows what their security services are wired into, or the system overlays they run. Their military runs its own parallel networks too. Their stuff is primo grade-A, Jasper." King's voice betrayed his nervousness, as it even talking about Chinese technological capabilities might bring the hoodoo down on them.

"That good, huh?" Jasper looked askance at his younger brother then set his empty coffee mug down to one side. Elizabeth Jade Carver had made the first move, and it was a good one. Masterful even, thought Jasper. One of the finest pieces of play action he had seen since his days sacking quarterbacks for the Longhorns. He smiled with satisfaction. Now it was his turn.

"So, let's say for now that we can't follow her in Beijing. Now that might not be such a drawback after all," he drawled.

"How's that, Jasper?" asked Marvin, torn between curiosity and a growing sense of foreboding that wherever this was leading, Marvin Thibodeaux was going to find himself at its very centre.

"Because, my friend, if the Jade Dragon has the egg, Elizabeth means to take it back with her to Michelangelo. There's no chance she'd be in Beijing if those two dragons ain't seeing eye to eye."

"And if not? If he ain't got it?" asked King, now as intrigued by the conversation as Marvin, and eager to hear the response his elder brother was cooking up.

"Then she's checking in and finding facts. And that means she'll be on the move again." He turned to King. "You can leave her be in Beijing, but you damned sure better know the minute she ups and leaves China."

The steward quietly placed a fresh mug of coffee at Jasper's elbow, and he nodded his thanks. "Marvin, get your boys together. Tell 'em to saddle up. Lock and load. Y'all go and sit in Hong Kong and be ready to move when she does. Wherever that may be. And King? Tell Marvin what gear you need. You're going with him." Jasper grinned maliciously at the two men. "Come on now, boys! Y'all didn't think I'd let you off Scot free for being sold a bill of goods by that clever little English girl, now did you? There is always a price, gentlemen. Always a price."

Jasper dismissed them and watched Marvin and King rise from the table and file out of the room. He turned his chair to the window and surveyed the shadows as they inexorably lengthened across his city, the sky still the searing azure of another scorching afternoon. He recalled that the last quarterback to have successfully faked him out on the football field had paid for his audacity the very next play, when Jasper had bull-rushed the offensive line and hit him so hard that he broke the young man's leg in three places. Never played football again, thought Jasper. More's the pity, the young man had shown some real talent.

"There's always a price, Elizabeth Jade Carver. Always a price," he said out loud to the whole of Houston and no one in particular as he slowly sipped his coffee.

*

That metallic sensation in the back of the throat, thought Marvin, as he hurried to his own desk to begin the calls and make the preparations for the response that Jasper had ordered. Like now, he could always taste it when the anticipation began to build and the adrenalin to flow. It had been quite some time since he and the team had seen any real action, and he knew that his key guys chafed at the drudgery of the various logistics and housekeeping duties with which they had been tasked for these many months. Especially the tedium of keeping the Oil Dragon's New Mexico lair stocked and fuelled. Marvin understood, but his sympathy had its limits. At the end of the day, you did what your commander ordered, no questions asked.

Unlike most of their competitors, Wolverine Petroleum had never used 'military contractors' to secure their facilities or keep their people safe whenever instability flared in the far flung corners of the world where they found their oil. Jasper Moffett had built this behemoth on the back of enormous risk taking, even if the dice were loaded, mused Marvin, so from the earliest days of their great expansion they had used a cadre of their own specialists. Drawn from Special Forces around the globe, employed on full-time contracts and handsomely remunerated, Marvin's team was thus fiercely loyal. Marvin cared not what passport you carried, or where you might call home one day. His criteria were simple: the men and women who joined his group to work for Wolverine were demonstrably the very best. Most, but not all, now made their homes and lives in metro Houston, but every single one of them knew to drop everything and report for duty the moment they received Marvin's call.

He spent the rest of the afternoon and on into the evening closeted away with his files, making a series of video calls and sending out emails to check on his team's readiness and their equipment requirements. One of Wolverine's many warehouses under Marvin's control contained a veritable arsenal, so availability was not an issue. He would have to get everything across to Asia, but the logistics for this type of operation were tried and tested, and they would take one of Wolverine's pair of Boeing Business Jets. The BBJ's were heavily remodelled 737's, split into two luxurious cabins for the passengers and with all the space Marvin needed in the hold to carry the couple of pallets of cargo. They'd have to refuel and take on a new Wolverine flight crew in Anchorage, so the total journey would be on the order of nineteen or twenty hours. However, compared to how some of these guys used to ply their trade, everyone would be able to sleep and be in good shape on arrival. They'd take only personal baggage off the plane with them on arrival in Hong Kong, and the BBJ could hangar at one of the private jet facilities at the international airport, just another rich man's plane on standby.

Marvin maintained active shell company accounts with each of the four major US hotel chains for just this kind of eventuality, and booked multiple suites at their Hong Kong flagship properties in Central and Wanchai, using a different account for each one. His team would split up on the ground to await developments, but one of the advantages of the city was that they could all be back at the airport within an hour. He didn't really care what any of the team got up to in the down time; they were all professionals and would behave with intelligence and care. The same might not be true of King Moffett, whose head could be easily turned by the diversions available in a city like Hong Kong. Jasper had known exactly this, and that one of Marvin's minor punishments would be to police his wayward younger brother and make sure that whatever excursions King undertook, whether physical or virtual, did not cause them either embarrassment or difficulty.

By the time Marvin finally closed things down for the night, everything was in place. Even King and his various flight cases of tech were all accounted for. Equipment and people would all be in position in Hong Kong within thirty-six hours. When Elizabeth Jade Carver next left Beijing, Marvin would be ready. Fool me once, shame on me, fool me twice …

17 Zhongnanhai

The Jade Dragon's compound was a large *siheyuan*, laid out in the traditional manner of four buildings around an inner courtyard, such as a noble or a senior mandarin might have enjoyed as their residence in pre-Revolutionary times. The main house stood on the north side, facing the gatehouse to the south, with ancillary buildings on both east and west, the whole compound surrounded by a high wall. The ample courtyard at the centre was a paved garden, well shaded by willow and ginkgo trees which now stood silent and unmoving in the still evening air, reflected in the light of the large red lanterns which hung from the eaves of all the buildings.

And there he was, Joseph Livesey, her grandfather. This odd, itinerant man whose absence from her life had gone unremarked until so recently, but who had then hurled EJ into this extraordinary adventure with his apparently unshakeable belief that this was her birthright and that she was therefore ready to meet its challenges. The breath caught in EJ's throat and she hesitated in the gateway. He stood between a pair of gnarled and ancient dwarf pines in two large earthenware pots which flanked the entrance of the north house, and was dressed in a simple short-sleeved white shirt, dark pants and sandals. Exactly the uniform that several million other men were wearing in Beijing that warm night, thought EJ, though something of a step down from the elegance of Meng Hua's silks. He remained a tall man, unbowed by age. The dirty blond curls of his youth were now white, and that piercing stare, so noticeable in the photograph of him and Selwyn Ormerod which EJ still carried with her, was softened by a pair of bifocal spectacles, but the smile was unmistakeable even if it betrayed a certain nervousness at this meeting. A meeting which, thought EJ, now filled her with trepidation too. He looked rather abashed, lost for words now that the moment of reunion with his granddaughter was finally upon him.

"Follow your instincts, Elizabeth," murmured Meng Hua at her side. She turned to the silver elf, possibly seeking further guidance, but he merely smiled his encouragement and retreated a pace into the shadow of the gatehouse. Nevertheless, that brief reassurance and an elf's smile had been enough. EJ felt her tiredness and doubts melt away and her confidence restored. She recomposed herself, and turned back toward the courtyard and her grandfather.

"Hello."

"Hello, EJ. Good flight? Welcome to Beijing."

And then, as if struck by the sheer absurdity of it all, her grandfather laughed and the tension of the moment evaporated. Instinct indeed took over, and EJ ran forward to fall into a long embrace that spanned sixteen wordless years of separation. Eventually, she stepped back and brushed the tears from her cheeks. She took her grandfather's hands in both of her own – weathered now, marked with liver spots and maybe not as big as her memories had made them.

"I guess Michelangelo's not the only one who needs glasses now," she teased him gently.

"No, I suppose not, EJ. Ah, you know, 'Rage, rage against the dying of the light' and all that."

"So, what should I call you? Grandfather? Granddad? Just Joe?" she asked him.

"To be honest, I don't think I have any say in the matter. After the past several days I've put you through, I think you've earned the right to address me however you see fit," replied her grandfather. The two of them turned toward the open sliding doors of the north house.

"Hmm, I think you're right. I'll give it some thought, shall I?"

The softly lit room they entered was not really a room at all, but a sort of vestibule, for immediately ahead of them was the head of a flight of shallow marble steps which descended into the glow of yet more lanterns. EJ could see that the north house functioned as the entrance to the Jade Dragon's domain, a necessary link to the surface world. She ran her hand along one banister, carved into a representation of dragon's scales from a smooth, warm, light green jade, its finial fashioned into a dragon's head, so that the banisters appeared to be dragons swirling up the length of the staircase from the depths below.

"I know we've lots to talk about, and I have about a million apologies that I need to make to you, but right now our host is downstairs. Best not to keep him waiting." Joe Livesey took his granddaughter by the hand once more and together they started down the marble stair to the presence chamber of the Jade Dragon.

The steps flowed in one long, single flight, the walls to either side decorated with large landscapes of mountains and flowing pines painted in the Chinese manner, some in colour some just in ink, and the scent of incense intensified as they descended. EJ realised that they must be heading underneath the ornamental North Lake. The stair ended in a broad, low-ceilinged room with a polished wooden floor. The walls were a series of deep crimson lacquer panels, each framed in gold. Along the sides were placed groups of brocade divans and large silk cushions around low tables. At the far end, some eight or ten yards away, and curled upon a low dais chased in gold and ivory, sat Guanzhong Nai'En, the Jade Dragon. He had large blue eyes framed by heavy white eyebrows, and whiskers like icicles which ended in long barbels that gave him the appearance of sporting a Fu Man Chu moustache. He was really rather small, thought EJ, maybe only about twenty feet long. The word that came to her mind was 'sinewy': Neck, body and tail flowed into each other in one long, snakelike coil of muscle, very different from Michelangelo, or even Riz, who both tended toward the more heavy-set and crocodilian in body shape. A column of serrated scales ran down the Jade Dragon's back to end in the spear-like tip of his tail, while his muscular legs ended in long, wickedly sharp talons. EJ realised that each scale on his body was a tessera of jade, and as he moved, he shimmered through every shade of the precious stone, from the darkest sea-green to a white that was almost translucent.

"Welcome! Shall I tell you what you are thinking, Elizabeth Jade Carver? Unlike other dragons I am a mind reader!" The Jade Dragon's voice in EJ's head filled her mind with flashes of forty centuries of the rise and fall of dynasties, abundant harvests and crippling famines, but most of all, the sense of a rather spry and self-satisfied older professor, quite certain of his own importance and ready to make sure that everyone else is aware of it too.

"It is racial stereotyping, you know. Or so I have been told," the Jade Dragon continued.

"I beg your pardon?" replied EJ, blindsided by the comment, but feeling herself begin to blush nonetheless.

"You are thinking that this handsome beast before you, looks just like all the Chinese dragons you have ever seen in paintings … and on porcelain … and in all the festivals … and really, everywhere you've ever set your eyes on a Chinese dragon! See! Racial stereotyping!" exclaimed the Jade Dragon cheerfully in her mind, his voice ringing with amusement and a certain smugness. With that, he blew a perfect smoke ring toward the ceiling and grinned at them.

"OK. You win. Was it that obvious? But that's not racial stereotyping at all! Not if all the pictures and statues are based on you," asked EJ, playing along.

"Oh, Elizabeth, you must forgive an old dragon his party trick. Of course! So many years, and so many visitors. Always the same thought in their heads! Though, I admit, very few of them had your own experience of dragons, and you do have a point about my being the original model for all the art! Anyway, how is my old friend Michelangelo? You saw him only a few days past, while your grandfather here has been away from Anglezarke for so long this time."

EJ turned briefly to her grandfather, who simply shrugged as if the Jade Dragon always behaved this way. Right, thought EJ, in for a penny, in for a pound …

"You dragons do seem to get straight to the point, don't you? You and Riz should have a chat sometime. You'd get on like a house on fire. I'm sure you know all about Al-Khwarizmi?" Nai'En nodded his assent. "Anyway, to answer your question, Jade Dragon, when I left Michelangelo, he was … well, I suppose he was just Michelangelo, if you know what I mean? He was still complaining that his back hurt, and his eyesight isn't up to much. I think it's looking at those screens all day long, don't you?"

She could feel her grandfather sniggering with delight beside her, but the Jade Dragon was not to be diverted and ploughed on with evident enjoyment.

"You are absolutely correct! I have been telling him for many years that he should take better care of himself. The last time your grandfather was here, I sent him back to England with plenty of my own herbal medicines for Michelangelo, together with strict instructions for their use. The same preparation that has kept me in prime condition for all these centuries! Yet, I am sure that he has not been following my advice. He is a most stubborn dragon at times."

EJ felt completely at home listening to one senior dragon berate another for his poor lifestyle choices. It was like one of those dreaded annual visits, usually at Christmas, to an elderly aunt or uncle whom every member of the family actively avoids during the rest of the year. The knowledge that Nai'En apparently accepted her as one of the inner circle of the dragon family made her swell with pride. The Jade Dragon flowed down from his dais and crossed the room to them.

"Come, sit! Your grandfather tells me that you have been most resourceful, but I want to hear all the juicy details from you. Such fun you have had! But first, you have had a long journey, so you must sit and take some tea." Nai'En swirled around them eagerly as he guided them to the nearest set of divans. EJ and her grandfather sat down and a pair of elves appeared from behind the dais, this time dressed in pale aquamarine silks and carrying trays of fruit and mooncakes, together with a celadon tea set. The pair knelt beside their table to serve them while Nai'En hovered impatiently. The two elves were clearly used to their master's ways and performed their duties unhurriedly, nodding occasionally with a smile as Nai'En chivvied them. Finally satisfied with the preparations, he begrudgingly allowed them to retire. The Jade Dragon folded his front legs before him and laid his head on the nearest large cushion.

"Good, now you may tell me how you tweaked the nose of our favourite Texan gentleman!"

And so, for the next hour EJ sipped tea, nibbled on mooncakes filled with sweet red bean paste, and recounted the whole story, from the moment she opened a strange package in her bedroom above the pub, all the way to her VIP arrival in Beijing that evening. She omitted nothing, since she knew that this was as much for her grandfather's benefit as it was for the Jade Dragon's.

"… and then the two guards stepped aside and Meng Hua introduced himself. And so here I am. I'm sure Wolverine have already worked out that I gave them the slip in Paris," she concluded. She placed her teacup back on the table, tapping her thanks with two fingers as her grandfather refilled it once more. Nai'En puffed a series of small smoke globes toward the ceiling, and it was her grandfather who broke the contemplative silence.

"It's just as we had discussed, Nai'En. Ever since you and Michelangelo sensed the Oil Dragon's strength begin to wane. Moffett wants this egg, and EJ here has done a first-class job of selling him the idea that her reappearance is the key. This connection that EJ has forged with Al-Khwarizmi is a huge bonus for us! Are we sure that the Oil Dragon knows nothing of him?"

"It would appear not. Even Michelangelo and I failed to sense just how powerful Al-Khwarizmi's evolution has been. It is now so long since the Oil Dragon cast himself adrift from the rest of us. He is unaware." Nai'En turned to EJ. "It took Michelangelo and I a long time to understand this. We are both ancient dragons, and though we have changed over the centuries, ours has been a slow evolution and we remain much as we have always been. The Oil Dragon is the same, though his essence now weakens. Al-Khwarizmi is different. He is everywhere at once and yet nowhere in particular. It is only recently that he has begun to understand that he is now the most powerful of us all. Your friendship with him is most gratifying." Nai'En tapped out a slow rhythm on the wooden floor with one claw and closed his eyes again before he continued. "The egg will appear soon. Ask me not why I know. It is a feeling, no more. But I am sure that if you asked Michelangelo, he would agree. You have done well, Elizabeth. You and Al-Khwarizmi must continue to monitor Wolverine's activities."

"Did you meet with the Central Committee today?" asked EJ's grandfather.

"I did. The less enlightened members have been disabused of their idea that they should seek this egg for China's benefit. The General Secretary voiced his displeasure that I should have been made aware of such ignoble and venal thoughts, and certain individuals have been instructed to thoroughly reassess their ideological purity and their loyalty to both Party and State."

"You mean he went berserk and started banging heads together," translated EJ out loud.

"Excellent, Elizabeth! I had no idea your grasp of Chinese politics was so nuanced. We dragons understand that we could no more control an egg than we could change the dawn or move the moon in its orbit. It is elemental. It will appear. What then happens remains to be seen. Unfortunately, men are fickle creatures, always believing they can bend this world to their will, as if they are gods. As you yourself have now seen with Mr. Jasper Moffett and his underlings."

"But you just said that there are men in the Chinese government who want do exactly that. Take the egg for themselves. Why do other governments not want to do the same thing?"

"A perceptive question. My government's acceptance of dragons – of me – is centuries old. I am, if I may borrow an English idiom, part of the furniture. No other country has such a rich story of dragons at its very centre as China! For the past several years, the General Secretary has valued my counsel. Our relationship is strong, but make no mistake, it is still men who wield power here, not some old Jade Dragon who enjoys making a nuisance of himself. Other countries would do well to heed the wisdom of their dragons, but it is to our advantage that until now they do not. We must hope that the egg appears soon, and that the circle of those who seek it remains small."

Nai'En jumped nimbly to his feet and shook himself, like a rather large dog. His mosaic of jade scales glittered like iridescent chainmail.

"Elizabeth, know that in this city you are under the seal of my protection at all times. You may move around as you please, though, as I am sure your grandfather will tell you, it would be advisable to stay within my compound as much as possible. Maybe a few days away from the cameras will be to your liking?"

EJ looked across at her grandfather. "Thank you, Jade Dragon. I think I've plenty to keep me busy right here."

Nai'En nodded and then turned back to the dais at the far end of the chamber, and the dim passages that led away behind it.

"I believe the General Secretary will be taking tea on his veranda. I shall go and surprise him! He will greatly enjoy hearing more about your exploits."

"More? You've been telling the General Secretary of the Chinese Communist Party all about me?" exclaimed EJ, mortified at the idea that one of the most powerful men on earth knew all about what she had been up to.

"My dear Elizabeth!" laughed Nai'En, "I am under polite but firm instruction to bring him nightly updates. He is most impressed."

With that, the Jade Dragon turned and disappeared into one of his tunnels to make the short trip under the lakes to the government compound in Zhongnanhai. EJ sat, her teacup forgotten in mid-air and her mouth agape.

"Takes a bit of getting used to, doesn't he?" added her grandfather in a statement of the obvious. "Still, he has mellowed over the years. Back when China was just reopening, he really was hard work. Michelangelo funded several projects for him, and that broke the ice. You can trust Nai'En, EJ. He'll make sure we find the egg." With some effort, Joe levered himself up off the low divan. "Why don't we go up to the house and see what Meng Hua's elves have made us for dinner?"

EJ rose too and together they climbed back up the long marble stair to the north house entrance. Joe led her around the back of the building to a long wooden terrace built over a pond stocked with huge golden carp. Every so often, the surface would ripple and swirl, and one of the ancient fish would roll across the moon's reflection before slipping back beneath the dark waters. A dining table had been laid for the two of them. EJ was suddenly aware how ravenous she felt, despite the tea and mooncakes with the Jade Dragon, and hurried forward to lift the lids from the nearest serving bowls.

"Eight Treasures Rice! And Beggar's Chicken!" she exclaimed with delight.

"I see our Molly ordered from the chippy for you," chortled her grandfather. "Come on then, I'm starving. Let's dig in."

They ate in companionable silence for several minutes. EJ poured them each more tea, then put the teapot down and regarded her grandfather.

"Selwyn says you're out for revenge. You and Michelangelo. The Jade Dragon too, by the sound of it. He seems to think I should be happy about it."

"Happy about it? Absolutely not. Nor should you be. A terrible idea, revenge. It slowly eats away at you, a bit of your soul at a time, until there's nothing left." Joe placed his chopsticks carefully across his bowl, then took off his glasses and rubbed the bridge of his nose. He looked past EJ and over the carp pond. "I suffered for many years. Made those around me suffer a damned sight more, I can tell you. But you have thrived, turned into a young woman of so much ability and such promise. Even the worst things in life can turn out for the best, if you give them enough time."

"So, if you're not out to punish Jasper Moffett, then what is going on?"

"Jasper Moffett's punishment is of his own making. His oil wells will dry up. The mighty Wolverine Petroleum will collapse and he'll become just another failed tycoon, all his power and influence gone forever. Believe me, for a man like Jasper Moffett, that's a fate worse than death – to fade slowly from view, just like the dragon that made him. A footnote to history."

EJ took a small orange from a plate in front of her and began to peel it.

"I get that. I get the whole 'the world's changing for the better and it's our job to help it' stuff. It's just like Riz – one moment he's lord of the sands and bored out of his tree, the next minute he's silicon incarnate and every computer on earth is his personal playground. I understand all that, Joe. Just don't go telling me that part of you doesn't want to see Jasper Moffett destroyed. He killed my parents. I don't care about his oil company!" She paused and took a deep breath. "What happened to them, Joe?"

He turned to EJ with a sigh and asked, "Do you really need to know?"

She made no reply. Finally, he continued, for he had known all along that he would have to answer EJ's question. It was a bill that had remained unpaid for sixteen long years.

"Tom, your father, had grown up with Michelangelo, just as I had. Then by the time he went off to university we'd already started Anglezarke and were busy running all kinds of projects, mainly in Africa. Tom decided to jack in college and work full time in the field on our projects. He was like that – once he got an idea into his head, then you couldn't shift him." EJ smiled at the image. "He met your mother out there. In Tanzania, if I recall. Oh, what a pair they were! Jenny was just like Tom, just as fierce, just as committed. And they did great things together. It was just how I had envisioned Anglezarke when we started – really making a difference in people's lives, without all the red tape, corruption and what have you."

EJ could feel herself drawn in by her grandfather's enthusiasm, and her own swell of pride at Anglezarke's achievements. However, there was also a twinge of disappointment with herself that, although she knew Joe's story was about to take a much darker turn, she was impatient to hear the ending.

"Anyway, when Jenny became pregnant with you, they decided to come back to Anglezarke. Tom began to travel back and forth much more, while Jenny worked closely with Selwyn and me. I'm still not sure how Tom got to know

242

about Wolverine, or how he worked out what they were up to. He and Michelangelo had always been close, and the two of them put the pieces together. He was a zealot, our Tom. Lived for Anglezarke and what we were doing, so the thought of using a dragon for pure profit and power went against everything he stood for.

"He'd decided to expose Jasper Moffett and Wolverine. He was going to bring a film crew in and open everything up, make Anglezarke public. I tried to dissuade him, and you can imagine how Selwyn Ormerod reacted, but Michelangelo had agreed and so in the end we went along with it. God knows how it would have turned out … A couple of days before they were due to start shooting, Tom and Jenny went into Manchester for the evening. They hadn't had a night out together since the day you were born, but there was a concert at the Free Trade Hall. I can't remember who was playing that night, but Tom had managed to get tickets."

Joe Livesey paused and wiped his face. He took EJ's hand in his own and then continued.

"To this day, I don't know how Jasper found out, but he did. Maybe word leaked out among the expats in Africa, or the Oil Dragon had sensed something and warned him. When you've been round dragons as long as I have, EJ, nothing surprises you anymore, no matter how unlikely it might seem. Anyway, he wasn't about to let some young upstart aid worker turn his world upside down, was he? We know that he had been up on one of their platforms in the North Sea, and that he drove down from Aberdeen with his hatchet man, Thibodeaux. The he followed Tom and Jenny into Manchester. We'll never know if he tried to speak to

Tom, change his mind. Doesn't matter now. Maybe never did. They drove your parents off the road on the way back over the moor. Fuel tank ruptured on impact. At least that's what the police report said. That was it."

Joe's grasp of EJ's hand had tightened as he relived that terrible night, but now he let go, picked his glasses up off the table and put them back on.

"You asked me if this is revenge. The thing is, EJ, we've all come so far since that night. Maybe I didn't need to have hidden you away with George and Maureen, but in the days that followed the car crash we didn't know what was going to happen, and you needed to be looked after by more than a grieving old man and a bunch of dwarves. If Tom had been right, and the world had learnt about Michelangelo and Anglezarke, would it have made things any better? Jasper Moffett would still have found a way. He'd have kept his secret dragon telling him what to do and where to drill. It's only now that the world has turned. Now Michelangelo and Nai'En and the rest of the dragons can sense the sea change that's happening. That's why you're here. Michelangelo knew it was time for you, and Nai'En can sense it too. Somehow, you are a key to all of this, not just some distraction to keep Jasper Moffett guessing."

18 AliBaba

Three days had passed since EJ's arrival in Beijing and she had found the rhythm of life in the Chinese capital to her liking. This had been the first day that she had ventured beyond the Jade Dragon's compound. She had left after breakfast to visit the Palace Museum in the Forbidden City, that enormous repository of the history of Imperial China and its cultural and artistic glories. The previous day, Nai'En had reacted enthusiastically when she had told him her plan for the day, immediately announcing in that grandiose but endearing way with which he seemed to approach everything, that he would arrange a private visit to be accompanied by a whole cadre of the museum's senior curators. EJ had successfully argued that she should maintain a low profile and mix in with the other tourists. In the end, Nai'En had reluctantly agreed, but only after extracting a promise from her that she would return to Beijing when all this was over and allow him to show her his city in the way he wanted.

One of the guards had driven EJ the short distance to the edge of Tiananmen Square. The sight of her dismounting from a blacked-out Range Rover had elicited curious stares from several passers-by, but by the time she had crossed to the museum entrance, EJ was just another young backpacker armed with a water bottle and the Lonely Planet guidebook. She had contentedly wandered the labyrinth of galleries and gardens, and it was already mid-afternoon by the time she decided to call it a day. EJ left the palace complex through the northern Shenwu Men, the Gate of the Divine, and was unsurprised to see one of the Range Rovers idling across the avenue in front of Jingshan Park. It felt oddly reassuring to know that she was back in the camera's eye once again, even if the surveillance was rather more anonymous that she was used to. A Beijing city policeman was making a heroic attempt to avoid eye contact and blend into the bushes behind him, rather than enforce the no parking regulations on such an intimidating vehicle.

Back in her bedroom in the north house once more, EJ was already showered and changed for dinner with her grandfather. Meng Hua had offered to take them out that evening to sample some of Beijing's myriad street delicacies in the night market on Wangfujing Street, not far to the south-east of Tiananmen Square. EJ was interrupted by a polite knock on her door. She opened it to find one of Meng Hua's elves, who bowed with a smile and presented her with a small package before withdrawing. EJ could immediately see that it contained electronic equipment of some sort. Uh oh, she thought, and began to count out the seconds under her breath, "One one thousand, two one thousand, three ..."

Right on cue, the four notes of Beethoven's Fifth chimed out. EJ had basically left her iPhone alone since her arrival. She'd assumed that Riz, Stan and the rest of her personal network infrastructure would remain active in the background, but there had seemed to be little reason to check in with them while she was under

Nai'En's security umbrella. Something must be up, and there was really only one 'something' that mattered: The dragon egg. Well, that's dinner cancelled for a start, she thought. She picked up the 'phone from where she had left it charging on the side table by the bed.

"Hey, EJ. You get the package?"

"Hi, Riz. Yes, one of the elves just brought it up," she answered.

"Cool beans! Open it and plug it in. Keep your iPhone plugged in too. I need to be able to jump across and reprogram this thing."

EJ undid the packaging to reveal a small pico projector. The whole thing was little bigger than a paperback book and hardly any weight at all. She found the enclosed charger and USB cable and did as Riz had instructed. A pair of small blue diodes flicked into life and then the avatar on the 'phone froze, as EJ now expected whenever Riz's attention was diverted. A couple of seconds later, the tiny projector burst into life and a shimmering hologram of the Silicon Dragon appeared on the table in front of her. The image flickered a little and lacked some of the definition that the bigger equipment provided, and she heard Riz's cheerful voice through the 'phone's loudspeaker.

"EJ dude! Been a while, huh? Hold on a sec while I calibrate this puppy."

"Hiya. I thought you were allergic to Chinese servers?" replied EJ sarcastically. "What's up? As if I need to ask."

EJ could feel the tingle of anticipation building. She pulled aside the curtain of her bedroom window which looked out onto the courtyard garden and could see a more than usual number of both men and elves. Their movements were brisk and purposeful.

"Must be important for you to Alibaba me a mini projector. I assume you've charged my card for this?"

"Yeah, yeah. You'll get billed later. Anyway, first off, ain't this just too cool? I mean, off the charts cool! You remember my boys on the PCH who came up with all this good stuff? Well, allow me to present their latest version of the software. They've only gone and made it portable! Neat or what? Though audio is still a work in progress, so I'm bogarting your 'iPhone for the time being."

"OK, it's cool. But you're not lighting up backtraces in every security agency in China just to bring me your latest new toy, are you?"

The Silicon Dragon's grin faded, and when Riz spoke again it was in that older, pre-Californian accent that EJ knew signified that he had something serious to report.

"No. You are correct. Something is happening. I felt it, so Michelangelo and Nai'En will already know. They are much more ancient than I. They are attuned to the old rhythms. The Jade Dragon appears to have alerted the Chinese authorities already. They are focused on a volcano in Java called Merapi. It has begun to erupt in an unusual manner. The Chinese seismology people already have a great amount of data, but an hour ago the Central Committee ordered every cyber agency in Beijing to drop everything and go out and grab whatever they could find – every analysis or report – that anyone in the world is putting together. Americans, British, Russians, doesn't matter from whom. The order from on high is an immediate full course press. No exceptions, no excuses."

"And Nai'En put them up to this?"

"Betcha dollars to doughnuts."

Their conversation was interrupted by another knock on the door. This time, EJ opened it to find her grandfather and Meng Hua stood expectantly.

"Did I ever tell you I'm a mind reader?" she asked, stopping them both in their tracks before they could utter a word. "Dinner is cancelled and Nai'En wants to see us downstairs. How's that?"

Meng Hua lowered his gaze and nodded briefly. "My master believes that the event for which you have been preparing has now begun. He indeed requests your presence."

EJ stepped to one side of the door. "Yeah, I already know. Joe, Meng Hua, may I introduce the Silicon Dragon. Riz to his friends."

"Hey guys! Love your work. Wish we could chat more and get to know each other, but right now you three need to go downstairs, and EJ, you need to bring me along. I've got stuff you all have to hear."

"Is there a signal down there?"

"Oh sure. I scoped it out earlier. Hey Meng Hua, that's some heavy duty shielding you've got in place round here, my man. Impressive."

The silver elf watched Riz cycle through his full repertoire of neon blues, yellows and pinks. "I shall take your approval as a compliment, Al-Khwarizmi.

Come EJ, and bring the Silicon Dragon. My master will be delighted to make his acquaintance at long last."

*

Meng Hua had shown EJ that indeed there were power and networking outlets in Nai'En's underground chamber, though they had been so cleverly concealed as to be impossible to find with just the naked eye. He had then withdrawn and left her and her grandfather to await the Jade Dragon who, he explained, was still detained in Zhongnanhai, but would rejoin them shortly. A pair of elves served them tea and assorted sweetmeats. EJ and Joe sat down on the divans to wait.

"I talked to Michelangelo earlier. Well, I talked to Mortensen, but he relayed what Michelangelo was saying to him. Michelangelo's sure. Selwyn is on his way up to Anglezarke from London," said Joe, while EJ plugged in the projector and her iPhone.

"Why don't we talk to Michelangelo directly? We got round that problem with Riz's help back in Anglezarke. Riz, are you here?"

The projector flicked on and California's favourite dragon sprang to life on the tabletop.

"Oh man, I love this! Those guys worked out that if you change the coding to a multiphasic cycle then you could get a holo effect through a single projector. Bingo! Portable hologram, dude!"

"Ok Riz, it's really super, but enough of the techno babble. You remember how we created a voice for Michelangelo back in his cavern? Could we do the same and relay it here?"

"No problem. Just need someone on his neural link to type in what they're hearing him say, like young Manbun did."

"Right. Message Daniel right now and get him down to Michelangelo. We'll set it all up while we wait for Nai'En to return."

Joe looked on admiringly while his granddaughter took charge and shot off a rapid series of messages to Daniel Mortensen and the IT team back in Anglezarke. Then she talked briefly with Stan Mortensen in London, who promised to coordinate and monitor the three-way signal between the locations.

"Your handsome elf friend has granted me full IP access on this end. Temporarily, of course," said Riz. "So, we're good to go."

There were several seconds of dead air, and then the donnish voice that EJ had settled on for Michelangelo back in Anglezarke came through on the iPhone's speaker.

"One two, one two. Mary had a little lamb. Am I on?"

"Hello, Michelangelo! We hear you loud and clear," laughed EJ.

"My dear Elizabeth. And is Joseph with you there?"

"I'm here, Michelangelo," added EJ's grandfather.

"Joseph, it has begun. Nai'En will confirm it. The Jade Dragon has instructed his government to send the analysis of the volcano to me."

"And you can understand it?" asked EJ.

"Yes Elizabeth. It is a picture. It is colours and movements, not so very different from all the other pictures that I watch. I will sense it better than the humans, better than Nai'En. The dwarves will study it too. After all, it is a mountain and their instinct for such matters remains strong."

The Jade Dragon chose that moment to make his entrance. He fairly flew out of the mouth of his tunnel and jumped onto the dais before it, immediately striking a somewhat triumphant pose which, EJ decided, would look appropriate on a porcelain vase.

"Good! Good, you are here. And Al-Khwarizmi has joined us, I see."

Nai'En's voice in EJ's mind was almost breathless with excitement. This is a huge deal for these dragons too, thought EJ. They're behaving like little kids at Christmas, or maybe like expectant fathers.

"I sense that Nai'En has returned. The dwarves tell me that they have received the data files from your government, old friend. They are large, but will be on my screen shortly," said Michelangelo.

Nai'En's eyes widened, and EJ felt a small thrill of victory that she had managed to surprise the old dragon.

"Can't we get Nai'En speaking out loud too, Riz?" asked EJ.

"Sure, but someone needs to input what he's saying. How's your typing? Just write it in the 'phone so I can run it through the program in real time," answered Riz.

"Yes, Elizabeth! Quickly! I am sure that I have a most melodious voice."

EJ had to hand it to Riz. He somehow decided on a rich tenor with a mildly mid-Atlantic accent. Nai'En seemed delighted with the result.

"Remarkable! I always imagined, Michelangelo, that you and I might sound this way. Your doing, Al-Khwarizmi Ibn Shams ad'Din? I bid you welcome. A first time for you to enter my home. Legally, that is."

Riz's hologram bowed its head. "Ah yes, Jade Dragon. About those other times … just high spirits, you know, dude."

"It is of no consequence. Not now. You were either very foolhardy or very sure of yourself, Al-Khwarizmi. Which is it now? The latter, I'll warrant. Which means that you have been watching our Texan friends, I presume."

Riz visibly brightened, and EJ marvelled once more at the complex unspoken hierarchy that the dragons seemed to follow. What would Riz be like if Nai'En is right, and he finally works out that he's the most powerful of them all, she wondered.

"Okay. They were pretty slow out of the blocks to figure out that EJ tricked them in Paris, but by the time you landed here in Beijing they had already started to mobilise. Right now, Marvin Thibodeaux is sat in Hong Kong with King Moffett and a team of twelve ex-Special Forces honchos. Flew in on a Wolverine jet direct from Houston. I took a look around their ride, now it's on the ground, and they've got enough guns and equipment on board to take over a small country. They haven't budged. They're waiting, EJ. My guess is they'll see where you head first."

"Jasper Moffett has moved his pieces as close as he can to shadow you, Elizabeth," said Nai'En. "Our own systems flagged Thibodeaux and his associates when they passed through Immigration at Hong Kong airport."

"But have they been watching me here?" asked EJ, with a great deal more curiosity than concern.

"From what I've been seeing, they've been real kid gloves so far. Even though Jasper's brother, the computer whiz, is holed up in the suite with Thibodeaux. I don't know if the Chinese systems have picked up more, but I would say that they are happy to take an occasional peek, just to keep tabs on you," confirmed Riz.

"Then I concur that they will react if you leave China," Michelangelo stated with certainty. "I have seen the analysis, Nai'En. We are correct, the indications are all there. The egg will appear on the mountain in Java. We are fortunate. The volcano is the land of the Coal Dragon. Joseph and Elizabeth, you must leave for Indonesia tonight."

"Will Wolverine know I'm on the move?"

"I think so," said Riz. "King flagged you this morning in Tiananmen with the same piece of software he used in London. Plus, I can always throw them a hint if they start dragging their feet."

"I have spoken with the General Secretary," added Nai'En. "He has put an aircraft at my disposal. Make your preparations. We will speak again before you leave Beijing tonight."

19 Mangrove

"It's the sixteenth rig in twelve hours! Every superintendent reports the same thing. One minute they're pumping just fine – pressures are good, boards are green, everything five by five – then nothing! Like someone just flicks a switch or turns a valve and the well just ups and dries. Got me ten thousand petroleum engineers running round like chickens with their heads cut off. Ain't gonna be long before the press gets hold of this, and that'll really be the frosting on the cupcake. I know you boys ain't off chasing wild geese, but some good news from your end would be mighty useful right now, Marvin. What's the lowdown on Miss Elizabeth Jade?"

It was still before first light in Houston, while in Hong Kong the harbour glittered with the evening reflections of the giant advertising hoardings that adorned the soaring towers of Central and their cousins across the water on the Kowloon side. Marvin had turned the spacious living room of his suite into their command centre, and was on the latest episode of a video conference call with Jasper that had been almost continuous for the past forty-eight hours since his departure from Texas. He had been seeing the same production reports and knew that Jasper was not handling the tension at all well. For the first time that Marvin could remember, Jasper had begun to look his age as the litany of well failures mounted. They were running out of time, sat metaphorically twiddling their thumbs while Wolverine lurched into the worst crisis in the company's history, teetering on the brink of failure, and they were powerless until the dragon egg appeared.

"King's been real careful. Swore he wasn't going anywhere near Chinese state servers, but you know him. Curiosity finally won out and he managed to slip that FBI recognition program into the Beijing surveillance net. Something about finding a network terminal in one of their ministry offices that no one had bothered to update. Anyway, that gave him the in that he needed, so to cut to the chase we finally caught our first glimpse of her this morning. She got out of a car on the edge of Tiananmen Square. Went sightseeing. The Forbidden City."

"Sightseeing? Well, better than nothing. At least you've picked up her trail. She go anywhere else interesting?" asked Jasper, visibly buoyed by the news.

"Nope. Another car and driver met her and took her home. Didn't travel far, says King, a ten-minute ride. So now we've got tag recognition on two vehicles and narrowed her location down to about half a city block. We ran over the satellite imagery and it's got to be the Jade Dragon's compound. It's sure big enough, and it's close to the Palace and the central government. She ain't moved from there since she got back this afternoon."

"That's good work, Marvin. You tell King to stay on it. These wells kicking one after the other … I don't mind telling you it's got me a mite rattled."

"But you think this is the dragon egg. You think it's begun, just like the old bird said it would, back in the canyon," stated Marvin with certainty.

"It's the only explanation we've got that fits. Otherwise, we're plum out of luck."

"Then I think I already know where she'll be heading. The news channels over here are full of a major eruption in Indonesia. I've checked, and there's nothing of that kind happening anywhere else in the world that I can see."

Marvin watched Jasper leave his seat and knew that he'd gone over to the dining room to check the news feeds on the screens there. Five minutes passed, and then Jasper reappeared on camera.

"I've told the seismology guys in Saudi and Aberdeen to run everything they can find on it. They'll pass it all over here in the next couple of hours and I'll cc the whole shooting gallery to y'all. So, what do you do now, if you're right?"

"Gotta be patient, Jasper. Can't be running off half-cocked, get the plane in the air without knowing for sure."

"I wish you were wrong. Wish there was something else we could do, but I agree with you. You get your team primed and out at that airport, ready to go. Elizabeth will have the jump on you, but she's got to travel from a ways north, so y'all shouldn't be far behind her."

At that moment, King Moffett burst into the room, a laptop in one hand and a Coke can in the other. "She's moving, Jasper! I've got a three-car convoy heading south through Beijing at high speed, and two of those tags pinged. They're the same ones that she used today, and they left the compound location about ten minutes ago. It's gotta be her."

"King, are you sure the girl's in one of them?" asked Jasper slowly.

King threw his Coke can into the trash with a moue of frustration. "Hell, Jasper, you know I can't say for sure until I get eyeballs on her! But by my reckoning, those cars are heading for the new airport to the south."

"We flew in there once, Jasper. You remember?"

"Yup. Hadn't been open for long, if I recall. Moved most of their government and military traffic to the southern field. Less congestion. Can you watch them all the way, King? If you're right and she's headed for a plane, then we need to know."

"They'll like as not catch me, Jasper, soon as I touch that airport system. It's state-of-the-art. Scary good. They'll be on me like white on rice."

"Then stay off the airport. Just confirm she's in one of those vehicles. It's time to use the brains the Good Lord gave us, boys," instructed Jasper, who seemed more alert now than at any time in the past two days. "You track the departures. You'll know the flight when you see it. It'll be something private and fast, no obvious flight plan but heading near enough due south. In fact, if you and Marvin are right, then Miss Elizabeth Jade Carver should fly straight over the top of you in a couple of hours. Maybe she'll wave."

*

King Moffett's touch had indeed been featherlight. The sophisticated systems engineers who oversaw China's most sensitive networks had remained oblivious to his intrusions, though some time later the Jade Dragon took a perverse pleasure in hinting to the General Secretary during one of their evening chats that a thorough sweep of the security servers might uncover certain anomalies. The Silicon Dragon was not so easily fooled, though Riz had the advantage that he not only knew what he was searching for, he could also examine the results of King's work directly. Nevertheless, it had been Riz who had made sure that the Range Rovers tripped King's surveillance. Since they had no need to hide the convoy's destination, and every reason for the cars to take the quickest route possible to the air force base adjacent to Beijing Daxing International Airport where the aircraft was being made ready for them, it was reasonable to expect Wolverine to work out what was happening without the need to nudge them further.

The Jade Dragon had been telling EJ and Joe for the last ten minutes that they needed to leave immediately … that they had no time to waste … that they must rest on the plane to be fresh for their arrival in Java. In his excitement, Nai'En was completely oblivious to the delay he was causing. EJ went up to the dais and kissed the old dragon on the cheek.

"Thank you. We must go now," she murmured to him.

EJ's small gesture effectively stopped Nai'En in his tracks, and he leant forward and looked at her closely.

"You must tell me everything, Elizabeth! Al-Khwarizmi will report to me, and of course to Michelangelo. Omit no detail, however small. The Coal Dragon knows of your journey. You will be met when you land. Joseph! Take good care of your granddaughter."

"I will, Nai'En, but we really should be on our way," replied Joe.

"Yes, yes! So why are you wasting precious time talking to me? Leave now. Meng Hua will accompany you. He has the necessary clearances for the airfield, and they know him well. I must return to the General Secretary's side."

EJ glanced across at her grandfather, who just rolled his eyes as if to say, "Well, what did you expect?"

They turned toward the foot of the marble staircase. EJ heard Nai'En whisper in her mind, "Farewell, Joseph, my old friend." She turned back. Nai'En stood immobile and he and EJ contemplated each other silently, before the old dragon broke her gaze and hurried into his tunnel and away.

Up at ground level, they crossed the courtyard quickly to the gatehouse, and after brief words and nods of thanks to the household elves and the guards, joined Meng Hua aboard the middle of the three Range Rovers. EJ kept hold of her rucksack, which was now tantamount to a Riz command centre, with all the bits and pieces at her disposal to summon the Silicon Dragon, but their other luggage was already safely stowed. The convoy pulled a tight turn and sped away from the compound, blue VIP lights flashing on the front grilles. This was no clandestine getaway, but designed for maximum visibility and effect. EJ could feel the speed of the powerful cars, even in the narrower lanes near the Jade Dragon's *siheyuan*, but once they made the turn onto the broad West Chang 'An Avenue and were heading for Beijing's inner ring road, she could see that traffic was being held at every intersection to allow their passage.

"This evening you are guests of the General Secretary and the Central Committee. He has instructed that the roads be cleared for you. Quite the honour," explained Meng Hua. EJ checked his expression for any hint of irony, but found none. "We are heading to the Air Force base at Nan Jiao, adjacent to the new airport. Your aircraft is being fuelled as we speak, so once we arrive it should take no time to get you in the air and on your way," he added, then turned forward to watch the deserted highway ahead, and the car lapsed into silence once more.

A little over twenty minutes later and they were approaching the International Airport. A pair of military policemen waved them down a side exit from the main expressway which led to a perimeter gate of the People's Liberation Army Air Force base at Nan Jiao. The cars slowed to manoeuvre through the concrete tank traps at the checkpoint, then sped across the airfield toward the complex of hangars on its western side.

A long, sleek private jet, which looked like it was moving quickly even while it was on the ground, sat in a bright pool of light on the apron in front of the hangars. The three Range Rovers pulled up alongside, and EJ could hear the low whine of the aircraft's twin turbines begin to rise in pitch. The two drivers of the lead and chase cars jumped out to assist with transferring the baggage to the plane's hold.

"The General Secretary confiscated it from one of our newer billionaires," explained Meng Hua, and even the silver elf couldn't hide a wry smile. "He felt that it conveyed a poor image of the state of Chinese capitalism, and demonstrated a lack of humility. The gentleman in question was most happy and honoured to donate it to the State.

"The pilots will keep their commercial transponder on. The flight will be clear even on public trackers, so Wolverine will not miss it. Hong Kong will delay them for a while, it is easily done at such a busy airport, and then report to the General Secretary's office once they take off."

EJ, Joe and Meng Hua descended from their vehicle and walked across to the boarding steps. "It has been my honour to serve …" began Meng Hua, but before he could continue, EJ silenced him with a fierce hug. Caught by surprise, after a moment's hesitation the silver elf returned the gesture warmly. "We will see each other again soon, Elizabeth Jade. The bond between our houses is strong."

"Yes, we will. Thank you for everything," EJ replied quietly. She broke away from Meng Hua and rushed up the steps before either the elf or her grandfather could see the tears pricking at her eyes. Without noticing the plane's opulent interior, she ran straight to the washroom at the rear.

When EJ returned to the cabin, the aircraft had already begun to taxi to the end of the runway. Her grandfather looked at her quizzically. "Are you ready for this, EJ?" he asked kindly.

Oh, I'm ready, thought EJ, replying to Joe with only a smile and a nod, but she couldn't shake the sense of foreboding that Nai'En's parting look had left with her. Much was indeed about to change, and EJ knew that it was not all for the better.

*

Sunlight flashed off the leading edge of the Gulfstream's wing as the jet banked over the South China Sea. The light in the cabin woke EJ, who had been dozing fitfully, still troubled by her thoughts from previous evening. She looked across the narrow aisle at her grandfather. He remained asleep on the flat-bed seat, covered in one of the plane's supply of light quilts, his seatbelt loosely fastened. The first two days of her stay in Beijing, she and Joe had hardly spent a moment apart. Their conversations had merged into one long description of her daily life and its rhythms in Norton Magna, about which Joe Livesey proved, unsurprisingly, to be exceedingly well informed. The work, thought EJ, of Gibby – and George and Maureen for that matter – who must have been reporting to him regularly.

EJ had marvelled at the man's discipline, that he could stand to observe from afar and resist interfering when, as she now understood, he and Michelangelo had all the resources necessary to bend the world, and her, to their will. That they had not done so until the past few weeks was no longer any great mystery: Michelangelo and her grandfather had known that this showdown was inevitable, but it had been Nai'En who had opened her eyes in one of those rare jolts of comprehension that seem to tilt the world on its axis when they occur: The confrontation that the two dragons sought was not with Jasper Moffett at all, but with the Oil Dragon. Michelangelo and Nai'En had both told her, sometimes directly and other times not, that the actions of men meant nothing to them. The dragons would outlive them all, their individual connections to the earth and its myriad rhythms a permanence that neither men, nor even the longer-lived dwarves and elves, could either match or overcome. The Oil Dragon's treachery, his sale of his very essence in exchange for his life, meant that a course set long ago was now approaching its conclusion. EJ understood now that her mixed feelings about her parents' death and revenge, about which she and Joe had talked at dinner on that first evening and then never yet spoken again, reflected her own strange relationship to the dragons themselves. Joe Livesey had understood when she was very small that her bond to Michelangelo was unique, and he and the Golden Dragon had held true to their beliefs for all this time.

The flight from Beijing would take about five and a half hours in total. Though there was no stewardess on this flight, the galley to the rear had been well stocked with thermoses of tea and coffee and a selection of cold cuts, sandwiches and pastries. Not quite up to the standards of the hawker stalls at the Wangfujing night market, thought EJ wistfully, but neither she nor her grandfather was going to starve. EJ roused herself from her seat and went aft to fix some breakfast for them both. She made up a tray of croissants and Danishes, and brought them back to the coffee table in front of the long leather divan seat in the centre of the Gulfstream's cabin, together with a thermos of coffee and plates, cups and cutlery.

Joe had woken while she was at the plane's rear, and he came back now from his seat to join her.

"Oh lovely! Don't know about you, EJ, but I'm famished. An old colleague once told me you should always eat on a plane whenever food is offered. Excellent advice to live by, if you ask me," said Joe, deliberating over which of the Danish pastries would be his first victim. "Has your neon friend Al-Khwarizmi been in touch?"

EJ was sat with both hands wrapped around a mug of strong coffee, and so consumed was she by her own thoughts that it took a moment for her to register Joe's question. She hadn't thought once about Riz since they had spoken with all three of the dragons back in Nai'En's presence chamber, which now seemed an age ago.

"No, I haven't talked to Riz since Beijing. Let me plug everything in and get him here."

The jet was amply supplied with power sockets and wi-fi. EJ hooked up the 'phone and projector, then tapped open the Riz app.

"Hey Riz! You got anything for me?"

The projector immediately flicked into life and Riz's hologram appeared on the seat opposite them.

"EJ dude! Joe, always a pleasure. Man, do you guys know where you are? That General Secretary dude has some sick taste in rides. A G650ER! Man, this is about as dope as a jet can get! And some young billionaire dude just upped and gave it to the PRC? Like wow! What kind of stunt did he pull for the headmaster to confiscate his toy?"

They had seen nothing of the aircraft's pilots when they boarded, but at that moment the cockpit door opened and a young Chinese woman wearing the gold star on blue shoulder boards of an Air Force Major came through. She sat down on the corner of the divan and contemplated Riz for a few moments, before she turned to EJ and Joe and said in perfectly unaccented English,

"Yes, I was told before we left Beijing not to ask any questions, so I will not. Anyway, good morning. I hope your flight has been comfortable. I'm your pilot, Major Wang Mei-Ling. I thought you would wish to know that Indonesian Air Traffic Control has instructed us to land at Semarang, about a hundred kilometres north-west of the mountain. The ash cloud is blowing south-east on the prevailing wind, so the other landing strips at Yogyakarta and Solo are closed to civilian traffic. I'll begin our descent in about ten minutes."

Major Wang rose to return to the cockpit, but looked back at Riz and added with a grin, "And the 'stunt' as you call it, little dragon, was serious enough that he coughed up a seventy million dollar aeroplane without a single word of complaint."

Riz's hologram fairly fizzed with mock indignation as the cockpit door closed. "Little dragon! Doesn't she know who I am?"

"Probably not," laughed EJ, "and I'm sure the Major could care less. So, let's get back to business. What's happening with Thibodeaux and his boys?"

"They're on the way. King kinda lost you for a while when you didn't appear at the airport – I mean, wow, he's batting 0 and 2 with you and airports, isn't he! Anyway, he rallied nicely and I made sure there were a couple of decent stills of the cars turning for the airfield instead. I even enhanced them so he could just see you in the back seat. That did the trick," answered Riz, evidently enjoying himself.

"Then what did they do?"

"What do you think? Packed up in about five minutes flat and booked it for the business jet terminal at Hong Kong International. Traffic was heavy last night so Hong Kong ATC held them on the ground for a while, but they're in the air behind you. ETA about four hours after you land."

"They worked out where we are headed then," stated Joe grimly.

"Oh yeah. I still read Jasper's emails, dude. His seismology guys were doing backflips about this volcano. I mean, these guys are serious about their geology. Even Jasper. I grabbed a copy of their analysis and sent it over to Michelangelo. He said to tell you that it confirms what the Chinese had shown him, but Manbun – sorry, Daniel – said it was way better."

"There you go. Never chuck a rock at a dwarf. They'll bore you to tears," chortled Joe.

EJ heard the Gulfstream's engine note change and felt the plane begin to slow into its descent. She looked out of the window behind her. A tropical morning haze bathed the land from its lush green coastline to rise high on the shoulders of the peaks and perfectly conical volcanoes that formed Java's spine. As the aircraft rapidly shed altitude, she could see the skirt of mangrove along the silty shore, small waves breaking in an irregular line in the tangled vegetation. The suddenly the Gulfstream's shadow was rushing up to meet them and, with a brief squeal of rubber as the wheels hit the hot tarmac of the runway, they landed.

"You've got to be my eyes and ears here, Riz," said EJ to the dragon's hologram, "but it's time for you to make yourself scarce." She unplugged the projector and stowed everything away again in her rucksack.

The Gulfstream turned off the main runway and passed in front of the terminal building, already busy at this early hour with half a dozen passenger jets. They taxied rapidly to the military side of the field, where a pair of large Russian-built helicopters stood in front of a line of dark green hangars.

"How well do you know the Coal Dragon, Joe?" asked EJ, unbuckling her seatbelt and collecting her belongings.

"It's been a few years since I was last here, so not a lot, really. The relationship is cordial enough, but Anglezarke has never done that much with her," answered her grandfather.

"Her? The Coal Dragon's a she?"

"Oh yes. Didn't you know?"

EJ felt a little ashamed that the possibility had never occurred to her, and Joe Livesey could see that she was struggling with the concept, so he added with a grin, "You assumed all dragons were male. Well, nominally male. I know, the whole dragon gender thing is a bit of a mystery, but the Coal Dragon is most definitely female."

"Alright. Question is: Can we trust her?" EJ asked.

"I think we'll find that out in about two hours' time, won't we?"

20 Sulphur

The transition from Major Wang's glorious Gulfstream to a rock-strewn jungle trailhead among the towering teak trees of Mount Merapi's rainforest was so rapid and efficient that a powerful sense of dislocation left EJ's mind reeling. When the aircraft had come to its final halt inside the open hangar, an impeccably turned-out Indonesian Army officer, of some seniority if the amount of gold braid and his other insignia were anything to go by, had boarded. After he had smartly saluted both Major Wang and then EJ and her grandfather, he had politely requested their passports and invited them to disembark. A dark green Toyota Landcruiser together with a pair of Military Police motorcycles was already drawn up next to the Gulfstream, and the soldier drivers were busy transferring their luggage to the larger vehicle.

Outside, the smell of marsh and seashore mixed with the fumes of jet fuel in the cloying tropical heat. Beijing in high summer had been hot and humid, with the constant threat of an afternoon thunderstorm, but as EJ stepped down from the plane she could already feel her shirt begin to cling to her back in the dense, humid air. The Army officer was away for only a couple of minutes before he returned to hand them back their documents with another crisp salute. EJ lowered the car window and waved to Major Wang, who was already closing the jet's door ready for departure. The Chinese government aeroplane would clearly spend as little time as possible on the ground, and as the motorcycle outriders started their engines and sirens, and their one-car motorcade moved off, EJ wondered if either country would ever acknowledge that their flight had even taken place. Not for the first time, she decided that life among the dragons appeared to take place in the wrinkles, the spaces where the edges of ordinary existence didn't quite meet up correctly – a sort of demimonde where normal expectations were almost always wrong and very often completely ignored.

Police whistles shrilly warned all around them of their approach as they exited the airport gates. After the soundproofed elegance of the business jet and the managed order of the military airfield, EJ's senses were assailed by a riot of colour, noise and smells as they shot into the everyday chaos of Semarang's morning rush hour. Their two outriders raised the volume of their sirens and added high-pitched bleeps and blarts when required, as they expertly carved a path for the big Landcruiser through the packed shoals of motorcycles and minibuses, cars and trucks, rickshaws and pedestrians, each intent on navigating their own way through the controlled mayhem. EJ marvelled at how against any logic it all seemed to work, though she would have been hard pressed to explain it; a system without any system in which everyone seemed to eventually reach their destination.

Their own progress was quick and, blue lights flashing, they soon turned onto an expressway and sped through the tollgates which had been opened at their approach. The wide, new highway immediately began to rise steeply and they left the narrow coastal strip upon which the port city stood to begin their ascent into Java's central mountains. The two motorcycles fell aside from the Landcruiser, their jobs done, and they crested the top of the highway's first long uphill drag. Filling the view ahead through the windshield stood Mount Merapi, huge even now, some eighty or ninety kilometres distant. The volcano's darkly wooded slopes remained shrouded in cloud, but a prodigious plume of white-grey smoke billowed from its summit to be blown away to the south-west on the wind.

Some ninety minutes later, the Landcruiser finally bumped and jounced up the last rutted track of red-ochre dirt and came to a halt in a clearing. Through the blanketing mist, the vehicle's powerful headlights illuminated the foot of a trail between two enormous teak trees, but the forest on either side remained hidden in gloomy shadow. EJ, Joe and the young Army Captain who had been their driver all climbed down and stretched their legs. The young officer had remained silent for most of the drive out of the city and up to the clearing, speaking only to the soldiers who manned the gates at a series of checkpoints on the ascent of Merapi itself. They had each rapidly jumped smartly to attention at the sight of the travel warrant that he had brandished, hurrying to open the barriers and let them through. He now turned to EJ and Joe and politely suggested that they might want to open their luggage and find jackets or other warmer clothes before they continued the ascent on foot.

"My orders are to leave you here to take the trail you can see ahead. The guardians will collect your bags for you, and make sure that you reach your destination. The trail can be steep, but it is broad and you should have no difficulty following it," he explained. He helped them unload their cases, and then with yet another crisp salute jumped back aboard, and the Landcruiser bounced away over the ruts and potholes. In a few seconds, even its bright red taillights were swallowed by the mist beneath the trees, and EJ and Joe were on their own.

The sounds of the forest returned, as if this small remaining patch of Java's ancient rainforest had collectively held its breath until the Army vehicle had retreated back to the teeming world of men below. They were surrounded by life, that overwhelming cycle of growth and decay that powered each and every living thing around them, from the implacable march of the many billions of microbes and mycelia to the whoop of a howler monkey as it crashed joyously through the canopy away to their left. As EJ's ears rapidly attuned to their surroundings, she could hear the leaves of the teak trees, huge and thick as leathery dinner plates, as they scraped and rustled against each other high above. One moment, the mist would muffle everything, and EJ felt as if she stood at a great distance, straining to make out any detail. The next, the forest seemed to rush back to crowd in upon her from every angle, and every drip of water, insect's call or falling leaf came to her amplified in crystal clarity.

EJ zipped her favourite Italian leather jacket tightly and wound a silk scarf around her neck. The temperature in the clearing this high on the mountainside was closer to the moors of Anglezarke than the stifling heat of the airfield. She looked over at her grandfather, who grinned back at her. Nothing fazes him, she thought. He simply lives for this.

"Alright then. Let's go and find the Coal Dragon and see what she has for us," he suggested, shouldering his own rucksack and heading for the trailhead between the trees.

"Did you come up this way the last time you visited her?" asked EJ.

"Similar, but not this path. The mountain's got a lot more active, a lot more dangerous. The Army has all but the lower slopes cordoned off, just as you've seen. All the villagers that lived higher up have been relocated. Right now, there's just you and me up here, EJ," he replied.

EJ wondered whether this deep, old forest that clung to the steep ravines and gullies around her would have thrived if men were still active in it. Maybe the volcano was more dangerous now, but man's absence certainly appeared to have made a difference. The Army Captain had been quite correct; the trail was certainly steep, but it was well built and maintained. She watched her grandfather stride off up the path with all the confidence of a mountain goat, and said a silent prayer that they were both fit and healthy enough for the challenge.

The trail wound up the mountainside in a loose zigzag, and as they climbed higher the mist and cloud began to thin and, in some places, disappear altogether, allowing EJ to look down through breaks in the trees and catch brief glimpses of the lush world they had left behind. After about two hours they called a halt. Joe sat down on a convenient boulder for a breather and EJ surveyed the scene around her. She reckoned they were close to the mountain's tree line. They had long left the great teaks and ironwoods far below, and the trees around her had thinned and grown smaller in stature. More alpine, they were now predominantly some species of tropical spruce or pine. Out of the corner of her eye EJ sensed movement, then clearly heard through the foliage the approach of a large animal making no attempt at stealth. She watched in incredulity as onto a jutting flat rock at the edge of the trail, a little elevated and some ten yards away from her, there emerged the unmistakeable shape of a Komodo dragon. The giant lizard was jet black and some ten or twelve feet long, but caparisoned in burnished golden armour, that covered its snout and head in a type of helmet, then as a breastplate down and across its powerful chest and forelegs.

"Granddad," EJ whispered urgently, "we've got company!"

Joe turned round and regarded the great lizard. As he did so, more Komodo dragons appeared along the sides of the trail, until they flanked both its sides at intervals of roughly fifty feet. Each was as large as the first and outfitted in identical armour. They stood now unmoving, two files of menacing statues arrayed as both a guard of honour and an unmistakeable threat of terrifying violence.

"Ah yes. The guardians. I forgot our young Army friend had mentioned them," said Joe conversationally, apparently entirely at ease.

"Bloody hell, Joe! You mean you knew? You could've told me! I almost had a heart attack," hissed EJ, livid that her grandfather had left her unprepared.

"Yes … I suppose you're right," he admitted sheepishly. "I should have said something earlier. Anyway, if this lot are here then their mistress can't be far away. I think we're expected."

They headed up the trail once more. As they passed the Komodo dragons, each of the sentinels moved back into the trees, but EJ could sense them keeping pace on either side, a cordon sanitaire that dared anyone, or anything, to enter at its peril. The trail made one further switchback then dropped away into a jagged ravine, a broken scar on the flank of the mountain. EJ swayed to regain her footing as scree beneath her shifted and a trickle of pebbles bounced away down the path ahead. She nearly jumped out of her skin as a pair of Komodo dragons passed on either side within a couple of feet of her, to be followed in procession by the rest of the troop. The mist in the ravine wavered to drift and part, and a cultured voice with that rather bored upper class drawl filled her mind.

"Aren't you going to introduce your granddaughter to me properly, Joseph?"

"Ah Madame, such a pleasure to finally see you again!" exclaimed Joe, striding off down the hill with a broad grin, his arms out wide ready to embrace whatever lay waiting ahead. After her exploits on the streets of Mayfair, EJ reckoned she knew a thing or two about bad overacting, and that she was witnessing it right then and there.

"Joseph! Still as suave as ever, I see. Shall we cut the flannel?" replied the Coal Dragon, even though her tone of voice showed that she was evidently tickled by Joe's antics. Joe stopped in his tracks and waited until the Coal Dragon nodded her assent before he continued forward and entered the ring of guardians which had now formed around her.

At the foot of the slope stood the ruins of an ancient Hindu shrine, it's stupas now fallen in on themselves, the panels of bas relief carvings of deities and demons shattered and jumbled. She was sat on a slab of surviving basalt pavement, a huge coil of lustrous black scales which each shone with the deep, anthracite glow of polished jet. A broad snout like that of an alligator offered a mouthful of brilliant white teeth like boars' tusks, and a long, bright red tongue curled and tasted the air like a serpent. Her eyes were round and the size of dinner plates, quite unlike the crocodilian eyes of Michelangelo, and betrayed a quick intelligence. On her head, she wore a jewel-encrusted golden tiara in the style of a Javanese Sultaness of old, from which hung a series of beautifully worked swags of gold hammered into stylised leaves and flowers, that rested beneath her chin and down her chest in a series of enormous necklaces. Enough gold, thought EJ, to settle the national debts of several small nations. EJ could feel the Coal Dragon's cool, calculating gaze upon her, and immediately knew that this was one very clever dragon indeed.

"You're right, of course. Madame, allow me to present my granddaughter, Elizabeth Jade Carver."

"Come down the hill, dear. Let me see you. I'm almost as short-sighted as Michelangelo, not that I'd ever dream of wearing those ridiculous spectacles!" said the Coal Dragon, and EJ scrambled down the slope to stand beside her grandfather within the ring of Komodos.

"Now that's much better. Let me take a look at you. Elizabeth Jade … the prodigal Elizabeth Jade. I am Madame Kartika Basuki Hendra Farida Sastrowardoyo. Most people refer to me as Madame … if they know what's good for them, eh Joseph? However, I think that you may call me Tika. After all, we girls have to stick together."

"I'm delighted to make your acquaintance, Madame … Sorry, Tika," answered EJ, playing along. This was like one of those Javanese shadow puppet shows that she had once read about, she thought. Behind Madame's bonhomie lay a far more serious purpose. This dragon, EJ decided, would need to be watched very carefully.

Madame descended from her basalt perch and flowed over the few yards between them until they were face to face. EJ did not flinch but held the great serpent's gaze. Madame smelt of rich spices and the sharp odour of burnt cloves – a heady, fragrant melange that EJ immediately knew was yet one more of her seductive weapons.

EJ stuck her hand in her pocket and closed it round the reassuring oblong of her iPhone. The knowledge that she was not alone, could summon Riz in an instant, was a powerful source of confidence as the mysterious Javanese dragon continued to take her measure. Then Madame turned away from her in a feint of boredom and loss of interest, and focused her attention on Joe.

"Barely a word in all these years, Joseph, and suddenly here you are without so much as a by your leave. You know, I'd begun to think that the great Michelangelo had forgotten all about me."

"Now that's hardly fair, Madame. Anglezarke has always respected your desire for independence," Joe replied diplomatically, allowing just the right amount of bruised disappointment to seep into his voice.

The great serpent whipped back around to EJ and in one smooth motion raised herself like a cobra.

"Of course … and such a pleasure for me to meet the next generation. I have been told, Elizabeth, that you have an uncanny affinity for we dragons. Is that true? You see, I am sure that today marks a new chapter in my relationship with Anglezarke, one filled with opportunities for us both. Wouldn't you agree, Elizabeth?" goaded the Coal Dragon.

EJ was on her mettle. Even a sideways glance at her grandfather now would be an unforgivable sign of weakness – not the desired outcome, stood as they were in a ring of huge carnivores. EJ took her time. She looked around for a convenient spot to rest her rucksack, then carefully unwound the silk scarf from her neck. Madame made no move, but watched intently.

"You're so right, Tika. Opportunities. Possibilities. New beginnings even. I don't have my grandfather's training or long years in the diplomatic service, so you must forgive me if I come over a little blunt to begin with, but I'm sure I'll get the hang of it in time."

"Not at all, Elizabeth dear. So refreshing for me to deal with someone who speaks their mind. The Javanese can be so tiresome. Never get to the point."

"Good. So, since you know damned well why we're here, why don't you tell me what you intend to do about it?"

EJ heard the Coal Dragon's ringing guffaw, a joyous peal of laughter that couldn't fail to raise a smile on any who heard it. Then it cut off as abruptly as it had begun.

"You mean the dragon egg? It's just over the ridge behind me. A bit of a hike, but not too far. It popped up in a fumarole last night. Right about the time that Nai'En was running back and forth in his tunnels and telling you to drop everything and appear at his side, I shouldn't wonder. Such a demanding old soul! What do I want for it, I wonder? Gold? Jewels? Respect? My dear, I have all of that and more! I want nothing for it, nothing at all. Come with me. No, not you, Joseph, I think you can make yourself comfortable with my guardians here. Just Elizabeth. We're going for a little walk. Back soon!"

Madame swung lithely back onto the basalt slab and slithered toward a gap behind the broken shrine where a narrow path led upward to the ridge beyond. EJ felt her grandfather move forward, but put an arm out to restrain him.

"No, Joe. Do as she asked. She's not going to hurt me."

Her grandfather looked pleadingly at EJ, but relented and turned away, unwilling to let her see the helplessness in his eyes, or the conflict, now that they were apparently so close to their goal. Madame had already slipped out of sight through the gap, and EJ heard her sarcastic call in her mind.

"Don't dawdle, dear!"

EJ grabbed her rucksack, jumped up onto the basalt pavement and hurried to catch up. The path narrowed, hemmed in on either side by boulders and broken rock. EJ could make out Madame's shape some twenty yards ahead through the mist, and knew that the Coal Dragon could sense exactly where she was and had no intention of stopping to wait for her. The mist thickened and the smell of sulphur strengthened steadily. The incongruous pair crested the ridge and headed further into the debris field on the mountainside. There were neither trees nor foliage here, a place of near-permanent half-light. EJ needed her wits about her to dodge the gouts of steam that shot and spilled from the many fissures and crevices, for this was a smashed and broken zone, a result of one of Merapi's many earlier eruptions, where rock of all shapes and sizes lay thrown and jumbled like the gigantic spoil of some long-abandoned mine.

Ahead of her, Madame had stopped and now sat curled, tight and rigid, all her attention fixed on the fumarole ahead of her. The vent was calm, wisps of sulphurous steam rising gently into the silent air, and at its centre sat the egg. For some reason, EJ thought it looked exactly as she had imagined – almost the same colour as the rock around it but quite smooth, and a little larger than an ostrich egg – and asked herself why she should have expected such a drab object. She came forward to stand at Madame's side.

"What do we do now?" she asked.

"You take the egg, Elizabeth dear. It's what you came for, isn't it?" answered Madame with a throaty chuckle. The dragon turned to look at the young woman by her side, and when she spoke again the haughty edge of sardonic humour had disappeared from her voice in EJ's mind, to be replaced by a sincerity as warm and patient as a mother's.

"Joe's perfectly safe with the pets, as he knows full well and you had worked out for yourself. You wonder about my little show back there? Call it a test. One that you passed with flying colours. I told you already, I want nothing. I am the

Coal Dragon. My time nears, but I accept my fate, as all dragons do. All except one."

"So, you know about that. Did Michelangelo and Nai'En tell you everything? You know they are following me too?"

"Yes, Elizabeth, but I also know that a dragon egg marks a new beginning, it is not some magic spell to prolong a dragon's life. You would be well advised to remember that."

"Not the big, bad dragon lady after all, are you, Tika?" EJ added carefully.

"No, Elizabeth. Just another dragon who knows her place in this world. I know Joseph thinks I can be standoffish, or 'independent' as he so diplomatically puts it, but he is a man and thinks in a man's terms. Just because I don't need Michelangelo's gold," and Madame shook her own bejewelled throat, "does not mean that I have no contact with him or the other dragons. And you can see by your own arrival that my influence here can be considerable, when required."

EJ studied the dragon egg, which sat like some prehistoric pearl on the sulphurous half-shell of the steaming vent, and felt the 'phone in her pocket vibrate urgently. There was no Beethovian jingle, and when she pulled it free, no grinning avatar nor flashing neons and sparks. There was only a message:

they're here. hurry!

"The famous Al-Khwarizmi, I presume?" asked Madame in a voice laced with curiosity.

"Yes. I guess the other dragons really did tell you everything. Riz says they're here. Wolverine are here."

"Then it is time. Gather the egg and remember what I told you. It cannot save the Oil Dragon. Deep down, even he must know that. Whatever tale he may have spun his master, the egg will not save Jasper Moffett or his oil. He will discover that for himself soon enough."

EJ approached the vent and leant across to place one hand against the egg. She could feel a pulsating warmth, an inchoate murmur and presence in her mind.

"Do you hear it?" asked Madame quietly.

"I think so. Nothing clear, but there's something there," replied EJ, rapt by the sensation that this was an experience that few, if any, had ever had before her.

"We dragons all felt it when it appeared. Especially I, since I was the closest, but even Michelangelo so far away knew immediately. It beats with the rhythm of the Earth."

"Is it … alive?"

"Honestly, Elizabeth, I haven't the foggiest. There's a dragon there. Somehow. But what happens next is a bit of a mystery. We don't exactly sit on them like chickens and wait."

EJ lifted the egg free with both hands and felt its presence even more strongly. She brought it over to Madame, who flicked her long red tongue across its surface.

"I get the strongest feeling that this dragon will be more single-minded than any of us. That will be something to experience. Who knows, maybe I'll be around long enough to witness it," laughed Madame.

Then they heard the gunfire.

21 Tsunami

Marvin Thibodeaux's disquiet had grown steadily from the moment he, King and the rest of the team had rendezvoused in the Business Jet Terminal at Hong Kong International. The reason was King Moffett. The rest of his team were professionals who had been flying into trouble spots their whole careers. They expected problems and delay – SNAFU – and had learnt to take them in their strides, reducing each moment down to its essentials: First order of business was to get comfy on the Boeing, grab three or four hours of sleep and be refreshed and ready on arrival. Once they had landed in Indonesia, the team had needed only a few minutes to put together their go bags and check their weapons before they had transferred to the pair of heavy choppers that Marvin had requisitioned from Wolverine's local exploration and production company.

King had been another matter. He had made a ruckus on the ground in Hong Kong with anyone and everyone as the delays had mounted, which had irritated Marvin but he had kept his counsel because he still needed King along for his computer skills. He sat across from Marvin now, hunched forward over his laptop, his face a masque of concentration as he typed occasional commands into the scanning software he was cycling across frequencies and base stations to triangulate the position of EJ's iPhone on the mountain ahead of them. No, what really sent a shiver of apprehension down Marvin Thibodeaux's spine was King's enthusiasm for what he termed 'the action'. Like all Texans who spent a good deal of their time on the brush and scrub of their ranch properties, King was an experienced hunter and a competent shot with a rifle or a handgun, but the rainforest of a Javanese volcano was a far cry from bagging deer and wild pigs in the Texas hill country. Marvin could no longer shake the feeling that, whatever happened on this mountainside, he was running a fool's errand.

Their two pilots had logged hundreds of hours of flight time in Indonesia's wildly unpredictable weather, and had patiently circled until a break in the cloud had allowed them a window to bring the heavy aircraft in close enough to a narrow ridge above the tree line where the dozen passengers could jump out and assemble. King had checked his screen once more and, as the two helicopters lifted away to land and refuel, pronounced that they were about a kilometre above and to the west of the last position he had for Elizabeth Jade Carver. He had slammed the laptop lid and stuffed it into his backpack, before ostentatiously flicking off the safety on his AR-15. Most of the team had the good manners to look away in embarrassment, rather than catch Marvin's eye, but his own disapproval had already been painfully sufficient. With a small sigh, Marvin had ordered the team to head off in the direction that King had indicated.

*

"Quickly, Elizabeth! Climb on my back!"

EJ hugged the dragon egg to her and levered herself aboard Madame. She managed to wedge the egg between herself and the back of Madame's broad neck, grabbing a pair of the golden swags that fell from Madame's tiara to hold like the reins of a carousel horse as the Coal Dragon began to gather speed. What had seemed impossibly precarious, turned out to be quite stable – the great serpent kept her front half rigidly upright and propelled them along with the powerful muscles behind her passenger. They came to a halt among the boulders before the last low ridge behind the ruined shrine. EJ dismounted and laid the egg down carefully against a nearby rock.

"One of the guardians is dead. I sense this," said Madame, the voice in EJ's head a quavering mix of anger and sorrow.

"And the men? What about them?" asked EJ softly.

Madame's eyes were two huge golden saucers in the half light, and she raised her tongue to taste the tendrils of mist that swirled into the gap between the rocks where they waited.

"Yes, I taste human blood also on the wind," she confirmed to EJ.

At that moment, EJ's iPhone rang. It had been such an age since she had used the 'phone as anything other than a convenient connection to Riz, that it took her a couple of seconds before her brain processed what was happening. As realisation dawned, EJ hurriedly pulled it from her jacket pocket. The screen showed no number, but she hadn't really expected one.

"Hello?"

"Miss Carver, I'm going to assume you know who I am and why I am here," came a lilting Cajun drawl.

"Yes, Mr. Thibodeaux. I do."

"Good. Let's not beat about the bush then, Mademoiselle. I have two men dead and another badly injured. Under normal circumstances I could be a patient and reasonable man, however, if you are in possession of the dragon egg, I strongly suggest you bring it to me now from wherever you are hiding. I know you're close by, I could hear that 'phone of yours ringing. Come on down now, Miss Carver, or I order my men to kill every goddamned lizard on this mountain."

"I understand, Mr. Thibodeaux. Please tell your men to hold their fire. I will bring you the egg."

"A wise decision, Mademoiselle. You have sixty seconds."

The call from Marvin Thibodeaux ended with an abrupt click, and EJ looked at the Coal Dragon beseechingly.

"You heard all of that?" EJ asked her.

"Yes. Take the egg now. I will stay here. The guardians will not move unless I order it. They will allow him to approach you."

Madame bent lower and brushed her snout against EJ's cheek.

"I understand you are in the habit of kissing dragons. This kiss is for courage. Remember our conversation about the egg."

EJ hugged the dragon briefly then knelt to pick the egg back up. She advanced from the shadowed rocks and down the slope to the basalt pavement. The mist in the ravine now wavered and cleared as she crossed the broken stone slabs. Some fifty feet away, Marvin Thibodeaux stood with his group of remaining gunmen arrayed around him in a ragged circle, the muzzles of their automatic weapons swinging back and forth nervously as they scanned the trees for the next attack. On a boulder a little to one side, one badly injured leg heavily bandaged and his pale face contorted in a rictus of pain, sat King Moffett. EJ recognised him from the pictures that Riz had gathered from one of his Wolverine forays. King held his rifle supported on his other knee and aimed at her grandfather, who stood in front of him.

"Thank you, Miss Carver. I admit, I did not expect to meet your grandfather today. Unfortunately, Mr. Moffett here, in addition to being in a good deal of pain from his run-in with a giant lizard, is concerned. I apologise, but he considers it prudent to ensure your good behaviour."

"Are you alright, Joe?"

"I'm fine, EJ. Don't give this scoundrel the egg!" her grandfather replied heatedly.

EJ nodded as if in agreement, then knelt slowly and placed the egg on the ground at the edge of the basalt pavement. She rose and took a couple of paces back.

"Let's all just take this nice and easy. No one else need get hurt, Mr. Thibodeaux. Bring my grandfather to me here and take the egg. The Komodos have been ordered to remain still, but should any of your men start to shoot, none of you will leave this mountain alive. Is that clear?"

"As crystal, Miss Carver."

Marvin passed his rifle to the nearest of his men and gave his group a quiet order, for they visibly relaxed and slowly lowered their guns to a less threatening angle. He settled his black Stetson on his head and politely motioned to Joe Livesey to accompany him. Marvin turned back toward EJ, both hands opened before him in a gesture that he was unarmed, and she nodded curtly for him to approach. The two men walked across the short distance until they were stood in front of EJ and the dragon egg.

"EJ, what are you doing? Jasper Moffett cannot be allowed to have this egg," pleaded her grandfather. "It's not right!"

"I know what I'm doing, Joe. Madame and I have discussed this. Mr. Thibodeaux will take the egg," replied EJ carefully, never once taking her eyes off Marvin. There was a flurry of movement at the edge of her vision near the trees. The Komodo guardians were close. She knew that Marvin and his men had sensed it too, and suddenly the tension in the heavy silence around them ratcheted up another notch.

"Take it now, Mr. Thibodeaux. This ends here."

Marvin bent at one knee and placed his hands on the dragon egg.

"Can you feel it, Mr. Thibodeaux? You've been around a dragon long enough. Can you sense the presence?"

Marvin regarded EJ curiously and lifted the egg into his arms.

"Yes, Miss Carver. I believe I do."

"Good. I want you to remember that sensation Mr. Thibodeaux."

He inclined his head, then turned to walk back across the clearing. Marvin had only taken a few steps when Joe leapt toward him with a bellow born of the years of silent torment that he had endured at the hands of this killer and his amoral master. Before he could reach Marvin and wrestle him to the ground, another shot rang out. King Moffett had fired, and time for EJ stood still.

She watched her grandfather stumble and drop to the ground. She saw one of Marvin Thibodeaux's men club the rifle from King Moffett's hands and the younger man sprawl from his boulder. She knew she was screaming, and could see Marvin spin round to fall to his knees at the side of the prone body, his mouth wide as he shouted for his medic, the veins standing out like ropes on his neck, but she could hear nothing as a mental wail of anguish of such intensity from Madame rocked the clearing in a tsunami of force as if another eruption had begun. EJ ran blindly to where her grandfather lay, his head cradled in Marvin Thibodeaux's lap, but it was too late.

Marvin sat in stunned silence, his hands slick with Joe Livesey's blood. He tried to say something, once, twice, but no words would come. EJ held her grandfather's hands and felt the Coal Dragon loom over them. When Madame spoke, her voice betrayed the sorrow of every mother to have ever lost a son.

"Marvin Thibodeaux, this is not of your doing, but you shall carry the blame for this murder, as you do for others. King Moffett, hear me now, for your sentence has already been passed. You carry a Komodo's bite. It shall consume you. Now, all of you, leave my domain!"

Marvin sat transfixed by the great dragon as she swayed in all her majesty above him and pronounced her judgement. His hat forgotten, his hairpiece askew, he looked at EJ, tears coursing down his cheeks.

"I am sorry. This was not … He should not … This should never have happened."

She did not look up at him as he gently laid her grandfather's head down on the ground, slowly got to his feet and retreated. EJ closed Joe's eyes and lovingly wiped a smear of blood from his cheek. Then Madame curled around her in an enveloping embrace and lifted her away from Joe's body. They sat beside him together, a pietà of misery and pain, and EJ's tears glistened on the Coal Dragon's jet-black scales as she keened in shock and anguish. Madame raised her once more and carried her away behind the shrine and into the mountain.

"Come. The guardians will watch over him. The villagers have been summoned from below. The women will wash and prepare him. It is our way. We will cremate your grandfather before sunset as a Prince of Dragons."

*

EJ had not left Madame's side since the Coal Dragon had brought her from the ravine. She had paid little attention to the respectful activity around them, nor to Madame's brief words of instruction or acknowledgment, but had sat in the dragon's warmth, her left hand curled around the pendant at her throat, a touchstone to Anglezarke and her dead grandfather.

The chamber opened onto a gully adjacent to the larger ravine, and here above the mists the mid-afternoon sun now warmed the chimney of stone. Ahead rose more of the peaks in the grand necklace of volcanoes that held Java together, and EJ watched the peaceful vista while the sun slid away to the west and the flanks of the great mountains darkened to blues and purples. How long had she known her grandfather? Just five days or a lifetime? How much more had been stolen from her in those terrible seconds? What more could Jasper Moffett take from her? She closed her eyes, but crowding out the happy images of her grandfather and the few days they had shared in Beijing was a colder vision of a great dark dragon and its master, helplessly in thrall to a dragon egg that would provide them no salvation. EJ could feel her pain and loss crystallise within her and knew that the events on Mount Merapi had set in motion a vendetta which would define her. It would be her gift to her grandfather and her long-dead parents.

"Come, child. The women will bathe and dress you. You shall make your farewells as a Princess of my House."

Madame's words were gentle but firm. Now, from deeper within the cavern complex, EJ could hear the gongs and drums of the gamelan begin to play, and soon it seemed as if the very rock around them was singing in unison with the instruments. Two of the young village women appeared at Madame's side and with smiles and gestures conveyed EJ to a smaller chamber, where the volcano's hot springs fed a series of pools and a narrow waterfall spilt down one wall. EJ stood motionless and allowed the women to undress her and then lead her to one of the steaming pools, where they scrubbed her with black volcanic sand until her skin tingled and glowed. She then stepped under the waterfall to have her breath taken away by the shock of the ice-cold water as it pummelled her, fully aware of the symbolism of the cleansing. The women wrapped her in a large batik sheet and moved her to the adjacent chamber, where more girls bathed her skin and hair in coconut oil then anointed her with essences of ylang-ylang and frangipane and wove fresh blossoms through her hair. They dressed her in a silk kebaya and placed slippers embroidered with gold and diamonds on her feet. In the final chamber, Madame awaited her. Two young men, bare chested and wearing sarongs with long keris knives sheathed at their waists, brought forward a tiara, necklaces and armbands in glittering gold and encrusted with gems. While they began to dress her, Madame spoke to her alone.

"These gems have lain unworn for centuries, entrusted to me as the spirit of this sacred mountain. Let this day of sorrow also mark a rebirth. Elizabeth Jade Carver, of the Dragon House of Anglezarke, you are now joined to me, Kartika Basuki Hendra Farida Sastrowardoyo, as a Princess of this, my House. Come Elizabeth, it is time."

At the rear of the cave, two large doors of intricately carved teak were opened, and Madame and EJ advanced together along a short corridor which gave into the cremation chamber. The cavern was a spacious vent open to the sky. As EJ looked heavenward, the last rays of sunlight disappeared from the lip of rock above her and the chamber was lit by only the two tall braziers on either side of the entrance where they stood. Ahead, dressed in the finery of a Javanese prince and covered in necklaces of flowers, Joe's body lay atop a pyre of sandalwood that had been built in the centre of the cavern. The air around it rippled with the hot gases from the vent below. The gamelan orchestra were knelt to one side of the chamber, and now began to play a more jagged rhythm, music which evoked a feeling that certain notes were missing or subtly out of place. EJ laid her hand on Madame's cool flank then stepped forward to pull a burning branch from the nearest brazier. The polyrhythm of the gamelan began to shift once more and gain in tempo, and with a silent declaration of love and fealty, EJ tossed the torch into the base of the funeral pyre. The gases ignited and as Joe Livesey's mortal remains were consigned to the flames amid the scent of sandalwood, EJ turned and walked away.

22 Smoke Rings

EJ had wandered the caverns in a daze after the cremation, until two of the village girls had found her and guided her back to a bedchamber that had been prepared for her. They had carefully helped her disrobe, though EJ had barely noticed. Then they had given her a sweet, spiced drink and put her to bed. She had quickly fallen into a deep sleep, filled with fractured dreams. Now awake in the milky light of dawn, she vainly grasped at fleeting fragments of images and sensations, but they were soon lost, soothed away on the vibrations of the rock as the great mountain strained and shifted, the unending tug-of-war of all the great earthen forces that struggled in Merapi's depths. Perhaps the self-defence mechanisms of her subconscious and the dignified beauty of the cremation ceremony combined to shore up the ramparts of her psyche, but the horror of the previous day's events now seemed so very distant, a cinema reel that had lost its ability to shock and repel.

Looking around the bedchamber, EJ was unsurprised to see her and Joe's suitcases set neatly against one wall, nor that her clothes of the day before, soiled and bloodstained as they had been, now sat laundered and perfumed on the low wooden bench at the foot of the bed. She rummaged for her toiletries and padded out into the corridor. After a little trial and error, she managed to find the hot spring chamber, and lay back in one of the pools to allow the scalding water to work its subtle magic on her. On her return to the bedchamber, she found a simple breakfast of fruits, rice and hot tea had already been left for her. Beside the breakfast tray was a wooden plate, on which sat a well-worn Rolex wristwatch, its case scratched and its dial faded. It was her grandfather's. Hands wrapped around her teacup, EJ simply looked at it for some minutes, unsure whether to touch it or not, before she put down her cup and picked it up. Surprised by its weight, she turned it over. On the caseback was an inscription:

To Tom
HAPPY 21st BIRTHDAY

EJ closed her eyes, but this time there were no fresh tears. The watch bracelet was too big for her wrist. She'd get it resized and vowed that once she put it on, it would never leave her wrist again. For now, she stashed it safely in one of the compartments of her rucksack, then pulled out her 'phone. There was still plenty of charge in the battery. It was time to make some calls.

She grabbed her jacket and rucksack and headed down toward the cavern system's main entrance behind the ruined shrine, wrapping her silk scarf around her neck against the chill morning air. She came outside and heard the rasp and heavy tread of a pair of the Komodo guardians as they fell into step with her on the mist-laden pavement. Much had changed, not least her position and status on this mountain, so she no longer felt unease in their presence for she understood that the guardians would now accompany her at all times. The farther side of the ravine appeared to be catching the best of what sunlight there was at this hour, so she headed that way and found a path that led upwards through a mix of rock and scrub until she found an outcrop of stone that overlooked the ruined temple below. She sat, and as she did the breeze parted the mist to leave her bathed in blinding sunlight. To her left, rose the peak of the great volcano, while out beyond the far edge of the ravine, the rest of Java lay covered in a rippling blanket of cloud. EJ pulled out her 'phone once more. There were messages of all kinds, and missed calls from Selwyn Ormerod and her parents, but Riz must have run some interference for her to reassure them all that she was safe and unharmed, for the messages became more respectful and loving, promising her time and space and hoping to hear from her when she felt able. She read them, but set them all aside unanswered – mind made up that whatever need be said would best be said in person. EJ tapped the Riz avatar.

"He's gone, Riz. Joe's gone. They killed him."

"I know. Michelangelo knows. We all felt Madame's cry. I'm sorry."

"Thank you for keeping them all off my back. Selwyn and everyone."

Riz's avatar cracked a wan grin and there were the faintest flickers of sparks at his fangs and a ripple of neon. That's better, thought EJ, high time we both got back on track.

"I'm going to get him, Riz. For Joe, and for my mum and dad. But most of all for me. You're still in this with me, right?"

"EJ! Of course, dude! What do you want me to do?"

First of all, I've got to get back to Anglezarke. I need to see Michelangelo. I need to talk to him."

As usual, Riz froze momentarily, and EJ smiled as she imagined a billion tiny Rizes flashing into every corner of the worldwide web before coalescing back into the Silicon Dragon on her screen.

"There's a Gulfstream available in Singapore … or I could book you commercial."

"How long for the Gulfstream to be here?"

"… Four hours."

"Do it." There'd be some explaining when the dwarves in the Accounting department at Anglezarke saw her travel expenses, she thought wryly, but she doubted there'd be any problem. "What happened to Thibodeaux and his guys?"

"They got out. I piggybacked Jasper's comms. King Moffett was in a bad way already," answered Riz's avatar.

"I don't suppose he asked after the two dead mercenaries, did he?"

"As if! Collateral damage. Only the egg mattered."

"Collateral damage? Dinner more like," snorted EJ derisively, and glanced over at the nearer of her two Komodo bodyguards, which sat immobile occasionally tasting the breeze with a long, dark tongue.

"How do I find the Oil Dragon, Riz?" she asked.

"No worries, dude. Jasper has no secrets from me. I know where he has him hidden."

"Good. He'll take the egg to the dragon. That's where I need to find them. Together."

"Michelangelo and Selwyn Ormerod will try to stop you," warned Riz.

"Selwyn? Probably, especially after yesterday. Michelangelo? No, Michelangelo will understand," she replied.

Riz's avatar nodded. The Silicon Dragon might be a law unto himself out there in the computer playground, but EJ knew that the dragons were of one mind – the Oil Dragon's treachery was a crime against them all that remained unpunished. Her gaze was drawn by the flash of sunlight on gold below in the ravine, and she looked down to see the phalanx of guardians move out into the clearing ahead of Madame, herself resplendent in the sunshine as the sun glittered on her tiara and necklaces.

"Got to go, Riz. Get the jet down here for me. We can talk more when I'm on the plane."

"Roger that, EJ."

*

"I sense you are resolved, Elizabeth," said Madame kindly as she approached, though EJ could not help but notice the hint of weariness in the Coal Dragon's voice.

"Good morning, Tika. Yes, I know what I have to do."

"You would put yourself in mortal danger once more? For us, the dragons? Or for some higher purpose? Or are your own reasons now sufficient? Joseph's failing was that he thought he could reconcile all three, and that was never possible," said Madame, with a bluntness that caught EJ off guard.

"You know better than to question what has been stolen from me. It makes no difference whether by man or dragon. They are one and the same now," replied EJ coldly.

"Then you are decided. Very well."

The largest of the Komodos moved forward from Madame's side, its talons clicking on the basalt as its long tail swished from side to side, came to a stop in front of EJ and bowed its head. Strapped to its back was an ancient teak chest.

"Open it, Elizabeth."

She did so. Inside were two silver caskets, chased in gold, one considerably larger than the other. EJ looked questioningly at Madame.

"Before you finish the task that you have accepted as your burden, you must return your grandfather to Anglezarke. He has been purified by my mountain, but his resting place is there, beside his family. Michelangelo will guide you."

EJ ran her hand across the larger casket which contained Joe's ashes, feeling the cool metals immediately warm to her touch.

"The jewels you wore yesterday are your regalia for whenever you return here, but they shall not leave the mountain. In their stead, you shall wear a single jewel, by which you shall be known to all dragons."

EJ removed the smaller casket from the chest and unclasped it. Inside lay a ring of plaited white gold filigree set with an opal so dark as to be black, but riven through with a heart of scarlets, golds and orange, as if the flames of the volcano itself had been bottled inside it. She gasped in wonder, and slid the ring onto a finger of her right hand. The fit was perfect.

The Komodo retreated and Madame swirled down to wrap EJ in her coils. The Coal Dragon and the princess of the mountain spun in a dance of embrace, and EJ's tears were for the parting to come, but also for joy and the new-found strength that coursed through her veins. The huge opal on her finger swallowed her gaze, the pulses of flame at its heart pulling her deeper, while all other sound in the ravine was lost to her and what remained was the cadence of Madame's voice in her mind.

"You will return to me soon, Elizabeth. An Army helicopter will be here to take you off the mountain. The guardians have removed your luggage to the landing site. The Oil Dragon will know this gem. It is a lightning opal, a dragon's gem. He will recognise you for what you are, a Princess of Dragons ... and he will fear that knowledge. He will fear you."

*

EJ leant forward and tapped the driver on the shoulder.

"I think you'd better drive slowly through the village," she advised him.

The driver looked back in his mirror at the elegantly dressed young woman in the black suit who seemed to have been holding a one-way conversation with her iPhone since she had slid confidently into the backseat of the big Mercedes at Manchester Airport's Business Jet Terminal. She lifted her eyes from the 'phone for a moment, patted the ornate silver box on the seat beside her, and smiled.

"You'll see what I mean."

He followed her instruction and slowed at the bottom of the hill to cross the stone bridge into Anglezarke. It was only just past eight o'clock in the morning but already a beautiful day without a cloud in the sky. Despite the gorgeous weather, he was dumbfounded that so many people were already out and about. Then he saw the swags of black crepe in the shop windows, and the front doors of houses open as people emptied out to line the pavements in respectful silence, and he understood. There was no other traffic. He slowed the car to a walking pace and the villagers formed up behind them in a cortège as they passed. At the mill gates, EJ saw Mortensen and Daniel at the head of a throng of dwarves, many wearing old fashioned dark suits and mourning ties, black armbands affixed, best jewellery on everyone. The car began the slow climb up the hill in that long sweep beside the mill's railings toward the church on its rise, and on the other side of the road more men and women came out of the houses on the Church Terrace and from the streets that ran off it down the hillside, to stand with heads bowed as Joseph Livesey came home for the last time.

EJ had landed that morning around six. She had spent most of the flight either on the phone or in an animated conversation with Riz's hologram, much to the amusement of the solitary stewardess that had accompanied her, as she and the Silicon Dragon worked through the details of the day to come and the steps that would follow. They had stopped to refuel in Dubai, but EJ had slept through that. Once on the ground in Manchester, she'd spent an hour or so in the terminal to shower and change, before stepping smartly into the limousine that she and Riz had booked for her onward journey to Anglezarke.

Beyond the churchyard, the car turned to crunch slowly along the gravel drive to the front of the house. The driver pulled up in front of the portico, jumped out and trotted round to the passenger side to open EJ's door.

"My condolences at your loss, Miss Carver," he added, offering a hand to steady her as she leant back into the car to retrieve the silver casket that held Joe's remains.

"Thank you. You should stay and have something to eat. I don't think you'll be going anywhere soon," replied EJ, nodding over her shoulder. Sure enough, the whole village had trooped in after them and filled the driveway, before they silently filed onto the lawns and through the low gate into the meadow beyond.

EJ had spoken at length from the plane to both Selwyn Ormerod and Mortensen, who had taken joint charge of the preparations and explained to her the instructions that Joe Livesey had left with them for when this day arrived. The man and the dwarf, one the epitome of classic elegance in bespoke black that emphasised his patrician demeanour, the other respectfully dashing in a velvet suit of such a deep purple as to be almost midnight and wearing a bolo tie clasped by an amethyst the size of a golf ball, came forward now. EJ warmly hugged each in turn and listened to their murmured sympathies, then handed them the silver casket. She stepped away and ran to the front steps to fall into the open arms of George and Maureen, who at her instruction had been chauffeured up from Norton Magna the day before.

"Oh, my love! How are you? We're ever so sorry, but we're so pleased to see you too!" gushed Maureen, showering her daughter with kisses, while George held her tightly and dabbed at his eyes with an enormous white handkerchief. EJ kissed him fiercely, then extricated herself from the pair.

"I'm happy you could both be here."

She turned to the rest of the group assembled at the portico. Molly Mortensen stood with Stan and Lemmy, the silver and gold in her hair and the rings on their fingers flashing in the sunlight. Gibby was off to one side, and EJ touched the pendant at her throat, a silent gesture of comradeship with the old man who tapped his signet ring in acknowledgment. Behind them all stood Meng Hua, who came forward now to bow deeply to her.

"Please accept my deepest condolences and those of my master and the General Secretary."

"I am honoured that you are here today, Meng Hua."

"Your grandfather was a revered confidante of Guanzhong Nai'En, and a man whom I knew well and respected greatly. It is you who do me honour, Elizabeth," said the elf in that refined accent that EJ admired so much. Meng Hua was dressed in a simple Mao suit of midnight blue brocade, the contrast with his silver hair even more striking than usual.

EJ clicked her tongue softly, and Balthazar and Akitafelt came from behind the house to stand beside her. Selwyn and Mortensen waited expectantly in front of the car, and at a nod from EJ they now moved off across the lawn toward the meadow gate, Mortensen carrying the casket of ashes with Selwyn Ormerod at his side. She rested her hands lightly on the two hounds and followed a few paces behind them, and then came her parents, Meng Hua and Gibby, and the rest of the small party of those closest to her.

The assembled villagers of Anglezarke moved silently aside to allow the funeral party to pass, then fell into step behind. They crossed the meadow and then through the five-bar gate in the drystone wall, where the track began to rise through the heather and gorse that covered the far side of Michelangelo's hill. EJ breathed in the deep, earthen scent of heather blossom and heard the complaints of the bees and other insects disturbed by their passage. Her mind felt curiously detached, the familiarity of the place and those now with her bringing their own kind of clarity and calmness. The well-worn path, now more often used by cattle than man, led diagonally up the face of the hill to crest in a shallow bowl that formed a natural amphitheatre, the grass kept cropped short by the constant attention of sheep and rabbits. Some sixteen years previously, a single granite boulder shot through with quartz and feldspar that glittered in the bright sunshine, had been set at the centre of this bowl of land. EJ now knew that beneath it lay the remains of her parents, and this morning they would place her grandfather beside his son and daughter-in-law.

People continued to enter and take whatever place they could around the hilltop, and EJ smiled to notice that her driver had decided to tag along and join them. EJ released her grip on the two hounds, who padded down to take up station either side of the granite stone, and took George and Maureen's hands instead. Joe would be delighted it was such a beautiful day, she thought, gazing North over the long sweep of the Ribble Valley to where the peaks of the Lake District rose in the hazy distance and the sun gleamed off the shallow waters of Morecambe Bay. The day was so clear that when she turned to the southwest, she could make out the far purple heights of Snowdonia and the curve of the North Wales shore. Joe would complain that we were all going to an awful lot of fuss and bother too, she mused.

Joseph Livesey had stipulated – at some length and with a good deal of vehemence, according to Selwyn Ormerod – that there were to be no eulogies, nor music, nor, heaven forbid, any poems at his funeral. The gathering of the village in silent tribute at this final act was fitting. The crowd now complete and attentive, Selwyn and Mortensen moved to the front of the stone and opened the casket to pour its contents into a hole that had been dug at its base, which they then covered with a sod of turf. The pair stepped back, heads bowed, each in their own private contemplation of their fallen friend. Molly came forward and handed EJ the bouquet of canna lilies that she had carried with her from the house, and EJ knelt and placed them before the stone.

"You know my promise," she whispered.

EJ stood and brushed some stray wisps of grass from her trousers, then looked to the heavens. The whole assembly now did the same, some squinting, others shading their eyes with a hand for a better view. High, high above, almost lost in the glare was a dot, little more than a dark smudge in the clear blue sky. As they watched, it began to resolve itself into the shape of a dragon. A dragon which now fell in a dive, its wings held close. Michelangelo dropped toward them, and just when it appeared too late pulled out of the dive with a primordial roar to swoop over them so low that everyone instinctively ducked and many fell to the ground with shouts and screams. They all got to their feet, craning their heads to follow Michelangelo as he flew on into the west, then burst into spontaneous applause which grew and grew.

"I didn't know he could still fly," commented EJ to Selwyn Ormerod at her side.

"My dear girl, neither did Michelangelo," he replied, with evident relief.

*

EJ contemplated the dark lightning opal at her finger. Here in the dim light of the trading chamber under the hill, the gem glowed like the banked fires of a furnace, but it filled her with resolve.

"It is extraordinary, isn't it?" she said to Michelangelo. She was sat with her back against his flank, feeling the comforting rise and fall of the dragon's breathing as he lazily blew smoke rings into the rafters. The usual background hum of Anglezarke at work, even at this late hour, was absent. The big screen was quiet, only the news ticker scrolling along the bottom, and all the trading desks stood empty.

"The gem you wear is of great rarity. And great value. No dragon bestows such an honour lightly, least of all Madame," replied Michelangelo. He shifted his weight to accommodate himself better against his cushions and EJ heard a small groan of relief.

"Are you sure you're alright? I mean, it was very impressive and a lovely send off, but wasn't it just a wee bit reckless?" asked EJ, unable to suppress the giggle at the edge of her voice. She felt the gentle rumble of Michelangelo's laughter in her mind.

"I believe you are teasing me, Elizabeth … though I admit that I shall be paying for this for days to come. I ache terribly."

"See! I told you. It's not teasing at all," laughed EJ, then added in a more sober tone, "You know what I have to do, don't you? I'll leave before dawn."

"I do not stand in your way, Elizabeth. Though I shall worry for your safety, as I have always done. Your grandfather and I set you on this road, but it is you that have chosen which of the paths to follow, and where that path must end."

"Joe was right, you know. Just before they killed him, he said that Jasper Moffett cannot be allowed the dragon egg, even if it won't do him or the Oil Dragon any good. I have to face them."

Michelangelo blew more smoke rings heavenwards. To say more was redundant. The Golden Dragon and Elizabeth Jade Carver, Princess of Dragons, were of one mind and one purpose. EJ raised herself and kissed him lightly on the cheek, then headed for the staircase that led to her doorway in the hillside above the garden, where Balthazar and Akitafelt awaited to guide her home. She turned at the head of the stair and looked back at him.

"Madame said I would return to her," she told him.

"I know she did. Madame is a perceptive and intelligent dragon. Elizabeth Jade Carver, Princess of Dragons, I too shall await your return to me here."

23 Thunderbird

"Riz! I mean, come on! Haven't you ever heard of privacy?"

EJ opened the door to her bedroom to find Riz's hologram sat on the low coffee table in front of the sofa. She swore under her breath and vowed not to leave the projector plugged in next time, but they both knew that her indignation was for form's sake only – Riz would not wait for her without good reason.

"Yeah, yeah. Whatever, dude. You checked the business news?"

"The ticker was running on Michelangelo's screen, but I wasn't paying much attention."

"King Moffett's dead. Went public about twenty minutes ago. Material information, so Wolverine had to announce to the New York Stock Exchange."

EJ grabbed her iPhone and did a quick search herself.

"Says here 'died in an unfortunate accident on the family ranch' … 'mourn the loss of a brother and valued colleague' … 'immeasurable contribution to the company's success' … yadda, yadda, yadda … "respect the family's privacy, no further statement at this time'. All the usual," she read out.

"The Komodo bite did for him, just like Madame said it would," replied Riz.

"Looks that way. Or Jasper shot him for killing my grandfather. I wouldn't put it past him. Doesn't matter really, does it? He's dead and good riddance … What have Jasper and Marvin been saying to each other?"

"Jasper's postponed his trip to the canyons until after the funeral. He emailed Thibodeaux a few minutes ago to tell him. He's angry, but now he's got the egg he reckons a couple of days won't make any difference."

EJ grinned. That was just the answer she had hoped for. All the preparations that she and Riz had made on the flight home the night before should run more smoothly now that she would have one or two extra days to play with.

EJ had instructed Stan Mortensen to bring her Ducati and leathers up with him in the van from London, together with a new military-grade backpack and a lightweight desert camouflage version of a sniper ghillie suit (minus most of the tapestry of shape-altering strings and fake foliage with which they were normally supplied) that she had had delivered to Albemarle Street from an army surplus store in Essex. After lunch with everyone at the house, and while Selwyn and Mortensen had taken George and Maureen on a tour of the mill and the village, she and Stan had huddled for a few minutes and she'd laid out as much of her plans as she thought he needed to know. Stan promised that he'd manage the satellite uplink to her phone – if he could keep her online halfway up an erupting Javanese volcano then any location in the US, however remote, was child's play. EJ had hugged the young dwarf and warned him not to go running his mouth off to his father or Selwyn Ormerod, though she had few illusions on that score.

The gorgeous black Tom Ford suit that she had worn to the funeral was already hung in her closet, and EJ had lovingly run her fingers over the rest of her favourites as she and Molly had emptied her suitcases. Molly had spirited away her grandfather's luggage, but EJ had prised a promise out of her that nothing in Joe's bedroom would be touched until EJ had a chance to go through it herself. Molly had eyed her curiously, but stayed quiet. The only thing of Joe's that would travel with her this time was his wristwatch. When she had mentioned it to Mortensen, he had asked for it and taken it away with him to the mill. Within a couple of hours, he had returned it to her, cleaned, serviced and perfectly resized. EJ was still getting used to the novel weight on her wrist, but the Rolex was a pleasantly reassuring reminder, and she glanced at it almost as often as the ring on her finger. She checked the time now and turned back to Riz's hologram.

"I'm all packed, apart from your projector. I'll get a few hours' sleep and then leave for the airport before dawn."

"Everything's booked as we discussed on the plane. I've got you in Business class via Amsterdam on the KLM to Salt Lake City. Then it's a short flight down to Tucson."

"You'll monitor the cameras? I don't expect they'll be watching me anymore, especially now their main computer guy is dead, but you never know if the dearly departed King left any of his algorithms running."

"Yeah, I'll make sure to dump anything that pings you. Dude, forget about the roads and airports, do you really think you'll get out of Anglezarke unobserved?" asked the dragon with a chuckle.

"No! Stan will have cracked as soon as his father raised an eyebrow to him! This time round it's different, Riz. Selwyn and Mortensen have always looked out for me, and they won't go against Michelangelo," replied EJ.

"OK. Whatever you say, dude. Ride safe. I'll be watching you."

*

In the end, EJ was half right. She padded downstairs with her two rucksacks, boots in one hand. She paused in the hallway. The black and white tiles reflected the moonlight, and the only sound apart from her own breathing was the ticking of the long-case clock. EJ headed to the kitchen, smelt the fresh coffee and knew she was busted.

"George and Maureen told me before they left that they expected you to do this, you know. I said you'd wait a couple of days, but they were adamant that once you got something in your head you'd leave immediately," said Selwyn Ormerod, sat in slippers and a silk dressing gown at the dining table. "At least come and have some coffee before you go."

"Good morning, Selwyn." EJ set her bags down at the back door and sat to pull on her boots. Selwyn filled a second mug from the pot of coffee on the table.

"They know me better. As soon as Mum knew the 'bike was here, she'd be sure. If it were either of them, they'd do the same."

"Yes, I expect you're right. I suppose you and Al-Khwarizmi have worked out all the details again? I know Michelangelo wants his traitor, but are you sure, EJ? Don't forget, they killed your grandfather."

"That was unworthy of you, Selwyn. I was there, remember? The fool who killed Joe is dead himself, as you well know. It's time to pay his master a visit. Details? Apart from the travel and hotel, there aren't any. I just plan to break into one of the most secret places on the planet. It's like Lord Nelson said, 'Never mind manoeuvres, go straight at 'em'."

Selwyn watched her silently over the top of his coffee cup.

"In that case, God's speed. I do have one request: Call me every day. You or Al-Khwarizmi. You'll be in his territory this time. I know we can track you, and Stan Mortensen has commandeered half the IT department at the mill to make sure we do, but you need to stay in touch this time."

"You're right. I will." EJ drained the coffee from her cup and checked her watch. "Time I was off if I'm to make the Amsterdam flight. Are you coming outside?"

Selwyn accompanied her out into the courtyard. Balthazar and Akitafelt sat attentively either side of EJ's Ducati. She strapped on her helmet and put on her gloves, then Selwyn helped her settle the pack on her back. EJ started the engine and sat, her hands resting on the two dogs' heads.

"Don't worry, Selwyn. You know I have to do this."

Selwyn Ormerod pulled the dressing gown about him more tightly against the early morning chill and squinted up at the lightening sky.

"Of course I'll worry. It's what I do. Go on, get out of here before I change my mind."

EJ laughed, and with a final ruffle of the hounds' ears, kicked the Mostro into gear and rolled around the corner out of the back yard and away.

*

It had turned into a very long day. As soon as the seatbelt sign had extinguished after take-off, EJ had changed into sweats and a t-shirt and extended her seat to its full length. She promptly fell fast asleep, the emotional toll of the past few days having finally caught up with her. The crew had left her undisturbed for most of the long flight, only waking her for the light meal they had served a couple of hours before their arrival in Salt Lake City in the early afternoon. The short flight to Tucson had landed on time, but it was still close to six in the evening when she had stepped from the airport taxi at the city's one and only Ducati dealership. No matter. EJ had known they were staying open especially for her: A well placed email to the President of Ducati USA himself meant that he had instructed his staff in Tucson to roll the red carpet out for the owner of the powerful Desert Sled Scrambler which EJ had bought, then had customised and shipped at considerable expense from Los Angeles to Arizona.

While the 'bike was checked and fuelled, EJ changed into her red leathers in one of the offices behind the showroom. Ducati had provided a helmet identical to the one that now sat locked to her Mostro in the long-term parking at Manchester Airport. After EJ and the chief mechanic had run through some further checks, and with the eastern sky already spangled with stars, she had kicked the 'bike into gear and headed out onto Tucson's broad streets.

She took her time, getting used to the balance of the new 'bike, running north on US Route 77 to her base for the next several days, a spa resort she had found outside the town of Catalina some thirty miles away from Tucson itself. She and Riz had rented the largest of the resort's retreat villas for a week. She wasn't interested in any of their new age wellness, and the villa was far too large for her alone, but it meant that she was secluded and had a high speed wi-fi connection that Riz and Stan could make as secure as a military network. As Selwyn had reminded her earlier that same day, she was in enemy territory now.

She had swum a few laps in the villa's plunge pool to stretch her muscles and ease some of the inevitable kinks of the day's travel away. Now showered and swaddled in one of the spa's thick towelling robes, she took a bottle of mineral water and a glass out to the low chairs near the fire pit on the villa's pool terrace. The clear night of the Sonoran Desert was a swirl of stars above the saw-edged line of mountains to the west. The low flames of the fragrant mesquite logs burning in the fire pit reflected in the opal at her finger, deepening the ring's own scarlet and golds.

"Do you think you could turn the light show down a bit, Riz? They'll think I've got a rave going on out here."

She had plugged the projector in on the terrace as soon as she had unpacked, and Riz's hologram now sat on its haunches on the outdoor dining table, tail primly curled around itself, rather like a large golden retriever – if, that is, golden retrievers could pulse in neon pink and yellow.

"What are Jasper and Marvin up to?"

Riz dutifully dialled back the intensity. "Dude, just another day at the office for Jasper. Literally. His security log says he'll fly out to the ranch tomorrow morning for King's funeral service. The next two days are left open."

"So, the world will think he's sat in the countryside in quiet contemplation, but really he's coming out here."

"Sure looks that way, EJ. Reading his emails, especially to Marvin and his other brother, the finance guy, your man Jasper is one worried hombre. Wolverine's wells are kicking left, right and centre. Production numbers are way down."

EJ nodded. She stroked the dragon pendant at her throat and stared into the glowing embers in the fire pit, thinking about her grandfather's cremation at the heart of the volcano and Madame's conviction that the dragon egg was not the panacea that Jasper Moffett expected. EJ had held the egg in her arms on that mountainside. She knew.

"He's out of time. Soon as the funeral's over, he'll fly here to see the Oil Dragon and he'll bring the egg with him. The Maps app says it's about a four-hour ride from here to those canyons. I need to be there for when he arrives tomorrow."

*

The ashes in the fire pit were still warm, the outside temperature nudging into the high seventies though sun up had been barely half an hour earlier. EJ rested her arms on the edge of the plunge pool, slowly turning her hand one way and then the other, so that the lightning opal flared and glowed. The cordillera to the west remained a patchwork of mottled greys and browns, but with each passing minute the rising sun uncovered more of its features. EJ had woken early and made coffee, then come back out to the terrace to enjoy dawn in the beguiling solitude of the high desert and let her mind wander. She imagined that if you were writing this out as a film script then today would be the day of the great confrontation. Ragnarok, the gunfight at the OK Corral. The sort of final battle between the forces of good and evil that you'd expect in some sweeping fantasy saga. She floated in the pool and wondered if Jasper Moffett understood that things would not play out that way. Such a straightforward ending took no account of the dragon egg. Even Michelangelo and Nai'En did not realise that it was the egg alone that would decide the outcome – they had not held it, felt it's strange, patient presence. EJ now understood that all of them – she, Jasper, the assorted dragons – were just spectators privileged to witness this great elemental drama as it reached its final act. EJ looked again into the lightning opal. She saw the flames of a funeral pyre inside a Javanese mountain, and the flames of a burning car on a Lancashire moor. She looked yet deeper, and the flames writhed and licked the dragon egg until it exploded in a blinding flash of white and gold. She slipped back under the surface of the pool to break the spell, then turned and swam to the steps. Wrapped in a towel, EJ sat with her knees hugged to her chest on one of the low recliners and drank her coffee.

*

She followed US Route 77 north as it tracked the San Pedro river, a shallow, lush strip of cottonwoods and willow amid the Sonoran scrub. Every so often she caught a glimpse of the river's placid surface, so out of place in this otherwise harsh landscape. At the town of Winkelman, the San Pedro fed into the larger Gila River, and she continued north, roughly adjacent to its own series of water meadows, now much diminished in the searing summer heat. Before the town of Globe, she swung onto US Route 70 and began the steady climb toward the state line and the mountains of southern New Mexico, an occasional car or pickup truck flashing by her on the smooth highway, the even thrum of her off-road tyres a hypnotic accompaniment. Together with a custom engine cover and meshes for the 'bike's air intakes to limit the inevitable damage when she headed onto the desert trails to Wolverine's black site, she had fitted a GPS bracket, and with her iPhone plugged into the bike's electrics she could monitor the route and know that Riz was only a tap away. Her connection data showed that Stan had her on the satellite link into the Anglezarke servers, no matter how deep into the mesas she climbed.

As the morning wore on, the distances between towns began to lengthen and the towns became smaller. Riz flashed her a message to turn off the highway onto a dirt trail that headed into the desert toward an escarpment, its worn stripes of red and grey sandstone vivid, and she pulled to a halt in the shade of a small stand of piñon pine. The track was well-used – there were clear tyre prints from a big vehicle, probably one of the pickups that everyone in the region seemed to drive. It must have been heavy too, for the tracks were deeply indented into the soft sand.

"They must bring in supplies along here. How far to the gate, Riz?"

"About five miles. Electronic locks. High fence. Cameras."

"You've got it covered?" she asked, knowing this would bring a reaction from the Silicon Dragon.

"Dude! Show a little faith, huh?"

EJ dismounted and took a long drink from the water bottle she had brought. She dragged the desert camo suit from the depths of the rucksack and slipped it loosely over her leathers, making sure it wasn't liable to foul on the 'bike's wheels or other moving parts; couldn't do much about the Scrambler standing out, but by now the desert dust had turned its bright red body work a streaked and dusty pink. Still, no point coming this far to leave anything to chance, even if she had complete faith in Riz's electronic wizardry.

"Let's go do this then."

*

Jasper Moffett was not a man to dwell on failure or the number of eggs you had to break to make an omelette, but he could not shake the feeling that King's gung ho stupidity, and the ultimate price he had paid for it, were only the beginning where this dragon egg was concerned. For the past several days he had thought of nothing other than the full-blown crisis that had engulfed his company. Laying his younger brother to rest in the family plot on the ranch that morning had only succeeded in souring an already pessimistic mood.

He picked up the dragon egg from the seat beside him as the VTOL slowed and its engines swung up to bring the aircraft down onto the landing pad in a cloud of ochre dust. Jasper glanced over at Marvin Thibodeaux, stirring from his seat. Marvin had recounted how on the mountainside Elizabeth Jade had instructed him to place his hands on the egg, and the feeling that something had spoken to him on an almost elemental level. Try as he might, Jasper had not felt a flicker.

The dust cloud settled and the aircraft taxied forward into the hangar in the hill. The two men grabbed their hats and descended, Jasper carrying the dragon egg, then took their practiced roles in prepping the ATV and loading supplies. A couple of minutes later, Jasper rolled them out and away down the side ramp and, following Marvin's guidance headed over the ridge through the mesquite and cactus to beard the Oil Dragon in his lair.

EJ had watched the aeroplane approach from beneath an overhang of rock about a hundred yards from the landing pad. Riz had guided her from the screen up the series of low ridges and mesa from the main gate, which he'd popped with a flourish and a grin full of sparks, and EJ had lost herself in the pure enjoyment of the challenging terrain. It had been too long since she'd ridden any motocross. She climbed and skidded up boulders and across shale, through thick scrub and along dry washes, concentrating hard on keeping her balance and finding the right path. She'd stayed off the main trail as much as she could – more for the fun of it than anything else – after all, even if Wolverine's surveillance cameras could pick her up, Riz would wipe clean any record of her presence.

Riz had brought her as far as the landing complex. Once she had taken a brief look around, EJ had decided to find some shade and await Jasper's arrival. Here below the overhang, she had made herself comfortable, eaten the sandwiches she had fixed in the villa's well-stocked kitchen, and plugged the projector into the 'bike's 12-volt socket. Riz's hologram sat now off to one side on the sandy floor.

"How soon do you think I should follow?"

"I've done some scouting. There's a whole net of sensors and cameras. They all feed into a small data centre in the hangar, with an uplink to Houston. That's how they know where to look for the Oil Dragon. The sensors are no problem, I can fix them, but give them a good head start."

"I guess the signal must be pretty good here, right? If they're running a big surveillance net," EJ added.

"Dude, no worries about losing contact out here. I'll be all over you like a cheap suit."

EJ could have sworn she saw the hologram snigger. Riz was enjoying himself.

She allowed a further ten minutes, then repacked the electronics and checked that the iPhone was on signal. With Riz back on the screen, EJ slipped back down the hillside until she regained the main track then turned back toward the landing pad and the deeper canyons beyond. She rode as slowly as she dared until she was clear of the hangar to keep the engine noise low. She picked up her pace a little but kept to as low a gear as possible on the upper trails through the stands of desert juniper and cactus. It was easy to follow the ATV's fresh tracks in the dust, and she had covered about twenty miles when Riz flashed her a signal to stop. EJ cut the engine and slowly rolled to a halt. A low ridge ahead and a light wind in her face shielded any noise of the 'bike from the canyons beyond, and she parked in a rare patch of shade against the grey and rust sandstone. EJ dismounted and shrugged out of the camo suit and her gloves and helmet. She unclipped the iPhone from its bracket and stowed it in a pocket of the rucksack, which she shouldered. She slowly traversed the ridge, keeping her angle shallow and watching her footing, Riz whispering directions in her earpiece. The ground flattened to a narrow mesa at the ridge's crest, and she could see the ATV parked about fifty feet away to the side of a low stand of desert trees. She tugged the zipper at her throat so that her dragon pendant was clearly visible.

EJ of course had no way to know that she was entering the same large canyon where the Oil Dragon had first told Jasper Moffett about the possibility of a dragon egg. She descended the same path slowly, noticing the security netting and sensors above her, aware that each sound she made was amplified by the canyon walls. Well before she reached the canyon's sandy floor, she could quite clearly hear Jasper Moffett's voice. His conversation with the Oil Dragon did not appear to be going at all well.

"… Meanwhile I'm losing billions! Now, I'm well aware that means diddly squat to you, Jacky Boy, but best get your head around it right quick. You said bring me the dragon egg and I'll destroy it! And then we'd all go back to living happily ever after! Now you tell me you have to contemplate. What is this? You need to get in the mood, you old vulture?"

EJ continued down, and then she could see the three of them. Jasper and Marvin stood facing the Oil Dragon, Marvin dressed in his customary black, Jasper stood arms akimbo in jeans and a plain white shirt, his Stetson held in one hand. She looked at the Oil Dragon and gasped inwardly. EJ had never seen a dragon that looked so damaged … so weary. Then she felt the voice in her head, heard for the first time that voice of rasping cruelty that had mesmerised Jasper Moffett so many years before, and she understood that the Oil Dragon's brain was as rapier sharp as ever.

"Ah, I see that we have company. I had wondered if you would join us, Elizabeth Carver. Only the Golden Dragon would be so bold as to seek me out."

The two men turned. Marvin Thibodeaux strode across to the foot of the path to intercept her.

"You should not have come here, Miss Carver. This is no place for you," he hissed to her urgently.

"Elizabeth Jade! As I live and breathe. I am delighted to finally make your acquaintance in person. You are without doubt the most persistent young woman it has been my pleasure to know in many a long year. Now, what brings you here this fine day? You have caused me a great deal of trouble, but, as you can see, my associate here is having a crisis of conscience over the egg that you so kindly discovered for me," called Jasper, a broad grin on his face.

Before EJ could answer him, the Oil Dragon spoke in her mind once more.

"Approach me, Elizabeth Carver. Jasper Moffett has told me that you found the egg. Perhaps you understand it better than he."

EJ gave Marvin a brief smile and he made no move to stop her walking past him to where Jasper stood, the dragon egg placed on the sandy floor between him and the Oil Dragon. Despite Jasper's smile and the levity of his greeting, EJ could see that he seethed with anger. It was time to find out if Madame had been right.

"Good afternoon, Mr. Moffett. How was the funeral? My condolences, by the way… You know, it's only recently that I found out who you are. I mean, I'd heard your name often enough – who hadn't? – but I wasn't all that interested in oil or business. More into fashion and so forth." She saw that the last little jibe had stung. "Of course, all that was before I discovered that you murdered my parents. And now you've killed my grandfather as well."

The grin had disappeared from Jasper Moffett's face, but he remained silent and allowed her to continue. She raised her hand and watched the dragon's dark eye fix on the ring on her finger.

"You know this gem, dragon. You know too what I now am. Tell them! Tell them, Jacinto Saavedra Cervantes i Domenech! I am a Princess of Dragons." At her challenge, the Oil Dragon brought its huge head close to her, and she could smell the acrid corruption of its flesh, the scarred eye socket ravaged and livid.

"Listen to me carefully, Mr. Moffett. You too, Marvin Thibodeaux. This dragon will not destroy the egg. He cannot destroy the egg. The egg will bring him the atonement he craves. What he becomes, no one yet can know."

"Princess of Dragons? How dare you! Why, you're no better than your damned idealistic parents. Yes, I killed 'em. Do you know what your father said to me, Elizabeth Jade? He told me that he and the saintly Michelangelo would rather destroy it all than see me earn one more red cent off this here dragon. And he smiled at me when he said it, young lady, like it was the simplest thing in the world. Now what did he think I was going to do? Let him get away with it?"

EJ was about to turn to leave, but stopped and looked back at Jasper.

"My grandfather always wondered whether you spoke to them that night. I guess now I know."

Jasper lunged at her with a roar, but the Oil Dragon was faster. Before Jasper had managed a single stride the Oil Dragon whipped his tail around like a harpoon and speared him, the wicked barbs bursting through Jasper's chest. Jasper stood transfixed, and looked down in astonishment. Silently, the snarl of anger disappeared from Jasper's face and he raised his gaze to EJ and, in that fleeting final look before the light of recognition in Jasper's eyes dimmed, EJ understood the shared experience that had defined them for so long. The dragon lifted Jasper from the ground to hold him transfixed and examine him like a butterfly on a pin, turning him slowly from side to side while Jasper's lifeblood drained from the mortal wound. Apparently satisfied with the result, it was as if the Oil Dragon then simply lost interest, and it dropped Jasper's dead body to the floor.

"It is as Elizabeth Carver, Princess of Dragons, has said. What becomes of me now, I do not know. The earth turns, Jasper Moffett. Only the earth shall decide."

Neither EJ nor Marvin had moved a muscle in those few brutal seconds, but Marvin now sprinted forward and pulled her away from where she stood, her face sprayed with Jasper's blood. He dragged her backwards away from the Oil Dragon to the foot of the path, and EJ stood with Marvin's arms wrapped protectively around her. They watched in wonder as the Oil Dragon slowly slumped to the ground. Its breathing became ragged and dark blood now seeped from its newly reopened wounds. Jacinto Saavedra Cervantes i Domenech laid its head beside the egg, and the dragon egg burst open in the blinding flash of searing white and gold that EJ had envisioned that morning. She and Marvin both shielded their eyes instinctively and when they turned back there was no more Oil Dragon. Where it had been sat a new dragon, flexing its wings and revelling in the play of light across the muscles of its broad chest. It held its head cocked to one side, and was eyeing them with curiosity.

EJ reacted quickest and pulled her iPhone from her backpack. She pressed it into Marvin's hand and tapped the Riz avatar.

"Riz, patch the video to Michelangelo's screen! And into Nai'En too, if you can. They have to see this! Mr. Thibodeaux? I need you to film this, OK?"

Marvin nodded like an automaton, still stunned by what had happened in the space of a few seconds. EJ walked over to the dragon. Its scales glowed like molten glass, as if each held a tiny sun. At the same time, shades of green, blue and aquamarine swirled and pulsed over its body with the ebb and flow of an ocean tide. The new dragon bent its head to her. Its voice, when EJ heard it for the first time, could have stretched across galaxies, or been the trill of a moorland brook.

"You remember what you were?"

"Yes, I remember all that went before, Princess of Dragons."

"And do you know what you have become?"

"As yet, I do not. I cannot. The earth will form me. I will be as intended. For now, in this place, I am renewal, the thunderbird."

"You will leave here."

"Yes, these canyons were my cage. No longer. You alone will know where to find me."

EJ raised her hand with the lightning opal ring once more to stroke the great head and saw the answering flash of lightning in the dragon's eyes.

She turned for the final time and walked back to Marvin Thibodeaux.

"Well, Mr. Thibodeaux, what do we do now?" she asked.

"You, Mis Carver, need to leave here. Few people know of this place. I have your solemn word that it will stay that way?"

EJ nodded in agreement and extended her hand. Marvin took it, but instead of shaking it, brought it briefly to his lips. "I told you on that mountain, it should never have happened."

"I know. What about the body?"

Marvin sighed. "He was what he was, Miss Carver. Never tried to be anybody or anything else. There's few of us are lucky enough to get that chance, don't you think? You leave all this to me. I'll take care of it and leave you and the dragon out of it."

He handed her back her iPhone and EJ started back up the path out of the canyon. Without turning, she said to him,

"I'd sell all my Wolverine stock if I were you."

She could still hear Marvin's laughter echoing off the canyon walls when she stepped back out into the sunlight.

24 Pelican

The aroma from Selwyn Ormerod's cigar mingled with the sharp scent of the turned rows of freshly cut hay beyond the hangar of trees that shaded *The Grouse and Hare*'s garden. His Montecristo's plume of smoke slowly weaved among the motes of dust and pollen, which glittered in the dappled sunlight of the warm September afternoon. Selwyn was seated at a small, white wrought-iron table beneath a spreading copper beech, the scant remains of one of Maureen Carver's splendid game pies on the plate before him attracting the attention of a pair of fat wasps already drunk on the fruits of late summer. He blew a soft cloud of smoke toward the plate and the two insects rose indignantly from the table with a buzz of resignation. Gibby, his lunch companion, had already retired to the snug of the Lounge Bar, The Times crossword in hand, to leave him alone at the table to wait for EJ. She was on the broad, stone-flagged terrace next to the pub, dressed for service in black t-shirt and slacks, with a white apron at her waist and a tea towel casually slung over one shoulder, her blond curls held back by a black bandanna. She chatted amiably with the last table of diners as they prepared to take their leave, and glanced enquiringly at Selwyn as she felt his gaze rest upon her. He smiled and returned his attention to his cigar.

Michelangelo and Joe had been right all along, he thought. Seeing her now, who would believe that this remarkable young woman had borne witness to the extraordinary episode of death and rebirth in that hidden New Mexico canyon just a few weeks before? Or that the Elizabeth Jade so competently waiting on table in an English pub garden, could also be a Princess of Dragons in that parallel demimonde in which she and Selwyn both had the privilege to spend their lives? Notwithstanding that he knew for a fact that her clothes today were Off White originals and would have likely cost most barmaids half a year's wages. She had developed an uncanny ability to blend in with her surroundings, no matter the circumstances.

Jasper Moffett's unexpected demise hard on the heels of his younger brother's own death had predictably sent global financial markets into an almighty tailspin. The flood of glowing tributes at the loss of such a titan of industry had left a bitter taste in the mouths of those few, like Selwyn, who had known him for his true self. Yet just as predictably, once the hysteria had peaked and the wild gyrations of oil and share prices had been tempered, the world had found other more immediate matters to grab its collective attention. The uncertain future of the world's most powerful oil company without its leader and driving force had returned to the business channels and the pages of the financial press. That small community of bankers, brokers and traders who treated such speculations as if their very lives depended on them, continued to debate and parse the implications, as some profited while others railed at their loss of fortune.

Selwyn Ormerod had been privy to several such conversations between the great and the good: In the hushed confines of the mahogany-panelled library of his London club; sat with merchant bankers in the boardrooms of the City of London; and, on one flying visit across the Atlantic, over glasses of iced tea on the lawn of a billionaire hedge fund owner's estate as they watched yachts tacking to and fro on Long Island Sound. Eventually the conversations had all resolved themselves in the usual manner: The initial wave of fear and panic had given way to greed and the scent of opportunity. Far be it from Selwyn Ormerod to reveal that Anglezarke Holdings and Michelangelo had already reaped enormous sums out of the Wolverine panic, nor for that matter that a goodly proportion of those profits had then been put to work pouring balm onto the troubled waters, restoring a sense of proportion to the same markets which had, however briefly, unleashed the Four Horsemen to wreak havoc across the globe. Of course, Wolverine Petroleum would no longer dominate the world's energy markets, as great chunks of the behemoth's sprawling empire would be sold off over the coming months to shore up its ravaged balance sheet and save the company, if not its reputation. Not a bad day's work, in the end, thought Selwyn.

Today's leisurely pub lunch was the first time that Selwyn had seen EJ since her return. His own busy schedule in the aftermath of the Wolverine debacle, allied to an innate sense that she still needed some space, had kept him more distant than he might have liked. Now, with the final group of lunch guests safely ushered to their cars and their table cleared and reset ready for the evening, EJ had shed her apron and towel and walked down the garden to join Selwyn at his table. She took the seat opposite and pushed an errant blond curl back behind her ear.

"Up to standard?" she asked.

"Naturally. Your mother's one of the finest cooks in the entire Home Counties, as well you know."

"Of course. You were lucky I saved you a decent helping of that pie. It's usually all gone well before you got here."

EJ looked aside, staring off through the trees behind Selwyn. Here we go, he thought. It's taken you long enough.

"So, what do you think I should do?" EJ asked, coming straight to the point and shifting in her seat to look him in the eye. "Just about everybody else has given me advice. Mum, Dad, Gibby, half the pub. Oh, I know they mean well … but they weren't there, up on the mountain or in the desert. None of them have a clue, do they? Only you and Michelangelo."

Selwyn watched her stroke the dragon pendant at her throat, its jewels glittering and the lightning opal on her finger sparkling in its depths like the stirrings of a volcano.

"And what does your other favourite dragon think about all this?"

"Riz? To tell the truth, he's not been much help. Taking life seriously has never really been his strong suit, has it? Not when you can spend your time flitting in and out of every computer system on earth. I think he's having too much fun, even if he'll still show up whenever I call." EJ grinned, but her eyes betrayed a shadow of regret.

"Right then," said Selwyn. "I think I know you well enough by now. You've already worked out for yourself what I'm going to tell you. Or else you wouldn't have asked."

EJ smiled and her eyes came alive again with their more usual humour.

"Yeah, pretty much. Still, go ahead and say it."

"Alright. Go and see Michelangelo. Spend some time with him. Then get on a plane and go and see Madame. And then, when they've both shown you how much you matter to them, go and get that other motorbike of yours out of that lockup in Los Angeles and find the new dragon. He needs you more than any of them, and I suspect you'll find that you need him just as much."

"That's it?"

"Absolutely. Throwing yourself back into this life was good for you. Gave you time to breathe, maybe to come to terms with who you've become. What you've become. But you can't change who you now are, EJ."

"I can sense them all, Selwyn. All the dragons. Even the ones I've never met. Did Madame know this would happen?"

"I haven't a clue. You know her better than any of us. If I had to guess, even given the circumstances of how you first met her, I don't think she could have been certain. But to anoint you a Princess of her House is not a step that she would take lightly, so I think she must have had some idea."

"That's what I think as well. With Michelangelo, Madame, Nai'En even, it's as if I can always feel them with me. If I concentrate a bit, I can even sense where they are and what they're doing."

"And the new dragon?"

"That's the strangest of all. With him, I don't even have to try. It's as if he's part of me." EJ gently stroked the pendant at her throat once more. "Right now, he's somewhere in Northern California, in the mountains. He's been heading North, moving up into the old forests, what's left of them."

"So, what's the problem?"

EJ hesitated.

"The problem is I had everything planned out. Before this all began. Before you, and Michelangelo and Anglezarke. A Levels, and Cambridge … and whatever … and then find something interesting to do with the rest of my life."

EJ's smile returned, only to fade once more.

"I mean, I guess I've managed the last bit already. But somehow it all seems so topsy-turvy, and now I don't know what to do. Out there, in Java or facing Jasper in the canyon, I couldn't second guess myself. It was all in the moment. But now, I feel … Oh, I don't know! A bit lost?"

Selwyn poured himself the remains of a bottle of Riesling then set the bottle back in the ice bucket to the side of the table. Lifting his glass, beaded with condensation in the warm, still air, he took a thoughtful sip, then reached into the inside pocket of his jacket and drew out an envelope.

"I had a quiet word with your father when I arrived. He reminded me what he had said at the very beginning, the day you received that pendant from me, that this was a chance for you to find out who you really are. Insightful chap, your father."

He passed the letter across to EJ.

"So maybe I can make this a bit easier for you. I had a chat with the Master and Senior Tutor of our old college, mine and Joe's. They are delighted to offer you a place – to read French or History seem to be their preferences, though the final choice remains up to you – but they will defer it for at least a year, if that is what you want."

EJ tore open the envelope and read the enclosed letter twice through. She had received her A Level results at the end of August and, to a chorus of 'I told you so's' from the entire village of Norton Magna, had secured straight A's in all her subjects. Without looking up, she asked in a quiet voice,

"They'd really do that? For me?"

"Certainly! Your exam results are first class. You're the granddaughter of a distinguished former member of college. And a number of alumnae wrote to the Master to plead your case. Once I explained to them what I wanted."

EJ finally looked up, and Selwyn saw the tears in her eyes.

"Oh, come now. Really, it's just a gap year. Almost everybody takes one nowadays. Admittedly, in your case there's a chance it might drag on a bit. Who knows? Given your recent track record, you'll probably end up saving the world or some such nonsense."

And finally, EJ laughed.

Beaming with the self-satisfied air of someone who recognised a job well done, Selwyn excused himself from the table to make his farewells to Gibby and, he said, pop into the kitchen to give Maureen Carver an enormous hug of appreciation for her splendid cooking. EJ sat on, staring into the glowing depths of the lightning opal on her finger, a few final tears blurring her vision once more. The hubbub of conversation and the clink of glassware now a memory, the cooing of the wood pigeons and the soft, afternoon buzz of insects expanded to fill the silence and reassert their ownership of the space around her. After what had seemed an age, but was in reality only a few minutes, she roused herself, checked and tidied her appearance with the help of her iPhone camera, and went back inside to look for her parents.

She found them in the Lounge Bar, sat with Gibby at his corner, four champagne flutes and a bottle of Pol Roger chilling in a bucket before them. As they saw her come in, George Carver lifted the bottle and opened it with a practiced flourish. EJ stood and watched: Selwyn – or Gibby, or both – had clearly let the cat out of the bag. They looked, she realised with a grin, like any other family whose child had just received a place at university, and the normality of this little tableau seemed finally to evaporate all her recent angst and uncertainty.

No one had yet spoken. Her father rose from his bar stool to bring her a glass of champagne, and then the afternoon dissolved into a whirl of hugs and kisses, tears and laughter, liberally seasoned by some of Gibby's more risqué reminiscences of Cambridge life. In no time, the Norton Magna bush telegraph, of which the pub was the principal nexus, had been humming, and soon half the village had appeared to add their congratulations, leavened with generous helpings of 'never-doubted-it-for-a-minute's'. George declared to a cheer of approval from the assembled throng that for today at least the licensing laws be damned, and he would put on a barrel to mark the occasion. Maureen was already ferrying platters of sandwiches from the kitchen – she must have had an inkling of her own – and, as the shadows lengthened and the western sky dissolved into a dusk of orange and purples, the party had been in full swing.

*

The following morning, EJ woke with a surprisingly clear head, though she doubted that anyone else in Norton Magna, including her parents, would be able to say the same. She padded downstairs in stockinged feet to make a pot of strong tea and sit at the kitchen table with an assortment of the sandwiches left over from the night before as her breakfast. She'd heed Selwyn Ormerod's advice, though her instincts told her to go to California and find the new dragon first. Thus, once showered and changed into her leathers, rucksack packed as an overnight bag, EJ slowly rode out of the yard and around the Green, trying not to disturb residents or wildlife by keeping the Ducati's revs as low as she dared, and headed into London.

It was one of those glorious September mornings that only Britain's fickle climate could occasionally conjure up. The brick and Portland stone of Mayfair seemed to glow and the banners of the shops and boutiques rippled in the light breeze like battle standards. EJ removed a glove and placed her palm to the biometric reader on the garage door in the mews behind Albemarle St. She rolled the Ducati in to where Stan and Lemmy were waiting. As the door clicked back into place, Stan pressed the lift control to take them down to his IT domain.

"Hi, EJ. Selwyn's not here. Left early this morning – said something about Zurich – but he told us we should expect you. What's up? Oh, and congratulations!"

EJ set her gloves down on the fuel tank and undid her chinstrap to take off the scarlet helmet and shake her damp curls free. The two dwarves were evidently pleased to see her – even Lemmy had a smile that morning – and waited for her to dismount. She leant over to flip the catch on one of the panniers and pulled out her rucksack.

"Morning, lads. Thank you. Let me get Riz on the 'phone and down here. Lots to do today."

If anything, the dwarves' smiles had broadened. Stan rubbed his be-ringed hands together and said to the departing Lemmy, who had already turned to go back inside,

"Aye, reckoned as much. Right, Lemmy'll put the kettle on."

EJ wheeled her 'bike to one side and pulled it up onto the centre stand. She unclipped her iPhone from its cradle and with a couple of thumb taps, the grinning, fizzing neon avatar of Al Khwarizmi Ibn Shams ad'Din flashed onto the screen.

"EJ! Dude! Understand congratulations are the order of the day!"

EJ knew enough by now not to question how Riz should already know, though she felt a small part of her lizard brain give an atavistic shudder each time he demonstrated his omniscience where she was concerned. Riz, undeterred of course, ploughed on without expecting an answer, though his tone was immediately more serious.

"Michelangelo says you've been struggling. Decompression, he called it. You sure you're ok, dude? You really up for this?"

"You talked to him about me?" she asked, surprised.

"Oh, we've got to chatting all the time, man! Regular three way gossip-fest – me, the big guy and Nai'En. I mean, you know how deep you guys were in the fallout of the Wolverine business. Been visiting some with your dude Selwyn too – on the mini rig Stan the Man fitted upstairs. Course, now it's kinda all gone quiet on the western front, I've been amusing myself with a bit of surfing of my own. Some rad stuff out there, EJ, if you know where to look."

The idea that Michelangelo and Nai'En had now accepted Riz into their inner circle would definitely take some getting used to. Still, probably a big plus overall from her standpoint, thought EJ. More immediately, she needed Riz's talents for her own purposes. There'd certainly be plenty of time to delve into the details of the dragons' growing relationships over the coming days.

"So, you're not busy on anything for them now, are you?" she asked, instantly regretting it as the colours of Riz's face dimmed and she blushed at his evident disappointment in her.

"Riz, forget I asked that. The last few weeks have been … difficult."

Riz brightened. "EJ! Come on, dude! Just delighted you're back in the saddle, so to speak. What you got for me?"

"Do your 'Beam me up, Scotty' routine and flip down to the garage holos and we'll talk."

EJ felt the momentary sense that all the oxygen had been sucked from the room and the now familiar fizz in the air as ions seemed to realign themselves, then there he was, right in front of her, the hologram more tangible than she remembered.

"Whoa! Has this thing been upgraded again?"

"Oh yeah. Forgot you hadn't seen the new beta yet. You remember my boys on the PCH? They, er, came into some new funding. Still, pretty cool, huh?"

Stan and Lemmy returned with their laptops, and a tray of tea and chocolate digestives. EJ noted the familiarity with which they greeted Riz, and realised that his appearances in Albemarle St. had reached the level of commonplace.

"This one here all the time, then?" she asked Stan.

"Oh aye. Can't keep the bugger away. Part of the furniture almost," he replied with a chuckle. Lemmy nodded sagely and went back to the door to drag in a couple of office chairs.

EJ pressed the control to take the garage lift back up to street level so that she could climb the narrow staircase to the coachman's rooms to change out of her leathers and into the silk shirt and slacks and the soft Italian leather jacket that had become her go-to outfit for trips into town, then gratefully accepted a mug of tea and a biscuit from Lemmy, took a seat and laid out the situation. Over the next hour, EJ, the two dwarves and Riz slipped back into the comfortable routine they had developed.

She explained, a little haltingly at first but with growing confidence as the reality of traveling to find the dragon in California took concrete shape, how she could now sense all the dragons, especially the ones she already knew, and most especially, the new dragon. He was still where she had felt him last, high in the Trinity Alps wilderness of granite peaks and glacial lakes in the far north-eastern corner of California. She'd need good hiking gear – professional or military grade – to get up to him, though the trails were well maintained by the Parks Department and the distances involved from the trailhead were not onerous. EJ reckoned she could, at a push, be up and back in a day, but they'd plan as always for the contingencies. She also wanted her other 'bike, the Scrambler, from its lockup in LA. After some toing and froing, they decided that to minimise her time away she would fly directly to Sacramento rather than have her ride nearly the length of the state from Los Angeles.

From that point, Riz and his box of tricks took over: First class on Air France to LAX the following afternoon, with an onward to Sacramento; a shopping list of top-grade outdoor gear for the hike, including a tent and sleeping bag;

weatherproof battery packs for the pico holo rig; and half a dozen hard black plastic Pelican flight cases to ship all her gear – Riz found a custom shop in the East End which could cut the foam inserts for the equipment cases to fit the outdoor stuff and the projector rig, as well as her bike leathers, boots, gloves and helmet – which this trip would all be going with her – and sent them over detailed drawings.

For the Scrambler, Riz found a transporter in Beverly Hills that specialised in moving the very high-priced vehicles and other toys of sports, rock and movie stars. They would deliver the 'bike upstate to a Ducati dealership in Sacramento, where it would be fully serviced and have new tyres fitted, then dropped off at her hotel before her arrival. And the hotel? Riz booked something called the Happiness Suite in a quirky boutique place downtown in Old Sacramento for the entire week. EJ took a look on one of the laptops and was tickled to find that the room had a real fireplace.

Stan and Lemmy collated all the virtual paperwork on the laptops in readiness for the slew of deliveries and packing. Everything had to be ready to go by 5pm to be handed over to the courier company – one which you wouldn't find in the Yellow Pages or its digital equivalents – but which for an eye-watering sum of money guaranteed to have everything waiting for EJ at her hotel in Sacramento by the following afternoon local time.

Stan and Lemmy looked up from their screens at EJ and Riz.

"That it then?"

"I think so. Anything else would be too last minute for you guys, so leave that with me and Riz. You get all this together and off to California. We'll handle the rest. And thank you."

"Right. Guess we won't see you in the morning. Be safe, and …"

"If you can't be safe, be lucky. Yeah, yeah."

The two dwarves closed their laptops and Stan took them down once more to the IT level. EJ turned back to Riz, who sat cycling his colours to the muffled blastbeats of the heavy metal from Stan and Lemmy's oversize audio system, his teeth sparking along in time.

"Love those guys, dude. Solid as."

"Couple of last things while the boys here take care of the grunt work. Book me overnight at Claridge's with a car for Heathrow in the morning, and get me an appointment at Huntsman for this afternoon."

Riz gave a brief flicker.

"Done and done. The Concierge is looking forward to seeing you again, and the tailors have cleared the decks for you from 2pm. Oh man, that new dragon is something else. Can't wait. First time I was just doing the film and relay, now I'll see him up close and personal. Later."

EJ thought she could almost hear the holo pop as it sprang out of existence. Riz instantly reappeared on her iPhone screen and winked at her.

"Get outta here!" she laughed, as the Silicon Dragon finally flicked out.

H. Huntsman & Sons had been all she had hoped, though it had taken a surprising amount of courage to walk through that famous oak door. Inside the expert staff had taken over, putting her at ease with their quiet professionalism to envelop her in a world of exquisite cut and glorious fabrics. Bank balance reduced, she had walked away a changed woman. Claridge's had been, well, Claridge's: The welcome by name, the beaming Concierge, her corner suite, the spray of orchids and lilies on the mantle – all a very exclusive way to spend the night in Mayfair.

She'd left the hotel early the following morning in yet another powerful, black car to Heathrow, though this time without the background noise of subterfuge to distract her. An incident-free flight to Paris, then the lounge and lunch before boarding her flight to Los Angeles. There was only one other passenger in First Class, dressed impeccably in what the stewardess informed EJ in a stage whisper was, if she was any judge, 'bespoke Cifonelli, 'ead to foot'.

The step down in quality to the one-hour regional carrier flight to Sacramento was jarring, especially after the drag of US Immigration and the deconstructed third world chaos of LAX, but her bags arrived quickly and a Lincoln Town Car whisked her efficiently to her hotel downtown. The Happiness suite lived up to its name – occupying the upper storey of the building, what would have been attic space in a private house had been cleverly converted into a self-contained unit with its own kitchen. And yes, it did have a fireplace in which a fragrant pile of pine logs smouldered.

The high-priced courier company had been as good as its word, as had the Ducati dealership: six black Pelican cases sat at the foot of the bed, while her newly-serviced Scrambler was parked to one side of the hotel entrance. A quick Riz-call found a well-regarded pizza joint nearby, and replete with excellent sausage and mushroom, EJ stripped, showered and slid gratefully beneath the light goose-down duvet, asleep almost before her head hit the pillow.

25 Sapphire Lake

Sacramento, the City of Trees. A good omen, and at this early hour the cool air was redolent of the sharp scent of eucalyptus and the lavender-like fragrance of the Jeffreys' Pines in adjacent Southside Park. EJ had woken in half light, eerily aware of the creeping weight of the time difference. As the glowing dawn washed through the windows, she had inventoried the contents of the flight cases, packed the hiking gear in the large rucksack and laid out her leathers, boots and gloves on the bed ready for departure. The morning sky was now already that near crystalline azure that only ever seemed possible in California, at least until the smog of the state's cities inevitably seeped across like a nicotine stain. Maybe it would be different up in the mountains, thought EJ. She certainly hoped so.

The lobby had been deserted when she came down to step outside and check over the Scrambler. The dealership seemed to have done a thorough job – she'd take them on trust until she got on the road and could make her own judgment. A couple of other early risers, radiating Californian good health, were already down for breakfast in the dining room. EJ ordered avocado toast, bacon, eggs and coffee from the enthusiastic young waiter – the ride north to the trailhead for the Trinity Alps would take her about four hours, with a final stop at the Ranger Station in

348

Weaverville to pick up the required wilderness and camping permits that Riz had requested by email. A healthy base of carbs and caffeine was definitely a good idea. She smiled at the memory of the sandwiches she had made and carried with her that last time she had ridden the Scrambler into the wilds to Jasper's secret canyon. They'd ended up a bit squashed, but had been a Godsend. At least today she'd be riding through a series of good-sized towns where she could break her trip, and Weaverville itself looked like a decent bet for lunch.

Back upstairs in the suite and changed into her crimson leathers and boots, EJ hooked up the pico projector to test the new outdoor battery packs. Riz appeared immediately, to perch like a rather prim neon cat on the end of her bed.

"Beautiful day for it, dude. Practically in my backyard too. This is gonna be out of sight."

"And good morning to you too. Glad you're so chipper. Michelangelo get in touch with you?"

"No, man. No one. Keeping themselves to themselves and their powder dry. Reckon they want to see what you turn up with the Freshman first," replied Riz. "Say, what's the plan for after the visit with cuz?"

"See how long this takes first. Then head back to England, to Anglezarke. Need you to record the whole thing today, movies and sound. Do the ride too – Michelangelo'll only want to see the visit, but I want everything."

"Yeah, no worries. You about ready to hit the road?"

EJ nodded and powered down the projector unit. She slipped the electronics into a soft padded bag that she'd carry in one of the Scrambler's panniers, then bent forward to tighten the clasps on her boots. Helmet and gloves in hand, she headed downstairs.

*

A different kind of ride. Even with the rucksack bungeed behind her, the Scrambler felt a better fit – more a part of her and she of the 'bike than in Arizona, when she really had been just learning its weight and balance. Everything felt more responsive and her own touch sharper, more assured.

The flow of traffic into Sacramento on Interstate 5 from the city's northern suburbs and satellites was already building to the morning rush, but EJ's route north took her counter to it. She could have run most of the way on I5, but to make things more interesting, she and Riz had put together a route via Yuba City and Chico to the north-east which roughly followed the winding path of the Sacramento River as it flowed south into California's Central Valley. She would swing back onto the Interstate for forty miles or so between Red Bluff and Redding as the Valley narrowed to the north, before heading west from Redding to climb to Shasta and then on to Weaverville and the Trinity Alps.

Traffic was regular, with noticeably more passenger vehicles in populous California than she had experienced in the high sierra. The forty-mile stretch of I5 to which she returned after a couple of hours, eventually to make the swing west to Shasta, was pleasant enough: The semi-trailers headed for America's vast interior, loaded with containers from California's ports or refrigerated fruit and produce from the Central Valley, were a breeze compared to the wall-to wall cliffs of steel of the heavy trucks on Britain's crowded motorways.

At Redding, EJ left the Interstate on CA299 and the landscape finally began to change as she started the winding climb to Shasta. The low banks of alder and buckeye that had framed the highways in the Valley gave way to a mix of mature pine, spruce and fir. EJ flicked up her visor and enjoyed the resin-laden air as her surroundings became more alpine. In New Mexico, the roads had kept a perverse logic, narrowing and less travelled the deeper she had penetrated that brittle, majestic landscape. California seemed more at ease with itself, a different kind of welcome.

The Scrambler was no touring 'bike, so she'd kept her eye on the fuel gauge and stopped a couple of times en route to refuel and stretch her legs. In Shasta, she topped up the tank once more, then pushed on to Weaverville, intent on starting the trek into the Trinity lakes by early afternoon.

Weaverville had the air of a comfortable Western town. Spreading either side of the state highway which described a long slow 'S' through its middle as Main St., its many Douglas firs and Ponderosa pines overtopped the two-storey buildings of its commercial centre strip. EJ pulled over at the Weaverville Ranger Station and could see the first forest-clad barrier ridges of the Trinity ranges rising to the town's north and west.

The Ranger Station was a single storey rancher of brick and clapboard, painted in forest green and khaki beige. EJ decided that there must be some US Government directive that dictated the exact Pantone shades, as the place screamed 'Forest Service'. Despite this brief burst of British cynicism, the enthusiastic young ranger manning the front desk could have been neither more welcoming nor more helpful. She quickly produced EJ's permits and suggested she ride up to begin from the Stuart Fork trailhead, where she could securely park the 'bike at any one of the campsites there. When EJ asked her about lunch options, she gave her a hearty recommendation to backtrack a couple of hundred yards to load up on bagels and coffee at Mama Llama's Eatery.

*

The young ranger had been spot on, thought EJ, locking the Scrambler to a substantial pinewood post beneath the conifers at the Stuart Fork; Mama Llama's knew a thing or two about lox and cream cheese on a bagel. So much so, that she'd taken a bag of an extra half-dozen to go, together with a pound of cream cheese and a pound of smoked salmon. Well, she thought, it's not like I'm not going to walk it all off in the next day, is it?

She released the bungees that held the rucksack and changed into the hiking gear – breathable inner socks to avoid blisters, warm woollen outer socks, lightweight Goretex hiking boots, a long-sleeved shirt, waterproof pants and camo jacket in a pattern apparently favoured by the British Special Air Service.

Food, water, med kit, tent and sleeping bag all stayed in the rucksack, to which she added the pico projector and its batteries in their carrying bag. Leathers and bike gear securely stowed, and the 'bike's alarm system armed, she clipped her iPhone to the front of the jacket, and fitted her earpiece under her bandanna.

"Dude, who'd have thought you could get great bagel in the middle of the boonies, huh?" said Riz, doing that weirdly disarming trick of appearing to read EJ's mind.

"As if decent restaurants were two a penny when you were holed up in the Sahara."

"Yeah, point taken. Still, pretty cool little joint for a small town."

"Agree. Anyway, are we good to go? Or do you have anything new for me?"

"All good, dude. Have another bagel, why don'tya? Weather's solid – nice fat Cali high pressure system set fair to stick around for a couple of days – long enough for us to get in and out anyway. Bit chilly at night up here, but nothing you can't handle. Kit's all in good shape, batteries five by five. Whadda'ya say, time to rock'n'roll?"

Of course Riz grinned. And the teeth sparked, and the neon rippled; the Riz that EJ had so missed. Even out here in California's Trinity Alps, as physically removed from his electronic playground as could be – though EJ knew he was only ever a nanosecond away – Riz was in his element and loving it. EJ glanced down at the lightning opal on her finger which glowed like coals banked in a forge, and shot him a broad grin.

"Yeah, dude. I can feel him. He's close. So close. Let's do this."

*

The trail was easy to follow, running close by the stream of the Stuart Fork, well maintained and marked at regular intervals by cairns of granite shards. The first six or so miles were under forest canopy, but then the conifers thinned to open into an alpine meadow of tall grasses, now sere and yellow as the cooler Autumn temperatures set in. Ringed by pine and fir, Riz informed her that this was known as Morris Meadow. To EJ's left rose the first of the granite peaks, their lower flanks sparsely forested as if enormous boulders shrouded in lichen.

The weather was playing nice, just as Riz had predicted in his impromptu forecast. The summer campsites which dotted the trees at the edge of the meadow now stood deserted, certain proof to EJ if she had needed it that she was alone. Well, physically. She patted the iPhone and gave a silent prayer of thanks to Riz, Stan and the satellite uplink that she knew was tracking her.

From Morris Meadow to Sapphire Lake took her a further three hours. As she crested the final rise, EJ turned to look back down the valley, Morris Meadow a broad golden strip set into the darker forest. Beyond, only the last half-mile or so offered any real difficulty as she carefully negotiated her way over the moraine line of granite rubble that fronted the bowl of Sapphire Lake. The long ellipse of dark blue water sat in an almost perfect glacial U of saw-toothed granite, upper ridges already dusted with early snowfall. The shadow of the western rim crept across the lake's leftmost shore, the smooth water a placid mirror of granite, pine and sky.

Twenty yards ahead, a flat shoulder of rock cantilevered out above the water. She picked her way through the boulders and low alpine scrub, careful not to turn an ankle at this late stage. EJ hopped down and unclipped the iPhone from her jacket.

"We'll set up here, Riz. On this ledge. Quickly, he's so close."

The lightning opal glowed on EJ's finger as she set down the rucksack and pulled out the bag with the pico projector and its batteries and power cables. Five seconds to hook up, thumb the power switch and watch the little blue diode wink into life. Riz flickered once as his holo flashed into existence.

"Dude, even I can sense him. So, you want full Spielberg?"

"Yep, best res you can manage. Multiple storage. You know the drill."

Riz's teeth sparked once, and EJ turned and walked to the edge of the granite ledge.

"I have come. I am here. For you."

Water streamed from the head and shoulders of Jacinto Saavedra Cervantes i Domenech as he rose from the lake like the conning tower of some steampunk submarine, then flexed his wings, muscles rippling beneath a skin now weathered to a dull platinum, the blues and aquamarines still visible but like afterimages compared to his moment of renewal. They regarded each other silently and EJ could feel the sharp mind pervading her consciousness, the draw of those ancient eyes, their swirl of light and experience like the spiral arms of two vast gravity wells.

"You have returned, as we both knew you must, Princess of Dragons. And you, Al-Khwarizmi Ibn Shams ad'Din, I sensed your presence at my rebirth. Now I bid you welcome."

In that moment, EJ's feeling of oneness with Jacinto Saavedra Cervantes i Domenech clicked into place, an exquisitely engineered key fitting a lock so smoothly in her mind. The return, her trek to his high alpine lake, had been the missing pieces that assuaged the emptiness and sense of loss of these past weeks. Melding into one with Jacinto, EJ could feel herself unfurling, expanding into the space and beauty of the world of the dragons more completely than she had ever done before. She knew him, his elemental presence, his long centuries in this world compressing to an instant's understanding. She also understood that this dragon now knew her own essence, more than any other being could. There was nothing to hide, no secrets, indeed the very idea was absurd, beyond all realms of possibility.

*

EJ checked the Rolex on her wrist: It was just after eight o'clock in the evening, eight days since her little heart-to-heart with Selwyn in the garden of *The Grouse and Hare*. She had landed back in Manchester that afternoon from Charles de Gaulle, the last short leg of her return flight from the West Coast. The same driver who had picked her up for her grandfather's funeral had been there to meet her, the only one of the small gaggle of chauffeurs in the Arrivals foyer without the customary hand-printed name sign. The remnants of the first Atlantic gale of the autumn were still blowing in from the Irish Sea, and EJ and the driver had sprinted through the gusting volleys of rain to the black Mercedes sat idling in an illegal parking spot in front of the entrance, studiously ignored by both airport security and armed Police stood only yards away. EJ had seen the car's lights flash and heard the clunk of the door locks. Not waiting for the driver, she had wrenched the door open herself and dived for the dryness of the passenger cabin. She had no checked baggage, only her rucksack and a TUMI garment bag made from some kind of ballistic nylon. Having thrown these into the boot with as much of a semblance of care as he could muster, the driver had run round to his door and within seconds they were moving off to merge into the stream of glowing red taillights on the loops of the Terminal complex and then north to Anglezarke, their only sound the rhythmic swish of the big car's windscreen wipers.

She now sat with the lights dimmed at the large round dining table in the kitchen of the Anglezarke house. Michelangelo's house? Joe's? Hers, she supposed, probably via some arcane structure of companies or trusts, though she still had some trouble getting her head around that whole concept. On the table in front of her sat a large raku bowl of miso ramen, three thick slices of glistening roast pork and half a soft-boiled egg fanned elegantly across the noodles in their oddly milky broth, one of the blue and white striped mugs filled with hot

Japanese o-cha to the bowl's left. Molly had looked suitably smug when she had placed the meal before her, evidently pleased by EJ's raised eyebrow in recognition of hitherto unknown culinary depths. Eyes twinkling nearly as much as the rings on her fingers, Molly had grabbed her coat and left soon after, spinning EJ some tale of pressing family matters to attend.

EJ closed her eyes and inhaled the intense, earthy aroma of the Japanese noodles in front of her. In its own way, the last week had been the most extraordinary, the most revelatory, of all her experiences since she had become a part of Anglezarke again. Although, she admitted to herself, some parts of it – the planning, the equipment, the travel and, most of all, the possibilities afforded her by the combination of near limitless funds and a dragon that could get into any computer on Earth – were becoming almost alarmingly routine.

EJ ate, then laid down her chopsticks atop the empty ramen bowl and drank the last of the tea. The wind outside continued to rattle the windowpanes, but the rain at least had eased off over the past twenty minutes. She pushed back her chair, cleared her place, took the empty bowl and mug to the sink and rinsed them. Then she went upstairs to her room to find a jacket and scarf. It was time to see Michelangelo.

Molly had left the lights dimmed and laid out a well-worn wax jacket on the edge of the bed, just like the one EJ kept hung up beside the kitchen door of *The Grouse and Hare*. EJ rummaged through the wardrobe and fished out a Rubinacci silk scarf in a red and white motif that made it look like a particularly chic keffiyeh. Satisfied with her look in the mirror, she pushed an errant curl of hair behind her ear, checked that she had her iPhone and trotted back downstairs then through the kitchen and out into the back yard.

Balthasar and Akitafelt flowed round the corner of the house like black and white mercury. EJ strode toward the garden gate and the two hounds slipped into their usual stations at her side as she crossed the wet yard, its flagstones glistening in the floodlights. The diodes on the biometric reader flicked from red to green and the trio moved in the nimbus of path lights across the vegetable garden and on under the trees of the orchard, heavy drops shaking down onto them as the dying gusts of wind moved through the branches while ragged cloud scudded across a pale moon.

Mortensen stood in front of the door, swaddled in a long riding coat and with a tweed cap on his head, the glow of a small and evil-smelling cheroot betraying his presence. He stepped forward as EJ approached, tossed the cigar away into the wet grass, and hugged her.

"Too long, lass. Welcome back. Hurry up, we ain't got all night – everyone's waiting for you."

EJ looked at him enquiringly, but Mortensen just gave a brusque shake of his head and broke into a lopsided grin.

As she followed him inside and down the corridor to the main cavern, the familiar scent of leather and tobacco put her at her ease. At once, she felt Michelangelo in her mind, the sense of golden bells pealing nearby.

"Elizabeth, I see that Mortensen has found you at last. I am pleased. Do come and join us. I think you will be most impressed … and we have much to discuss."

At the balcony into the cavern, Mortensen stepped to one side and with a flourish like a ringmaster, invited EJ to survey the scene before her.

She stood open-mouthed. The main lights were dimmed, but every desk and the gangways between them were occupied by Anglezarke's dwarves and humans. She spied Molly among a gaggle of Mortensens to one side, laughing and waving to her; The Mrs. Winters and Summerbee appeared to be sharing a joke with one of the dwarf traders across another aisle; Stan, Lemmy and Daniel sat huddled together in a sort of command centre, its multiple screens a mirror of the huge frontal display, full of readouts and power meters, quietly relaying commands into their headsets; and everywhere there was a hum of excited chatter. Selwyn Ormerod, impeccable in a moss green tweed suit and white shirt open at the neck, stood to one side of Michelangelo and beckoned her to join them. But EJ hardly registered any of this, because there on the dais in front of the screen, arrayed in a rough semicircle, stood Nai'En, Madame and Riz. A chorus of overlapping welcomes, each bubbling with excitement, boomed through the audio system; Nai'En's cultured mid-Atlantic tenor, Madame's upper class drawl, Riz's best surfer dude, and that donnish baritone which she had chosen it now seemed so very long ago for Michelangelo. And then, to top it all off, the room erupted into applause.

One desk next to Michelangelo's pile of enormous cushions remained empty, and Mortensen led her by the hand down to it.

"Yours, lass. Pride of place."

EJ tossed her jacket and scarf onto the chair then ran to throw her arms round Michelangelo, showering his neck and cheek with kisses and feeling that surprised thrum of happiness from the Golden Dragon.

"But how?" she asked him.

"Ah, you should ask Al-Khwarizmi. I suspect this all began with his impromptu visit those weeks ago. He really is a most remarkable dragon, when he puts his mind to it," replied Michelangelo.

She turned to Riz. She knew that he was always holographic, and had immediately understood that Nai'En and Madame must be present in simulacra too.

"So? This is why you've been avoiding me!"

If Riz's neon could have burnt any more brightly, even the Silicon Dragon might have redlined his circuits.

"Aw, don't be mad at me, dude. Anyway, I'm pleading not guilty on this count."

He flicked his tail and pointed it at Selwyn Ormerod, who guffawed with laughter.

"On this occasion, EJ, I'm afraid Riz is correct. More my doing than his, though he was instrumental with a couple of important introductions – you know I wouldn't recognise one end of a silicon chip from the other. Anyway, Anglezarke Holdings has recently closed an interesting new investment in a small Californian venture – what Riz, I believe, refers to as his 'PCH boys'. We now own a minority equity position that gives us a seat on the board, as well as first use rights for anything they may develop. Naturally, you are our nominated director."

EJ suppressed the urge to swear like a trooper as she flashed back to a conversation with Riz when they were last in Albemarle St. and turned to the Silicon Dragon, hands on hips.

"So that's what you meant by 'er, new funding', you sly beggar!"

"Come on, dude. Sorry, yeah? But Selwyn and the boys were still crossing T's and dotting I's. As he said, I just made a couple of introductions. Anyway, look at this! Seems to have worked out pretty well, huh?"

EJ grinned and moved across the dais to Madame's hologram. She was just as EJ had left her, every jet black scale and swag of gold a perfect three-dimensional representation, the great eyes at their most kindly.

"Tika! Oh, I'm so happy to see you! If I hug your holo, will you know?" she said, caressing the Coal Dragon's flank.

"Elizabeth, dear, I haven't a clue! But I will certainly see it. Al Khwarizmi has cameras all over the place, so Nai'En and I are fully involved and can watch everything. He really is such a darling for this, and I've almost forgiven him completely for his past hastiness. We must be getting terribly old – I don't know why we hadn't thought of this before. It's awfully overdue, you know."

"But you're still on the mountain?"

"Of course! One of my young men is a whizz with computers. He's typing my words as he hears them. Beyond that, I'm afraid I'm just an old Coal Dragon.

Though I must say, it is a delight to be here and I do hope we can do it again soon."

Riz, vibrating at his own special frequency now and set to burst with pride, broke in.

"It's what you and me have been doing since Beijing, just on a bigger scale now that the new algorithms let us multilink. Still in beta and taking a ton of bandwidth – Stan and the boys are routing everything Anglezarke's got right now, as well as bogarting a couple of comms satellites. We'll have some of the kinks ironed out soon, but hey, pretty sweet, huh?"

EJ walked the couple of yards to Nai'En, and the Jade Dragon bowed his elegant head in greeting.

"Elizabeth Jade, Princess of Dragons. It is all to your liking? I, of course, was not consulted, but the result seems most satisfactory."

EJ could practically feel the other dragons roll their eyes, but laughed and kissed the Jade Dragon fondly. Michelangelo rapped the floor with one burnished ivory claw.

"Now that we have all inflated Al Khwarizmi's ego to the point of ignition, shall we return to the matter in hand? Elizabeth, you have spoken once more to Jacinto Saavedra Cervantes i Domenech?"

"Of course you know his name. Why did you never use it before?"

It was Nai'En who answered her.

"We have never forgotten his name. We are dragons! Now that he bears it with honour once more, and has accepted you as a Princess of Dragons, we may speak it once again. Is this not so, old friend?"

"Indeed," replied Michelangelo. "Our shame is now assuaged. The question is, to which we all hope you may now have an answer, has Jacinto Cervantes Saavedra i Domenech returned to our kind, to the community of dragons? Or has he chosen a different path, for only he has ever passed through rebirth in this manner and we must respect this. Elizabeth, can you enlighten us?"

EJ returned to stand at Michelangelo's side.

"Riz, run the tape."

The main display filled with Riz's point of view from where his hologram had sat that late afternoon on the granite overlook at Sapphire Lake. The high definition of the recording drew a gasp from the audience of dwarves and humans in the dealing room, and even Stan, Lemmy and Daniel stopped what they were doing to stare up in fascination. Jacinto Cervantes Saavedra i Domenech sat before EJ in the deep blue shallows of the lake. A tapestry of silver water tumbled down the cliffs in thin cascades beyond his right shoulder, and the jagged ring of granite peaks was striated with purple edged in pink as the late afternoon waned into twilight. The human and dwarven audience felt the pull of those ancient eyes as the dragon spoke.

"Now you understand, Princess of Dragons."

"Yes, but I want to hear it from you. It was never about your rebirth in that canyon … or Jasper Moffett's death. It was days earlier. What happened to me on the mountain when Joe died … when my grandfather was murdered?"

"Yes. The murder of your grandfather, Madame's scream of anguish. In that moment you and I were bonded forever. By pain. By loss. By suffering."

"When I lifted the egg that first time, it was you that I felt. You were already there. Aware."

"I was present. I felt it all as you did. How could I not? You and I are one, Elizabeth Jade Carver, Princess of Dragons. As you feel so do I. I sense you, whether far or near."

"And Madame understood all this?" EJ asked.

"Understood? I cannot say. The senses of dragons go far beyond your human spectrum, as you now understand. Kartika Basuki Hendra Farida Sastrowardoyo, Guanzhong Nai'En and Michelangelo de St. Exupéry-Antoine are ancient dragons, elemental as I," and Jacinto Saavedra Cervantes i Domenech inclined his head toward Riz. "Even your companion Al Khwarizmi Ibn Shams ad'Din, so different now from what he once was, is ultimately of this earth, as he and I both know. All dragons' knowledge is as mine, and time touches each of us but briefly, if at all."

EJ looked at the lightning opal on her finger which flashed with the crackle of an electrical storm. She held it up to Jacinto, mirroring her gesture in the canyon.

"Yes. In joining you to her house, Madame achieved something more. She joined you to us all. You are not a Princess of Dragons, you are *the* Princess of Dragons. Of all dragons. That is the gift you brought me to avenge my shame. It is to you that I owe my rebirth, my freedom. Now you will use this gift to find all the dragons."

EJ turned and looked back to Riz, motionless as a gargoyle on the granite behind her, recording every moment, imprinting Jacinto's words from his mind. The sparks and neon ripples had faded almost away. Here in the presence of Jacinto Saavedra Cervantes i Domenech at Sapphire Lake, the Silicon Dragon, for all his ones and zeroes, was once more that ancient dragon of shifting sands and scirocco winds. EJ brushed an errant curl of hair back behind her ear and turned back to the dragon before her.

"I struggled. I knew that I had to come here, was being drawn back to you, but it was only when that was pointed out to me that the understanding became easier." She nodded toward Riz. "Then I could come back to all of you."

"Has it ever been your path to choose, Princess of Dragons?"

EJ's hand had strayed to the dragon pendant which lay warm at her throat.

"Mine to choose," she replied, "though not really a choice at all. I sense them, as you do. Some are pressured as you were before — their fit in this world becomes more difficult, more tenuous. Yet I will find them all. The ones which seek me out, as Riz did, and the ones which do not. Only I can do that."

"The great dragons with whom you are already well acquainted are skilled in the ways of this world of which we are all a part. They will stand as one with you. As shall I."

A shiver of ripples moved across the lake's surface and EJ looked up toward the far ridge, now fading to a deep purple as the first stars began to appear in the early evening sky. She wondered what her grandfather would have made of all this. Could he have had any inkling? She chuckled to herself. Of course not. This was her story to take forward, had been all along, though she knew that Joe, more than anything else, would have given his eye teeth for the adventures that beckoned her, and that brought a smile. Jacinto Cervantes Saavedra i Domenech laughed, a rolling release like the thunder of a waterfall or the ripping of a comet across the sky, filled with pure joy and exultation. She sat on the ledge at the edge of the water and the great dragon bent his platinum neck toward her and laid his head at EJ's feet. She wrapped her arms about him and buried her face against his.

*

The screen faded to black. EJ quietly left Michelangelo's side to stand at the centre of the circle of dragons. The audience of men and dwarves now stood as one and bowed toward her and the dragons to her sides, and quietly filed out of the cavern until only Selwyn and Mortensen remained, with Daniel, Stan and Lemmy still at their station to maintain the holo links and sound.

EJ surveyed the group that remained — the four dragons and Anglezarke's two most trusted lieutenants — and realised that they each waited expectantly for her to take the lead. It dawned on her that the new desk at the centre of the room, indeed at the right hand of Michelangelo, meant far more than the symbolic and somewhat sweet gesture that she had supposed amid Mortensen's dramatics. They had all already known that her visit to Jacinto Cervantes Saavedra i Domenech, and this evening, marked the beginning of a new chapter in the life of Anglezarke and the dragons; one which the death of Joe Livesey had set in motion. She flashed back to previous occasions in this great room with Michelangelo and her irritation that she wasn't being taken seriously, had been kept in the dark about the true extent of her involvement. No longer. Around her now was complete, if tacit, agreement that the four dragons — five if you counted Jacinto — and the whole edifice of Anglezarke would now fall in behind her intentions.

EJ looked at each of them in turn. Selwyn and Mortensen looked relaxed yet somewhat detached, appearing to reflect on the enormity of the changes that the past months had wrought. Riz continued to grin, though in deference to the company he had clearly dialled back the wattage on his personal light show. Nai'En and Madame both watched her with patient fondness and gave small nods in her direction. She turned around to Michelangelo, sat behind her on his nest of cushions.

"You all knew it would come to this."

"Yes, Elizabeth," replied the Golden Dragon. "However, Jacinto Cervantes Saavedra i Domenech is mistaken in one important respect, the choice has always been yours to make. We four would never presume otherwise."

"Indeed, Elizabeth," added Nai'En. "Though as you yourself now know, the consequences of your grandfather's murder and Madame's actions did change everything. It quickly became clear that you can now sense the dragons as only we do. An unprecedented gift."

Nai'En bowed toward Madame and then to Michelangelo.

EJ crossed the short distance to Madame and brought her hand up to stroke the holographic cheek of the Coal Dragon.

"Dear Tika, was Jacinto right, or did you know this would happen?"

"No, my dearest Elizabeth, Princess of my House." Madame broke into a throaty chuckle. " Us girls, dear, sometimes we do things in the heat of the moment. Anyway, it appears to have worked out alright, doesn't it? These two old dears would have analysed it to the nth, wouldn't they?"

EJ grinned and kissed Madame fondly. She stepped back and took a deep breath before addressing them all.

"Actually, Jacinto was right. Well, maybe not about the choice bit … but I think he's still getting used to being able to sense all of you again after so many years in exile. I do feel him more than you, and certainly more than all the other dragons I've yet to meet. It's like there's this image of the whole world at night in my mind, and its lit up with all these points of light. Some are still faint, but others are much brighter — like you, Michelangelo, here in Anglezarke, or you, Nai'En in Beijing, or you Tika in Java."

EJ turned to Riz.

"Or you, Riz. You're like a swarm of fireflies around the whole globe. But even then, I can concentrate and see your core back in Cupertino."

"Dude, that is so awesome!" said Riz, in a hushed tone.

"Anyway," continued EJ. "What I'm saying is that Jacinto and Michelangelo are both right. I can't change what I have become and how I can now sense all dragons, but I can decide what I do with this."

Michelangelo moved forward and brought his head close to her.

"And you have made your choice."

"Yes. Jacinto Cervantes Saavedra i Domenech can no more deceive me than I him. He is no longer the dragon he once was. We know each other's hearts. When he said that I would find the other dragons, all he did was speak my own truth, my own mind."

Michelangelo raised himself and surveyed the ring of dragons,

"Then, Elizabeth Jade Carver, Princess of Dragons, I pledge myself once more to you."

"As do I, Princess of Dragons," intoned Nai'En, bowing his head gracefully toward her. "Come to Beijing soon. I shall remind the General Secretary that we shall take tea together. He is anxious to meet you!"

With that, Guanzhong Nai'En's hologram gently faded away. Madame let out a snort of laughter.

"Oh, he's always been such a one for the grand gesture! Elizabeth, Princess and scion of my House, find us all. Who knows quite what we'll ever do with all these new dragons back in the fold? Still, interesting times, eh! You have my love and loyalty, dear."

EJ ran across to Madame's hologram and threw her arms around her as best she could.

"Thank you, Tika. For everything."

The Coal Dragon gently dissolved into a blur of pixels and then away.

Riz made a half-hearted attempt at clearing his throat, as if nervously required to make a speech.

"Riz, dude!" laughed EJ. "We're cool, right?"

"Yeah, EJ. We're cool. You know where to find me."

"Give you a shout in a couple of days, OK? I want to spend some time here with Michelangelo first."

"You got it, EJ. Later."

Riz's gently pulsing neon pinks and Ferrari yellows blurred away as he disappeared back into cyberspace.

Selwyn Ormerod and Mortensen, together with the dwarves who had been manning the holo and audio uplinks, had quietly made their exits. Only EJ and Michelangelo remained in the cavern, dimly lit by a few lamps high above them.

She came across and sat down, leaning her head back against his side, feeling the rise and fall of the Golden Dragon's flank and hearing the tiny clinks of golden scales as he shifted slightly to accommodate her.

"So, Elizabeth."

"So. Is this what you expected?"

"No, Princess of Dragons, in truth it is not. I have asked much of you and put you through many trials, for which we both have paid a heavy price to arrive here. A price I would gladly have avoided, but such is not in my power and it is a burden I shall now bear."

EJ remained silent for a while, thinking of her grandfather who had begun all this, and the brief time she had been allowed to know him. Michelangelo blew a stream of smoke rings up into the shadows.

"He'd be very proud, you know," she told Michelangelo.

"Yes, Elizabeth," replied the Golden Dragon. "I believe he would."

Afterword and Thanks

I am deeply grateful to the following three readers of early drafts: Miranda Ogley, who knows exactly where Norton Magna could be; Joan Whittle, who knows where Anglezarke ought to be; and Julian Hill, who, at a loose end for something to read one day on a flight, remembered that I'd given him an early copy of the manuscript - The Trinity Alps chapter is for him.

My thanks also to David Kao, my da loh, who provided the details for the Chinese banquet with his usual enthusiasm and flair.

Above all, this would never have been possible without the love and support of Anisha and Gabriela. They were there at the inception and supported it throughout. Thank you.

*

This all began with my father. I suppose that's true for so many of us, whatever the values which define you. In my case, a love of reading and language has always been my touchstone. All my father's fault.

He was self-made academically, one of those post-war Grammar school boys from a working class background in Lancashire, steeped in Beethoven and Shakespeare, who drove themselves to excel in exams. He had received the offer of a place to read English at Oxford when my grandfather was made redundant by the mill. My father had to set his own plans aside and become a teacher at a prep school in Yorkshire to make sure that there was at least one wage coming into the house. The place at Oxford became a memory, and though he went on to earn a good degree from London University, he had the better fortune that he had already found his calling, to become a gifted teacher of English and Art History with a particular flare for bringing stories to life for the youngest boys. Eventually, he crowned his long career by becoming Headmaster, though even then he continued to teach as often as his other duties allowed.

He always taught English to Form 1Q in the first year of the boys' grammar school where I also attended. I was not in his first form class, but already knew by heart most of the stories which he had conjured over the years to keep the eleven-year olds entertained. Indeed, I was not alone, for there were other boys in my year whose older siblings had been transported and entertained by my father's imaginings and had regaled their younger brothers with his stories and characters. The stories themselves changed from year to year, but the characters that populated them had become such favourites that even the other teachers knew their names.

The most beloved of these was Michelangelo, the dragon that lived at the bottom of our garden. Michelangelo de Saint-Exupéry-Antoine, to give him his full, splendid name. Quite how my father discovered him in his imagination I will now never know, for he died many years ago and I had never got round to asking. I know that our imaginings are very similar – he made me read The Hobbit when I was barely seven years old – so I've always instinctively known enough about Michelangelo and all his other characters that I didn't really need to ask.

If you are the sort of reader who actually bothers with afterwords and thanks at the end of a novel and you've managed to get this far, then allow me to clear up some matters. Anglezarke is not a collection of my father's first form stories: I couldn't remember any of them if I tried. I began to write bits and pieces of this tale when my own daughter was born. We were living in Central Java in Indonesia at the time, and I had little to occupy myself, so like many before me I turned to a blank page and, thankfully, found that a melange of my own varied experiences, my voracious appetite for books of all kinds, and my father's cast of characters gave me something to play with.

Although I can let you in on a little secret: sometimes, if you're very patient and you allow things to develop in their own time, you really can find dragons at the bottom of the garden, and they can lead you on the most surprising of journeys when you do …

I would be delighted to hear your thoughts and feedback, which you may send to me at *anglezarkebooks@protonmail.com* or you can find me on your favourite social media *@anglezarkebooks*.

About the Author

Nicholas Whittle was born in Preston, England and educated at Cambridge and Columbia Universities, where he earned degrees in Asian Studies and Business Administration. He has spent most of his career based in South East Asia, working in senior management and corporate finance roles in commodities and energy. He enjoys literature, fine art, fashion and food, though not necessarily in that order. *Anglezarke* is his first novel.